THE NEXT DEAD GIRL

All Tish Lewis knew was that it was dark.

And cold.

How long had she been in this place? And where exactly *was* she?

She had long since stopped screaming. No one had come in response to her screams.

Why? Why was she being held?

Ransom? That's what she thought at first. Someone had kidnapped her and was demanding money from her father. But that was before she began to hear the chanting through the door. The terrible singing.

That was before she heard the scream.

It was a girl's scream. She knew that. And she thought she knew who the girl was, too.

Her roommate, Joelle.

Tish began to cry again. She was starting to lose hope that she'd ever get out of this room alive. What worried her most now was *how* her death would come, not if. They had taken her for a reason—they'd taken Joelle, too, and Tish was certain it was Joelle's scream of death that she had heard. They'd taken both girls to kill them.

But who "they" were and why they wanted to kill them was unknown. And it was the unknown that Tish feared most . . .

ALL THE PRETTY DEAD GIRLS

JOHN MANNING

PINNACLE BOOKS
KENSINGTON PUBLISHING CORP.
www.kensingtonbooks.com

PINNACLE BOOKS are published by

Kensington Publishing Corp.
850 Third Avenue
New York, NY 10022

All Kensington titles, imprints, and distributed lines are available at special quantity discounts for bulk purchases for sales promotions, premiums, fund-raising, educational, or institutional use. Special book excerpts or customized printings can also be created to fit specific needs. For details, write or phone the office of the Kensington special sales manager: Kensington Publishing Corp., 850 Third Avenue, New York, NY 10022, attn: Special Sales Department; phone 1-800-221-2647.

This book is a work of fiction. Names, characters, businesses, organizations, places, events, and incidents either are the product of the author's imagination or are used fictitiously. Any resemblance to actual persons, living or dead, events, or locales is entirely coincidental.

ISBN-13: 978-0-7860-1798-0
ISBN-10: 0-7860-1798-8

First printing: April 2009

10 9 8 7 6 5 4 3 2 1

Printed in the United States of America

Prologue

1

The white Lexus was doing exactly one mile over the speed limit when it crossed the Louisiana state line.

It had started to rain just outside of Jackson, Mississippi—a steady downpour the wipers simply couldn't keep up with. Visibility was impaired enough to force Sue to slow down to a crawl as she passed through the city.

Sue's shoulders tensed as she watched the red taillights of the Jeep Cherokee in front of her. She had been driving almost nonstop for nearly two days now. The other girls on campus had been thinking about their exams, about what they'd do on their upcoming holiday breaks. But Sue's mind had been on one thing and one thing only. Getting away. There had been no other choice.

She snapped on the radio, trying to relieve the tedium of the drive and the steady, pounding rain. "Have yourself a merry little Christmas," a voice sang from the radio. "Let your heart be light . . ."

Christmas. It was almost Christmas. It didn't feel that way to Sue, with the warm, muggy rain.

"From now on, our troubles will be out of sight . . ."

She was crying. She switched off the radio. She preferred the silence.

Sue glanced back in her rearview mirror. She wasn't really sure who—or what—she was looking for. In the rain, she couldn't see anything but headlights anyway. But somehow it made her feel better to look back every now and then. Her nerves, already shot, began to fray a little as she kept taking her foot off the gas pedal to avoid slamming into the car in front of her.

"Come on, come on," Sue muttered under her breath, drumming her fingers on the steering wheel. The wind and rain whipped against the side of the car with a long, screeching howl.

It seemed to take hours to get through Jackson, but once she did, the thick traffic began to disperse. Finally, she was able to start getting her speed back up. As soon as she clocked seventy-one, she clicked on the cruise control and removed her foot from the gas pedal with a sigh of relief. Her right hip was getting sore, and she shifted a little in her seat. Cars and trucks flew past her in the left lane, throwing up streams of water onto her windshield. No matter how tempting it was to speed up, she resisted the urge and kept relying on the cruise control. She couldn't risk being pulled over.

It was just paranoia, she knew. Surely, there was no rural Southern sheriff watching for her. In all likelihood, there wasn't anyone at all on the road looking for her. But better safe than sorry.

I just don't know, Sue reminded herself, *and until I do know, it's better not to take any risks—and not to trust anyone. If I try to tell anyone—they'll just think I'm crazy, and they'll turn me over to Gran and Granpa. I can't risk that.*

A sob rose in her throat, but Sue fought it down. *Don't cry again, that's a waste of energy. I have to* focus. *I have to keep my mind clear and not give in to emotion. I'm almost there. It's only a few more hours at most, and then I can take a break, get some rest, and maybe find some hope . . .*

But for how long could she afford to rest? Sooner or later, she knew, they'd come for her. They wouldn't just let her get away.

She still had over five hundred dollars in cash in her purse, but there was no telling how long that would last. She was afraid to use her credit cards and her debit card. She'd paid cash at that horrible cheap motel just outside of Richmond, Virginia, where she'd grabbed a few hours of desperately needed sleep before hitting the road again. She couldn't leave any electronic traces behind—that would make it too easy for them to find her. She'd left her cell phone back at her dorm room in upstate New York, buying a cheap disposable pay-as-you-go one at a Wal-Mart somewhere in northern Pennsylvania as she headed south. She'd worried about her license plates, wondering if there was a bulletin sent out with a description of her and her car—but if it came down to it, there was the gun in the compartment between the seats. She wasn't sure if she would actually have the nerve to use it, but it was there in case she needed it.

I hope I don't have to use it, she thought, glancing down at the armrest where it was hidden. But she would if she had to.

The highway was wet and the rhythmic sound of the water being thrown up by the wheels against the car made her even sleepier. She was exhausted. It had been almost sixteen hours since she checked out of that miserable motel and hit the road. Outside of stopping for gas and a quick run to the bathroom, she'd been driving—and her legs and back were stiff. She could feel knots of tension in her back, and her left elbow was sore from resting on the car door. Her eyes burned with fatigue, her throat was dry, her lips chapped. She'd kept the window cracked, hoping the rush of cold air from outside would keep her awake. She glanced at her watch. It was almost two.

It can't be much further, she reasoned. *On the map Hammond looks like it's almost in Mississippi.* She glanced at herself in the rearview mirror and grimaced. Worse than how she looked, she could smell herself and it wasn't pleasant—she smelled like sour socks. Her feet were sweating in her shoes. And now her stomach was growling. She hadn't eaten since seven in the morning, when she'd stopped at a Hardee's somewhere in north Alabama. She'd managed to choke down some sort of fried egg on a dry biscuit, washing it down with numerous cups of coffee. All she'd wanted to do was just put her head down on the table and go to sleep right there. But she'd forced herself to get a refill to go, and kept driving.

Got to keep going, Sue told herself, repeating the litany like a catechism. *Don't know when they might come after me, don't know how much time I have, got to get there before they figure out where I've gone, got to get there while it's still safe—if it ever was safe there in the first place.*

She allowed herself to smile when she saw the big sign with the fleur-de-lis in the center, reading WELCOME TO LOUISIANA and BIENVENUE EN LOUISIANE underneath. She thought about stopping at the welcome area, but there were too many cars and trucks parked all around, and a quick glance down at her gas gauge, inching ever closer to the red, convinced her to keep going. She decided to take the next exit with a gas station, fill up the tank, use the restroom, and get something to snack on, maybe another cup of coffee. Her stomach rebelled at the thought of more coffee—especially gas station coffee. *Maybe a soda,* she thought. *I'm almost there, it can't be more than another hour, maybe I can make myself stay awake till I get there without more coffee.*

After crossing the state line, she took the next exit, pulling into a deserted Texaco station. It was a typical roadside gas station, two islands with numbered pumps, a little food store for snacks, and restrooms. Through the rain she could discern Christmas lights strung along the outside of the building, blinking red and green and yellow. Signs all over the glass front announced sales on beer, soda, and the availability of Louisiana lottery tickets. The jackpot for the next drawing was fifty-three million dollars.

A lot of good that would do me, Sue thought.

She noticed off to the side of the station a battered-looking Toyota was parked, with bumper stickers plastered all over the trunk and rear bumper: YOUR MOTHER WAS PRO-LIFE. GOD CREATED ADAM AND EVE NOT ADAM AND STEVE. JESUS DIED FOR YOUR SINS. SUPPORT THE TROOPS. A metal fish symbol was affixed to the lower trunk close to the bumper and next to the license plate, just below a huge yellow ribbon.

She felt an inexplicable surge of panic.

Get out of here, get back on the highway, stop at the next station, there's got to be a better place than this, raced through her head before she got a hold of herself again. *I need gas, and I have to go to the bathroom.*

Just be goddamned careful, that's all.

Sue pulled to a stop at the pump closest to the store entrance and stepped out of the car, shivering against the chill in the air. The rain was letting up. She stretched—she hadn't been out of the car in over four hours since stopping at a rest area—and her knees and back popped in places. It felt good to stand up. She bent over to stretch her back a little more, and twisted at the waist a bit.

She walked over to the door and pushed it open, greeted by the high-pitched wail of a Christmas carol—*Rockin' around the Christmas tree, have a hap-pee holiday*—and a blast of hot air. Sue smiled at the girl behind the counter and headed for the bathroom. Once inside, she locked the door.

The bathroom smelled vaguely like pine. It was relatively clean—she'd used worse on this trip—but she wiped down the seat anyway before dropping her jeans. She let her head rest on her hands. *Almost there,* she reminded herself as her eyes began to droop.

Washing her hands, she ran the sink water until it was hot, then splashed it into her face. She grabbed her brush out of her purse and ran it through her blond hair. *What a mess,* she thought, grimacing at her reflection. *Whatever happened to that pretty college freshman?*

She never really existed, Sue thought with a terrible sensation in her chest.

When her hair was in some sort of order, she dropped the brush back into her purse and looked again at herself in the mirror. *That's better. Not pretty, but at least presentable.* Her hair needed to be washed—a shower would be heaven—but she dried her face and walked out of the bathroom.

At the counter, a fresh pot of coffee was almost finished brewing. The coffee in the other pots looked like mud, scorched by hours on their burners. Her stomach growled again. A glass case full of doughnuts next to the coffee stand enticed her. She opened the case and picked up two glazed doughnuts, slipping one into a bag and taking a bite out of the other as she waited for the pot to stop brewing. She finished the rest of the doughnut, dropping a third into the bag, and poured herself a large cup of the fresh coffee. After adding creamer and sweetener, she took a sip. *Not bad for gas station coffee,* she thought.

The girl working behind the counter was about Sue's age. She was short and carrying an extra thirty pounds, give or take. A home perm had frizzed her mousy brown hair around her head. She looked as if she'd received an intense electrical shock. Her cheeks were thick, narrowing her brown eyes until they were almost invisible. Acne scars pitted both cheeks.

Her lips were thin and painted orange. Her plump arms were freckled where they extended out from her blue smock, and on the upper left arm in blue script the name *Jason* was tattooed. The smock was open, revealing a black T-shirt with *A Touch of Class* silk-screened in gold over her breasts. A charm bracelet jangled as she punched numbers into the register. On her heavy left breast a name tag read MYRNA LEE.

"New York plates," Myrna Lee said, gesturing with her head out the window. "You're a long way from home." Her voice was high-pitched and her accent thick. "Don't see many of those around here."

Sue offered the clerk a small smile. "I want to get twenty in gas, too." *Act normal, like anyone else. That's the most important thing. Don't act funny in any way.*

The register beeped as Myrna Lee typed that in. "Twenty-three forty-seven." The clerk grimaced, her lips pulling back to expose crooked yellow teeth. "Where ya heading, so far away from home?"

She's just making conversation to be polite. Or—she could be one of them . . .

A chill went down her spine. "Los Angeles," she lied, handing over a twenty and a ten, trying to keep her hand from shaking. "Going to go live with my boyfriend."

Myrna Lee took her money, but kept her beady eyes fixed on her face.

"How far is the next town, or where I can get something to eat?" she asked the clerk, who finally averted her eyes. She felt could feel her heart pounding.

"We-ell, let me think." Myrna Lee put her change down on the counter and tapped her chin. "There's Amite, Shiloh, Independence, then Tickfaw, and then Hammond. I reckon it depends on how hungry you are. There are more choices in Hammond, I'd imagine. College town."

"And how far is that?" *Don't act too interested in Ham-*

mond. Even if she isn't one of them, they could always ask her, and you don't want to give too much away.

"Twenty, thirty minutes maybe. It ain't far."

"And New Orleans?"

"New Orleans? 'Bout another hour past Hammond." Myrna Lee grimaced again. "It ain't the same since the hurricane, though. You just keep taking 55 past Hammond, and then you go east on I-10. You pick it up out in the swamp. I-10'll take you right to New Orleans."

"Thanks."

"Don't mention it. You have a happy Christmas now."

Sue wished her the same, then picked up the doughnuts and coffee and walked back out to the car. Hooking the nozzle into the tank and setting the latch so she didn't have to hold it, she wolfed down the doughnuts. Then she took another long sip of the coffee. When the gas tank clicked that she was full, she replaced the nozzle back onto the pump and climbed back into the car.

She sat there for a few moments after starting the ignition. It was still raining, and an eighteen-wheeler flew past on I-55, throwing up a huge spray of water.

"Almost there," she said out loud, and then felt panic starting to creep into her brain.

What if this was all for nothing? What if there's nothing she can do to help me? What if she's not even there? What if there's nothing anyone can do to help me? I don't even know why I'm going to see Dr. Marshall—but she is an expert, and the girl said she could help me. But this could still all just be a fool's errand, the delusions of a crazy girl, a crazy girl who claims she—

"Stop it," Sue said, pounding the steering wheel with both hands. "This isn't going to help."

Her eyes filled with tears. Sue sat there for a full minute and let the panic sweep over her. Her body began to tremble, and she put her head down on the steering wheel and let the tears come. After a few moments, she took a deep breath and regained control of herself. "Okay, that's enough of that," she said aloud.

She glanced out the window. Myrna Lee had come outside and was staring at her, smoking a cigarette. Sue wiped at her face, smiled, and gave Myrna Lee a friendly wave, even though fear was starting to inch its insidious way back into her mind. *So much for acting normal,* she thought grimly as she slipped the car into gear and rolled out of the parking lot. *I need to put some distance between me and this place.*

There was no traffic coming, so she sped up as she headed back onto the highway. The eighteen-wheeler was just taillights in the mist far ahead of her. She got the car back up to seventy-one miles an hour and turned the cruise control back on, then allowed herself to relax a little bit. But within a few miles, she was back to glancing in the rearview mirror every minute or so to make sure no one was behind her.

I'm being stupid, Sue reminded herself again. *Even if they are coming after me, how would I know it was them behind me? I wouldn't know until it was too late, until they had me—*

"Stop it," she said, and turned the radio up louder.

Angels we have heard on high, sweetly singing o'er the plain . . .

She wished so much she had managed to grab her iPod, or at least a handful of CDs.

Every muscle, every bone, every joint in her body ached with fatigue. Sue's eyelids began drooping again. The coffee hadn't helped at all, other than to churn up more acid in her stomach. She grabbed the pack of Rolaids she'd bought a hundred years ago, it seemed, in North Carolina and chewed on two. Rolling the window all the way down in spite of the rain, she took a long deep breath of cold air. Her hair blew back into a mass of tangles and her teeth began to chatter, but it was better than falling asleep again.

She flew past the exits for Amite, Tickfaw, and Independence, glancing down at the directions she'd printed off the Internet just before taking off on this nightmare drive. The first Hammond exit wasn't the right one, so she kept going. The traffic was getting heavier, but it was the second turnoff she wanted. She slowed down at the bottom of the off-ramp and turned left, heading into Hammond. She passed a Lowe's, a Wal-Mart, and the numerous fast-food places that always gathered in small towns near the highway exit. Her stomach growled again and she thought about going to a drive-through, but dismissed the thought as quickly as it came. *I'm almost there. I can worry about getting something to eat after I've gotten out of this goddamned car and talked to Dr. Marshall.*

Even though it was early afternoon, the wet streets were packed with cars crawling along as she passed parking lot after parking lot. *Christmas shoppers*, she thought. Once she had loved Christmas. Once it had been a festive time for her, but now it terrified her.

She dreaded what might come on Christmas Eve.

She passed a Raising Cane, a Sonic, a Wendy's, and the sight almost made her cry again. *No, no, you're almost there, keep going*. The road swerved to the right and she followed the curve, and started passing into a residential area. The street she wanted was two blocks past the railroad tracks, and she turned right, watching the house numbers. She struggled to keep her eyes open and focused. She'd gone two blocks when she found the house she wanted, and turned into the driveway, parking behind a black Chevrolet SUV.

The house was a three-story clapboard Victorian, complete with a cupola. Dormer windows peered out from what was probably a half-attic. A porch ran the distance of the house and curved around it, disappearing behind in the back. The windows were large, and the whole place needed painting. The lawn was also in disrepair, with exposed areas of dirt. Towering pines shot upward with lower branches sparse and brown.

Yet the windows were lit up with blue Christmas lights, and a huge Christmas tree, unlit, stood in a window at the corner of the house. Gray smoke rose from a chimney. She smiled. *Someone must be home.*

Still, she sat in the car for a couple of moments, and felt the fear start to snake through her body again.

What if this was all for nothing? What if she has no answers for you? What if she thinks you're crazy, and calls them to tell them you're here? What if there's nothing she can do to help you?

"No," Sue whispered, gripping the steering wheel with both hands until her knuckles whitened. "Stop it. You're here."

She steeled herself, and got out of the car. It was raining hard again, so she grabbed her backpack and ran up to the front door. Without any hesitation, she rang the bell. Footsteps sounded within the house, and she sagged against the door frame with relief.

The door opened. The woman who stood in front of her was in her early fifties, wearing a red and black checked flannel shirt over jeans and fuzzy blue house slippers. Her short dark hair was shot through with gray, and reading glasses were perched on the end of her nose. Her eyes widened in surprise.

"Sue?" Her eyes grew wide. "What on earth are you doing here?"

She pulled the younger woman into a hug.

"But thank God you're all right! I've been worried sick about you."

Sue couldn't say anything. All of her weariness suddenly seemed to overcome her. She just clung onto Dr. Marshall.

The older woman stepped back and looked at her. "Are you okay, Sue? You look terrible! What's wrong? Why are you here?"

"Just really tired, Dr. Marshall." Sue gave her a weak smile. Her legs felt like they might buckle at any moment. "I had to come. I had to see you."

Dr. Marshall stepped aside and Sue brushed by her into the house. "Ever since I got that e-mail from you, I half expected this," the older woman said. "Sue, are you sure you're okay?"

"I don't know if I'll ever be okay again." Once inside Dr. Marshall's house, Sue began to tremble. "I need your help. And I'm so tired—so very tired."

"Well, yes, of course I'll do whatever I can. Come on in." Dr. Marshall gestured into the living room. "Have a seat here. Can I get you anything? You must be hungry." She followed the younger woman into the room, standing over Sue as she nearly collapsed on the sofa. "I haven't been to the grocery store—but I'm sure I can make you a sandwich or something." She stared down at Sue, pushing her glasses up her nose. "Sue, you look *terrible*. Are you sure you're all right?"

Sue laughed bitterly. "I'm alive, aren't I?"

The room was warm, comfortable. The furniture didn't match, and there was a thin layer of dust on the tables. A fire blazed in the fireplace. Books were piled everywhere, and overflowed from bookshelves on the walls. A frayed Oriental rug covered the hardwood floor in the sitting area.

"Has anyone—" Sue's words stuttered as she looked up at Dr. Marshall. "Has anyone been looking for me?"

"The college called here last night, wondering if I'd heard from you." Dr. Marshall looked at her intently. "Would you like some tea? Coffee? A soda?"

Sue sat upright. "What did you tell them?"

"Well, you told me in your e-mail not to say anything to anyone." Dr. Marshall shrugged. "Sue, what's going on? What kind of trouble are you in? Apparently, your grandparents are frantic." She leaned forward. "Don't you want to call them?"

"No." Sue replied definitively.

I didn't tell anyone I was coming here—but they suspected I might come here. How could they have known? I got rid of the cell phone, and the phone I bought was untraceable . . .

Then it hit her.

They must have hacked into my e-mail account.

She fought back a sob. *I'm not safe here, I'm not safe anywhere, they'll find me wherever I run to . . .*

"Let me get you that tea and sandwich, then we'll talk." Dr. Marshall headed out of the room, and Sue's body slumped with fatigue and defeat against the back of the sofa.

Maybe Dr. Marshall won't be able to help me, but at least I'm here. They might be able to trace me here, but I won't be here that long. If they know I'm coming here, they're probably already on their way. I could be putting her in danger. But if I tell her before I go, I might be safer. And once someone else knows, if anything happens to me . . .

She didn't finish the thought. She didn't want to think about that.

She reached down, opened her backpack, and pulled a manila envelope out of it. The envelope was full of printouts, two separate groups rubber-banded together, which she placed on the coffee table. She could hear Dr. Marshall in the kitchen. She had everything in that envelope memorized, but she started reading the printout on top again.

VIRGIN SIGHTING IN MONTERREY
(from the Mexico City Sentinel)

LOS ZAPATOS—Thousands of the faithful have
come to this tiny town in the desert of Monterrey
to watch and pray for the Virgin Mary's
intercession.

Three young girls, all aged thirteen, went to
their village priest just over a week ago to tell
him of their miraculous vision. They were looking
for a lost goat when, on a hilltop, the three girls
heard a voice and looked up. According to the
priest, Father Fernando Ortiz, the girls claimed
that the "sun turned into a silver disk and moved
across the sky until it was directly over their
heads, where it began to spin, growing smaller
and smaller until it winked out and darkness fell
over the hills. Then, a small light appeared, and
grew until it took the form of the Holy Mother,
who then spoke to the girls. The Holy Mother
asked them to pray for the repentance of
mankind, and also spoke to them of other things,
about which she swore them to secrecy."

While the girls have steadily refused to tell
anyone what the Virgin Mary told them, they
have returned to the hillside every day, where
they claim she reappears to them and gives them
other messages, again swearing them to secrecy.

The news of the visions spread throughout the
province, and now every day when the girls
return to the hillside, they are joined by
thousands of faithful Catholics, who maintain
a distance from them while the girls are
experiencing their visions of the Virgin Mary.

A spokesperson for the Archdiocese of Mexico

City refused to comment on the sightings, saying
only that the Church is taking these visions very
seriously and is planning on conducting its own
investigation into the sightings.

Sue paged through the clippings for the thousandth time.
They were culled from newspapers and press services all
over the world, and each one of them told a similar story—
all within days of each other.

A young Catholic girl in a small rural village in Vietnam
was marked with stigmata. There was another vision of the
Virgin Mary in a remote village in the Philippines. In each
case, the children were given a message and sworn to secrecy
by the Holy Mother. In Poland, in Canada, in sub-Saharan
Africa, in India. Stigmata, visions of the Virgin Mary—or if
she appeared to non-Christian children, she was described in
terms of their own religion. "A holy lady." "The goddess of
the sky." One Chinese girl claimed a visit from Quan Yin, the
female manifestation of the Buddha. The tabloids were having
a field day. ARE THESE THE END TIMES? one headline screamed.

Sue's hands shook as she paged through the clippings. All
of the articles and stories in the first grouping were from
twenty years ago. The second pile was from the last two
months. They all consisted of the same type of thing: occurrences of stigmata and sightings of the Virgin.

Sue ran her hands through her unwashed hair. *Maybe I
have lost my mind. None of this will make any sense to anyone. All I have to go on is the word of two women, and both
of them could be completely insane.*

But if they're insane, that doesn't explain—

She choked back another sob.

Dr. Marshall came back into the living room, carrying a
tray with a teakettle and two cups. There was also a sandwich on brown bread. Placing the tray down on top of sev-

eral magazines on the coffee table, she poured a cup of tea for Sue and passed it over to her. She smiled apologetically.

"I'm sorry, dear, all I had was peanut butter. I hope that's okay. Maybe we could order a pizza or something?"

Sue picked up the sandwich. "No, this is fine for now." She wanted to add, but didn't: *I don't have a lot of time.*

Dr. Marshall poured herself a cup of the tea, then picked up the pile of papers. She frowned as she paged through them all. "Sue—what are you doing with all of this?"

Sue let the tea warm her as she leaned back into the sofa. "Sometimes, I think I'm going insane, Dr. Marshall. I think I've completely and utterly lost my mind. But if I'm not—if I'm right—if everything I've been through, been told, and found out is true, I would *rather* be insane." She laughed. "I don't even know what to think anymore."

"But I don't understand." Dr. Marshall riffled through the pile of papers again. "Why did you come here? Why did you bring this with you?"

"Because you're the only person who *would* understand." *Because a woman in a psych ward told me to come here, that you could help me, that you were meant to help me, crazy as that might sound.*

Dr. Marshall set the papers down and picked up her teacup. "This is all very interesting. Obviously, I'm very familiar with all of this, since I'm writing a book about sightings of the Virgin Mary." She smiled. "I've even been to Los Zapatos, when those young girls were having their visions."

"And what did you think?"

"Sue, dear, I fail to see how this—I mean, you came all this way to talk about sightings?"

"Please, just tell me what you think about the visions in Los Zapatos. And everywhere else."

Dr. Marshall sighed. "The Church has never recognized

any of these visitations as miracles, you know." She took another sip of her tea. "Of course, if it had been just fifty years earlier, the Church would have been all over these incidents. Back then, they seemed to like to publicize them, to whip the devout into a bit of religious frenzy. But things have changed, and now the Church isn't so sure . . ."

Sue closed her eyes.

Dr. Marshall studied her with concern. "But what does any of this have to do with you, Sue? Why have you run away, made your grandparents worry? This is not like you. Are you sure you don't want me to call your grandparents, let them know you're okay?"

"After I tell you—" Sue bit her lip. "Just let me tell you, okay? Then we can talk about my grandparents, if you want to."

But I am not calling them, Sue told herself, *and if you call them, I'm out of here.*

"All right." Dr. Marshall removed her glasses and rubbed her eyes. "I won't call your grandparents just yet. But talk to me, Sue. Tell me what's going on, what's got you acting so differently. Explain it to me."

So Sue told her everything.

2

She talked for just over three hours. Dr. Marshall didn't interrupt, didn't ask any questions. She just let Sue talk until she finished, betraying no emotion on her face.

The clock on the mantelpiece read just past five thirty when Sue finished her story. The sun had gone down, and an automatic timer had turned the lights on. Every so often as Sue talked, Dr. Marshall had stood and put another log on the fire. The tea service still sat on the coffee table, the water gone cold, the cups untouched for quite some time.

They sat in silence, the only sound the occasional crack and pop from the fireplace.

"So," Sue said finally, "do you think I'm crazy?"

"I'm not sure what to think, to be honest." Dr. Marshall replied, standing up and picking up the tray. She carried it out of the room.

She does. She thinks I'm crazy.

Sue shivered, wrapping her arms around herself. The streetlights outside had come on, throwing strange-looking shadows into the room.

Maybe it was a mistake to come here. Maybe there's no one who can help me.

But if it hadn't all happened to me, I don't know if I would believe it either.

Dr. Marshall walked back in, carrying two wineglasses and an open bottle of Shiraz. She poured herself a glass and placed the bottle and second glass on the table. She settled back into her chair. "Help yourself," she told Sue.

"No, thanks."

"Sue—" Dr. Marshall looked at her with stern eyes. "Surely you're aware of how fantastic your story is."

"Yes. But that doesn't make it untrue." *She doesn't believe me,* Sue thought, clenching and unclenching her fists.

"But you don't have any proof, do you?" Dr. Marshall asked gently. "That's the problem, isn't it?"

"You don't believe me." Sue felt her eyes fill with tears of frustration. *It had been a mistake to come here.*

"No, that's not quite true." Dr. Marshall cleared her throat. "I don't *want* to believe you. But I conducted a few investigations of my own before I left the college, and so parts of your story ring true."

Sue moved forward in her seat. "Do you know then? Do you know what was going on there?"

Dr. Marshall took her glasses off and set them on the coffee table. "No, Sue. Like yourself, I have no hard evidence." She shook her head. "But if your story is true . . . Sue, it's frightening. Absolutely frightening. And without proof, I don't know what we can do. No one will believe this, no one."

"My grandparents lied to me. I can prove that."

"But that doesn't prove your story," Dr. Marshall went on. "Your grandparents could easily explain away why they didn't tell you the truth. I can think of any number of reasons myself they wouldn't have told you."

Sue stood up and walked over to one of the windows facing the front yard. A truck drove by as she watched. *Show her,* a voice within her whispered. *That's the only way to make her believe. You have to show her.*

She resisted the voice, as she had any number of times since that horrible day.

"You really should call your grandparents and let them know you're all right." Dr. Marshall was talking behind her. "They're worried sick about you."

"No." Sue replied. "They aren't worried about me. Didn't you listen to anything I said?"

She turned to face Dr. Marshall, who sat in silence now.

"I explained why they want to find me." She laughed bitterly, shaking her head. "It has nothing to do with concern about me."

"Sue . . ."

She wiped her eyes. "I'll go. But promise me you won't call them. You won't tell anyone I was here."

"Sue, you're exhausted. I can't just let you go—"

"You can't stop me." Sue was hard, angry. "Promise me you won't call my grandparents."

"All right. I won't call them, if you don't want me to. But I insist you not leave here until after you've rested a bit, gotten something more solid to eat than a peanut butter sandwich." Dr. Marshall held up her hands. "And besides, I didn't say I didn't believe you, Sue. It's just a lot—a lot to take in."

"Swear to me you won't call them." Sue was fierce. "I'll lay down, take a nap, whatever you want, but swear to me you won't call them!"

"All right, I swear." Dr. Marshall gave her a smile. "I won't call them. But once you've gotten some rest . . ."

I never want to see or speak to them again, Sue thought, *and no amount of sleep is going to change my mind.*

3

Sue fell asleep almost the moment her head hit the pillow.

Dr. Marshall closed the bedroom door and walked back downstairs into the living room. She refilled her wineglass and sat watching the fire for a moment. Picking up the pile of papers from her coffee table, she thumbed through them again. She'd read all this material before. She had most of it in her files and had, in fact, accessed information the news media had never gotten their hands on. She'd even been to visit many of these sites—and some that weren't included in Sue's folder.

She rubbed her forehead, remembering the terrible conversations she'd had with that police officer back in Lebanon, the college town where she'd spent several mostly unhappy years.

Dr. Ginny Marshall had come back to Hammond to finish her book. She'd been working on *Sightings of the Mother* now for almost twenty years. All too frequently, she'd get distracted from it, getting stuck in mindless academia and forced onto other, more mundane projects that resulted in other books. But she always came back to this book. No matter how many times she'd given up on it, put it out of her head, boxed up her materials and hidden them away, somehow *Sightings of the Mother* always came back to her. She called it her personal Vietnam, *the book she'd started without an exit plan*. It was a joke she'd use when she was still married to Jim.

Los Zapatos, Mexico—that was where she'd started. Twenty years ago, when she was fresh out of graduate school and looking to start her Ph.D. Her marriage to Jim was still new and fresh, still in the honeymoon phase. He'd passed the bar and was working insane hours at his new job with a firm in Boston. She was teaching a couple of theology courses for undergraduates at Harvard, determined to get her Ph.D., tenure, and a name for herself in her field.

Research into the sightings of the Virgin Mary was an odd choice for a Ph.D. dissertation. Still, Jim was all for it— back then, her career was just as important to him as his own, even though the trip to Los Zapatos would strain their already strained finances. But it was also an adventure: flying to El Paso, renting a car and crossing the border, driving through the deserts of northern Mexico to that godforsaken little town. The roads were bad and there were times when Ginny feared she'd run out of gasoline in the middle of nowhere. The Mexican people of the region weren't very friendly to her either; to them, she was the *gringa* with the bad accent. The Mexicans looked at her with suspicion in their dark eyes. They weren't used to Americans, despite their proximity to the border. And Los Zapatos itself . . .

Calling it a *town* was a misnomer. It was a village, dirty and poor, with dusty unpaved streets and poor sanitation. The faithful who flocked to the village were better prepared than she was; they'd brought their own food, their own tents and sleeping bags. None of the villagers would speak to Ginny. But the pilgrims, from all over Mexico, they were different. They were happy to tell her about the Virgin and their faith—even if none of them could see or hear the Virgin. They only came to watch as the three young girls had visions, and to pray, and to leave flowers at the Holy Site.

The parish church was adobe and baked hard by the harsh sun. The priest, Fernando Ortiz, was only too happy to speak to Ginny in his own cultured Spanish. He was very proud of his origins in an upper-middle-class Mexico City family, and even more proud of the tough parish he had been sent to. His faith was strong, he assured her, and only made stronger by the Virgin's miraculous appearance to three of his parishioners.

"Father, I would like to speak to the girls." Ginny requested, seated in a hard chair in his hot office inside the little church.

The tall handsome priest shook his head. "Impossible. The archbishop has refused permission for them to speak to reporters."

She tried again to explain she wasn't a reporter. She was a scholar. But her arguments fell on deaf ears. She understood the only information she'd get would come through this intermediary, this upper-middle-class priest from Mexico City.

"So let me understand," she said. "The Holy Mother has forbidden the girls to tell anyone what they've been told, isn't that correct?"

Father Ortiz gave her a warm smile. "The Holy Mother has forbidden them to tell anyone other than their priest, Señora."

"So, you know what the Virgin has said?" She leaned forward. "Are you sworn to secrecy, too?"

He leaned back in his chair. "I cannot tell you the Mother's message, no. That is for my archbishop's ears only. I go to Mexico City to meet with him next week." He smiled at her. He was young, maybe not even Ginny's own age just yet, with strong white teeth and thick black hair. "The Holy Mother talks to the girls, who are allowed to talk to me, and I can speak to the archbishop, who can only speak to His Holiness the Pope in Rome."

"So I came all this way to try to understand this phenomenon . . ."

Ginny wasn't averse to flirting with him, even if he was a priest. She smiled, looking up from under her long lashes.

He seemed to know what she was doing, and he smiled despite himself.

"Señora, I cannot tell you the Holy Mother's message, but I can tell you this, because I like you." He gestured for her to lean closer to his desk. "You might want to make yourself right with God."

"I don't understand."

He gave her a smile. A sad smile, she thought. A smile that was both sad and rapturous at the same time. But he would say nothing more.

That afternoon, Ginny joined the pilgrims and walked out to the field a few miles outside of the little village, over dirt paths beaten down by the footsteps of others before. The sun was high and hot, and her shirt was soaked through with sweat before they reached the hillside. It was a nondescript place, buzzing with flies and dusty. She wiped sweat from her forehead. Close to a hundred people gathered on the hillside; a woman in a black veil offered Ginny a drink from a bottle of water.

The pilgrims stood in silence as three young girls, not quite teenagers, appeared on the opposite hill. The crowd buzzed with excitement for a moment, then all fell quiet again. Ginny watched the girls climb to the top of the opposite hill, then sink to their knees and turn their faces up to the bright blue sky, their arms outstretched. She watched as their eyes grew wider, and their faces began to glow as they smiled in joy. Not a muscle did they move for almost ten solid minutes. Then the glow faded from their faces and they rose, dusting off their knees. There was a murmur of excitement in the crowd as the girls climbed down their own hill.

That was it. The girls were hustled away by a flock of black-robed nuns.

Ginny stayed in Los Zapatos for a few days more, buying water and food from other pilgrims, sleeping next to the battered Volkswagen she'd rented, writing down notes and her impressions in the spiral notebook she'd brought along. Father Ortiz was no more forthcoming during any of their subsequent meetings, though he reiterated each time his plea to make herself "right with God." Though Ortiz was stubborn, Ginny found herself liking the handsome young priest more and more.

On her third day there, a long black limousine appeared on an unpaved road that led into the village from the south, stirring up whirlwinds of dust. The limo stopped in front of the little church, its back doors opened from within, and all at once Father Ortiz and the three girls scurried from the front doors of the church. The four of them slipped inside the limo, the nuns depositing battered boxes of clothes and books into the trunk. Then the limo doors closed and the vehicle began its slow drive out of Los Zapatos toward Mexico City. The nuns made the sign of the cross as they watched it drive away.

Ginny knew the girls never returned to Los Zapatos. Indeed, the Church never put its stamp of approval on the sightings. No one was really sure whatever happened to the three young girls who claimed to have seen the Virgin. Not even their parents ever knew. It was presumed they were hidden away somewhere. After all, Rome had centuries of practice in keeping its secrets.

Now, holding the printouts in her hand, Ginny became aware that she was trembling just a little bit.

You might want to make yourself right with God.

She looked up at the ceiling. The room Sue was sleeping in was almost directly overhead.

Her story is so fantastic, Ginny thought. *I don't want to believe it*

But she also knew it could be true.

The police officer's story . . . and the words of the girl, Bernadette deSalis . . . they all came together now in some kind of horrible, terrifying logic.

She was trembling even more now.

And it's no coincidence that Father Ortiz has shown up again after all these years . . .

Ginny stood and moved over to her desk, clicking open a file on her computer. It was the opening chapter to her new book. Ginny scrolled down to the last few paragraphs.

There is no question that the Bible has been rewritten and revised and edited numerous times throughout the history of the Christian religion. These revisions have always had a purpose: whether it be to shut out women from the church; extend its political power; or to make the ritualized dogma more palatable to the newly converted.

The Book of Revelation has often been used, throughout history, to promulgate the dogma of the church, as well as to stigmatize political enemies. Political leaders from Charlemagne to Phillip II of France to King John of England, to Adolf Hitler and Stalin in modern times, have been called "the Antichrist." But the coming of the Antichrist and Armageddon, while often viewed by the faithful as a horror, are ultimately the end game of all Christian theology—when the faithful are carried off to Heaven for their just reward. So, why do most Christians fear the Rapture?

There has long been a rumor that several chapters of the Book of Revelation were removed and hidden away by the early Church. These chapters were not written in the mysterious language of prophecy, and very clearly explain who and what the Antichrist will be. They outline in stark specificity the exact conditions of the world that will lead to the rise of this leader. These are what have been termed the "lost revelations."

It is believed by some that if these prophecies were ever made public, they would shake the very foundations, not only of the Church, but of Western civilization itself. Some scholars believe these expunged chapters of Revelation are locked away in the most secure vault in the Vatican and, like other prophecies, can be accessed by only the Pope himself when he succeeds to the throne of St. Peter. It is even said sometimes that St. Peter himself decreed that these dangerous prophecies regarding the end times be suppressed.

Ginny Marshall closed the document. Now it wasn't just her hands that were shaking. Her heart was pounding, and the electricity in the house was beginning to flicker on and off.

It must be the rainstorm, she told herself.

It can't be anything else.

Three Months Earlier

4

"Damn it!"

Sue Barlow swore as she drove right past the exit for Lebanon. She stabbed at the brakes, but it was too late.

I'll have to turn around at the next exit and come back, she thought, annoyed with herself for missing it. *But they should have it better marked.*

The sun was shining bright that day, and the trees on either side of the highway were a vibrant green. But it was upstate New York after all, and here and there Sue had spotted a few patches of pinkish gold, evidence of autumn's impatience to put an end to summer's run. She'd missed the exit for Lebanon, in fact, because she'd been admiring the rolling hills of trees as far as the eye could see. She'd also been speeding, she realized now. She'd come around that last curve at nearly eighty-five miles per hour, humming along with the CD of *The Magic Flute.*

Now she could make out another exit ramp about a mile down the highway. With a quick shake of her head and a rueful laugh at her stupidity, Sue pressed the gas pedal down harder and the car picked up speed. She reached the second off-ramp in the blink of an eye, and a joyful giggle erupted from her throat. Speeding up the incline, she made sure no cars were coming in either direction before she coasted through the stop sign at the top. She shot across the bridge and headed back down the ramp in the other direction, rocketing back onto the highway.

I love this car, Sue thought again as the speedometer reached eighty with an amazing ease.

The brand-new white Lexus two-door was a graduation gift from her grandparents. They'd surprised her with it that very morning as she got ready to leave for her first day of college. They'd taken her down to the parking garage beneath their building and there it sat, gleaming.

"You'll need a car up there anyway," her grandmother told her, seeming to try to rationalize their extravagance, her soft Southern accent still pronounced despite years of vocal coaching. "And this way, we don't have to worry about you taking trains, or sending Radcliffe up to get you for holidays."

Radcliffe was their driver. He routinely carried Sue's grandparents to every occasion, big and small, in the austere black Lincoln town car parked in the spot next to the Lexus.

"Thank you, thank you!" Sue exclaimed, giving both her grandmother and grandfather giant hugs before running over to the car and slipping inside. It was love at first sight. She'd always wanted her own car, even though she didn't really need one in Manhattan—the traffic was always horrendous and she'd been getting around on the subways or grabbing cabs ever since her grandparents decided she was old enough to go out unsupervised. When necessary, her grandparents had given the nod for Radcliffe to chauffeur her around in the town car, but riding around with a uniformed driver always made Sue uncomfortable. *Putting on airs,* as her grandmother liked to say. So when she turned sixteen, finally old enough to drive, Sue had asked for a car of her own—but while her grandfather had agreed she might take driving lessons and get her license, he'd refused outright to get her a car.

"You are too young," he'd told Sue in no uncertain terms—and Sue had learned early in life not to argue with her grandfather. His word was law in their family.

Still, she'd been kind of hoping that she might get a car for her graduation from Stowe Academy. There had been hints, like commenting on other cars to get Sue's reactions to them. She'd scrunched up her nose at the Mini Cooper, and declared the Range Rover to be "too masculine," but she'd licked her lips when they'd passed a white Lexus much like this one. Yet when graduation rolled around, she was left confounded. Her graduation gift, her grandparents announced, was a three-week holiday in Paris.

As much as she'd enjoyed their strolls down the Champs d'Elysée, however, Sue kept wondering about a car. And finally, here it was, her own wheels, just in time for her move to college, when she would finally be out from under her grandfather's thumb. *No more rules or restrictions*. Sue felt like singing.

Of course, it wasn't like Wilbourne College didn't have its own set of rules—part of the reason, Sue suspected, that her grandparents had pushed the school so insistently on her. That and some other reasons, of course. Life in the dorms, Sue had read in the school manual, was pretty strict. No parties, no alcohol, and certainly no boys. But compared to living in her grandparents' apartment on Central Park West in what some of her friends from Stowe called "the concentration camp"—she was indeed free.

And now, driving herself more than three hundred miles to her new school, speeding along the highway and coasting through stop signs, Sue exulted in that freedom.

It was hard not to be excited. She was eighteen, and on her own for the first time in her life. She'd been looking forward to college for as long as she could remember. And she now had her own car to boot.

And nothing had prepared her for the joy of hurtling down a highway at over eighty miles per hour, the stereo blaring, the wind down and her hair getting tossed about in the wind. Nothing had prepared her for how it felt to have a warm sun coming through the windshield, her expensive sunglasses perched on her nose, stopping whenever she felt like it, passing slower cars without a second thought as she drove farther and farther north. *Now I know why people are so attached to their cars,* she thought with another grin. *It's all about freedom,* she thought as she glanced into the rearview mirror. For eighteen years, her life had been defined by the walls of her grandparents' apartment. While she had her trips to Florida and Paris, they were always arranged and controlled by her grandfather. For the first time, Sue was on her own.

If I wanted to, she thought giddily, *I could just keep driving, see wherever the road leads, see parts of upstate New York I've never seen, head to the border and cross over into Canada. I can go wherever I want to whenever I want to.*

College was the first step to adulthood, and this was just a small taste of freedom. But the practical side of her mind soon stepped in.

Don't be silly, you can't just keep driving on. You have responsibilities and dreams and ambitions—and college is the first step.

Sue had a feeling she was destined for big things. She was smart—all her teachers at Stowe had told her so—and certainly her grandparents had raised her with the expectation that she would be special. They might have been strict—rarely letting her roam through the city with her girlfriends, never allowing her to bring a boyfriend home—but that was only because she was all they had. Manhattan was a dangerous place for a girl to grow up. Girls disappeared all the time—as Gran was always reminding her. "Always pay attention and keep your eyes open and be aware of your surroundings," Gran had lectured.

Last night, in their final heart-to-heart, Gran had delivered a new warning. "Remember, Susan, just because you're going to college in a small town in the country doesn't mean that you can let your guard down for a minute. You're a pretty girl. Very pretty. Very special. And lots of people get very jealous of pretty, special girls."

Heading back along the highway, Sue couldn't help but laugh out loud at her grandmother's words. Both Gran and Granpa were very old school, so out of touch with modern life. Of course Sue loved them—they'd been the only parents she'd ever known—but it would sure be refreshing to see the world without the filters they imposed, to make her own decisions and follow her own rules. That is, as much as Wilbourne College would allow.

She made sure she didn't miss the southbound exit, coasting to a stop at the top of the ramp. A battered old Chevrolet pickup truck from sometime during the days of hippies passed by, the rusted-out back filled with crates of apples. Sure enough, there was a peace symbol on the bumper, as well as a sticker reading IMPEACH BUSH. Sue smiled, rolled her eyes, and turned left. In her mind she could hear her grandfather. "Hippies started the decline of this great country," he'd say. "They were all nothing but Communists, and this country has never recovered from their foolishness."

Sue shook her head. In Granpa's mind, anyone who disagreed with him on anything was a Communist—even though *Communism* in the way he'd always feared didn't really exist anymore. More than once, Sue had considered pointing that fact out to him, but she always bit her tongue. It was better not to say anything than to argue with Granpa. He thought he was always right, and keeping peace in the house was the most important thing. His rages, though infrequent, could be terrible—and she and Gran had always done whatever they could to make sure he didn't fly off into one of them. Nobody, nothing was safe when Granpa was angry.

Sue shuddered, wondering why her thoughts had turned so dark all of a sudden. Why think of any of that now?

According to the directions she'd gotten off the Internet, Lebanon was just about two miles from the highway. She'd been there once before, when she and her grandparents had come up in April to check the place out. Of course, Radcliffe had driven them then, and Sue had been forced to stick close to Gran's side the whole time. Now she was looking forward to seeing what Wilbourne was like without her controlling chaperones.

She sped up, ignoring the posted speed limit of fifty. The two-lane road was smooth and dark, as if it had been recently repaved. She drove past rows and rows of apple trees spreading out on either side of the road, the sweet smell of the ripening fruit heavy in the air. She wrinkled her nose. She'd never been a big fan of apples.

When she saw the sign WELCOME TO LEBANON—HOME OF WILBOURNE COLLEGE, she slowed down to sixty. At almost the exact same moment, she saw the flashing red lights in her rearview mirror and heard the "whoop-whoop-whoop" of a police siren.

"Aw, shit," Sue grumbled, slowing down and coasting to a stop on the side of the road. *Granpa's going to kill me, getting a speeding ticket on the first day away from home. That's a big lecture about responsibility and insurance rates just waiting to happen.*

In the armrest between the front seats was an envelope containing proof of insurance and registration papers. Before she'd left, her grandfather had shown them to her and given her a lecture about obeying the traffic laws. "I don't want to get a call from the state police that you've flipped the car or something," he said, shaking his finger at her. "A car is a big responsibility, young lady, and I want to know that you're up to our trust and faith in you."

Sighing, Sue flipped the armrest up and retrieved the envelope. She was reaching for her purse when the cop tapped on her window.

She rolled it down partway. That was something else her grandfather had impressed on her: *If you're in the car alone and you get pulled over, make sure you don't put the window down all the way and don't unlock the door. Be respectful, but always remember that cops aren't all nice men either.*

"Yes, Officer?" Sue gave him what she hoped looked like a respectful smile.

"License, registration, proof of insurance, ma'am." His voice was deep but soft. He was wearing a brown uniform and sunglasses. She couldn't tell how tall he was since he was having to bend down to talk through the crack in the window. His legs looked long, and his shirt seemed to hang on his upper torso. His bare forearms were cobwebbed with veins. He seemed young, barely old enough to be a police officer, barely older than Sue herself.

Flirt with him. Becca Stansfield, one of Sue's friends at the Stowe Academy for Girls on the Upper West Side, had sworn she'd never gotten a ticket despite her complete disregard for traffic laws. With her thick mane of red hair and huge breasts, flirting came easy to her when she was pulled over for speeding out on Long Island, where her family had a beach house. Sue's grandparents disapproved of Becca—her mother was an actress notorious for her divorces and her many lovers. But Sue found Becca fascinating. Becca seemed to know everything there was to know about boys and sex, and she was losing her patience with Sue. "You're missing out on so much," she'd say with a flip of her hair.

"Guys are a lot of fun, and pretty as you are, you could have them eating out of the palm of your hands. Live a little! Surely, you can break curfew once in a while or sneak out of that mausoleum."

"Ma'am? Did you hear me?" the cop called again through the window.

"Oh, yes, of course, Officer. Just a moment."

She gave him a sunny smile as her eyes caught a glimpse of herself in the mirror. *Pretty.* That's what Gran always said, and Becca seemed to agree, but Sue's ash-blond hair wasn't thick and didn't bounce with as much verve as Becca's did, no matter how much conditioner or treatments Sue gave it. Pretty? Sue was never really convinced. There was the matter of that small bump in the middle of her nose from the time she'd broken it at age twelve in gym class. She considered her face was too narrow for her wide mouth, and her left eye was slightly larger and set a little higher in her face than the right.

But her eyes, a vibrant green with gold flecks, were her best feature. Of this much she was confident. She turned back to the window and gave the policeman a smile she hoped was seductive. "Was I speeding, Officer?" she asked, using just a pinch of her grandmother's Southern accent.

I'm so lame, she groaned inwardly. *I don't even know how to flirt.* Still, she kept the smile pasted on her face and tried to think how Becca would act in the same situation.

The officer examined Sue's documents, then handed them back through the window. "Yes, ma'am, you were," he said. "I clocked you at sixty-five in a fifty zone." He took off his mirrored sunglasses, and his eyes were a chocolate brown. "That's a pretty hefty fine, Miss Barlow."

"Oh." She bit her lower lip. *Granpa is going to kill me— he might even take the car away. A huge ticket on the first day I have the car.*

"You haven't been driving long, have you?" His teeth flashed in a smile. Sue shook her head no.

He's kind of cute, Sue thought. She didn't have a lot of experience with guys. Not once since kindergarten had she ever gone to school with boys. While her classmates were always talking and giggling about boys, she'd always sat there clueless. Whenever she met her friends' boyfriends, she found them immature and childish—no matter how cute they were. The occasional guy that Becca would fix her up with always turned out be dull and uninteresting. The one boy she'd liked— a guy named Tom Parker she'd met at one of Becca's family bashes in the Hamptons—had been a studious, smart boy who told her he wanted to study astrophysics and understand the interaction between matter and radiation in outer space. Sue hadn't known what the hell Tom was talking about, but his intensity had been sexy, and she wanted to see him again. But he never called. She suspected her grandfather had found about it and turned the boy away. What was the use anyway? *Why would he want to go out with me when I have to be home by ten on a Saturday night?*

"You need to focus on your studies," Granpa always argued. "Boys are a distraction." Many times Sue had thought about protesting, holding out for even eleven o'clock as a curfew—but decided it wasn't worth it. She'd be in college soon enough, she reasoned, and besides, she never knew what to say or how to act around most boys anyway. She certainly didn't want her breasts pawed at the way Becca described. She didn't like how Becca and the other girls acted around guys, turning into imbeciles and behaving like fools.

She focused her attention on the eyes of the young man peering through the window at her.

"No, sir," she said, "I haven't been driving long. I just got the car last night, in fact."

She kept her voice deferential and respectful. Another

lesson from her grandfather: *When dealing with the police,
always be polite and show respect. They are doing their jobs.
Be cooperative, but never give away any information that
they don't ask for. And if you think you could be in serious
trouble, ask for a lawyer immediately. If there's any question
in your mind, ask for a lawyer. It's your right.*

"I suppose I could just let you go with a warning." The
officer was still smiling. "Seems like a bad way to start your
school year, with a ticket and all."

"That would be so great." All the tension built up inside
of her since she heard the siren was swept away and she gave
him a real smile. "Wilbourne students are probably a real
pain in the ass for you, huh?" she asked in a sympathetic
tone.

He shrugged. "Not really. There's hardly ever any trouble
up on the campus, and girls aren't as big of troublemakers as
boys, you know. This your first year then?"

She nodded. "Freshman. Guilty as charged."

"You'll like it here. It'll take some getting used to after
Manhattan, because it's awful quiet around here." He shook
his head. "You're probably going to miss your boyfriend."

"I don't have a boyfriend."

He took off his sunglasses and leaned on the door, bringing his face closer to hers. He *was* good-looking, Sue decided. He had big brown eyes with thick lashes, a strong nose,
thick full lips over strong white teeth. He looked strong, but
in a lean narrow-hipped kind of way rather than those thickly
muscled jock idiots Becca Stansfield preferred. There was
some stubble on his cheeks and chin.

"My name's Perry Holland," the cop said.

Taking a chance, Sue buzzed the window all the way
down. "Sue Barlow." She giggled. "But then you knew that
already, didn't you?"

"Nice to meet you." They shook hands through the window, and then fell silent for a few moments. Perry watched her face for a few moments more before standing back to his full height. "You'd best be getting on to school, Ms. Barlow."

"Sue."

"Sue." Perry nodded. "Be seeing you around."

I hope so, she thought as she put her window back up. He winked at her before putting his sunglasses back on and walking back to his patrol car. Sue sat there, watching him in the rearview mirror as he made a U-turn and headed back down the shady lane in the direction of the highway.

Sue giggled. *Becca would be proud.*

The campus was on the other side of Lebanon, and she made sure she followed the speed limit as she drove through the center of town. There was a town square with a courthouse, and little businesses lined the streets that surrounded it. Church spires poked up through the trees. People milled about on the sidewalks, some of them still in their church clothes. Sue drove on, the businesses and houses growing farther and farther apart until she was out of the town and in the country again. Through the bushes on the side of the road, Sue soon became aware of a brown brick wall. It was high and imposing, and Sue realized she had reached the campus. The wall seemed so coldly impenetrable to her— keeping people out of Wilbourne, and keeping the girls in.

After another mile, she saw the massive brick entryway into the campus. A huge wrought-iron arrangement of curlicues and flowers branched from one brick column to the other, and in Gothic letters was spelled out WILBOURNE COLLEGE. Driving through the gates, she followed the campus map the school had sent to her. She was looking for her dormitory, Bentley Hall. All around her, girls were meandering across the campus, some carrying books, most of them in little groups. A pang shot through Sue's stomach. *They all look like they know everybody already. I know no one.*

Up ahead, she saw the sign for Bentley Hall. The parking lot in front was already full, but Sue pulled up underneath a big oak tree and sat there for a moment.

This is it, she thought, *I'm finally here.*

Excitement and trepidation warred within her. She was thrilled to be on her own, but also suddenly frightened. She supposed the fear was normal. She'd grown up very protected, very sheltered. Now she was taking her first steps on her own.

But there was <u>something else, too.</u>

She glanced up at the windows of Bentley Hall. They seemed so dark. Almost as if the glass were painted black. *They're tinted for privacy,* she supposed. But for some unknown reason, those black windows terrified her.

Watching from inside her car, Sue felt as if she had entered another world. All noise from the outside world was cut off by the sturdy construction of the Lexus. As she watched the girls stroll past, their lips moving in conversation without making any sound, Sue shivered. Why was she suddenly so afraid?

Get over this, she told herself. *You're here. Go for it!*

There were no signs prohibiting parking, so she figured she could leave the car here, at least for now, at least until she got her parking sticker and found her way around. Sue took a deep breath and got out of the car. She stood there for a moment and looked around. The grounds of the campus were immaculately kept. A huge fountain in the middle of a big expanse of lawn bubbled to her left. Bright yellow marigolds and sunny pink petunias bordered the paved pathways leading from Bentley Hall to the other buildings, most of which were red brick, with a few hewn out of brownstone.

Sue's heart was thudding in her ears as she removed her suitcase from the trunk. Everything else she'd shipped on ahead of time. Ahead of her, there was considerable activity in the dormitory parking lot. Several girls were dragging boxes and suitcases out across the pavement toward for the front door. Sue was glad that Gran had insisted on shipping everything. She pulled up the suitcase's tow bar and started rolling it through the parking lot, and pulled it up over the curb.

Bentley Hall was enormous. Four floors high, made of neat red bricks and those large dark windows heading off in either direction from the main entrance. A wrought-iron statue of a woman in nineteenth-century clothing stood right beside the entrance. Sue stood there for a moment, staring up at what would be her home for the next four years. Her eyes went from window to window, wondering which were hers, wishing she could see some light—some life—behind one of them. The packet from the school had indicated she would be rooming on the second floor. She began moving her eyes across the line of second floor windows, when something just above— on the third floor—caught her eye.

What was that?

She stared back up at the window, but there was nothing there now.

She shook her head.

She could have sworn she'd seen a girl's face there.

And it looked as if the girl was screaming.

5

Sue made her way up to the second floor, wrestling her rolling suitcase into an elevator that was packed with other girls and boxes. The other girls all seemed to know each other, laughing and joking and teasing, and Sue felt very alone. She tried to smile at the other girls, nodding and saying hello. She told them her name when they asked for it. But mostly, she just went her own way, and the other girls let her. She knew she should make more of an effort to talk to them, to make new friends, but she couldn't get what she'd seen—what she thought she'd seen—out of her mind.

I must have imagined it, she told herself as she rolled her suitcase down the hallway on the second floor, looking for her room. *My mind was playing tricks on me, that's all that was. I'm more tired than I thought from getting up early and the long drive up here. It's my first time away from home, and I'm nervous and a little jumpy.*

But still, she couldn't get the image of that face out of her head.

Ahead of her, to the left, was Room 227. The door was already open, and dance music was playing loudly. Sue walked in, and saw her boxes and luggage stacked in one corner, near a window. The room was larger than she expected, with two twin beds set out on opposite sides of the room. Each side of the room had bookshelves built into the walls, and there were matching closet doors on either side of the room. Another door on one side led into what she assumed was the bathroom. That had been a reassurance for her when she'd read the material sent by the college. All the rooms in Bentley Hall had their own bathrooms. She wasn't sure how she'd managed to get a room in Bentley—her grandfather's influence most likely—but she wasn't going to question her luck.

"Hello?" she called out. "Anybody home? Hello?"

A dark-skinned girl walked out of the bathroom wearing a pair of low-riding jean shorts and a tank top. She was drying her face with a towel. Her hair was in long braids that hung down her back almost to her waist, and she had dark eyes and a large forehead. She couldn't have been more than five feet tall.

"Are you Sue?" the girl asked. Her voice was soft, low, the intonation almost singsong. She smiled and held out her hand. "I'm Malika."

"Hi." Sue shook her hand and looked around the room. "Is this my side?" She gestured to where her boxes were piled.

"I hope you don't mind." Malika said. "I got here Friday—and so I picked this side of the room. I like to be close to the bathroom."

"That's fine." Sue gave her a smile before wheeling her suitcase over to the pile of boxes. She climbed onto her bed and moaned. "I don't even want to think about unpacking." The bed was comfortable. She stared up at the ceiling for a moment.

Malika sat down at her desk and folded the towel. She

closed her laptop, and the music stopped. "I understand you're a freshman," she said to Sue.

Sue rolled onto her side. "Yeah. Aren't you?"

Malika shook her head, her braids flapping vigorously. "I'm a sophomore."

"I kind of figured I'd be with all other freshmen."

"No. Bentley is mostly sophomores and juniors."

Sue smiled. "Wonder how I got in here then."

Malika's dark eyes seemed to study her. She didn't reply.

"Well," Sue said, sitting up on the bed. "I guess I should just be glad. So what's your major?"

"Poli sci," Malika told her.

"That's going to be my major, too." Sue grinned. "Prep for law school."

Malika shrugged. "You and about half the girls here. Me, I want to go work for the United Nations, work in under-developed countries."

"Well, that's noble of you. Where are you from, Malika?"

"Tanzania." The other girl's chin went up proudly. "My parents both work for the United Nations, helping countries put together systems of law and develop their economies. It's God's work."

God's work.

Malika kept talking, but Sue wasn't really listening. The phrase had kicked up some memories for her.

"God's work" was a favorite phrase of her grandfather's, one he used so frequently, it had seemed to lose its meaning. The Barlows were regular churchgoers, devoted parishioners of Saint Matthew's Lutheran Church on the Upper West Side. Sue never remembered ever missing a Sunday service. Even when they were on vacation, they managed to find a place to worship. "God's work" to Granpa meant pretty much going to church, paying your taxes, voting in every election (for a Republican), and saying grace before meals. Sometimes,

Gran would joke about it. "What's Granpa doing?" Sue would ask, catching her grandfather nodding off in front of the television set. "He's doing God's work," she'd tell her.

"Did your parents drop you off?" Malika asked.

Sue smiled. "No. I drove up from the city."

"New York?"

Sue nodded. "My grandparents gave me a car. I'll have it here on campus, so if you ever want to get away for a bit—"

Malika smiled. "As if the deans would ever allow that. You'll see, Sue. It's pretty strict around here. They'll let you keep the car—but they just won't let you drive it."

An image of that tall brick wall encircling the campus flashed through Sue's mind. "I'll find ways to drive it," Sue vowed.

"So if your grandparents gave you a car, you must be a little rich girl," Malika said, smiling. "What did Mommy and Daddy give you?"

Sue felt numb—the automatic reaction she always felt whenever anyone asked about her parents.

"My parents are dead," she told Malika.

The other girl's face instantly became sympathetic. "I'm sorry, Sue. I didn't—"

"Of course you didn't. How would you know?"

She stood, moving from the bed to the window. She could see the tinting on the glass, but from the inside the windows didn't seem nearly so black. They let in the sun, for which Sue was glad. She gazed down at the green campus, the fountain bubbling in the center of the yard, watching little groups of girls moving across the grass.

"My parents died in a car accident when I was very young," Sue told her roommate. "I don't remember them at all. But my mother went to school here. I suppose that's the biggest reason why my grandparents sent me here as well."

"Do you have brothers and sisters?" Malika asked.

Sue shook her head. "Just Gran and Granpa. Only family I have."

"I can't imagine. I have three brothers and two sisters and I grew up with cousins and aunts and uncles . . ." Malika's voice faded away as she seemed to catch some sadness in Sue's eyes.

"Not me. My mother was also an only child, so there are no cousins."

"What about your father?"

"I don't know. My grandparents rarely speak of him."

But of her mother, there was plenty of evidence. Given that she had been Gran and Granpa's only child, she was pretty much enshrined in their apartment on Central Park West. Pictures of their darling Mariclare were everywhere. In one room were photos of Mariclare as a young girl. In another, dozens of snapshots captured her graduation from high school. There were pictures of her on beaches and in boats, in convertible cars and at the top of the World Trade Center, always laughing and looking happy. As a little girl, Sue had been jealous of this Mariclare, who had seemed to lead such a more outgoing life than she did. Mariclare—the apple of Gran and Granpa's eyes.

Studying the photos of her mother, Sue didn't see much of a resemblance to herself. Mariclare had thick red hair and wide blue eyes. She was model-pretty, with none of the flaws Sue saw in herself. Yet for all their devotion to their departed daughter, Sue's grandparents rarely spoke about Mariclare directly. It was too painful, Sue understood. On the rare occasions Sue got the nerve up to ask Granpa about Mariclare, his eyes would glaze over and he'd shut down completely. Her only source for information was her grandmother, who doled out information in small doses.

"Your grandfather still misses her—the pain has never really gone away," her grandmother, a slight woman with silver hair who always was dressed as though going to a luncheon, told her one day as they stood side by side in front of the shrine to Mariclare.

"Why isn't there a wedding picture?" Sue, thirteen at the time, asked.

Her grandmother smiled slightly. "Your parents eloped. I'm afraid your grandfather didn't approve of your father." She then added in a whisper, "He blames your father, you know. He was driving the car when they crashed." She wagged a finger. "So don't ever ask your grandfather about your father."

"But didn't my father have any family? Don't I have any cousins or grandparents on that side?"

Gran shook her head, her heavily sprayed hair not moving. "He had no people." She sighed, and picked up a photograph of Mariclare in her cap and gown at high school graduation. "Every day, I thank God you weren't in the car with them."

"Are you going to the opening ceremonies tonight?"

Sue's thoughts were brought back to the present by her roommate's question.

"Well, I haven't really thought about it. I was just thinking as far as getting here and collapsing."

Malika smiled. "Well, I'd like to skip it. But it's mandatory, honey. Didn't you know? If you don't go, they'll give you demerits or something. Besides, there might be a protest, and I don't want to miss that."

"Protest? Why?"

Malika shook a finger at her. "Susan dear, clearly you aren't reading the official statements the school sends out."

"Well, we got so many . . ."

"Joyce Davenport is here to welcome us all to the new school year!"

Sue smirked. "Okay, clue me in. Should I know who she is?"

"Do you not watch television?"

Sue gave her a small laugh. "Actually, no. My grandparents never allowed it. My grandfather would watch the news, but that was it."

It was Malika's turn to laugh. "Well, can't say you're missing much. Anyway, Joyce Davenport. One of Wilbourne's esteemed alumnae. And a scary forked-tongue mouthpiece for the far, far, radical right."

"Never heard of her."

"She is the High Priestess of the Rapturous Right in this country. Basically, what you need to know is that she's made a career out of smearing people she doesn't agree with. She doesn't debate them on the issues, she just calls them names. Traitors. Perverts. Faggots."

"So some of the students might protest?"

"Wilbourne isn't exactly a hotbed of liberalism," Malika said, "but there are enough girls here who oppose Davenport's brand of politicking that you see a few hecklers."

"Well, she has a right to her opinions, don't you think? Isn't there such a thing as freedom of speech?"

"Oh, of course. I don't want to shut her up. But if she has a right to spew her views, then the students have a right to say what they think, too." Malika shook her head. "She's really scary, Sue. Wait till you hear her. She's written some really terrible books about politics—even one defending Joe McCarthy, if you can believe that. They always trot her out on the twenty-four-hour news channels to say something outrageous about women's rights or minorities or gays. She suggested after 9/11 that the United States should just nuke the Middle East and be done with it. She calls the Palestinians savages."

"Sounds like a real doll." Sue suspected this Joyce Davenport was a favorite pundit of her grandfather's. Politics weren't discussed much in their household; indeed, as Sue quickly learned growing up, her parents weren't the only forbidden subject for conversations. If Sue ever voiced an opinion that differed from her grandfather's, she was told she was wrong—no questions asked. When she asked once why a woman couldn't be a minister in their church, Granpa had said simply, "That's God's will," and Gran had gestured with her hand to be quiet, to drop the subject, to not push Granpa too far. For when he was pushed too far, his anger could fill the entire apartment, leaving Sue and her grandmother suffocating for air.

Sue's grandfather was a formidable man, despite his stooped shoulders and white, wispy hair. He was a senior partner in a large law firm that specialized in representing major corporations. Sue had often heard Granpa thunder about the evils of labor unions, welfare, minorities, women in the workplace—and every pronouncement that came from his lips seemed almost like a command from on high. He was convinced there was a massive liberal conspiracy to turn the country into a Communist welfare state with "everyone on the dole!" When he was in one of his rages, he would slap the dinner table with his hand and dishes would literally go flying. "Tax and spend, tax and spend, taking money from the hardworking to give to the shiftless and lazy!" he'd bellow. "That is not the America the Founding Fathers envisioned when they created this great country! No prayer in school indeed! Abortion on demand! Is it any wonder God has turned his back on this great nation?"

Opposing all of these horrible liberals was doing "God's work"—and Granpa truly believed that was his mission in life. "And God has rewarded me," he'd say, "not only for my devotion to His commandments, but for doing His work." He'd gesture around at the massive dining room, the fine china on the shelves, the sparkling chandelier hanging over his head. "Look at the bounty He has blessed me with! Look at my beautiful young granddaughter, who will someday carry on my work!"

Indeed, when Sue was young, she would parrot whatever Granpa said. "Liberals are going to hell" or "Abortion is murder" she'd chime in her child's voice. How Granpa had beamed when she said such things around his friends.

Yet as she got older, and actually began studying these issues at the Stowe Academy, a few thoughts of her own dawned on her. She wasn't as liberal as Becca, who went through a "hippy phase," as Gran called it, and declared all inheritance laws should be abolished. But still, Sue began to see the value of labor unions, how they had protected the American worker— and while she struggled with the idea of abortion, she did think a woman should have the final say about what happened to her own body. But she knew she could never share such heresy with her grandfather. He believed she remained true to his ideals. So when she eventually decided to go to law school, he'd been pleased.

"That's my girl!" he'd said proudly. "You'll go straight from law school to an associateship with my firm—and then there won't be any stopping you, my girl!"

What she didn't tell him was she wanted to be a civil rights attorney.

There's plenty of time to cross—or burn— that bridge, Sue thought, as Malika kept up a steady tirade against this Joyce Davenport person. *After I get out of law school, I'll be free to do what I want.*

"Of course, you might like her," Malika was saying.

"You mean, the speaker?" Sue asked.

Her roommate's eyes twinkled. "Yeah. Who knows? Maybe you'll turn out to be a real firebrand right-winger."

"I like to think of myself as being part of the sensible center."

"The center's just for people afraid to take sides," Malika told her, only half joking, Sue thought.

"That kind of thinking only keeps people divided, in my opinion."

"Maybe so." Malika sighed. "But where Joyce Davenport is concerned, I just can't see reason. I can only imagine the hate she is going be spewing from the lectern tonight." The girl shivered. "When I think of her, I think of the devil."

"Okay," Sue said, smiling, "now that *is* extreme."

Her roommate's dark eyes had closed in on her. "You girls who've grown up in sophisticated cities think there is no such thing. But even though I have been well educated all my life, I am not so far removed from my origins. In my father's village back in Tanzania, there is a strong belief still in evil spirits. I believe they are real. And I think this school is full of them."

6

Sue spent the rest of the afternoon unpacking. Malika helped her set up her computer and get hooked up to the college wireless Internet system. Every so often, one of Malika's friends would stick her head in the door—she apparently was one of the more popular students at Wilbourne—and after the first two or three, Sue gave up trying to remember their names.

Around six, Malika took her over to the campus cafeteria for dinner before the welcome ceremony. The food wasn't bad, and Sue found herself relaxing a little bit, starting to feel at home. As the sun sank in the west, the wind got cooler and Sue began to wish she'd worn something heavier than a cotton blouse. A chill wind blew as they walked across campus to the auditorium and found seats near the back.

The hall was filled with girls talking, laughing, giggling, and gossiping, getting caught up with friends they hadn't seen since the previous semester. Sue was a little startled to see a few young men scattered throughout the audience. Although Wilbourne was a private academy for women, it did accept some men for graduate studies.

At promptly eight o'clock, a large older gentleman stood

up, waddled across the stage, and introduced himself as
Dean Gregory. He led them all in a short prayer—although
Wilbourne was nonsectarian, many of the instructors had not
abandoned their Lutheran roots. After the prayer was con-
cluded, Dean Gregory introduced some of the faculty also
seated on the stage. The names meant nothing to her, other
than Dr. Virginia Marshall, a professor of theology. Sue was
taking one of Dr. Marshall's courses; she'd read some of her
books for a paper she'd written at Stowe and enjoyed them.

Dean Gregory went on to officially welcome them to the
new school year, and expounded about how bright their fu-
tures were. He had the kind of voice that put an audience to
sleep, and indeed Sue's eyelids were starting to droop as he
droned on and on . . . until he introduced Joyce Davenport to
polite applause from the crowd. Sue sat up straight. Malika
gave her a little nudge.

Joyce Davenport walked across the stage to the podium
as though she owned it. She was wearing a tight black off-
the-shoulder dress that barely reached her thighs. Her long
thin legs were perched on top of a pair of what Becca Stansfield used to call "come fuck me" pumps. Her shoulders
were narrow and bony, and her arms long and thin. She had
thick, long black hair that hung down almost to her waist,
and it was all the same length. From the back of the auditorium, Davenport's face was just a white oval in the bright
lights.

She started speaking, and Sue winced. Joyce Davenport's
voice was shrill, and through the microphone it sounded
very similar to fingernails on a chalkboard. Other girls in the
audience started fidgeting and whispering amongst themselves, but as Davenport continued to speak—about her days
at Wilbourne and what they had meant to her—her voice
came down an octave or two and became almost hypnotic.
The fidgeting and whispering stopped, and Davenport's

voice became full of passion as she went on and on about how Wilbourne had prepared her for the real world, for great success and fame . . .

"No politics," Malika whispered. "She's staying away from politics."

"You sound as if you're disappointed."

Malika shrugged. "I was just hoping for a little drama."

When Davenport finished—to, again, polite applause—Dean Gregory led the students in a closing prayer and then dismissed them.

"I can't believe it," said one of Malika's friends, a plump brunette, rushing up to them outside. "Not a controversial word! I saw that bitch on CNN the other night and wanted to put my fist through the television. I was all ready to stand up and shout her down."

"And get ten demerits your first day back," Malika reminded her. "Sandy, this is Sue. Sue, Sandy."

The girls shook hands.

"It's time we radicalize this campus," Sandy was saying, even as she let go of Sue's hand. "I've petitioned the dean to let us form a group—"

"Excuse me," a woman said, interrupting them. All three girls turned to look at her. She was a thickset young blond woman in a white blouse and blue skirt. "I'm looking for Sue Barlow."

Sue glanced at her companions, then said, "I'm Sue Barlow."

"Ms. Davenport would like to see you. Will you come with me?"

"What?"

"How do you know Joyce Davenport?" Sandy asked, leering suspiciously at Sue.

"I don't," Sue said.

Malika just looked at her oddly.

The woman in front of them narrowed her eyes at Sue. "She's waiting."

"I don't know her," Sue protested.

"Apparently, she knows you," Malika said, her voice cold.

Sue turned to look at her. "It's got to be my grandfather. His firm . . ."

Malika just shrugged. "Go see what she wants."

Sue turned back to Davenport's emissary. "Okay, take me to her."

The woman smiled. Sue didn't like her smile. Not at all.

"Follow me," she said.

7

Sue followed the woman around the building and up a short flight of stairs that led to the back of the stage. They pushed through the curtains and down a narrow hallway. Finally, they stopped in front of a door, and the woman rapped on it before letting herself in.

"Ms. Davenport?" she called. "I have Sue Barlow."

"Send her in!" It was the same voice Sue had just heard over the microphone. Her heart beating a little faster, she walked into the room.

It was dingy and cramped, mirrors on both walls and a long counter on the wall to her left. The walls were plaster, and in places paint was missing where notices had been taped and later ripped down. The place smelled slightly musty, and the floor was yellowed with coats of wax. Round bulbs surrounded the long mirror. Behind a partition, Sue spotted the woman who had summoned her.

"Hello." Sue's words were awkward. "You wanted to see me?"

Joyce Davenport was sitting on top of a stool, smoking a cigarette and drinking white wine from a fluted glass. Her legs were crossed at the knee, hiking her skirt up to her upper thighs. A long run showed in her stockings on her left leg. She smiled and tilted her head, narrowing her dark eyes. "So you're Sue Barlow." She set the wineglass down and gestured to her. "Come closer."

Sue took a hesitant step forward.

Joyce stood up. Up close, her face was long and narrow, almost horsy, with a pinched nose and thin wide lips. Her eyes were brown and round, and the whites were shot through with red. Heavy makeup could not disguise the small lines around her eyes and mouth.

Joyce tossed her head to get her long hair out of her face. She threw her arms around Sue and hugged her, then stepped back and searched her face.

"Yes, I can see traces of Mariclare in you." The woman smiled deeply. "I was kind of hoping you'd be like a twin to her, but I can see her in your face—your eyes, you have the same eyes."

Sue's heart jumped. "You—you knew my mother?"

Joyce laughed. "Yes, I knew your mother. In fact, we were roommates here at Wilbourne. I was very, very fond of her. And I've been waiting for years to meet her daughter." Her smile got bigger. "And you are so pretty. Are you as smart as your mother, too?"

"I don't know how smart I am, or how smart she was, to be honest." Sue replied, staring at the older woman.

No matter what Malika had said about Joyce Davenport, Sue was suddenly thrilled to be standing before her. *She knew my mother! She was my mother's roommate!* Thoughts flashed through her head—here was someone, at last, with whom she could talk openly about her mother . . . to whom she could direct questions . . . from whom she could maybe get some answers . . .

"Well, you're here at Wilbourne, aren't you?" Joyce let out a hoot. "And they don't take idiots here!" She smirked.

"The occasional lefty moron, of course—you can't get away from that in academia, of course, especially here in the Northeast—but I have no doubt you're going to do just fine."

Sue managed a smile.

Joyce reached into a worn Louis Vuitton bag on the floor. "Unfortunately, I can't visit with you as long as I would like—I have to be in D.C. tonight, which means driving over to Albany and catching a flight, and I should be gone already—but I so wanted to meet you."

"I don't know much about my mother. I'd love to hear what you remember about her."

Joyce had pulled out a book from her bag. She opened it to the title page and scrawled quickly on it with a pen. "Here you go," she said, handing it to Sue. "A copy of my latest book, just for you. I wrote my cell phone number on there as well as my private e-mail address. I want you to call me night or day if you need anything, okay? Or e-mail me—I will always answer you. Anything for Mariclare's little girl."

"Did you know her long? And my fath—"

"Sweetie, I can't talk now. I promise to be back up here soon to really get to know you better. Maybe in a few weeks. Then we can talk *endlessly* about Mariclare. My schedule is just so insane right now." She slipped her bag over her shoulder. "But read the book in the meantime . . . and I'll give you a call to set up dinner when I can get back up here."

Sue tried to say something, but the words wouldn't come.

"Okay, move on out!" Joyce barked to her assistants, who suddenly came running into the room, scooping up boxes and suitcases. Joyce reached over to give Sue another hug. "So good to finally meet you, sweetheart." Then she swept out of the room, leaving Sue standing there alone.

Sue glanced down at the cover of the book. There was Joyce, dressed pretty much the same as she had been tonight, with her hands on her hips. She was standing in front of a chalkboard, where the word SMEAR was written in green chalk. Across the bottom were the words *How Liberals Have Perfected the Art of Libel.*

In the upper left-hand corner inside a black balloon, it read, *The latest from New York Times best-selling author Joyce Davenport!*

She opened the book to the title page.

For Sue, I hope this is the start of a beautiful friendship, Love, Joyce.

Her cell phone number and e-mail address, as promised, were written underneath the signature.

Sue walked out, holding the book, and headed across the campus. The auditorium had emptied out, and a cold wind had blown up. There was a full moon so there was plenty of light, but it seemed weird how fast the entire campus had emptied. There were no girls milling about now. Everyone was back in their dorm rooms, unpacking and preparing for the first day of classes, and anyone who wasn't would be shooed inside. It seemed Sue's grandparents weren't the only ones to set curfews. Sue walked faster, rubbing her arms to warm them up as she headed down the path to Bentley Hall.

She was lost in thoughts of her mother.

She'd always, always, felt something missing in her life. Her grandparents had loved her, but she'd never been able to feel close to them. Whenever she was at a friend's home— even Becca Stansfield's—she'd missed the camaraderie, the closeness she sensed between her friends and their mothers. Her friends might complain about busybody moms, they might fight with them, even call them monsters—but every time Sue listened to them complain, all she could think was, *I'd give anything to have a fight with my mother.*

Her eyes filled with tears, but she wiped them away.

Suddenly, she wished she'd asked Joyce Davenport in which dorm her mother had lived.

Stopping in front of Bentley Hall, however, Sue knew the answer to that question.

Her eyes flickered up to that third-floor window where she'd seen that face earlier. Where she'd *thought* she'd seen a face, that is—the face of a woman screaming.

That was my mother's room.

How she knew that for certain, she couldn't say. It was impossible to know such a thing, but she knew.

And the woman who screamed?

Had that been in her mother?

Had that been Mariclare?

The campus was suddenly very cold. Looking around her, at the deserted walkways and windows so black that seemed to blot out the light behind them, Sue felt as if she were the only one left alive at Wilbourne.

She pushed through the front door and headed for her room.

8

The town of Lebanon went dark no later than nine every night.

Every night of the week, with the exception of the Yellow Bird Café around the town square, the 7/11 near the high school, and Earl's Tavern out on the county road, every business within the city limits was locked up and closed no later than nine. The streets fell silent, and the only signs of life to anyone driving through town would be the occasional light in the windows of a house. It made the sheriff's life much easier, and the night shift for the deputies was generally slow and quiet, disrupted only by occasional acts of vandalism or a drunk driver every once in a while. Lebanon was a quiet town, and as the mayor, Robbie Kendall, was fond of saying whenever making a speech, "a fine place to raise a family."

Unlike other small towns around the country, Lebanon wasn't drying up and blowing away. Sure, every year after graduation, a high percentage of teenagers hit the road and never looked back—an interesting mix of the slackers and the top students. The top students went away for college, incurring years of debt in student loans, and the slackers headed for bigger cities—New York, Philadelphia, Boston, or Albany. Some of the college-bound kids came back after graduation if there was a job to bring them back—working in the Walgreen's pharmacy or teaching, for example. But the slacker kids didn't come back, and outside of their families, no one really cared. Those kids were lazy, a bad element, and the ones the adults in town automatically thought of whenever drug use came up in conversation. The sooner they left town, the better.

Yet enough of their classmates stayed around and went to work after getting their diplomas, settling into life in Lebanon as adults. They married and had enough kids to keep the population steady each year as another group of kids left. The town folk worked hard. They paid their bills, and rarely complained. If there wasn't a decent job in town, there were the paper mills and meatpacking plants forty minutes north on the highway in Senandaga, the county seat. The only people who didn't work were just lazy or drunks.

So far, the scourge of drugs plaguing other small towns had stayed away from Lebanon. Sure, some of the kids smoked pot or drank, but it wasn't a big problem and for the most part, other than an occasional car wreck, they didn't bother anyone. Lebanon High School provided a decent education, and had turned out some championship teams in football and girls' basketball. Robbie Kendall was right. Lebanon *was* a good place to raise a family. The last murder had been seven years ago, and pretty much everyone agreed Wade DeBolt had had it coming. If he hadn't been slapping his wife Norma around, she wouldn't have needed to shoot him.

Still, even if folks in Lebanon didn't need to lock their doors at night, they did anyway. *Better safe than sorry,* was the general thought, and above all else, Lebanon folks were practical. There was a great big crazy world out there, and who knows when someone from outside might blow into town and cause trouble?

There were nine churches in Lebanon, and they were all well attended every Sunday. The churches were the centers of social activity in town, with picnics and potlucks and dances for the teenagers. They were all Protestant—the few Catholics in town attended Mass up at St. Dominic's in Senandaga. There wasn't any friction between the different congregations, except at the Church League softball games in the summer, and that was just good fun. There were no minorities in Lebanon, other than the Asian family who owned the 7/11 and the video store. Some people considered the French Canadians a minority, but other than their weirdly accented English and statues of saints, most people never gave them a second thought. The majority of them worked at the factories in Senandaga, they didn't cause any trouble, and they pretty much kept their religion to themselves.

Lebanon took pride in not only being a good place to raise a family, but in being a *clean* town. People kept up their yards and houses. The homes in Lebanon were like the people themselves: nothing ostentatious or overly ornate; solid and strong, built to weather the humid summers and the bitterly cold winters. Property values were low, as they were in most small towns, but the cost of living was also quite a bit lower than it was even up the highway in Senandaga—let alone Manhattan or Boston. It was a town where everyone knew everyone else, where neighbors talked over coffee in the mornings, where you took care of your neighbors when they were sick or laid up, and people just did for each other in general.

Sure, there was a neighborhood—as there is in every town—far away from the town square, where the houses needed painting and the yards were mostly dirt, where it wasn't unusual to see a beat-up car up on blocks in the yard, but nobody ever had to drive through that part of town on their way to somewhere else. When they did, they just clucked their tongues and shook their heads at the lack of pride revealed by the run-down houses and dead yards and beat-up cars, but at the same time patting themselves on the back for not winding up in one of those houses. It was where the low-wage-earners lived, where every month was a struggle to pay the bills and buy food, where every ring of the telephone could be a bill collector calling with insults and threats. It was very easy to pretend that part of town didn't exist, which is what most people in Lebanon did. This part of Lebanon was collectively known as "the Banks," because it was the closest part of town to the shallow Frontenac River. It was generally presumed that any child from the Banks was destined for a bad end—drugs, alcohol, or an early shotgun marriage.

With the college that loomed just west of town over the rolling hills, the town maintained a friendly if distant relationship. The students were all well behaved for the most part (although there was some worry when the school started admitting male graduate students, but so far there'd been no trouble). Best thing about Wilbourne was that the people on campus spent money in town. They bought food at the A&P, got their cars worked on at Mike's Firestone or Bud's Shell, bought their makeup at the Rexall, ate at the local diners and restaurants, and opened accounts at the local banks. Many of them, true to the school's religious traditions, went to the local churches, where they dutifully dropped their money into the collection plates. And there were jobs on the campus as well—groundskeepers and janitors and cooks and secretaries and research assistants—that went to Lebanon locals.

Yet while, as a rule, the members of the college faculty were liked by the members Lebanon natives, they never really quite fit into the fabric of the town. They tended to subscribe to *The New York Times,* watch movies with subtitles, and their living rooms were filled with books most of their neighbors had never heard of—by authors like Proust and Sartre and

Faulkner, instead of Janet Evanovich and Nora Roberts and James Patterson. Dean Gregory himself was a deacon at the local Lutheran Church, and very dedicated to his position there. He was pretty well known and liked by the Lutherans, but outside of church matters, the other church members didn't have a lot to talk to him about.

The town also took great pride in knowing that Wilbourne College was one of the best in the country—even though no local student had ever been admitted through its gates. The majority of local kids who went to college went to the junior college or the branch of the state university in Senandaga, and there was no disgrace in that—both were fine schools, and affordable.

No one resented the college on the outskirts of town, and it had been there so long it was just thought of as another part of the fabric of Lebanon, like the town square, the high school, or the library. But it was something apart. There was no question about that.

9

The Yellow Bird Café was always the last business around the town square to close, and the only one that stayed open late on Sunday evenings. The Yellow Bird closed every night at ten, even on Sunday. Wally Bingham, who'd bought the place in the 1970s when he came home from Vietnam, didn't go to church and thought it might not be a bad idea to keep the café open late. Most people had huge meals after morning services, and sometimes wanted something different after evening services rather than the leftovers. So, on Sunday nights, Wally himself worked the grill. Marjorie Pequod, his night-shift waitress for nearly twenty years, stayed with him even on slow nights. She hadn't set foot in a church since she was a teenager, and would rather work.

Deputy Sheriff Perry Holland was glad the Yellow Bird was open late. As he pulled into a vertical parking spot right in front of the café, he could see Marjorie reading a paperback novel at the counter and Wally washing dishes back in the kitchen. The place was deserted. Perry turned off the car and sat there for a moment. He'd gone off duty at seven after a quiet day. He'd popped home to his small apartment for a

quick shower but, hungry as a horse, he'd known he'd be
heading out again. His kitchen cabinets were bare of food as
usual. Once again, he'd put off going to the A&P until there
was nothing in the house to eat. He glanced at his watch, and
sighed. The A&P was already closed, so it was either the Yellow Bird or one of the fast-food joints out at the highway
junction. *The Yellow Bird,* Perry decided.

The town was quiet as he headed over to the café—which
he pretty much expected. Lebanon was a quiet town, not much
excitement. Lights were on in the houses he drove past;
sometimes all he saw was the blue glow of a television set.
The worst Perry ever had to deal with since joining the force
nine years earlier was the occasional drunk driver, or a bunch
of teenagers who thought it would be funny to knock down
mailboxes with a baseball bat on Saturday nights. Violent
crime was pretty much nonexistent in Lebanon, other than
an occasional fistfight over at Earl's Tavern, which was usually over before he pulled into their parking lot. No, if Perry
wanted something to break the routine of his life, he had to
head up the highway to Senandaga—or the hundred miles or
so to Albany.

A bell rang when he pushed through the door. Marjorie
wasn't sitting at the counter anymore, and Perry sat down on
one of the round seats, placing his elbows on the counter.
The swinging doors from the kitchen bounced open and
Marjorie Pequod came out, a Parliament dangling from her
lips. She looked tired and grumpy. Her lipstick was an orange smear, and her face was heavily powdered and rouged
like always. She wore her graying dark hair pulled back into
a bun, and bobby pins glinted in the overhead lights. She
was thick in the waist, and varicose veins showed through
her stockings. She was wearing a pair of white leather flat
shoes that were splattered with ketchup. Her yellow uniform

was spotted with grease and God knows what else. Shuffling over to where Perry was seated, she whipped out her order pad and pencil from a pocket in her graying white apron.

"The usual?" she mumbled around the cigarette, not even dropping an ash.

Marjorie had worked at the Yellow Bird ever since the day her husband had run out on her, leaving her to raise their three kids on her own. She knew what everyone ordered. Perry wondered why she even kept that order pad.

For Perry, "the usual" was a well-done cheeseburger and fries swimming in chili with a Coke. He nodded. Marjorie scribbled it down, then tore the page off the pad and shoved it through the small order window, hitting the little bell sitting there.

Perry had been eating at the Yellow Bird since he was a child and his father brought him in for the first time. How he'd looked up to his dad, sitting there so strong and noble in his sheriff's uniform. Perry had wanted to be just like his father—and he was, going to the police academy and then joining him on the force. Now he was deputy to his father's sheriff—though he couldn't help but cringe a little when people would say, "Here comes Andy and Opie."

Ever since those days when he'd come in with his father, Perry had always ordered the same thing. With dutiful regularity, Marjorie poured his Coke from the fountain and set the red plastic cup in front of him. Stubbing out the cigarette in a dirty ashtray—Perry wasn't about to get her for smoking in a public place, as there was no one else in the place— Marjorie leaned her elbows on the counter so that she was nearly nose-to-nose with the young officer.

"How you doing, Marjorie?" he asked.

"Tired, that's how." She pushed a wisp of gray hair off of her shiny forehead, giving him a weak smile that didn't quite reach her eyes. "What you doing out so late on an off night, Perry?"

"No food in the house." He smiled back at her. "And this way I get to see you, Marj."

She rolled her eyes. "If things have got to the point where you look forward to flirting with a tired old bag like me, you're doing something wrong."

Doing something wrong. He bit his lower lip. He sometimes wondered about that himself. He was getting a lot closer to thirty than he cared to think about, and he was still single. He didn't have a steady girl, and rarely even dated anymore since Jennifer had gone back to Boston three years earlier. He looked younger than his age—he got carded whenever he went over to Albany to hit the bars—and he kept himself in good shape by going to the YMCA three times a week. But he was beginning to wonder if time wasn't running out on him somehow. All of his friends from high school were long married, raising kids, making mortgage payments, and settling into middle age.

Like she was reading his mind, Marjorie asked, "You still hear from Jennifer? You should of married that girl, Perry."

"I haven't heard from her in a while." He replied with a shrug. *Jennifer.* "I don't know, Marj. Maybe I should have."

The thought had plagued him ever since Jennifer Donnelly had gone back to Boston. *Maybe she brought up taking the job back there to get me to ask her to marry her,* Perry thought again. She'd come to Lebanon straight out of college, teaching home economics at the local high school. She was a South Boston Irish girl, and he'd loved the way she said *caah* for car. Jennifer had worked her way through college, getting student loans and scrimping and saving. She'd come to Lebanon determined to pay off her student debt as quickly as she could. She told him that the cheap rents in

Lebanon had been a major part of her decision to take the job at the high school.

They'd met right here, at this very counter. He'd been sitting here when she pulled up in a battered ten-year-old gray Honda Civic, and he'd almost gasped out loud when she got out of the car. Jennifer had thick dark hair worn short, a round face with an upturned nose, and the deepest emerald green eyes Perry had ever seen. She was short, not much past five feet, weighed one hundred pounds soaking wet, with a curvy body she liked to show off in tight jeans and tight sweaters. That day, she'd walked into the Yellow Bird with a broad smile on her face, sat down on the seat right beside him, and asked, "So, what's good here?"

I should have asked her to marry me. Perry let out a sigh as he watched Marjorie wipe down the counter with a dirty sponge.

He and Jennifer had been together for three years from that first night at the Yellow Bird, when she'd ordered the chili cheeseburger and fries he'd recommended, and it was a good three years. Perry had stayed at her place a few nights a week; she'd come over to his once or twice as well. They'd rent movies or watch television. He'd read while she graded papers. Sometimes, they drove up to Senandaga to go out for a nice dinner at the Outback or the Olive Garden before heading to a movie. After the first year, they'd settled into a nice routine, and before long the question was popping up from everyone—his family, his coworkers, people he'd known his whole life: *So, when you gonna do right by that girl and marry her?*

But whenever Perry would start to hint about marriage, even tentatively, Jennifer would always change the subject. Then one day, over a dinner of lasagna and some red wine, she gave him a big smile. "It's done, Perry," she said. "I paid off the last of my student loans today. What a relief to have that off my back."

"Well, that's great, honey!" He reached over with his glass and tapped his to hers. "Congratulations."

She cleared her throat. "And now that I'm done with that, Perry, I'm going back to Boston."

He'd replayed that dinner conversation in his head at least a thousand times in the last four years. *What did I do wrong? What did she want from me?* She'd insisted that she wasn't trying to force him into anything—but *why* hadn't she brought it up any time before that night? He loved her, he loved being with her, and he knew she loved him, but her decision was final. "I'm going back to Boston," she stubbornly said. "I'm not staying here."

Why didn't I offer to go with her? he asked himself again. *I could have found work there—there are plenty of jobs there. I could have gotten on with the Boston police. Why was I afraid to leave Lebanon?*

But she never asked me to go with her either.

After the school year ended, she packed her bags and kissed him good-bye. He'd watched her drive out of town, and out of his life.

His father still got mad about it if her name ever came up. "I'm not getting any younger, and I still don't have any grandchildren," he'd say every once in a while, smiling to make it seem as though he were teasing, but the set of his jaw and the tic in his cheek showed he meant it. Perry knew his dad was proud of him for following him into law enforcement—but a part of his dad worried that Perry was stuck in a rut.

"Well, Jennifer's not losing any sleep over not marrying me," Perry said. "That's for sure."

"You don't know that, Perry," Marjorie replied. "She

could be sitting there every night hoping you'll stop being stubborn and say the magic words to her." She shuffled his glass over to the fountain and refilled it. "Just tell me to mind my own business and I'll shut up."

"It's okay." He took another drink and grinned at her. He liked Marjorie, always had—despite her kids. *But you can't blame her for her kids—she did the best she could.* Her kids had been train wrecks. Marjorie's oldest, a daughter, had run off to Manhattan when she was seventeen and hadn't been heard from since. Frankie, her second, had been in Perry's class at Lebanon High. Frankie was a wild kid, coming to school reeking of marijuana. He'd been killed driving drunk the summer after graduation. Darby, her youngest, had been on the same road as Frankie—but seemed to have straightened out after Frankie was killed. He got a job right out of school as a mechanic over at Mike's Firestone, gotten married, and bought a house down in the Banks near Marjorie's. Still, everybody knew that Darby gambled, and word at the sheriff's office was that he was probably dealing in stolen cars. They had their eye on Darby Pequod.

"Marjorie's always had a hard life," his mother used to say, "but she never complains, bless her heart." They'd gone to Lebanon High together and were friends. And when the cancer was eating his mother alive a few years back, Marjorie had come over every day with wrapped sandwiches from the Bird.

"So what's gotten you so tired out today, Marj?" Perry asked her.

"First day of school over at the college." The locals rarely called it Wilbourne. It was just "the college."

"Yeah? A lot of students coming in?"

"In and out all afternoon, kept me hopping."

For a moment, the face of that girl he'd pulled over appeared in Perry's mind. What was her name? Barlow. Susan Barlow.

Marjorie sighed, but then she smiled. "Those girls are good tippers. I guess they had their welcome thing tonight, because it slowed way down after six thirty." She stretched, pressing both hands into the small of her back. "Man, my back is hurting. Be glad when I get home and can soak in a hot bath."

They both turned when the bell at the front door rang.

10

Virginia Marshall, Ph.D., was not in a good mood.

After leaving the welcome ceremony, she'd driven aimlessly around town with no real idea of where she was going or what she was doing, other than she didn't want to go back to her apartment. *Tonight was the last straw,* she thought over and over again as she cruised the quiet streets. She was fed up, tired, and sorely tempted to march into Dean Gregory's office the following morning and slap her resignation down on his desk. *Love to see the look on his weasel face if I did.*

The thought made her smile, and her blood pressure started finally to go down to a reasonable level. When she turned onto the square, she saw the lights on at the Yellow Bird. The bright lights looked inviting. *No point in driving around all night, I'll just stop in there for a cup of coffee.* She parked next to Perry Holland's deputy car, and walked in.

She waved at Perry and sat down at one of the booths that ran along the right side of the diner. "Just coffee, please," she called as she reached into her shoulder bag and pulled out a notebook. She carried it with her everywhere, using it to jot down notes and thoughts whenever they occurred to her. She didn't see the look Marjorie gave Perry—but she didn't need to. She knew she wasn't well liked in Lebanon, and that was just fine with her.

She hated Lebanon, and she hated Wilbourne College even more.

It had seemed like a good idea at the time, even though her colleagues at Harvard thought she was completely insane. No matter how hard they tried, though, they just didn't understand her need to get away from Boston, to get away from Harvard, to just get away. After watching her son die for two years of chemotherapy that didn't work, of medications and drug protocols and marrow transplants, of watching him try to smile and be brave for her through enormous pain and suffering, Boston was just too much for Ginny. Her colleagues didn't understand that every time she looked at one of her students, she hated them for simply being alive. Every time a young man walked into her classroom or through her line of vision, it was like the knife being twisted in her heart all over again.

Grief counseling hadn't worked, drinking didn't help, the pills did nothing except depress her all over again. And as Ginny suffered, her marriage crumbled around her as well. She *knew* her marriage was in trouble, she knew Jim needed her, needed more than a zombie who just wandered around in a coma not caring about anything, but she couldn't do anything, couldn't make herself care. Jim didn't understand her, didn't understand that she felt that "moving on" was just a politer way of saying, "Let's forget Eric ever existed," and when he finally sat her down and said, "Ginny, I'm not getting what I need from you anymore," she just looked at him and replied, "And it's never once occurred to you that maybe you aren't giving me what I need?"

So when Jim packed and left, Ginny didn't feel anything

other than a passing sense of relief that she didn't have to deal with him anymore. She just was numb everywhere, as though all her emotions and nerves had died.

She didn't think she'd ever feel anything again.

So when Wilbourne College made an offer, she'd decided to take it. It was a surprisingly good offer—considering what she'd already been making as a tenured professor at Harvard who'd published best-selling works on the history of the Christian religion. Something about being in the woods—and teaching girls, not boys—had appealed mightily to her. She'd driven over to Lebanon on a three-day weekend to meet the other faculty and get a feeling for the town and college. That first weekend, she found Lebanon quaint and charming—it reminded her of her own hometown, Hammond, Louisiana—and she liked the college. The campus was beautiful, and she liked the idea of working with a student body that was over ninety-five-percent young women. There'd be no reminders of Eric everywhere she turned. The change was exactly what she needed.

She resisted every temptation to remain on the faculty at Harvard—her department chair begged her to simply take a leave, to keep her options open. Her agent thought she was insane—"Ginny, part of your appeal to publishers is your position at Harvard. You can't give that up"—so she'd finally accepted emeritus status. But that was the only concession she made to her original decision to leave Boston behind. She sold her town house rather than renting it. She got rid of everything inside of it, not wanting to keep anything that would remind her of her son, anything that might keep the agony alive inside her.

I have to get on with my life.

That had been her mantra on the drive to Lebanon. She'd gotten a second floor apartment—small but cozy—just a few blocks off the town square. She arrived two weeks before that fall semester began, enthusiastic and ready to go to work. She had all of her research for her book—on hold for the whole duration of Eric's illness—packed in the trunk of her car. She was eager to get back to work on it. In the peace and quiet of this small upstate New York town, she planned on making it the best work she'd done.

Those two weeks before school started, Ginny found some good used furniture and set her apartment up exactly the way she wanted. When the town paper, the *Lebanon Herald,* called requesting an interview, she'd been more flattered than anything else. After all, when you've been interviewed by *The New York Times,* what did you have to fear from the *Lebanon Herald?*

That was her first mistake.

The reporter had been a woman who looked to be in her mid-thirties. Her name was Gayle Honeycutt. Gayle had been kind of nondescript-looking, very pale, with white blond hair and no eyelashes. Short and running a little to overweight, she had tiny hands and tiny feet and a simple, straightforward manner that Ginny found appealing, especially in comparison with other interviewers she'd faced over the years. Gayle accepted a cup of coffee, and settled herself into a wingback chair. She smiled at Ginny.

"I've never met someone who's been on the *New York Times* best-seller list," Gayle said meekly. "It's a bit intimidating."

Ginny laughed. "I'm just a normal person, Gayle. No need to feel intimidated. I've just been very lucky with my work, that's all."

"I don't really understand the point of your work," Gayle had said, clicking on her tape recorder and pulling out a pad of paper with prepared questions on it. "I mean, I'm sorry, but I just don't. I've read your books, but—"

"What is it you don't understand?"

Gayle had smiled. "Well, why don't you just tell me what you hope readers take away from your book?"

So Ginny had embarked on a spirited lecture about the importance of historical research into the Bible and religion. Her first book, the one that earned her the Ph.D., had been *Reclaiming the Sacred Feminine,* a study into how the early male-dominated Church had deliberately excluded women from its hierarchy. She explained to Gayle that the early Christians had twisted not only the Old Testament, but the teachings of Jesus himself to establish their own power base. She made a point to stress that she wasn't attacking anyone's faith—and that she herself believed in the teachings of Jesus. But historical evidence existed, she told Gayle, that showed how early Church leaders had, for political purposes, distorted and sometimes removed entirely large segments of the Bible.

"What if much of what you've ever been taught about Christianity is wrong?" Ginny had asked the reporter in her enthusiasm. Gayle had sat there dispassionately, taking notes. Ginny talked for more than hour, even if Gayle didn't ask many questions.

When the article appeared, all hell broke loose.

For one thing, the headline simply read: CHRISTIANITY, SAYS NEW PROFESSOR AT WILBOURNE COLLEGE.

Dean Gregory had called Ginny into his office, and lectured her for over an hour about "dealing with the press"—which, considering Ginny had much more experience with the press than he did, was more than a little insulting. Not once did he even give her an opportunity to defend herself. Gregory had always been enthusiastic and friendly before, but from that moment on, Ginny and Dean Gregory kept as far apart from each other as possible.

Ginny's name was soon anathema in the town of Lebanon.

She'd hear the townspeople whispering whenever she walked into a store: "That's the atheist, the heathen, the anti-Christian bigot." A group called the Concerned American Women, New York Chapter, somehow got hold of the interview and started a campaign to get her fired. Televangelist Bobby Vandiver thundered from his television program on one of the religious cable channels for days about the "Christ-hating professor" at New York's Wilbourne College.

At first, Ginny had considered it a badge of honor to be condemned by the man who'd blamed the "licentiousness" of New Orleans for causing Hurricane Katrina, and predicted fire and brimstone for Massachusetts for allowing gay marriage. And, much to her publisher's delight, the controversy simply sent all of her books jumping back onto the best-seller lists.

But then she started getting the death threats in the mail—and so many obscene and threatening phone calls, she had to change her number and keep it unlisted. She filed police reports and talked to a special agent from the local FBI office in Albany, who assured her it was unlikely that anyone would actually kill her, which was only slightly reassuring. It was a rough couple of weeks, especially considering school was starting.

To the college's credit, the vast majority of parents came down on her side. The board of trustees refused to yield or even listen to the angry fanatics—the school was private, after all, and not dependent on tax dollars—and even Dean Gregory issued a statement of support. Ginny suspected—given the way he'd started treating her—that his statement was more about refusing to be told how to run his college than any actual support for her. The storm lasted about three weeks, and then it died away. Bobby Vandiver and the Concerned American Women found a new cause célèbre—a teacher in Pennsylvania who'd invited a gay author to speak to her student group—but around Lebanon, Ginny Marshall was forever considered a "troublemaker."

She smiled as Marjorie brought her a cup of coffee and a small saucer full of creamers. In return, Marjorie gave her a half smile and walked away.

What had gotten Ginny into such a snit tonight was Gregory's treatment of her in front of that harpy Joyce Davenport. It was bad enough that he asked that publicity hound (for that's all Ginny considered Davenport to be) to speak at the campus welcoming event, but to dress Ginny down in front of her was too much to take. For in fact, during the media storm that had accompanied Ginny's start at Wilbourne, Joyce Davenport had written a column shredding her and her books, using Ginny as an example of "what's wrong with higher education in this country." It was the one instance where Ginny considered suing; the column was full of so many slanders and lies and half-truths, it was hard to believe any newspaper would publish it.

It had taken all of Ginny's self-control not to choke the bitch to death as soon as she saw her on the stage earlier tonight.

But the worst part had already occurred. There had been a faculty reception at the dean's house before the welcome address, a semiformal cocktail party that everyone was required to attend. Ginny had considered not attending the party, but that would give Gregory what he wanted: an opportunity to reprimand her. So she'd go—*and be perfectly charming to that bitch, and to Gregory and his mousy, smarmy little wife, too.*

Maybe, Ginny reasoned as she got dressed for the night, Joyce Davenport was different in real life. No one could be that malignantly cruel and deliberately ignorant, could they?

Maybe it was all just an act, a persona Davenport assumed to make money and get herself on television.

Ginny had arrived at the reception late, and slipped over to the bar, hoping to avoid both the dean and and Davenport. But no sooner had she asked for a glass of red wine when Gregory placed his hand on her shoulder.

"Joyce, I'd like you to meet Dr. Virginia Marshall," he said in his most charming voice. "She's one of our more famous faculty members."

"Yes, I know." Joyce's face was seemingly friendly. "Isn't she the atheist?" she asked sweetly.

"No," Ginny replied. "I am not an atheist. I consider myself a Christian."

"Well, that's what makes America great, isn't it, Dr. Marshall?" Joyce Davenport said, still smiling sweetly. "We can call ourselves anything we wish, even if it isn't true."

Ginny opened her mouth to reply, her face flushing angrily, but Dean Gregory cut her off before she had a chance to say anything. "Speaking of which, Ginny," he said, "I need you to stop by my office tomorrow around one. I'm more than a little concerned by this theory of religion course you're teaching this semester. I've had a chance to look over the curriculum, and I think we need to talk."

"What?" She stared at him openmouthed. He couldn't be serious.

"We'll talk tomorrow." He waved his hand in dismissal, and Joyce gave her a parting smile—not so sweet this time, Ginny thought.

"You need a refill?"

Ginny's eyes flickered upward. Marjorie stood over her with a pot of coffee in her hand. Ginny nodded. "Thanks," she said. Marjorie filled her cup to the brim, then returned to the counter where she was talking with some young man.

Ginny sipped her coffee. Gregory was one miserable son of a bitch.

Oh, I'll come to your office tomorrow, but you'd better be prepared to fire me, because you're getting it with both barrels. No one interferes with my curriculum—especially not someone who thinks Joyce Davenport is a fine example for my students.

11

All three people in the dining room of the Yellow Bird turned their heads when the bell over the door rang once again and Bonnie Warner stepped inside.

Bonnie was bone tired. She needed a quick cup of joe to take with her, to propel her the last couple of miles back to Wilbourne. She knew the outside gates to the college had already been locked, but that didn't concern her. It was the eleven o'clock lockdown of Bentley Hall that was more problematic. Once Bentley was locked down for the night, no one was getting in—or out.

"Coffee, please, to go," Bonnie said, standing at the corner.

Marjorie nodded, and turned to fill the order.

Bonnie's eyes made contact with the young man seated near her on a stool. She nodded at him.

"You got to Wilbourne?" the man asked.

"Yes," Bonnie told him.

"Out kind of late," he said.

She shrugged. "I have a job in town."

He nodded, returning to the last of the french fries on his plate.

All Bonnie needed was to chug down the coffee and hop back on her bike and she'd be back at the college in practically no time at all. She glanced at her watch. She still had plenty of time, but she knew tonight she was pushing her luck. But Amy had actually been making progress tonight— Bonnie couldn't just take off in the middle of explaining why x times y equaled z. Tutoring algebra was a delicate assignment. When the kid's brain was finally showing some signs of comprehension, Bonnie needed to stick with it and make sure all the points were made.

"Here you go, honey," Marjorie said, handing her the coffee in a large Styrofoam cup with a secure lid.

"Thanks," Bonnie said, paying her.

That's when her eyes lit on the woman in the booth, who was also watching her. Shit! It was Dr. Marshall.

She couldn't bolt. Dr. Marshall had seen her.

Bonnie took a long breath, then walked over to where Dr. Marshall was sitting.

"Hello, Bonnie," the older woman said.

Bonnie decided simply to throw herself on Dr. Marshall's mercy. She liked Dr. Marshall. She had a reputation for being fair. She wasn't whacked out on authority like so many of the other professors at Wilbourne.

"Dr. Marshall, please don't tell the dean you saw me," Bonnie pleaded.

The professor smiled. "Bonnie, you know only upperclassmen are allowed to be off campus at this hour."

"I know. But I have a job."

"A job?" Dr. Marshall looked perplexed. "Again, only upperclassmen can hold off-campus jobs."

"I know, I know. But I'm not a rich girl like so many of the other kids, Dr. Marshall. Somehow I've got to find a way to pay for books for the new school year."

Dr. Marshall looked at her kindly. "What kind of job do you have?"

"I tutor a seventh-grader. The kid's having major troubles with algebra. I saw the ad her mother placed in a local paper and so I called, and now I ride back my bike into town to see her. Her mother is so grateful, and the kid's finally making progress."

"I see. So you've been away from campus all evening?"

Bonnie nodded. "I missed the welcome ceremony."

Dr. Marshall smiled wryly. "Well, count yourself lucky on that score." Her smile turned warmer. "But you'll be reprimanded for missing it. They'll see you didn't sign in . . . "

"Oh, no, Tish Lewis said she'd sign me in."

"I did *not* hear that."

"I'm sorry, Dr. Marshall, but I need the job . . ."

"Okay, Bonnie, I won't say anything. But please—try to arrange your visits to the girl during daytime hours, so you won't risk getting caught again."

"Oh, thank you, Dr. Marshall."

The older woman thought of something. "But the outside gates are locked. I'll need to give you a lift and—"

"No, no, it's fine. One of the seniors gave me the code for the gate."

Dr. Marshall sighed. "Do *not* tell me her name. Then I'd be covering up for *three* wayward students."

"Oh, thank you so much, Dr. Marshall. You're great!"

"Just please rearrange your tutoring schedule, okay?"

Bonnie nodded. She waved good-bye to Dr. Marshall and turned to head back out into the night. As she neared the door, the young man at the counter called over to her.

"Hey, do you need a ride back to the college? It's pretty dark out there."

Marjorie was leaning over the counter next to him. "It's okay, honey. He's a cop. You can trust him."

Bonnie smiled. The man had a kind face.

"Thanks anyway," she said. "I have my bike."

"Well," the young cop said, "be careful."

"I grew up Brooklyn," Bonnie told him. "Believe me, I know how to take care of myself. Lebanon is like paradise compared to the streets I grew up on."

The bell jingled again as she left the Bird.

It wasn't that Bonnie really enjoyed tutoring Amy. The girl was resistant and resentful. Only tonight had she shown any progress. All summer Bonnie had worked with her, trying to get her ready for the fall term. While the other girls on campus had all gone home for the summer, partying in the Hamptons or taking trips to Europe, Bonnie had stayed here, working in the registrar's office on campus and tutoring Amy in the afternoons. It was really quite baffling. Amy and her older sisters called Bonnie a "rich girl" from Wilbourne—a "Wilbournian" according to townie lingo—while Bonnie's classmates looked down on her for having to work off campus.

Can't win for losing, Bonnie thought as she biked through the town square. *Halfway there.*

She was wearing a pair of shorts and a T-shirt; a baseball cap was pulled down low over her head. She glanced again at her watch. Okay, now she was getting close. It was ten-thirty-five. Twenty-five minutes before the doors of Bentley were sealed shut until seven the next morning. In the event of a fire, they automatically unlocked, but nothing short of a conflagration would get them to open up otherwise.

She pushed on, even though now her legs were starting to burn and her breath was coming in gasps. Six miles into town was a long way on a bicycle. Amy lived out in what was known as "the Banks," a poorer part of town that reminded Bonnie of her own Brooklyn neighborhood—minus all the trees, of course. She tried to explain to the kid that she wasn't rich like most Wilbourne girls, that she had grown up in a third-floor apartment over a Greek restaurant. Bonnie wished she could quit the job, but she needed the money. Her parents were sure not sending her any. In any event, the job could only last a few more months at most. There was no way Bonnie could pedal her bike all this way once the weather turned cold.

At last, she passed through the center of town and could see the gates of the school looming in the near distance. Bonnie's legs ached, and she slowed down. *Almost ten minutes to spare,* she thought, sliding off the seat and taking deep breaths to try to slow her heart rate down a bit. She'd walk the bike through the gate after punching in the code. Then she could slip through the shadows and scramble into Bentley just in time.

I'm going to take a long hot shower and wash my hair, then just relax. My first class isn't until eleven tomorrow, so I can sleep in, I might even skip breakfast and take my time getting ready. Maybe Tish has something nice she can let me borrow for the first day of class.

She was walking her bike alongside the tall red brick wall that surrounded the school. She was almost at the gate.

And then she heard something off to the side of the road.

The road was dark. The sky was covered with clouds, blotting out the moon and the stars. Across from the campus stretched deep woods. The noise came again. An animal maybe. Something crunching through the leaves.

Bonnie felt a flicker of fear in her chest, but dismissed it. *Right, Bonnie,* she scolded herself. *Like it's a bear. Probably a squirrel.*

She was no more than ten feet from the front gate. She heard the noise again.

Now, don't scare yourself, there's nothing out there—

That's when she was suddenly bathed in a red light.

"What the heck?"

Great. Just great. Apparently I've been caught in a new security system to catch girls who left campus after curfew.

Except the light didn't seem to come from anywhere. It seemed, rather, just to *be*: a strange, eerie red glow.

Bonnie turned, ready with her excuses.

But what she saw left the words frozen in her throat.

She tried to scream, but couldn't.

She dropped her bike. It clattered on the road beside her.

Bonnie ran, heading for the gates of the college as fast as her tired legs could move. She heard the steps coming behind her, crashing through the underbrush on the side of the road, and then directly on her heels.

This time she found she was able to scream.

12

Sue didn't sleep well. It wasn't that the bed was uncomfortable, or even that she was in a new and different place for the first in her life. It was the dreams. They had started almost from the first moment she'd set her head down on the pillow. Weird, crazy dreams that she remembered only in fragments now—a face screaming at a window, a long dark road, a blond girl in a baseball cap riding her bike . . .

"Good morning," Malika sang out when the alarm went off at seven-oh-five. "Rise and shine and greet your first day as a Wilbournian!"

Sue sat up in bed. "You're pretty perky in the morning. Not sure I can get used to that."

Malika was already dressed and sitting at her desk, sipping a cup of coffee while she read the news on the Internet. "I was very good not to wake you," she said over her shoulder. "Did you sleep well?"

"No," Sue grumbled. "Is there more coffee?"

Malika laughed. "I told you not to read Joyce Davenport before going to sleep."

"Well, *something* gave me weird dreams." Sue replied, standing, stretching, stumbling to the bathroom.

Could it have been Joyce Davenport's strident tone that so upset her and caused her mind to wander all night? The book had been a grab bag of interesting opinion and outrageous nonsense—sprinkled, as Malika had warned, with some heavy helpings of outright bigotry. Arabs were "savages" in Davenport's description. Mothers on welfare were, one and all, "freeloaders." But she also talked about personal responsibility and moral convictions—things Sue thought were often absent from political life today.

Still, it was Davenport's stridency that left Sue with a bad taste. There was nothing Joyce had said in the book she hadn't heard around the dinner table from her grandfather growing up, but the way Joyce put things—she stripped down all of her positions to their lowest and most basic levels and made them seem crass and vulgar. And those who disagreed with her were accused of smearing her—the very same tactic Davenport was using herself. No wonder that people were unable to have civil conversations about politics these days.

Malika rapped on the bathroom door. "I'm out to my first class. Good luck with yours, Sue. Oh, and by the way—the coffee is in the lounge."

In the shower, Sue thought more about Joyce Davenport. Not so much about her politics or her stridency, but the fact that she was the first person she'd ever met who'd actually known her mother.

Was my mother the same way? Did she think the same way Joyce does? What kind of a person was she?

She'd wondered about her mother so often, alone in her room, all through her girlhood. So many times, Sue had stood in front of the shrine to Mariclare, staring up at the pictures of her mother, and wondered. What kind of a person had she been? What kind of dreams did she have, what did she want from life, what were her hopes and fears?

Sue used to run her finger across one particular photograph of her mother. Mariclare was young, maybe nineteen, so fresh-faced and happy. *Was she excited when she discovered she was pregnant with me? Would we have been close?*

She was so pretty. So much prettier than Sue considered herself. Did boys line up to take her out? Was she kind, was she sweet, was she nice to people? Did she study hard and get good grades, or was she flighty and bouncy like some of the girls at Stowe?

And then there was Sue's father. How had Mariclare met him? Were they madly in love? What kind of parents would they have been?

So many times, Sue had wished that her grandparents would talk to her about Mariclare. *Couldn't they understand how much it means to me to know something— anything— about my mother? I know it must be incredibly painful to lose your only child, but wouldn't that wound ever heal enough? It surely wasn't healthy to never mention her, never talk about her. And they could help me so much . . . why didn't they understand that I need to know about my mother and my father?*

She shut off the shower, stepped out, and began towel-drying her hair. This was the result of her grandparents' years of silence. On Sue's first day of college, rather than thinking about her classes and what lay ahead, she was still ruminating over the same old questions.

That's what meeting Joyce Davenport last night had done. It had sucked out all the anticipation about college from her, and left her once again a little girl pining after her unknown mother.

Sue had so envied her friends at Stowe Academy. She was the only student there who was technically an orphan. She would fall silent whenever any of her friends would launch into a litany of their parents' latest sins against them, always thinking, *At least you have a mother, even if she does drink*

*too much or fight with your dad or won't let you stay out as
late as you want. She's your mother and when you need her
she's there. You don't have a grandmother trying to take the
place of your mother—a grandmother who's really too old to
take care of you and a grandfather who won't even let you
bring up the subject of your parents. You have brothers and
sisters and you don't have any idea of how lucky you are—
all I have are my grandparents and when they die—and they
aren't young now—I'll be all alone in the world.*

Her earliest memories were of standing in front of the
shrine to Mariclare, thinking how beautiful her mother was
and indulging herself in fantasies about the life she could
have had with her parents. They would have been a family—
a real family—a real family that her grandparents, no matter
how much they might love her, had never really given her.

Sue understood her fantasies were just that, but in her mind
it was so easy to imagine Mariclare as the perfect mother.
Mariclare would understand her. She'd be her best friend. She'd
take her shopping and out to see movies. They'd have lunches
together in the city, chatting about their lives. Sue would be
able to talk to Mariclare about anything, and Mariclare would
always understand. Mariclare would be wise and kind and
loving, with a soft gentle voice and a wonderful laugh—the
kind that made you smile when you heard it, because it was
so full of love and joy.

Whenever her grandparents were out, sometimes Sue
would lift one of the pictures down from the shrine and carry
it into the bathroom. She would hold the photograph up next
to her own face and try to see any resemblance there. She
never could. All through her teen years, Sue kept doing it,
but never did she see a trace of herself in her mother's face.

But Joyce Davenport said I had my mother's eyes.

Sue had always assumed she took after her father. But her
father was even more of a mystery to her than her mother.

Once, when she was ten, she found a photograph in a drawer. She recognized Mariclare, but the man she was standing with was unfamiliar. A man about her age, with blondish hair and a serious expression. On the back of the photograph someone had written the name James. When Sue had shown her grandmother the photograph, the old woman had snatched it away from her and told her not to go snooping in drawers. But the name lingered in Sue's mind. She was convinced "James" was her father.

I must have other relatives out there somewhere, she always thought. *There must be someone on my father's side who would know something.*

Dressing for class, Sue tried to refocus. This was the day she'd been waiting for—the day she'd dreamed about. Away from home, on her own. In college! She could spread her wings, be her own person, find out what life was like outside the oppressive glare of her grandparents.

But all the excitement of the first day of classes paled before the simple fact that she had met someone who actually knew her mother—and knew her well!

If only it wasn't Joyce Davenport.

"Maybe she isn't so bad," Sue mumbled to herself as she slipped her shoes onto her feet. "She probably goes for shock value because it sells books."

She glanced down again at the cover of Joyce's book. The bio on the jacket described Joyce as "witty and vivacious"— though Sue had found the book to be bullying.

She'd score more political points if she didn't come across so intolerant herself, Sue reasoned. Joyce reminded her of a girl she'd known at Stowe—Lorraine Harrington. Lorraine was just mean. She liked making fun of people— plain and simple. She often would mock another girl right to her face—making fun of her braces, or her clothes, or her accent. Thankfully, Sue had never been a target of Lorraine's

cruelty, but still she'd disliked her. In some ways, she disliked even more the girls who'd been friends with Lorraine—the girls Sue had thought of as the "flunkies."

Is that what my mother was like? One of Joyce's flunkies?

She stood and looked at herself in the mirror. She wore a
pink T-shirt over khaki pants. Her blond hair was tied back in
a ponytail. Kind of preppy, but not as prepped out as some of
these girls here. She flicked on a little mascara.

No matter what I might think of her, Sue told herself, *I am
going to have to call Joyce Davenport.*

"Now," she said, gathering up the books she'd need for
her first class, "where did Malika say that coffee was?"

The lounge. It was next to the bank of elevators, a tidy little room with two plaid upholstered couches, and a big television set mounted to the wall. Girls were all heading in and
out, grabbing Styrofoam cups of coffee from the big silver
urn set on a table. Sue briefly wondered if any of these girls
might be future friends. A few nodded at her as she entered,
but most were engaged in animated chatter with their
friends. It was going to be difficult breaking into cliques, especially being a freshman in a mostly sophomore dorm.

Sue filled a cup, dumped in some cream and sugar, and
took a sip. Not bad.

"Oh, my God!"

It was a girl's voice in the hallway. Sue couldn't see her
face, as other girls were gathering around her. A small hud-
dle gathered in the doorway of the lounge.

"No way!" someone else said.

"What's going on?" Sue asked, looking over at a couple
of girls beside her.

"I don't know," one of the girls replied, raising her eyes to
look at the group in the hallway.

Sue took a few steps toward the excitement, as the chat-
tering of the girls just outside the lounge grew louder. She

could see the first girl now. She was tiny. She looked like she couldn't weigh more than eighty pounds soaking wet, and her long brown hair tumbled over a WILBOURNE COLLEGE sweatshirt. She had apparently brought some news to the group.

"Yes, you do know her," the tiny girl was telling one of her friends. "She was in our lit class last semester—remember, she was the blond chick with the thick Brooklyn accent?"

"Oh, right," said the other girl. "She didn't like Jane Austen. I thought Dr. Michalak was going to have a stroke."

"So she skipped out on the welcome ceremony?" another girl was asking. "How did she get away with that?"

"Tish Lewis signed her in," the tiny girl told her. "You know Tish, don't you? I can only imagine how much trouble *she's* in."

Sue gulped down the rest of the contents of the cup. "Excuse me," she said into the group. "But I need to get to class."

"Honey," said one girl, "I'm not sure there are any classes at the moment."

Sue looked at her oddly. "Why not?"

The girls all looked back at the tiny girl in the sweatshirt. She gave Sue a quizzical look.

"And who are you?" she asked.

"I'm Sue Barlow. A freshman."

The girl's face softened. "Okay. Chrissy Hansen." They shook hands. "Welcome to Wilbourne. But I hope you don't go running right back to wherever you came from."

Sue smiled. "Why would I do that?"

"Something's happened to one of the students. They think she may have been attacked."

"Attacked?" Sue gasped.

Chrissy nodded. "Her name was Bonnie Warner. I was just out jogging, and down by the front gate there are police cars everywhere."

The girl to Chrissy's left shuddered. "This freaks me out."

"The campus is safe," Chrissy insisted. "Bonnie was attacked off campus."

"But right outside the front gate!" another girl chimed in.

"When did it happen?" Sue asked.

"Sometime last night. They found her bike this morning."

Sue looked at Chrissy intently. "They found her bike? Where is she?"

Chrissy took a deep breath. "That's just it. No one knows. All they found was her bike and her baseball cap." Her face had turned pale. "And a whole hell of a lot of blood."

"Blood?" Sue asked, her knees suddenly weak.

Chrissy nodded. "Everywhere. On the road. On her bike. But no sign of Bonnie anywhere."

"What—what do the police think happened to her?" The coffee was churning in Sue's stomach, and she was struggling to keep on her feet.

Chrissy shrugged. "No idea."

Another girl came bounding off the elevator just then. "Classes have been postponed until noon today," she blurt out. "Bonnie Warner is missing and they found her bike with a lot of blood—"

"We know!" Chrissy yelled. For such a little thing, she sure had a loud voice.

Sue staggered away from the group, feeling light-headed and queasy.

One of my dreams last night was about a blond girl on a bicycle.

13

Lebanon started its day early, around five A.M. as alarms went off in darkened houses all over town. Lights flickered to life, and sleepy-eyed people staggered into their days. Coffeemakers perked, margarine melted in frying pans, teeth were brushed, showers got the blood pumping. School-age kids heard their parents' alarms faintly through their dreams, and knew their turn to rise and shine would soon be here. In the big bus barn behind the high school, the yellow buses with LEBANON SCHOOL DISTRICT printed across their sides were fueled up. The *New York Times* truck rolled over the back roads to throw bundles of papers out in back of the *Lebanon Herald* office, where at around quarter to six, Jimmy Madsen, thirteen, and his mother would arrive in their SUV to pick them up. All the newspapers would be delivered in time for Jimmy to be at school when the first bell rang at eight.

In his apartment above the Yellow Bird, old Wally Bingham heard the *Times* truck rattle by. *Almost time to get a move on,* he told himself. Wally could set his clock by that truck, even though he didn't need to. He woke every morning right at five on the dot. Even after being out of the Army for almost thirty years, it was a habit he couldn't seem to break. No matter how late he stayed up, no matter how much he drank, no matter what kind of sleeping pill he took, every morning his eyes opened as the digital clock on his night-stand switched to 5:00.

The apartment was empty and silent, except for the sound of his coffeemaker brewing in the kitchen. Wally lay there in the bed for a few moments more, relishing the sound of the silence. After his wife Lena died ten years earlier, he'd thought about marrying again—but then he'd gotten used to the notion of being alone, for the first time in his life, and he *liked* it. He'd been the youngest of seven kids, had gone into the Army straight out of high school, and after he finally de-cided not to re-up and "retired," there had been Lena. They'd never had kids—they tried when he was still in the Army, but Lena never could get pregnant. "God just doesn't seem to want to bless us that way," Lena said whenever someone brought up the subject of their childlessness. Wally admired her ability to publicly shrug off a question he knew caused her great pain. No one knew how many nights Lena had cried herself to sleep over her inability to conceive, his arms hold-ing her until her body stopped shaking.

They had talked about adopting halfheartedly, but noth-ing ever came of it—and then came the illnesses, one right after another, until Lena finally just quit fighting and died. Wally thought he'd be lonely without her, but he wasn't. Not really. It seemed almost disrespectful that he liked the quiet, liked being alone. *But it's not,* he reminded himself as he stared at the ceiling, *Lena wasn't much of a talker anyway, and neither am I. And if people think it's strange I didn't marry again, they can go to hell. It's none of their god-damned business.*

He got out of the bed and did his morning routine: two hundred push-ups and two hundred sit-ups, before getting a cup of coffee and heading into the bathroom to shave and shower. Now that he was past sixty, his body and joints ached more than they used to, and the mornings were getting harder for him. The winters and cold weather were getting rougher—some mornings when it was cold he woke up with his joints so stiff, he was afraid he wouldn't be able to get up. He was dreading the onset of the coming winter—he didn't look forward to shoveling the sidewalk in front of the café, or digging his car out of snowdrifts, and the apartment didn't seem to warm up quite as much as it used to. The weather was going to start turning cold in another month or so—and as he shaved, Wally looked at himself in the mirror and thought the magic word that had gotten him through the last two winters: *Florida*.

The thought brought a smile to his face. He was closing the café for two weeks at Christmas, flying down to Pensacola, renting a car, and driving all over the state until he found the place he was going to settle in when he'd had enough of the winters and the snow. He wasn't sure where yet in Florida it would be, but this year he was going looking for it. He'd last in Lebanon maybe another year or two, and that was it. He wanted to head south while he could still get around and spend his mornings fishing and enjoying the sun. *I'm still in pretty good shape,* he thought as he got into the steaming-hot shower, *and as long as I can do my morning calisthenics, I'm doing okay. I'm in better shape than most men half my age.*

He opened the café every Monday, and his morning routine hadn't varied once in all the years he'd owned the place. The first thing he'd do was turn on the grill and the deep fryers, and while they were warming up, he'd get the coffeepots brewing. After the grill was warmed up, he seasoned it with a layer of lard, and brought out eggs and slabs of bacon and sausage from the big walk-in cooler. Monday mornings were always the busiest of the week, and this one promised to be no different. Might even be busier than usual, since it was the first day of school over at Wilbourne. As he picked up the crates of eggs, Wally looked around and made sure everything was where it was supposed to be. There was plenty of everything. There was nothing worse than having to send Marjorie over to the A&P to buy something at retail grocery prices.

The diner would open promptly at six thirty, and there were always a few people waiting outside the door when he unlocked it. Even with the competition from the damned fast-food joints out by the highway, Wally still had a good breakfast rush every morning. *Although Micky D's has cut into some of my factory crowd with their rubbery food and fucking acid coffee,* he thought as he tossed an English muffin into the toaster.

At six thirty sharp, he opened the door. Waiting to come in were a couple of people he didn't recognize—he suspected they were parents of a Wilbourne girl, heading back to wherever they called home—and just at that moment getting out of his car was Sheriff Miles Holland.

"Howdy, Sheriff," Wally called. Miles waved back at him as he locked his car.

Sheriff Holland was well liked and respected by most people in Lebanon. Wally was always offering him a free cup of joe, but Miles always refused anything for free; he paid for every bit of food he put in his mouth. *Now that is one rare cop*, Wally thought. Miles was an honest man, and that he'd raised his son that way, too, had earned the respect of everyone in town. Like his son Perry and Perry's regular standing order of chili-covered cheeseburger and fries, Miles always had the same thing for breakfast every morning—scrambled eggs, a couple of slices of bacon, buttered toast with apple jam, hash browns drowned in ketchup, and lots of black coffee.

Rosie, his morning waitress, had slipped in the back door. She was tying her apron around her waist as Wally headed to the kitchen to get Miles's eggs scrambling. "One couple in the front booth," he told her. Rosie nodded and hurried over to take their order.

Wally heard the tinkling of the bell as Miles came inside.

"Sure you don't want to switch to sausage this morning, Miles?" Wally called through the opening.

"Can't eat this morning, Wally," the sheriff called back. "I just need to get the coffee to go, if you don't mind."

"No breakfast?" Wally asked, coming around to the doorway.

"No breakfast?" Rosie echoed.

Miles smiled. He was a few years younger than Wally, but was starting to spread out in the waist. He had thin legs and a barrel chest, and he shaved his head bald. Wally noticed that his blue eyes—usually so clear—were bloodshot and bleary. Since his wife died a few years back, Miles had aged what seemed like twenty years and seemed to put on weight. But this morning, Wally thought, he looked worse than usual.

"No breakfast," Miles said, sitting down at the counter.

Rosie handed Wally the order from the couple in the front booth. He glanced down at it, then looked back over at Miles. "You look like hell," Wally blurted out as Rosie filled a Styrofoam cup with coffee. "What's going on?"

Miles sighed. "Got a call up to the college." He accepted the coffee from Rosie and handed over two dollars. "Keep the change."

"What happened up at the college?" Wally asked, his voice low, glancing over at the couple in the booth, wondering if they really did have a daughter there.

The sheriff took a sip of his coffee. " One of the girls went missing." He raised his eyebrows at his friend. "Been a while since that's happened."

"And they need the sheriff for that?" Wally grinned. "She's probably just off having a good time."

"I don't think so. Her bike was found by a delivery man this morning outside the front gate." He lowered his voice. "Blood everywhere."

"Jesus," Wally said.

"You gonna get cooking the order?" Rosie said, sticking in her nose.

"Some girl got murdered up at Wilbourne," Wally told her in a harsh whisper.

"Now we don't know that, Wally." Miles gave him a face. "I shouldn't have said anything." He looked over at Rosie, a thin woman in her late thirties who might have been pretty once, but now seemed dry and brittle. "But I want people to be on their guard if we've got some attacker running around out there."

"No body?" Wally asked.

Miles shook his head.

"How they taking it at the college?"

"Well, you know how they get up there about them girls. They act like it's a convent and every girl in there doesn't have red blood flowing through her veins." Miles sighed. "We've got the state forensics team heading up there, so I gotta be off."

"Take a few minutes and eat something." Wally coaxed. "Be easier to get through the morning with a full stomach, you know."

"Nah, I've been dawdling as it is." Miles shook his head. "I'll be back in later before I go into the office. I'll have my breakfast then." He stood and picked up the coffee. "Just didn't have the stomach for eating a lot of grease after seeing all that."

"Given the circumstances," Wally said, "I'll forgive you for calling my food greasy."

Miles grinned and gave him a thumb's-up sign. Then he was off.

Wally watched as he drove off. Miles waved as he backed out of his spot, turned on his flashers, and headed off down the road at a steady clip in the direction of the college.

Somewhere in his mind, Wally seemed to recall another incident at Wilbourne a long time ago. He'd have to ask Marjorie later if she remembered what it was.

For some reason, his hands wouldn't stop shaking all morning as he fried eggs and toasted bread.

14

"This is the last time I'm telling you to get up, Billy!" his
mother shouted from the doorway. "You get out of that bed
right now or you're going to be sorry! I mean it!" The door
slammed behind her hard enough to shake the house.

Sixteen-year-old Billy Honeycutt yawned and sat up in
bed, stretching his long arms out overhead as the yawn deepened. *First day of school,* he thought, a smile starting to
creep over his face. *First day of my senior year in high
school!*

His mouth tasted sour and his shoulder-length blond hair
was standing up in every direction from his head. He kicked
off the covers and stood up, stretching up to his full six-foot-
three height, feeling his back crack just a little bit. That felt
good. His muscles were a little sore, and there was a big bruise
on his right shoulder from football practice. He grabbed a
pair of underwear out of a dresser drawer and walked into
the bathroom adjoining his room. Stepping out of his underwear, he stood naked in front of the mirror flexing his arms.
Years of weight training for football and baseball had thick-
ened and strengthened his body, and Billy was proud of it.

He smiled at himself. There was a patch of blond hair in the center of his chest, and a trail of blond down stretching to the thick patch at his pelvis. He brushed his teeth and washed his face and checked to see if he needed to shave. Nope. He'd shaved yesterday morning before church; every other day was usually enough. He also didn't need to shower; he'd taken care of that last night before bed. His mother had made it a requirement before agreeing to let him work at the McDonald's down near the highway. *"You aren't getting into my nice sheets all covered in grease and smelling like onions,"* she'd said. *"You need to shower every night after you get home from work."*

Billy knew he was a good-looking guy—the way the girls at school fawned all over him, it'd be kind of hard not to notice. That had started back in grammar school, and he'd never once lacked a date or a "steady' girl at any time—unless he chose not to have one. Every so often, he'd break up with whomever he was seeing just to be alone for a while—to see how many girls showed interest in him. He was rarely disappointed. He started humming to himself. He wasn't thrilled about going back to school, but it was his senior year. Syracuse, Colgate, and Boston College had shown interest in him already. If he had his way, it would be Boston—even if it was a Catholic school. He liked the idea of being a college student in a big city like Boston—the other colleges were in towns he didn't think were big enough. He'd only been to Boston once, but he loved everything about the city, even though his eighth-grade history class had been forced to spend the day at historic sites. Yes, if Boston College wanted him, that's where he was going.

Billy smiled to himself. The first day of school also meant no more two-a-day practices, and he sure hated those.

He smudged some gel into his hair and pulled on a pair of

boxer shorts, heading back into his bedroom. The sight of his mother sitting at his desk almost made him jump out of his skin.

"Mom!" Embarrassed, Billy grabbed a pair of jeans off the top of the pile of dirty clothes just outside his closet door and pulled them on. "What are you doing in here?" He buttoned the fly and shifted from foot to foot.

She was barely five feet tall and almost as round as she was tall, and her face was set in a hard-looking line. "I need to talk to you."

Panicked, he started running through options in his mind. *Did she find the bag of pot in the wheel well in the trunk of my car? Did she find out Heidi and I have been doing it? Did she find my pack of condoms? She couldn't know we went out drinking Saturday night . . . what is this about?*

"Do you know a girl named Bonnie Warner?" She narrowed her eyes. "Tell me the truth."

"Bonnie Warner?" That came out of left field. "No, I don't think so—"

"Yes, you do. She was tutoring Heidi's sister Amy. You told me a girl from Wilbourne was coming by to tutor her. You mentioned her to me."

"Oh, yeah. Yeah, that's right." Billy remembered the name now. His girlfriend's bratty little sister was flunking math class and so some Wilbournian chick was helping her out. He'd seen her last night at Heidi's house, in fact. "So what's up with asking me about her?"

"She was there last night when you were there, right?"

Billy nodded.

"Did you talk with her?"

For the first time, Billy noticed his mother was holding a pad of paper in her hands, and was jotting down notes as he talked.

"Yeah, maybe for a minute or so." He gave her a cocky

little grin. "She's not really my type. Kind of dykey actually."

"Don't use words like that, Billy."

"Sorry."

"What time did you see her?"

"Mom, what is going on?"

"Just answer me, please."

He sighed. "I guess it was about nine thirty. Yeah, I remember she wanted to get on the road because it was getting late."

"And you didn't offer her a ride? A girl on a bicycle on dark roads that late at night?"

Billy made a face. "Mom, I hardly know her. She always takes her bike." He leaned in toward her and took hold of the pad in his mother's hands. "Tell me what is going on, please!"

"Bonnie Warner never made it back to her dorm last night." Billy's mother stared at him. "You don't know where she might have gone, do you?"

"No." He pulled on an Eminem T-shirt he knew his mother hated, and started digging through his sock drawer. "I don't really know her at all. You know how Wilbourne girls are—they think they're too good to talk to any of us. Like they'll catch something if they talk to us." That wasn't true about Bonnie—she had seemed nice enough—but he knew his mother hated the college and it was easy to score points with her by bashing Wilbourne.

She smiled faintly. "You don't know if she had a boyfriend? If she was seeing anyone? I've asked Heidi's mother, but she's just too rattled by the whole thing to talk much. Did she ever mention who she hung out with?"

Billy smirked. "So you're writing an article about her disappearance? Is that what this is?"

"Billy, please, just answer me. If you have any leads at all—"

"I told you, I hardly knew her, I never really spoke with her. She was always huddled with Amy talking about trigonometry or algebra or something obscene like that."

"Oh, all right." His mother flipped her notebook shut. "But see if you can get Heidi to call me sometime today. I'd like to ask her a few questions, see what she might know."

"She's not going to know much either," Billy told her.

"Well, hurry up and finish getting dressed. I have to get to the office, so have some Cheerios for breakfast. And I can't drop Meghan off at school, so you'll have to do it for me."

"Aw, *Mommmm—*"

"I don't want hear it." She pointed her index finger at him. "It won't kill you to help out a bit around here, now will it? I have to get to work at the newspaper so I can keep food on the table." She glanced around the room and her face reddened a bit. "And pick up this room! How can you stand to live in a pigsty like this? It stinks in here. When I get home from work tonight, this room better be straightened up, or I'm throwing everything in the trash, do you understand me? Starting with your letter jacket."

"*Mommmmm—*"

The door slammed behind her. Billy let out a long sigh, then pulled on his shoes and socks. He glanced around the room. Reluctantly, he picked up a few dirty clothes and tossed them into the hamper. The bed was still unmade. This would have to do for "straightening up."

He was humming as he headed out of the room. Just to be safe, he grabbed his letter jacket and took it with him.

15

Ginny Marshall was having one of those mornings that made her wish she could just go back to bed. *Or kill myself,* she thought with a rueful grin as she examined herself in the parking lot of the administration building, which housed her office. *Well, better yet, kill Dean Gregory.*

It started when her coffeemaker broke while she was in the shower. She came out in her robe, longing for her first cup, only to discover that something was wrong with the damned thing and the pot was smoking on the burner. She threw the whole thing in the trash.

Eyes and mind foggy, she headed downstairs to beg a cup of coffee from her landlady. Mrs. Seibert was a soft-spoken widow in her early seventies who spent, it seemed, most of her life working in the yard or on the phone talking to her grandchildren. She was a great landlady as far as that was concerned—she kept her distance, which was a huge relief to Ginny. When she'd first moved in, she was afraid Mrs. Seibert would be one of those lonely old women who would be pestering her constantly for company. And while the apartment itself wasn't as big as the town house she'd had in Boston, it was comfortable and cozy.

Unfortunately, on this particular morning, Mrs. Seibert had just gotten off the phone with her oldest granddaughter, who'd just gotten engaged—and Ginny found that her landlady wanted to talk. So Ginny just gritted her teeth and let the older woman pour out her woes and worries about her granddaughter at the same time she poured the coffee. Finally, Ginny was able to make her escape by pretending she'd be late for work.

But more was still to come. After grabbing her briefcase and heading out to the driveway, she discovered her rear driver's side tire was flat. Irritated and cursing, she changed the tire, getting oil and grease all over her hands and slacks, necessitating a change of clothes. After dropping the flat off at Bud's Shell, she finally headed out to the college.

All the way there, she kept rehearsing in her head what she would say in her meeting with Dean Gregory. *No other faculty member has to get his or her curriculum approved by the dean, or clear it ahead of time with you. Of course my classes are controversial. Their purpose is to encourage intelligent debate about religion and its history. I do not teach that the Bible is wrong, or that Christianity is wrong, but no one can argue that the Bible hasn't been edited, and the Christian Church has historically been used by a male-dominated society for political purposes and to pursue agendas that are diametrically opposed to what the Bible actually says and teaches. The Church has been anti-woman almost from its very beginnings—and the Book of Revelation in particular has been used and misused.*

And if logic and rationality didn't work, she could always play the Harvard card.

As the only faculty member who not only had her doctorate from Harvard, but also had been a full tenured professor there, Ginny knew she had some clout. She didn't like to swing that weight around, but if she had to, she would.

The thought made her smile. She wasn't big on confrontation in her personal life—nor was she big on "tooting her own horn," as her agent, Angela Cohen, often pointed out to her. But she would not stand for infringements on her freedom to teach as she saw fit.

Ginny enjoyed the drive out to the college—the smell of the apple orchards, the low-slanting rays of a pink morning sun. Even though it took less than half an hour, there was something almost zenlike for Ginny driving through the countryside. But the calmness that settled her anxiety over Dean Gregory was short-lived.

As she reached the college entrance, Ginny's eyes widened. All along both sides of the road were police cars with their lights flashing. She could see uniformed men wandering through the woods on the opposite side of the road from the college entrance. There were state police cars along with the Lebanon cops.

"What the hell?" Ginny stepped on the brake, rolling down her window. "What's going on, Sheriff?"

She liked Miles Holland. He was one of the few people in Lebanon who'd remained friendly to her after that damned article had appeared—and he'd been the one to suggest calling in the FBI when she got the threatening e-mails. "I won't put up with that kind of bullshit in my town," he'd told her. "If they're playing pranks, let 'em think about that when they're behind bars."

He smiled as he saw her now. "Morning, Dr. Ginny," he called, heading toward her car. He always called her "Dr. Ginny," with a slight teasing sound in his voice that always made her want to giggle a little bit.

"What's going on?" she asked again.

Miles was at her window now. "Seems like one of your students went missing last night."

"Missing?" Ginny put the car in park. "From the dorm?" She felt a knot forming in the pit of her stomach.

The sheriff scratched his head as he leaned in her window. "Best as I can piece it together, she never made it back from town last night. We found her bike by the front gate." He paused. "There was a lot of blood, but no trace of the girl."

Ginny felt sick. "Who—is she?"

"Name's Bonnie Warner."

"Oh, dear God."

Miles looked in at her. "You know her, Ginny?"

"Yes. Yes, of course. I saw her. Last night."

"When? Where?"

"At the Yellow Bird. I'd stopped in, and she came in to get a cup of coffee. She was concerned when she saw me, because she shouldn't have been off campus at that hour."

"What did you tell her?"

Ginny sighed. "I agreed not to report her. She had been in town, where she tutors a girl. She said she needed the extra money to buy textbooks."

Miles was nodding. "Yeah. I've been over to talk to the girl she was tutoring and her mother. Nothing seemed out of the ordinary."

"I should have insisted I give her a ride."

Miles looked at her kindly. "She apparently has been making the same bike ride all summer. There was no reason to think last night would be any different."

Ginny felt her stomach twist. "But apparently it was. You said there was blood . . . ?"

"Ginny, I'll call you later, or maybe have Perry come by. To get an official statement from you. Is that okay?"

She nodded. Miles called ahead to tell his men to let her car through. Ginny's head felt light, as if she might faint. Bonnie's face hovered in front her, her plaintive plea not to report her ringing in Ginny's ears. She liked Bonnie. The girl had been in her Bible and Women class the previous semester. Bonnie had been a good student, rather quiet, only speaking when called on—but she'd always had a valid point to make when she did speak up. In her term paper, she'd made some excellent points that had surprised Ginny with their thoughtfulness. Bonnie had obviously not only been paying close attention in class, but had done some outside research on her own.

Ginny sat behind the wheel of her car after parking in her designated spot. She couldn't move. She felt frozen in guilt. *Blood*. There had been blood. That meant something terrible had happened to Bonnie. She might even be dead.

Why didn't I insist on driving her?

Finally, she was able to get out of the car and make her way into the building. The theology department shared its office area with the history department. All of the professors had small offices off a hallway that jutted out in either direction from a central reception area. Both departments shared a single secretary, Hazel Westwood, who was on the phone when Ginny walked into the office.

"Did you hear, Dr. Marshall?" Hazel's nasal voice was especially hard to take this morning. "One of the *scholarship* girls is missing." There was a smug note of triumph in her voice, as if she were trying very hard not to smile.

Ginny glared at her. Though blue-collar herself, Hazel looked down her snub nose at the girls who attended Wilbourne on scholarships, as though they didn't belong among the high-class princesses on campus. More than once, when Hazel made a snide reference to "scholarship girls," Ginny had had to bite back a stinging retort.

"Yes," she told the secretary. "I spoke with Sheriff Holland down at the gate. It's terrible. I certainly hope she's all right."

"She's probably with a boy." Hazel laced the words with condescension and contempt. "That's how those scholarship girls are, you know. You can't make a sow's ear into a silk purse, after all."

Ginny bit her lip and walked to her office. Her voice mail light was blinking. She picked it up.

"Ginny, this is Dean Gregory. As I am sure you are already aware, one of the students is missing, and so I am afraid I'm going to be tied up all day and have to cancel our meeting. We'll need to revisit this, though, sometime in the future. As you know, we now have a new board of trustees, and they are quite concerned about the curriculum we're teaching. So at some point soon, we'll need to have a conversation."

She set the phone down thoughtfully. She didn't like the way Gregory said "conversation."

Gregory's postponement of their meeting, however, also put off the eventual confrontation she'd have with him over seeing Bonnie Warner at the Yellow Bird. The fact would be noted in the investigation, and Gregory would want to know whether Ginny had planned to report the girl or not.

Ginny closed the door to her office, sat down at her desk, and covered her face with her hands.

What happened to that poor girl?

She realized she was shivering, and that her office was freezing, even though the temperature read seventy-five.

16

Pierre deSalis never could quite pinpoint the moment when his life went wrong. As he lay in bed listening to all the noise in the small house he shared with his family, he gave up on trying to get back to sleep until they were all out of the house.

Only a few more years and all the kids will be gone, he said to himself. *If I can make it that long.*

Pierre had Sundays and Mondays off from the paper mill. On Sundays, Maddie nagged him out of bed so he could drive them all up to Senandaga for Mass. And during the school year, the noise of the kids getting ready for school woke him up every goddamned Monday morning. So he never got to sleep in. Never.

Pierre buried his head in his pillow and tried to count his blessings. His children were healthy. He had a good job. And if maybe things hadn't turned out the way he might have wanted when he was first married, he supposed things could be worse. Things could *always* be worse.

They'd been thirteen when they fell in love: a pair of rural farm kids without much future in Richelieu. They used to go on picnics and laugh and tease each other, always planning to move to the States once they were married. Right after high school, they'd tied the knot in the little Catholic chapel in Richelieu in front of their family and friends, and instead of going on a honeymoon, they'd packed everything they owned into an old battered Chevrolet station wagon and moved across the border. Pierre got a job at the paper mill in Senandaga, and Maddie worked at the A&P as a checker. Between them, they scrimped and saved every cent they could. There were no vacations. In several years, they'd had down payment money for a nice little house in Lebanon.

Their little house was a dream come true for them; at the time it seemed big, roomy, and perfect for children. There was a backyard, three bedrooms, and an unfinished basement that could also be converted into bedrooms if the family grew that big. Until that point, they'd been using birth control—a secret kept from their priest—but as soon as they moved into their house, Maddie had stopped taking the pills. Within a year she was carrying their first child, Pierre Jr.

It was a bit of a commute for Pierre every day to the mill, but the house made Maddie happy. Pierre considered the drive a small price to pay for Maddie's smiles, to hear her singing in the kitchen as she cooked or cleaned. That first pregnancy, she'd glowed and been beautiful—and been so happy.

But Pierre Jr. hadn't been born healthy. There was something wrong with his blood. They'd had to drain all of his blood, give him transfusions, and it was touch and go for two weeks. Maddie spent almost all of that time in the chapel at St. Agatha's Hospital, or talking to priests. She wouldn't talk to Pierre hardly at all. Finally, Father Michaels had told him, "Maddie blames herself for the baby's sickness."

Pierre, exhausted from lack of sleep and still worried, just gaped at the priest. "Why?"

Father Michaels had shaken his head. "She thinks God is

punishing her for the years of birth control, which you know is a sin, Pierre. I've told her God doesn't work that way, but she's hard to persuade."

After the baby came home, everything changed. Maddie filled the house with statues and paintings of the saints. She was always saying the Rosary, watching the baby like a hawk, and many nights slept in the baby's room on the floor next to the crib. Once, when Pierre complained, Maddie turned on him in a fury. "It's your fault the baby was sick!" she snapped. "You insisted on me taking those accursed pills!" And she stormed off, leaving Pierre staring after her with horror.

Shortly thereafter, she returned to their bed as though nothing had ever happened.

Then the other children started to come, and it was as though each pregnancy shut something down in Maddie. Every pregnancy drove her further and further toward the Church. They'd never been particularly religious—they went to church on Sunday, that was all—but now Maddie spent two or three mornings a week driving up to Senandaga for Mass. She started putting on weight, and stopped wearing makeup and fixing her hair. Every child after the first was born healthy, which was a relief—and even Pierre Jr., after such a rough beginning, was an extraordinarily healthy child. But if anything, Maddie only became more devout. And when she'd put the statue of the Blessed Virgin Mary in the front yard, Pierre had supported her against the neighbors who wanted them to remove it.

"We're Catholic," he'd told Jacob Cobb and his sour-faced wife Bernice when they'd stopped by to ask that the "eyesore" be taken away. "And there's no law against having the Virgin Mary in our front yard."

Maybe I should have given in to them then, he thought as he heard Maddie yelling up the stairs at their youngest to hurry up. *Maybe I should have put my foot down and made her take down all the pictures of bleeding hearts and saints all over the damned house. Maybe sometime I should have told her I wanted a wife and not a nun to live with* After the last child was born, it was a very rare day when Maddie agreed to have sex with him.

Yet Pierre never objected when he came home from work to find a new picture of Jesus or Mary hung somewhere, or when another little statue of a saint appeared on a ledge like magic. Maddie had also lost her sense of humor somewhere along the way, and he couldn't quite figure out when that happened. In the old days, she'd never complained when he sat up watching a ball game and drinking a few beers, but now she'd purse her lips and furrow her brow in that annoying, disapproving way. How many times did Pierre come across her sitting in the kitchen, eyes closed with her fingers counting off the beads on her rosary?

Damn it, I work hard and if I want a beer while I watch a ball game, I'll have one! Whatever happened to that pretty young girl who liked a beer every now and then, who loved to laugh and cuddle up to me in the bed at night after the kids were asleep?

None of the boys took to religion the way Maddie wanted. Pierre Jr. had stopped being an altar boy. Michael, their second son, was urged by his mother to join the priesthood. *That's about as likely as me sprouting wings,* Pierre thought with a smile. Michael had always had an eye for the girls. He was a handsome boy, a star of the football team, and girls were calling him on the phone all the time, much to his mother's distaste. Frankie, their third son, wasn't likely to become a priest either. Right now he was reading tracts on Buddhism, which his mother called "paganism."

But their youngest child, Bernadette, worried Pierre. Thirteen and quiet, she was always reading books about the saints and praying with her mother. Today was Bernadette's first day of high school, and she and her mother had sat up until nine last night saying the Rosary in order that the Virgin would protect the girl as she started out on a new journey.

"Where is that girl?" Maddie was asking now, bustling around the kitchen as Pierre came down the stairs. "I've called her three times."

"Maybe you both stayed up too late last night praying," Pierre ventured. Maddie just glared at him.

Pierre sighed, pouring himself a cup of coffee.

"Bernadette!" Maddie shouted from the bottom of the stairs. "Are you up?"

There was no answer.

Maddie gripped the banister and began hurrying up the steps. Pierre settled down at the table with his coffee. In seconds, he could hear Maddie's heavy footsteps across the ceiling down the hall to Bernadette's room.

Her scream made him stand abruptly, spilling his coffee all over the floor.

Jesus preserve us, Pierre thought as he ran up the stairs. He could hear Michael and Frankie bounding out of their rooms.

Maddie was standing in Bernadette's doorway, her mouth open and her hands clasped together so tightly, the knuckles were white.

Pierre peered into the girl's room. His daughter was lying on her bed, flat on her back, her arms straight out on either side of her.

There was blood on her feet and on her palms.

"Call an ambulance!" Pierre shouted down the hallway to his sons, pushing past his wife and hurrying to his daughter's bedside.

Bernadette turned her eyes to him. Her face seemed to be bathed in an eerie light.

"Papa." She smiled at him. "The Holy Mother spoke to me. She came to me."

"The wounds of our Lord."

It was Maddie, whispering behind him. Pierre glanced around to see her make the sign of the cross and drop to her knees. "It's a miracle! Praise Jesus!" She grabbed at her husband's hand. "Pray with me, Pierre!"

He pulled his hand away from her, and turned to his sons. They were standing in the doorway, their mouths open. "Didn't you hear me? Call an ambulance!" Still, they just stood there. *"Now!"*

Frankie turned and disappeared down the hallway again.

"Is—is Bernie all right?" Michael stuttered.

Pierre couldn't answer. He turned back to his daughter, placing his hand on her forehead. "How did this happen?" he asked her. "Did you cut yourself?" He forced himself to look at the wounds. They did not appear deep, but the blood was fresh and flowing freely.

"She spoke to me, Papa." Bernadette's face was wreathed in smiles. "She told me that I am blessed."

He grabbed a shirt near the foot of her bed and began wrapping Bernadette's hand, trying to stop the blood.

"No!" Maddie pushed him away. "Don't!"

"Are you crazy? She'll bleed to death!"

Bernadette looked up at him serenely. "No, Papa, it's a miracle."

Maddie began mumbling, "Hail Mary, full of grace, the Lord is with you . . ." *Hail Mary.*

In the distance, Pierre heard a siren.

For the first time in a very long time, he started to pray.

17

It was three days after Bonnie Warner's disappearance that Sue once again saw the face at the upper window.

And just as before, the face was screaming.

All of her books fell to the sidewalk as Sue stared up at the window, transfixed.

"No," she mumbled. "It can't be . . ."

A terrible thought entered her mind. Was the face always there? Always screaming? Maybe it was—because until now, Sue hadn't had the courage to look up at the window again. Every day as she'd left her dorm, she'd studiously kept her eyes averted, and it would be the same when she returned.

But today, on her way back to the dorm from class, when life on campus was just starting to return to normal after the scare of Bonnie's disappearance, Sue had summoned the nerve to look up.

And there, from that same third floor window, she saw a girl screaming as if in mortal terror.

"Malika!" Sue shouted, spotting her roommate across the yard. "Come here!"

"What is it?"

"Look up at that window! On the third floor!"

Malika turned around and peered upward. "Which window?"

"The one where—"

Sue's words trailed off. The face was no longer there.

"Where what?" Malika was asking.

Sue leveled her eyes at her. "This is the second time I've seen a girl at that window, and she's always screaming."

Malika grinned. "So, some weird chick is screwing around."

"No." Sue shook her head. "It's not."

"It's not, huh? So what is it, a ghost?"

"I know it sounds crazy," Sue said, trying to laugh.

"Sweetie, you are still jumpy about Little Miss Bonnie," Malika said. "Everybody is. Just let it go."

Sue let out a long sigh and looked up again at the window. Just a dim darkness behind the glass. Nothing there.

Nothing behind the window of the room I was somehow convinced was my mother's.

Maybe Malika was right. Bonnie's disappearance had indeed unsettled her. She kept remembering that dream she'd had the night Bonnie disappeared—of a blond girl on a bicycle. The coincidence unnerved her.

For three days, everywhere Sue went, someone was talking about Bonnie. The story of the missing girl and the bicycle covered with blood had made the national news and become the buzz of the campus.

Given Wilbourne's rather prim reputation, of course, the story was almost always discussed in a hushed whisper, and few of the faculty would address it directly. The vast majority of the students had known Bonnie Warner only by sight, if that. Those who actually knew her from either having had a class with her or from living on her floor at Bentley Hall were—for the last few days anyway—minor celebrities on campus. Bonnie apparently hadn't been an outgoing girl, preferring to spend her time in her room studying or surfing the Internet. There were a couple of girls—Tish Lewis, for example—who knew her better than the rest, but even they didn't know a whole lot about her. She'd had a Brooklyn accent so thick you could only cut it with a meat cleaver, and was on scholarship. But other than that, no one really knew much about her, except that "she'd seemed nice."

Driving the talk, of course, was an undercurrent of fear, an unspoken terror that someone was out there, watching the campus, stalking them . . . There were still bloodstains on the road—blood that had been identified as Bonnie's. So much of it had been spilled that police didn't think she could possibly be still alive. But there was no trace of her body anywhere. That made the whole thing even creepier.

Malika put her arm around Sue. "Come on," she said kindly. "Let's go to the caf and get you some food. You are trembling, baby."

Sue agreed to be led away from Bentley Hall. She didn't dare look back up at the third-floor window again. She wondered if she ever would.

But at the cafeteria, Sue's mind wasn't on food, Even as she grabbed a tray and took her place in the line, she was thinking back to a girl she'd known at Stowe. After the winter break of her sophomore year, Sue had found out that one of her fellow students had been killed in a weird skiing accident. There followed a terrified hush over the girls at Stowe, much like that which had fallen over the girls of Wilbourne. Everyone talked in whispers, just as they were doing now here in the caf, as if speaking in normal tones would somehow be disrespectful to the dead girl.

Her name was Lori Powers, Sue remembered with a jolt, *and I didn't like her very much, and my first thought when I heard she was dead was "Good!"*

Lori had been a loudmouth, always bragging and name-dropping. Her father was a playwright—musicals, and he'd had several shows on Broadway at the time. Lori had long thick brown hair and gray eyes, but was inclined to be over-weight and she talked several decibels louder than she needed to. Sue made a point out of avoiding Lori as much as she possibly could, but she remembered now—she had for-gotten—that on their last day of school before winter break, she'd found herself in an argument with Lori.

"Watch where you're going, you clumsy bitch!" Lori had shouted at her as Sue bumped into her in the hallway. Lori's books had gone flying. Sue instinctively knelt to help her re-trieve the books—but something had snapped inside her, and she started shouting back at her.

"If anyone's a bitch around here, it's you, Miss Lori Pow-ers!" Sue stood, refusing to help any longer. "You can take your attitude and loud mouth and go fuck yourself!"

The girls who witnessed this little scene were shocked. Sue was no demure little thing—far from it—but such lan-guage was out of character. She could never explain her rage in that moment. Lori, like many a bully, had no response when confronted, just gathered up her books, her face red, her eyes filled with tears. Sue had just stood there, arms akimbo, glar-ing at her, until Lori hurried out the doors of the school.

A few days later, she skied headfirst into a tree and died.

That's weird, Sue thought as she placed a glass of orange juice on her tray. *Lori Powers! I haven't thought about her in years. Poor thing. I never got to apologize to her.*

She added a bowl of Cheerios and another cup of coffee to her tray, and headed out to the eating area.

She sat at the end of a table where three girls were hud-dled. They glanced over at her before going back to their conversation as if she wasn't even there. Sue shrugged. She didn't recognize any of the girls anyway. *And they're probably just gossiping about poor Bonnie Warner.*

Malika settled her tray across from her and gave her a bright smile. She was just having coffee and a granola bar.

"What's your first class this morning?" she asked.

Sue opened her backpack and took out one of her textbooks. *The Sacred Feminine,* written by her instructor, Dr. Marshall. "Theory of Religion," she told Malika. "This is a really fascinating book."

"I know," Malika said. "I've read it. I had Dr. Marshall. She's awesome,"

Sue nodded. "Yes, I like her very much."

In fact, of all her teachers, Dr. Marshall was the warmest and most interesting. Dr. Lloyd was a dreary droner in English Comp, and Dr. Adamson in Biology was a spitter. She'd sat three rows back from the front and still she'd gotten sprayed. The rest were so dull that she hadn't yet memorized their names.

Malika's phone twirped from inside her backpack. She groaned. "My parents have been calling every day," she said, taking it out and switching the ringer to vibrate. "Ever since they heard about Bonnie. Just to make sure I'm okay."

Sue smiled. Her grandparents hadn't called. She was surprised—and both relieved and disappointed at the same time. Disappointed because, after all, it would simply show that they cared—but maybe they hadn't heard about it, as unlikely as that seemed. But relief was greater than disappointment, because Sue feared their reaction. *They might make me come home,* she thought.

Maybe I ought to call and tell them, and assure them there's no need to worry, Sue mused as she spooned some Cheerios into her mouth. *No, why wake a sleeping dog?*

When she was about seven years old, her grandfather, the

esteemed lawyer, had been involved in a case with a steel company battling its union. The union, her grandfather had said many times over dinner, was incredibly corrupt—so any notion that they were interested in the welfare of their members was ludicrous. Union leaders, he insisted, were only interested in money and power, and by God, he was going to break the stranglehold the union had over his client. As the battle went on, things kept getting uglier and uglier, until one day the FBI had shown up at her grandfather's office.

Her grandparents didn't tell her anything at first, but she'd noticed the armed guards outside their apartment.

"That horrible union boss has apparently threatened us," her grandmother told her grimly one morning over breakfast. "That's how these thugs operate. They can't get what they want by civilized means, so they threaten with violence. So, I know it's going to be rather, well, *embarrassing* for you, but your grandfather has hired a bodyguard to go with you everywhere—school, the park—anytime you leave this apartment, he's going to go with you to make sure no one takes you from us."

At first, Sue had thought it was kind of cool to have a bodyguard, but as the weeks passed, it began to annoy her. None of the other girls had one, and while it seemed to mark her as special at first, soon it made her stand out. That big hulking guy—he was named Sam Puglisi—was always there, even during recess in the playground as they played kick-the-can or Red Rover. If she went off to the swings or monkey bars by herself, Sam always followed, watching her. One day, she heard one of the other girls—Melissa Hardwick—make a snide remark about "Susie and her trained monkey," and the rest of the girls laughed. As soon as Sue got home that day, she'd asked her grandmother how much longer she had to keep Sam.

"Oh, Susie." Gran had sighed, a hand going to the rope of

pearls at her neck. "Until this whole thing is over, I'm afraid. I probably shouldn't tell you this, but those horrible people specifically threatened *you*. You're all we have, dear, and we have to keep you safe."

"But why can't Granpa just give them what they want?"

"Susan!" Gran's face went white beneath her makeup. "You mustn't think that way—ever. We cannot give in to this kind of behavior, *ever*. When monsters like this threaten you, you cannot back down—because then they will win, and these kinds of tactics are despicable. You're very precious to us, darling, you know that, but if your grandfather backs down, if he gives in to this, he'd have to give up his practice. Because then bad people like this union boss would know all they had to do to beat him was threaten his family and he'd back down." She forced a smile on her face. "Is Sam so awful that you don't want him around you?"

"No." She did like Sam. He teased her and made her laugh, called her "his other little girl" because he had a daughter her age at home. "But the other kids—they make fun of me."

"The next time they do, you tell those nasty little girls that you have to have a bodyguard because your grandfather is doing important work." She sniffed. "Much more important work than any of *their* fathers are doing." Gran poured herself a glass of sherry with a shaking hand. "Now, run along and do your homework."

Melissa Hardwick is just mean, Sue thought as she went to her room. *The next time I see her I am going to tell her so. Granpa is doing important work, and I have a bodyguard so he can keep doing his work—and if she keeps being mean to me, I'll have to do something about it. Like pull her hair.*

But Melissa Hardwick wasn't in school the next day, or the next. She was sick, their teacher said, and they all had to pray for her to get better. But Melissa never came back to school. She died—some weird childhood disease that just seemed to take her without hardly a warning. They didn't explain it in school—and Sue's grandparents had never discussed it.

But her grandfather won the case, and one day the guards were gone.

Sue looked around the caf and shivered.

Why had she suddenly remembered both Lori Powers and Melissa Hardwick?

They were dead girls. Just like Bonnie Warner.

18

All day long, Sue continued to feel uneasy. She took notes in her classes and did her best to pay attention to the lectures—it was easiest with Dr. Marshall, who made them laugh and told them stories about the days when the female divine was worshiped instead of denigrated—but Sue's thoughts kept drifting back to Bonnie. And Lori. And Melissa.

Dead girls.

She knew there was no way she could avoid looking up at that window again when she returned to Bentley Hall.

It was turning cool. Summer ended early up here, Sue discovered. The sun was low in the pink sky, drifting behind a cloud cover growing increasingly heavy. It might even rain. In the air hung the tart fragrance of the apple orchards nearby. Sue cast her eyes toward Bentley Hall in the distance.

She'll be there, she told herself.

When she got close enough, she lifted her eyes to the window.

The girl behind the glass was screaming again, her silent plea for help.

Sue froze. This time she refused to look away. She stood her ground and overcame her fear and studied the face. It was a girl, all right, a young girl about her age, and her mouth was wide open, and screaming. This was no joke. She was terrified.

Yet all around her on the sidewalk, girls passed Sue without noticing, talking and laughing among themselves.

Can't they see her? Am I crazy? What's wrong with everyone? Can't anyone hear her inside the dorm?

In that one flicker of her eyes away from the window, the face disappeared.

Sue took a deep breath. She counted the windows. One, two, three, four—*fifth* window from the left side of the building, on the third floor.

She stood there for a moment, willing her heart to stop racing, taking deep breaths as she collected herself.

I'm going up there, Sue decided, *and get to the bottom of this*.

She hurried through the front doors, almost colliding with a squat brunette carrying an armload of books, bringing memories of Lori Powers back to her once again. Sue mumbled, "Excuse me," and gave the girl a weak smile before heading for the elevator. She hopped inside and pressed 3. Her heart raced as the elevator made its creaky ascent. When the doors slid open, Sue looked around. It seemed the floor was deserted. With a deep breath, she stepped off the elevator.

The third floor looked almost exactly like the second, an identical lounge across from the elevators. Except the lounge was deserted, as was the hallway in each direction. Never had Sue seen her own floor so still and quiet.

An itchy little pulse of fear began to thread its way down Sue's spine. The only sound on the floor was some distant music—so distant and so muted that Sue couldn't even make out what kind of music it was. With a heartbeat now so loud she could hear it in her ears, she made her way down the hall to the end of the building, then started counting doors. There. This had to be the one. Fifth from the end. Room 323.

Why do I feel that this was my mother's room?

She stood in front of the door and listened for a moment. She heard nothing from inside. Hesitantly, she raised her hand and knocked.

There was no answer.

She knocked louder.

Still nothing.

She was readying herself to knock again when suddenly there was a hand on her shoulder. Sue gasped out loud.

"Can I help you?" a voice asked from behind her.

Sue spun around. A girl stood behind her—kind of a Goth-looking girl, with long black hair and heavy black mascara.

"Oh, my God, I didn't hear you come up behind me—" Sue stuttered, trying to calm her heartbeat.

The Goth girl smiled. "Sorry, didn't mean to scare you," she said. Despite her severe look—she was dressed all in black, too—she seemed friendly, and gave Sue a big smile in apology. "Can I help you with something?"

"Well," Sue said, not sure how much she wanted to say, "I was wondering whose room this is." Even as she said it, she felt stupid. *What am I going to do, tell her I saw someone in the window screaming?*

The Goth girl looked at her. "Why?" she asked warily, her eyes narrowing.

"Well, I was just—"

The other girl shook her head. "Yeah, you and everybody else. It seems every girl on campus has come by that door sometime in the past three days." She looked at Sue more closely. "Hey, I recognize you. You sat at our table in the caf this morning, didn't you?"

"Well, I was there . . ." She remembered there were other girls, but couldn't place this girl's face—a face she wasn't likely to forget.

"I'm Joelle Bartlett," the girl said. "I'm a senior—you must be a freshman." She stuck out her hand, and Sue shook it.

"So, Joelle . . . tell me. This room . . ." Sue glanced back at the door over her shoulder.

"Yeah. That was Bonnie Warner's room."

Bonnie Warner. Sue felt so light-headed that it seemed she might faint.

"You all right?" Joelle asked.

"I'm—I'm—" Sue stuttered.

"Come on into my room," Joelle said. "I'm right across the hall."

Sue followed her inside, still feeling dizzy. Joelle gestured for her to sit on the futon propped against the wall. The room had the exact same setup as Sue's own, but Joelle and her roommate had added a lot of small touches that made it seem more homey and lived-in. A poster of Johnny Depp in his costume from *Pirates of the Caribbean* had been framed and mounted on one wall. Next to it was a movie poster from *Finding Neverland,* and a model of Edward Scissorhands stood on one bureau. One of these girls quite obviously had a Johnny Depp fixation.

A laptop computer was open on one of the desks, playing music Sue didn't recognize. The bathroom door was open, and Sue could see several candles burning in there. The fragrance of sage met Sue's nostrils. The room was neat and tidy, both beds made.

"You want something to drink?" Joelle asked. "I have wine, soda, water . . . "

"No, I'm good." Sue sat down in a chair and looked around the room. "I guess I just got a little woozy."

"It's okay. Everyone's shaken up about Bonnie's death."

Sue looked at her intently. "So you think she's dead?"

"Come on. You think she lost all that blood and is still alive?"

Sue shuddered. "Then where's her body?"

"I think it was a ritual sacrifice." Joelle seemed to know what she was talking about. "Some kind of witchcraft. They needed the body. The blood of a virgin."

"Oh, God," Sue said, shivering again.

"Sorry, I'm making things worse, aren't I? Did you know her?"

"Bonnie? No."

Joelle sat opposite her at the edge of her bed. "You're rooming with Malika, right?" Joelle poured herself a glass of wine and grinned at her. "She's very minimalist. Bare walls, everything in its place, deeply organized, right?"

Sue managed a smile. "Yeah."

"That would drive me nuts. I do like Malika, though. Very smart. She's going to go places." She sipped her wine. "Now, why were you knocking at Bonnie's door?"

"I—" Sue hesitated. "I—I thought I saw someone in the window from outside."

"Impossible."

"Why? Didn't Bonnie have a roommate?"

"No."

Sue found that odd. "Why not?"

Joelle was studying her with her dark eyes through her heavy mascara. "What did this person at the window look like?"

"It was a girl. I know that much."

"So there are lots of girls at windows in Bentley Hall. Why come up to this one?"

Sue steeled herself. "Because she was screaming." She paused. "I wanted to make sure she was okay."

To her surprise, Joelle didn't laugh or seem surprised. She just nodded. "You know why Bonnie didn't have a roommate?"

Sue shook her head.

Joelle took another sip of wine. "That room is supposed to be haunted. No one else would live there. Bonnie said she wasn't afraid of ghosts." She shrugged. "Maybe she was a little too brave for her own good."

"Haunted?" Sue looked at her, raising an eyebrow. "Okay, Joelle, I know I'm a freshman and all, but I'm not going to fall for that. You're playing a trick on me."

"I didn't say I believed it." Joelle laughed. "But that's the story. Every girl on the third floor hears it when she first moves in."

"How did the story start?"

"Who knows? Wilbourne's been around a long time. But I know it's been a bad-luck room for lots of girls."

"How so?"

"The girl who lived there when I was a freshman four years ago flunked out. Bright kid, straight A's when she got here. But once she moved in there, she started having bad dreams. We'd hear her crying out in the night. She couldn't concentrate and eventually flunked out."

"But that was four years ago. Girls have lived there since. And how have they turned out?"

"Okay, I guess. But now there's Bonnie."

Sue was sitting on the edge of the futon. "This is how legends get started . . ."

"Well, there have been other things that I've heard. Bad stuff that went on in that room before I got to campus." She sighed. "Of course, the worst story was the girl who got raped in there twenty years ago. Right here on the campus. You wonder why they're so strict about curfews and not allowing guests? This girl was brutally raped. She never came back to school—and the story goes her roommate moved out of there pretty quickly after that, because she heard things. . . ."

"Is this documented? This rape? Or is it just another story that's told?"

Joelle waved her hand. "I work part-time in the administration office and I hear things. There are secretaries there who remember when it happened. Listen, I'm just telling you what's been told to me. That room's supposed to be haunted. The stories got so bad last year that every girl refused placement there, so Bonnie asked for it and Mrs. Oosterhouse let her move in."

"Mrs. Oosterhouse?"

Joelle grinned. "Oh, that's right, you're new. You probably have met the dorm dragon yet." She let out a laugh. "She's the dorm supervisor. She has rooms down on the first floor. She can be a pain in the ass, but for the most part she's okay. Just don't cross her. Now where was I?" She refilled her glass.

"Trying to scare me to death."

Joelle chuckled. "Oh, yes, the haunting of Room 323. Some of the other girls say they've heard moaning coming from there, and screams—kind of like the face you say you saw, right? But Bonnie always said she never heard anything, and neither have I, and I'm just down the hall . . . and to be honest with you, the girls who say they've heard things, well . . . " Joelle put her thumb and index finger together and held them up to her lips, and made like she was inhaling.

"Let's just say they liked to smoke mind-altering substances, if you know what I mean."

"Well," Sue told her, "I've seen that face now several times . . ."

All at once, the door opened. A strawberry blonde burst into the room in a flutter of energy. "Oh, my God! Joelle, you have no idea what I have been through today!" She had a thick accent—it sounded as if she'd said, *Oh mah gawwwwd, Jo-ail, yew have no EYE-de-ah what Ah have bin threw todayah.*

She stopped when she saw Sue. "Oh, hi," she said, arching an eyebrow.

"Sue, this is the now-notorious Tish Lewis, my roommate," Joelle said, pouring another glass of wine and handing it to Tish. "She's from Dallas, if you couldn't tell the minute she opened her mouth."

"Fuck you, Joelle." Tish reached out to shake Sue's hand. "Nice to meet you." She gulped down the wine in one quick drink. "Hit me again, darlin'."

Joelle complied, then looked over at Sue. "You sure you won't have some? Don't worry, we won't tell. It'll steady your nerves."

"No, thank you, I've got to get going—"

Tish had plopped down on one of the beds. "Why did I *ever* agree to sign Bonnie in to the welcome ceremony? I will never do that again, *ever*, for anyone, under any circumstances. The way they treated me, you'd think I was a serial killer or something."

"I gather they didn't expel you." Joelle sat back down. "That's good to know."

"No, but just barely. One more infraction and I am so out of here." Tish shook her head. She blew out her breath with a whistle. "Which means I have to be really careful. I thought Oosterhouse's head was going to explode off her shoulders.

'I'll be watching you like a hawk, Ms. Lewis.' " Tish shuddered. "I swear, she was worse than the dean."

Sue stared at her, fascinated. Tish was of about medium height, pretty, with blue eyes and a pert nose. She had a slender figure and highlights in her hair, which was cut to frame her face. On her long legs she wore a tight pair of low-rise jeans, complemented above by a blue and silver Dallas Cowboys T-shirt that kept riding up to reveal a pierced navel. Her breasts were as large as her waist was narrow.

Tish sat up and clutched a pillow to her chest. She pointed at Sue. "Let this be a lesson to you, Susie Q. You're a freshman, aren't you?"

Sue nodded.

"Don't ever do someone a favor if it means breaking the school's precious rules, no matter how much you feel sorry for them. It will come back and bite you in the ass every single time."

Tish fell back onto the bed and stared glumly up at the ceiling. "I felt sorry for Bonnie. Does that make me a bad person? Does that mean I should be expelled? She had to *work*, for God's sake. She couldn't afford to lose her goddamned job. They should have excused her from the stupid welcome ceremony. We should *all* be excused from the stupid welcome ceremony. It's so lame. So I agreed to sign her in. Big fucking deal. How was I supposed to know she was going to disappear or run off or whatever the hell happened to her?" Tish rolled over onto her stomach. "I had to spend the past three days talking to the cops. Then Dean Gregory starts in yelling at me—and today Oosterhouse!"

Sue was getting ready to stand. "Well, nice meeting you. I should be—"

"Sue thinks she may have seen the ghost of Room 323," Joelle said.

"Really?" Tish set down her glass of wine and stared at her. "What did you see, Susie Q?"

Sue felt her face start to redden. "I don't know . . ."

"Go ahead and tell her, Sue." Joelle waved her hand, and winked at her. "Tish is one of those girls who's heard the screaming herself."

Suddenly, Sue looked at Tish with new eyes.

"Joelle acts like I'm crazy." Tish was glaring at her roommate. "But I know what I've heard, and I've heard someone screaming in that room." She shivered. "Before *and* after Bonnie's disappearance."

"You've really heard a girl screaming in there?" Sue asked.

Tish nodded. "Yep. Screaming for her life, I am telling you." She shot a look over at Joelle. "And I wasn't stoned either, Miss Know It All."

"Then why hasn't anyone else heard it?" Joelle scoffed, rolling her eyes.

"Do I look like Agent Mulder?" Tish snapped before turning back to Sue. "It was last semester, and it was scary as hell. I was the only person on the floor pretty much. I was just sitting in here minding my own business studying, and I heard this screaming." She shivered. "Oh, it was just terrible, horrible, like someone being murdered. I went out in the hall, and it was coming from Bonnie's room . . . only I knew Bonnie wasn't there, she was at work. I didn't know what to do, so I went down and got Mrs. Oosterhouse, and of course when we went into the room there was nothing there." She sighed. "Of course, Oostie thought I was nuts."

"And you've heard it since Bonnie went missing, too?"

Tish nodded. "Yep. First day of classes, in fact. Middle of the afternoon. I kept running around asking girls if they heard anything, but they all said no."

"I first saw the face at the window that day," Sue told her.

"It's not that I don't believe," Joelle said. "Especially not with the fact that I am certain Bonnie was the victim of some witchcraft ritual."

"Well, *that* much is pure speculation," Tish told her, finishing her wine.

"True. But if they slashed her up in front of the school, why take the body?"

"Evidence," Tish said.

Sue wanted to get back to the screaming from the room. "Other girls have heard it, though, right? Maybe no one recently, but others have . . ."

"Oh, yeah," Tish said. "A couple years ago, a girl claimed to hear the screaming so often, she finally forced the dean to agree to transfer her not just to another floor, but to another dorm entirely." Tish laughed. "She *was* a stoner, though. But maybe she smoked all that weed because she was so scared. Maybe the cause and effect is reversed."

"Well, something's queer about that room, that's for sure," Joelle said, "if Sue is saying she's seen someone screaming in the window." She gave Sue another wink. "And you appear to be perfectly sane. And no telltale aroma of weed on your clothes."

Tish had moved around on the bed so that she was lying on her stomach, her chin in her hands, staring at Sue. "Did you get a good look at the face at the window?"

"No, not really." Sue held up her hands. "I was out front on the sidewalk by the parking lot, and I just happened to look up, and I saw someone—a girl, I know that much—and then the next minute, it wasn't there anymore. So I thought I'd come up here, you know, knock on the door and make sure everything was okay."

"That room is haunted." Tish said, holding out her glass for another refill. "I told you so, Joelle."

Sue thanked the girls for their stories and bade them good-bye. Back in the hallway, she looked again at the door to Room 323.

What is it about that room?

What am I on the verge of discovering?

19

After dinner that night, Malika went to the library to study, leaving Sue alone in their room.

Might as well get it over with, she thought, picking up her phone and pressing her grandparents' number.

Her grandmother answered on the third ring. "Hello?"

"Hey, Gran, it's me, Sue."

"Sue, darling." Gran's voice seemed very far away. Sue guessed it was a bad reception. "How has it been going? Did the car do all right? Did you have any trouble?"

"Slow down, one question at a time!" Sue laughed. "Things have been going great. I like my classes. And I like the girls here."

"Wonderful, wonderful! We knew you would."

"And the car and the drive were great, too. I really enjoyed myself. Thank you again for the car."

"I'm so glad, dear," her grandmother said. "I have a feeling you will do very well at Wilbourne."

"I hope so," Sue said.

But her mind was still troubled by that room on the floor above her. She kept hearing Tish say, *I heard someone screaming, like they were being murdered in that room.* And then Joelle: *The girl who lived in that room twenty years ago was raped.*

She became aware there was silence on the line. "Gran?"

"Yes, I'm here, dear."

"You don't have to worry about anything. I know you probably are."

"I'm certain you're well looked after, Sue."

"No." Sue actually found herself a little annoyed about how obtuse her grandmother was being. One would think she'd have brought up Bonnie's disappearance right away. "I'm talking about that girl, Gran. Bonnie Warner. The one who disappeared."

"Oh? I wasn't aware of any girl disappearing."

Sue found that hard to believe. "Well, I'm sure Granpa has heard. It's been on the TV. Fox News has been sensationalizing it, like it sensationalizes everything, and I know he's always watching Fox News."

"Well, your grandfather has been very busy lately. I'm not sure he's had much time for television."

"I just thought you might be worried."

"Well, we always worry, Sue. But we know you're well looked after."

Part of Sue wanted her grandmother to express some worry. "She went missing," she said about Bonnie. "They found her bike covered with blood."

"Oh, how terrible," said her grandmother.

"So I didn't want you freaking out and trying to get me to leave school or anything. I know how protective you both can be about me, and I appreciate it, but really, Gran, everything is very safe here. I'm sure the dean is going to be sending letters assuring families that we are all well protected."

"Of course you are."

How very odd Gran seemed. Once, she'd hovered over Sue, a constant presence, ever fearful that someone might hurt her—that they'd lose their granddaughter the way they'd lost their beloved daughter. But now . . . she seemed so calm.

Sue should have been glad that Gran wasn't freaking out, that she and Granpa weren't planning to drive up here and take her back this very night. But she seemed to want to provoke something from Gran—something to prove she cared.

"They're not saying so," Sue said, "but everyone's pretty certain Bonnie is dead."

"What a terrible world we live in," her grandmother said softly. "I'll pray for her."

Sue sat there for a moment. That was all. There was no *"You need to come home immediately, young lady, enough of this nonsense, you can live here and go to school in Manhattan, it's too dangerous up there for a girl alone, you need to come home, you're all we have left and we can't take that kind of risk."*

What had happened to her grandmother?

"All right, dear," Gran was saying. "Look at the time. My committee is stopping by in a few moments—you know, that fund-raiser we're doing for the museum. But darling, I'm so glad you called. Call me later this week and I'll have more time and we can chat longer."

"Okay."

"Toodles, Sue."

Click.

"I love you, too," Sue said into the receiver.

How strange.

How very, very strange.

She had homework to do, but right now, she couldn't concentrate on it. She sat there for a few moments at her desk just staring straght ahead.

She pulled opened her top drawer.

Joyce Davenport's face stared up at her.

Reluctantly, she picked up the book. She looked down at Joyce's face.

Twenty years ago, the girl who lived in that room was raped.

Twenty years ago, her mother—and Joyce Davenport—had been students at Wilbourne College.

If the story of the rape was true, then Joyce would know all about it.

She probably also knew about the room supposedly being haunted.

She'd also be able to tell Sue if Room 323 had been the room she'd shared with her mother.

Sue opened the book to the title page, and stared down at the phone number written with a black Sharpie.

She picked up her phone.

No. Not yet. She wasn't ready to call Joyce yet.

I'll send her an e-mail tomorrow, Sue decided. *Just to thank her for the book, and see how she responds to that.*

She opened the book and started to read.

20

I am going to explode at any minute, Pierre deSalis thought, biting back the urge to shout at his wife, "Shut the Hell Up!"

Maddie was muttering to herself as she clacked through her rosary beads, hunched in her chair, leaning over Bernie's hospital bed. Her incessant muttering of Hail Marys and Our Fathers was driving Pierre crazy. But instead of telling her to quit it, he simply gripped the armrests of his chair and squeezed until his knuckles ached.

What he really wanted to do was put his fist through something—a wall, a door, some unknown person's face—but that wasn't an option. *I want to just grab Bernadette and get the hell out of here, get as far away from this goddamned hospital as we can go.*

He had a raging headache that felt like someone was driving a nail through his right temple. He was tired. He hadn't slept a full night since that morning when they'd brought Bernadette here. Every night since then, he'd only gotten to sleep by consuming a six-pack of beer in the living room, flipping through the TV channels without stopping on any of them for longer than a minute or two. Even then, when he finally made it upstairs, he'd stare at the ceiling for most of the night, drifting in and out of sleep. *Maybe I oughta switch to Jack Daniel's.*

Pierre didn't buy his wife's argument that all this was a wonderful miracle. It was a nightmare—and it was Maddie's fault. Her devotion to the Church, to the saints— somehow, some way, she'd been filling the poor girl's head with so much nonsense that it led her into this hysterical state. That's what the doctors called it—hysteria—with one psychiatrist telling him that such feverish belief can cause the body to react in certain ways. That explained the stigmata that had appeared on Bernie's wrists. But the big-shot priest from the diocese, some decrepit old Irishman, proclaimed that Bernie was "God's miracle." That was all Maddie needed. "My baby is a saint chosen by Our Blessed Mother," she had gushed. Rarely had she left Bernie's side, praying over her with those infernal rosary beads, forgetting she had three other kids—and a husband—at home.

Pierre glanced over at his daughter in the hospital bed. *When did she become so crazy with this stuff? When did she turn into a carbon copy of her mother?* Bernadette's eyes were closed. She was absolutely still—other than her fingers feverishly working the rosary beads Maddie had placed in her hands, seeming to follow her mother's recitations.

"It's possible," one doctor had told him when they first brought Bernie in, "that the girl made these wounds herself."

"You see?" Pierre shouted at his wife. "It's nothing miraculous. She cut herself!"

"Then why don't they heal?" Maddie shrieked back at him.

In fact, they *were* healing—but yesterday some of the wounds started releasing new blood, and that only convinced Maddie further that they were divinely caused. Bernadette's semiconscious state precluded her from being sent home, so for now the nurses had bandaged her wrists and feet tightly and tried to keep as close an eye as possible on her. But often Maddie was in the room alone with the girl, and she had plenty of time to—Pierre hated the thought—to unwind her daughter's bandages and break the scabs if indeed they were starting to heal.

That's how crazy she is, Pierre thought to himself. *She'll actually keep our daughter from getting well because she wants so badly to believe this is a sign from God.*

He had no proof she was doing anything of the sort. Right now, Bernie's bandages were pristinely white. The bleeding had stopped. If only she'd snap out of this state she was in—this half-awake, half-asleep religious delirium.

When had she become as crazy as her mother? Pierre thought again.

I wasn't paying enough attention, he told himself, recalling those nights when Maddie would insist their daughter kneel with her and pray for hours before they went to bed. *I should have been more aware of what was going on in my own house. But God help me, I didn't see any harm in Maddie being so religious . . . I never realized how far she was gone, and now it may be too late for Bernie. Why didn't any of the boys say anything to me?*

Except maybe they had tried.

"I'm out of here," P.J. had said to him the very day of his high school graduation. "I need my own place, Dad. Mom—well, I just can't take her anymore."

P.J.—Pierre Jr.—had looked at him that day and told him quite plainly that Maddie was crazy. Pierre just wasn't ready to hear it.

"Dad, I love her, but she drives me nuts with all her God talk. She knows she can't get anywhere with us boys, but she's always after Bernie about sin and hellfire and all that shit."

"Aw," Pierre said, "going to church is a good thing. It gives your mother some comfort."

When Bernie had been admitted to St. Agatha's Hospital a few days ago, P.J. had come by to see his little sister. She didn't seem to recognize him. Pierre noticed that P.J. didn't say a word to his mother. Since moving out of the house, he rarely visited. Pierre wondered if his other sons were counting the days until they, too, could escape.

I've failed my children, he thought, overwhelmed. He looked down at his little girl in the hospital bed. *She's lost her mind.*

Either that, or she actually saw the Virgin Mary.

And Pierre couldn't believe that.

No, this was all because of Maddie—Maddie and her goddamned saints and prayers. *Maddie and her goddamned rosary*—which she continued to clack away at sitting at her daughter's bedside.

"Stop it!" Pierre finally shouted. Unable to take it anymore, he reached over and grabbed Maddie's hands.

She looked up at him. "Let go," she whispered calmly.

Pierre didn't want a scene in the hospital room. So he let her hands go and she started again.

What was really uncanny, Pierre thought, looking once again down at his daughter, was the way Bernie's hands had stopped twitching on her own rosary the very moment Pierre had halted Maddie's.

Her eyes were closed. She couldn't have seen him do it.

She spoke to me, Papa. She told me that I am blessed.

Three days had passed since that morning, three days that seemed a lifetime ago. When the ambulance arrived, instead of going to the local hospital, Maddie had insisted they whisk Bernie off to St. Agatha's in Senandaga. *Her* daughter had to go to a Catholic hospital ninety miles away—no other hospital would do. The EMTs had looked over at Pierre to see if he agreed. He hadn't been in a mind-set to argue with his wife, so he'd nodded his consent.

Ever since, he'd spent as much time as he could in Bernie's hospital room. He'd taken time off from work—his supervisor was understanding, telling him to take as much time as he needed—but that couldn't go on forever. And unlike Maddie, Pierre remembered they had other kids, too, so he made sure he got the boys off to school every morning before heading over to the hospital. Maddie had often spent the night in the chair next to Bernie's bed. Usually, when Pierre arrived, Maddie was clacking away at her rosary or consulting with some visiting priest or nun, and she wouldn't even greet him. She was like a different woman, one Pierre did not know. Whatever had happened to Bernadette, it had finally pushed Maddie over the edge.

Pierre jumped a little as the door behind him opened. A slight woman, Indian by the look of her, came into the room. She was wearing a white lab coat over a pair of brown slacks and a matching blouse. Her hair was jet black and pulled into a bun behind her head, her skin was a rich brown, and her eyes were round and dark. "I am so sorry I am late," she said to Pierre and Maddie, offering a smile. Her English was perfect, her voice low and quiet. "I am Dr. Vaid." She held out her hand.

Pierre stood and shook her hand, mumbling, "Nice to meet you," but Maddie remained seated. If anything, she seemed to withdraw further into herself, looking at Dr. Vaid's hand as though it were diseased. Dr. Vaid merely raised her eyebrows, and looked back at Pierre briefly before turning her attention to Bernie.

"So, how is our little girl?" Pierre asked, trying to keep his voice steady, but he balled his sweating hands back into fists again. He took a few deep breaths, trying to remain calm.

"Ah, yes, Bernadette." The doctor sighed as she looked down at Bernie's still form. "She is not speaking today?"

"She's saying the rosary with me," Maddie said.

"But in a faraway place, no?"

Pierre nodded. "She's not communicative."

"Yesterday, she spoke to me when I examined her." Dr. Vaid was looking at her chart, then folded it and replaced it at the end of Bernie's bed. "She told me that she not only saw but spoke to the Virgin Mary, and the wounds on her hands and feet appeared miraculously while she was the presence of the Virgin. Moreover, she believes that the stigmata appeared as further proof of the visitation."

"Yes," Maddie said, finally putting her rosary aside and standing to face the doctor. "That's exactly what happened."

"Were you there?" Dr. Vaid asked.

"No," Maddie told her, "but—"

"Another doctor called her hysterical," Pierre said. "Bernie, I mean." He exchanged a look with his wife.

"Bernadette's original doctors called me in," Dr. Vaid explained. "They thought perhaps I might be able to see something they could not. I have treated these cases before."

Pierre was about to ask what "these cases" were, but Dr. Vaid went on.

"Physically, other than the wounds, your daughter is perfectly healthy. I spoke with her teachers, and they all described a happy girl, who has friends, who is interested in school. But on the other hand—"

Normal well-adjusted thirteen-year-olds don't think they've talked to the Virgin Mary, Pierre thought, finishing the doctor's sentence, glancing at his wife out of the corner of his eye. *Unless, of course, they have religious fanatics for mothers brainwashing them.*

"Her wounds," Pierre asked. "One doctor thought Bernie might have made them herself."

Dr. Vaid shook her head. "They do not appear to be self-inflicted. In fact, I would go so far as to say that self-infliction is not possible."

"So you're saying someone had to have *done* this to her?" Pierre glanced at Maddie out of the corner of his eyes.

"Well, it would have been most difficult for her to do this to herself." Dr. Vaid smiled sympathetically at both parents. "The other doctors have informed you of the severity of the wounds?"

"They told us she lost a lot of blood," Pierre replied.

Dr. Vaid held her hands together in front of her face as if in prayer. "The wound in her left wrist went straight through to the other side. I cannot imagine her being able to do that to herself, but let us suppose she did. She could not then have the strength to drive another object through her right wrist with an already injured left hand."

"Is this why the police want to speak with us?" Maddie asked. "They're thinking we did this to her?"

"I have no idea what the police want to ask you, Mrs. de-Salis. I did answer some questions for them myself, and they have seen my report."

Pierre was glaring at Maddie. *Could she? Could she have really done this to Bernie?*

"Why won't you even consider that this is a miracle?" Maddie burst out angrily. She had wound the rosary around her left hand and was tightening it so that her knuckles were turning white. "Just because you don't believe? Because you're from some Eastern religion with all your mediation and sacred cows and elephant gods? So you think a miracle involving Our Lady and my daughter can't be true?"

Dr. Vaid raised an eyebrow. "Mrs. deSalis, you look at my skin and listen to my accent and therefore assume that I cannot be a Catholic?" A hint of a smile played at her lips. "In fact, Mrs. deSalis, I have a very strong faith. Science does not after all preclude faith."

Touché, Pierre thought, watching with no small degree of satisfaction as Maddie's face turned red.

"So, I assume nothing, Mrs. deSalis. To do otherwise would be an injustice to your daughter." Dr. Vaid went on smoothly. "The questions I ask, as you well know, will be the same ones asked by the Church when determining whether this is a real visitation, a real appearance of Christ's wounds, or something else. I cannot say with certainty your daughter is delusional. I cannot make that diagnosis with clear conscience. Yes, there have been recorded cases where a hysterical person can manifest Christ's wounds. But from everything I can see, your daughter has never been a hysteric. Her teachers and friends all speak very highly of her. There has been no history of delusions. Tell me this, however. Was she a devout believer before this occurred?"

"Too devout," Pierre said, not looking at his wife.

"There's no such thing," Maddie snapped. "In fact, I'd say that Bernie struggled with what I was teaching her, but she was coming around to believe. It's hard to have faith—pure faith—in today's world, with so much temptation around teenaged girls."

"Well, then, there is the possibility that she was trying to please you in some way," Dr. Vaid observed.

"This isn't the work of my daughter!" Maddie shouted. "This is the work of Our Blessed Mother!"

Dr. Vaid had turned to look in Pierre's direction. "You don't believe it, do you, Mr. deSalis?"

Pierre didn't answer right away. "I don't know what's easier to believe, to be honest. That my daughter is a hysteric, or that my wife somehow caused this to happen, or that the Virgin Mary really appeared to Bernie and left the stigmata behind as proof." Pierre looked at the doctor with hard eyes. "What do *you* believe?"

Dr. Vaid smiled kindly. "I believe that your daughter honestly believes that she saw and spoke to the Virgin and that the Holy Mother caused the stigmata to appear as a sign of her presence." Dr. Vaid pressed her hand to the girl's cheek. Bernie's eyelids fluttered but did not open. "I am not saying her story is either true or untrue, simply that this is what she believes."

"When can she come home?" Pierre asked.

"If the wounds continue to heal, and if she becomes more alert, then I see no reason to keep her here." Dr. Vaid faced Pierre and Maddie. "But she will need encouragement to get well. I would try to engage with her. Bring her friends in. Mrs. deSalis, by all means keep praying your rosary. But *talk* with your daughter, too. Tell her things about the world. Bring her back to a state of alertness."

But that would mean to give up all this sainthood nonsense, to leave the miracles behind and go back to a normal life, Pierre thought. He wasn't sure that Maddie would do that.

Dr. Vaid approached Maddie and placed a hand on her shoulder. "Even if this is a miracle, surely Our Lady would not want this beautiful child confined to a hospital bed mumbling to herself."

Maddie nodded. She turned away, overcome with emotion.

"Thank you, Doctor," Pierre said, extending his hand, his voice thick.

Dr. Vaid shook it. "There are many things in this world that we cannot understand, Mr. deSalis. Perhaps it is not *for* us to understand. Medical science cannot explain everything. And when we encounter those things we cannot explain, we have two choices. We can either disbelieve, or we can have faith." She looked back at Bernie in the bed. "Scientifically, I cannot explain how your daughter received those wounds. Bernadette did not suffer any nerve or ligament damage in either her hands or her feet. That in itself is miraculous."

"I suppose it is," Pierre said, looking over at his sleeping daughter.

"Would it be so terrible if it were true?" Dr. Vaid asked.

Pierre looked at her. He couldn't answer.

Dr. Vaid patted his hand. She promised to speak with them again later that day, then bade them each good-bye as she quietly left the room.

Would it be so terrible if it were true?

Pierre kept his eyes on Bernie.

He didn't know. He just didn't know.

21

Half the booths in the Yellow Bird were empty when Billy Honeycutt and Mike deSalis walked in after football practice. The dinner rush was just winding down.

"Hey, boys," Marjorie Pequod called from the counter, where she was filling a cup of coffee for Jed Plunkett, who worked at Bud's Shell. "Grab a seat and I'll be with you in a minute, okay?"

"Sure thing, Marj," Billy called as they slid into a booth in the back.

He winced. His right shoulder and ribs were a little sore from a rather intense tackle in a scrimmage near the end of practice. His blockers had failed miserably to stop the defense from coming after him, and Billy had been gang-tackled, winding up under about five other players.

They better do a better job during the game on Friday night, Billy thought as he grabbed a pair of menus from the side of the table, passing one over to his best friend.

"Thanks." Mike's face was immediately hidden behind the menu.

"Dude, you okay?" Billy asked. "You've been awful quiet today."

"I'm fine," Mike said from behind the menu.

"Well," Billy teased, "I don't really mind you being quiet, since I'm pretty tired of listening to you go on and on about things, like how much you hate science class or how you want that Audi they're fixing up at Bud's or how you think Nancy Fox is just that—but still, it's pretty weird."

"Fine." Mike still didn't put the menu down. "Don't worry about it."

Billy sighed. *Okay, man, you don't want to talk about it, that's cool with me.*

He didn't even bother opening his own menu. He knew what he was going to get—what he always got at the Yellow Bird. You couldn't beat one of Wally's cheeseburgers, smothered in his own homemade chili. If Billy could eat Wally's chili cheeseburgers every night, he would. But then Gayle Honeycutt's idea of making dinner generally included opening a can of Franco American or microwaving some frozen pizza. "I have a job, you know," was Mom's standard response when either of her children complained about whatever mess she'd thrown together for dinner. "I am a *journalist*. I have *responsibilities*. So sorry I'm not here at home to play June Cleaver and wait on you both hand and foot."

Billy and Mike had been best friends since grade school. They'd always been the two tallest and most athletic kids in their class, and they'd gravitated toward each other. They both picked up sports easily—whether it was football, soccer, basketball, or tennis. They did pretty much everything together. Nobody could make Billy laugh the way Mike could. Mike had a funny response to everything, but never in a mean-spirited way. People genuinely liked Mike. He was a shoo-in to be Homecoming King. Billy knew that people tended to like Mike better than they liked him. Mike wasn't nearly as vain, he never bragged, and he never made anyone feel he was above them.

Billy knew the same could not be said about himself.

He looked over at his best friend, who had finally set down his menu and was thrumming his fingers on the table as they waited for Marjorie. Mike's thick mop of black hair was always messy and out of place. He never had a comb or a brush. He was sloppy with the way he dressed, too—sometimes wearing a shirt that clashed violently with his pants. He was always dribbling ketchup on his shirts. They'd had Sloppy Joes at school for lunch that day, and sure enough, there was a crusty red splotch just below the collar of his shirt. Mike was a good student—something else in which he parted company with Billy. He effortlessly breezed through his classes with straight A's. Mike never seemed to worry, never seemed to get angry or lose his temper. You could always count on Mike if you needed cheering up.

Until his sister went into the hospital Monday morning before school.

"Okay, boys, what will it be?" Marjorie asked, suddenly at their table, pad and pencil in hand.

Billy ordered his chili cheeseburger and a side of fries and a supersized Coke. Mike just had fries and a lemonade. "I'm not that hungry," he explained.

"So," Billy asked, after a few more minutes of awkward silence had passed between them, "how's Bernie doing?"

"I don't know."

"What do you mean, you don't know?"

"I mean I don't know."

"They don't tell you anything?"

Mike looked away for a minute and sighed. "Mom hasn't been home, and Dad—well, Dad . . ." He ran his hand through his tangled hair. "Dude, this has freaked all of us out."

"Well, what's wrong with her?" Billy asked. "She's going to be okay, right?"

Mike looked at him for a few moments before answering. "I don't want to talk about it," he finally said.

"I'm your best friend, man. If you can't talk to me about it . . ."

Mike glanced around before leaning across the table and lowering his voice. "You have to swear not to tell anyone, okay?"

"Sure, man."

"She's lost her mind." Mike made a circular motion with his index finger beside his right temple. "She's gone completely insane." He shook his head. "It's fucking freaky. She just went completely nuts Monday morning. I don't know if they are ever going to let her out of the hospital." His eyes filled with tears. "And Dad doesn't want anyone to know, so you can't say anything to anyone."

Billy's jaw dropped. "I swear, man. I won't say anything to anyone. But you gotta tell me what happened."

Mike just shook his head. "I don't know. No one does. It was horrible, man. Monday morning Mom was calling her to come down for breakfast, and she never answered, you know? Which isn't like Bernie, she's always the first one up, way before me and Frank, you know? And Mom kept calling and calling—and finally went upstairs to see what was wrong. Then she started screaming." Mike shuddered. "So we went running up to see what was wrong. And then we saw her . . . *man*." He swallowed and leaned across the table. "She was lying there in the bed, and there was blood everywhere."

"Blood?"

Mike nodded. "From her wrists."

"She tried to kill herself?"

"Nope. At least she says she didn't do it herself." Mike stopped speaking as Marjorie placed their drinks on the table, and waited for her to leave before continuing. "Are you ready for this? Bernie thinks she saw the Virgin Mary."

"What the *fuck*?"

The word exploded out of his mouth so loud that everyone in the diner stopped talking and turned to look at them. Mike glared at his friend.

"Dude, I told you, keep it down."

"I'm sorry. But now I know what you mean by insane."

"But here's the really freaky part. It wasn't just her wrists. She was bleeding from her hands *and* her feet. It's *stigmata*."

"Stig-whatta?"

"Right. You're not Catholic." Mike barked out a short laugh. "Stigmata—the wounds of Our Lord and Savior. You know, nails through the hands and feet?"

"Fuck." Billy's head was swimming. *"Crazy."*

"Exactly. Mom thinks it's a miracle, and I don't know what Dad thinks." Mike ran a hand through his hair again. "Bernie swears that's what happened, but she won't tell anyone what the Virgin supposedly told her. The Virgin, she says, swore her to secrecy. I've gone online and looked some of this stuff up. There are lots of cases of stigmata happening to people who believe it's a sign from God." He sighed and shook his head again. "It's all so damned crazy, you know? I mean, Bernie could have looked up all this stuff, too, but why would she? Why would she fake it? There's no reason for Bernie to pull something like this. She's just not like that."

"Dude, maybe she's looking for attention."

"I thought of that. Mom's always been a little nuts about the Church stuff—you've been to our house, you've seen all the saints and the candles." Mike gave another harsh laugh. "Lately, Bernie's been kind of that way, too."

"Maybe she's telling the truth."

Mike frowned. "Don't even say that, man, even as a joke."

"I'm not joking." Billy shrugged. Religion for him was more perfunctory than anything else, a part of his weekly routine. The Honeycutts were Methodists, and every Sunday morning the family got up, put on nice clothes, and headed over to the church. His mom especially liked going to church, because afterward she got to talk with everybody outside, hearing all the latest gossip. They never prayed at home, didn't read the Bible, never really talked about religion much. But his mother always told them that being Christian meant they had the "keys to the kingdom," whatever that meant. "Everybody else has to wait in line to be saved," she'd tried to explain. "We get into heaven through the fast lane."

Billy shrugged. "I mean, you got to keep an open mind, dude."

"I don't know." Mike sipped at his lemonade. "These are my choices. I either believe my sister is some kind of visionary, a saint, or that she's insane."

He leaned back against the booth as Marjorie slid their plates of food in front of them. She looked from one face to the other.

"You boys all right?" she asked, raising one of her penciled eyebrows.

"Fine." Billy gave her a weak smile. "Wow, this looks good."

She winked. "Well, if you need anything else, just give me a holler."

"You can't tell anyone," Mike hissed from across the table.

"I won't, I swear." Billy raised his hand. "Besides, who would I tell?"

"Heidi. You'd tell Heidi."

"I won't tell Heidi." Billy shook his head. "I don't tell her everything just because she's my girlfriend. What do you want me to do, swear a blood oath?"

"I mean it, man."

"Okay!"

They ate their food in silence. When they were finished, Mike pulled a ten out of his wallet. "Man, I got to get going. Dad's going to be home from the hospital at any minute, and I got to be at work at seven." Mike worked as a stock boy three nights a week at the A&P. He slapped the money down on the table. "Not a word to anyone, you understand?"

"Dude . . . I told you."

"Okay. See you at school tomorrow."

Billy's eyes followed Mike as he walked out of the diner, sidestepping to avoid a young woman who was just walking in as he was going out.

Now that is one hot babe, Billy thought.

She wasn't conventionally pretty like Heidi. Her nose had a little bump in it, and her face was a little narrow, but she had a great ass, showcased in a pair of tight black jeans. Her ash blond hair hung down to her shoulders. Billy watched as she took a seat at the counter and leaned forward to get a menu. Her sweater crept up a bit, showing smooth white skin just above the waistband of her jeans. Damn.

He didn't recognize her from Lebanon High, which could only mean one thing. *She's one of the Wilbourne girls.* Billy popped a french fry into his mouth as she glanced over at him. He smiled at her. She gave him a half smile in return and opened her menu.

He tossed a ten down on the table, finished his Coke, wiped his mouth, and stood up. One quick glance in the mirror on the wall confirmed his hair looked good and no ketchup smeared his chin. He strutted over to the counter.

Marjorie was watching him and gave him a crooked grin. She'd seen Billy make his moves before.

"Hey," he said, sliding onto the stool next to the knockout chick. "I'm Billy."

"Hi," the girl replied, not looking at him, keeping her eyes on her menu.

"Billy Honeycutt." He put his hand out. "And I don't recognize you, so my mental calculations tell me you must be a Wilbourne student."

Finally, the girl looked up at him. She didn't take his hand right away.

"Well," she said, "with all that mental calculation going on in your head, you might be a little exhausted. Why don't you have a seat?"

"I think I will, thank you." He grinned. "I suppose I should have asked first if it was all right to sit down.'

"And here I supposed all you country boys were perfectly mannered." Finally, she accepted his outstretched hand and shook it. "I'm Sue Barlow."

"Hello, Sue Barlow," Billy said. "And am I correct about you being a Wilbournian?"

"Your calculations were indeed correct. And where do you go?"

"L-High. I'm a senior—but don't hold it against me."

"Why would I do that?" Sue shrugged, raising her shoulders a bit and then dropping them, which briefly deepened the cleavage slightly exposed by the V-neck of the sweater. A gold heart with a solitary diamond hung there on a chain of gold links. *A rich girl,* Billy thought. Most Wilbournians were. "I'm a freshmen, so we're probably close to the same age," she said.

"I'll be eighteen in December." Billy tried to keep his eyes away from her cleavage. "But most college girls won't have anything to do with a high school boy."

"I just turned eighteen in June." Sue smiled, lighting up her entire face. "So there's really not that big of an age difference between us, is there?"

"Not at all, not at all." He waved Marjorie down. "Another supersize for me, please, and the lady here will have . . ."

Sue ordered a grilled cheese and a cup of coffee. Marjorie shook her head at Billy. He'd have to remember to get her to swear not to say anything about this to Heidi.

"So, Sue," he asked, sitting up as tall as he could on his

stool, "how do you like it here in our quaint little burg so far?" He could smell her perfume. It was driving him nuts.

"I don't know. " Sue shrugged, gratefully accepting the cup of coffee from Marjorie and taking a sip. Billy noted she was drinking it black. "I mean, Lebanon seems like a nice place, but in truth this is my first trip off campus." She rolled her eyes. "I snuck out. Thought I'd take a drive and look around. Curfew will be on us soon, and I felt the need to get out for a while."

"They must be cracking down since that girl disappeared."

Sue nodded. "Yes. Though I was pretty good getting past the gate. Put on a cap so I'd look like a driver for some big shot." She winked. "I drive a Lexus."

Billy laughed.

"The quiet was getting to me today. I mean, I grew up in Manhattan, and so—"

"Manhattan?" Billy asked. "Really?"

"Yes, really." Sue laughed, a light musical sound like tinkling chimes. "So, it's a little different here."

"I've never been to Manhattan," Billy confessed.

"Never?" Sue's eyes widened.

"No. I've always wanted to, though." He smirked. "Maybe you could show me around there sometime."

"Are you asking me for a date?" Sue grinned, tilting her head to one side.

"Yeah, I guess I am"

"Well." Sue fell silent, sipping her coffee, seeming to think about it. "I would enjoy getting off campus more. It's been feeling . . . confining."

"Well, cool."

"How about this Saturday then?" Sue asked. She reached into her purse and pulled out a small notepad. Billy watched her. She was moving fast—faster than he expected. How had a flirtation evolved into a date—on Saturday night yet? What would he tell Heidi? That's what happened, he supposed, when you hit on college girls.

Sue was scribbling something down on a piece of paper, then tore it out of the pad and handed it to him.

"That's my cell number," she said. "If I don't hear from you by Thursday, I'll assume you chickened out." She flashed a smile at him. "Like a high school boy."

"Oh, I'll call." Billy folded the paper and put it in his wallet, not wanting her to see that his hands had started to tremble a little. "I'll definitely call."

"Hey, Romeo," Marjorie said. "Your mother just called. She wants you home."

Sue smiled, looking down at her coffee. Billy felt his face burn.

Marjorie loomed over him. "She said pronto. She sounded pretty worked up. So skeedaddle. The Coke's on the house."

"Thanks," he muttered, sliding off the stool.

"Nice meeting you, Billy," Sue said.

"Yeah, you, too." He composed himself. "I *will* call."

She just smiled.

Billy dashed out of the café. How embarrassing was *that*? But he knew when his mother was "worked up," it meant he had better get there fast—or risk some major drama from her later.

He sped home, stepping on the brake when he saw Perry Holland sitting in his cruiser near the intersection of Elm and East Main. Billy waved a cheery hello, and Perry gave him a "slow down" sign with his hands. But as soon as he'd passed Perry, Billy's foot was again on the gas.

His mother was waiting for him in the living room.

"What's so urgent?" he asked. "Me and Mike were just hanging out . . ."

"Sit down, Billy," Gayle Honeycutt said in her no-nonsense

voice. "That's precisely what I want to talk to you about." She gestured for him to sit on the couch.

Billy obeyed. "We didn't do anything. I swear. We were just at the Bird having a cheeseburger and—"

"Did I say you had?" His mother sat opposite him in a chair and crossed her legs and leaned forward. "I want to talk to you about Bernadette deSalis. I want you to tell me everything you know. And don't you dare lie to me, or I'll ground you for the rest of the school year."

Billy gulped.

22

Joelle Bartlett had come looking for Sue Barlow, but Malika told her she'd gone for a drive.

"Poor kid," Malika said. "She's from New York, you know? And I think all this confinement on campus has left her a bit stir-crazy. She went into town."

Joelle nodded. "Yeah. I wouldn't mind getting away from here for a while myself."

She'd headed back upstairs. Tish was gone, too—who knows where Tish was, probably off smoking some weed somewhere—and Joelle had really wanted to talk with someone.

Someone who'd understand.

Someone who'd believe.

Because, for the first time, Joelle had heard the screams Tish and Sue had talked about coming from Room 323.

At first, she wasn't even sure if it was a scream. Maybe some girls were just carrying on. But it was dinnertime—most of the girls on the floor were over at the caf—and Joelle had poked her head out into the hallway to listen.

A scream.

A scream of terror.

And from right across the hall.

She'd gone up to the door and pressed her ear to it. Yes, a scream—and it was coming from inside. The heavy door muffled it, but it was a scream.

Except Joelle knew that no one was inside that room.

She was about to step off the elevator onto the third floor when another idea came to her. She hit the CLOSE DOOR button and then pressed 1. The elevator made a jerking movement, then began descending again. Joelle prayed Mrs. Oosterhouse was in her rooms.

She was. "Oostie!" Joelle called out in relief when the short, squat woman opened her door.

"I've told you girls not to call me that," Mrs. Oosterhouse said. "It shows a lack of respect."

"Oh, I respect you, I really do. I'm just so glad you're here."

For the first time, Joelle admitted to herself that she was frightened. Mrs. Oosterhouse seemed to notice. "What's wrong?" she asked.

"Have you let anyone into Bonnie's room?"

"Nobody but the police."

"There's someone in there. Right now."

Oostie made a face, squinting up her eyes into her pudgy cheeks. "Nobody can get in there. I have the only key."

"I heard someone just now."

"You're crazy, Joelle. That roommate of yours has finally made you as crazy as she is."

"No. Really. I heard someone—several times." Joelle swallowed. "They were screaming."

"Okay, this kind of talk has gone on too long in this dorm for me to take it seriously anymore."

Oostie tried to shut the door in Joelle's face, but Joelle put out a hand to stop her. "Please!" she cried. "I'm not making this up!"

"Do you know how often I get girls coming to me all upset about that so-called 'haunted' Room 323?"

"Please, Mrs. Oosterhouse! Please go check."

The older woman frowned at her. "If this is some kind of prank that you and Tish rigged up . . ."

Joelle sighed. "Tish has been in enough trouble lately. You think she'd try to pull something? I tell you, I heard someone in there! Screaming!"

Mrs. Oosterhouse gave her a dramatic sigh. She reached behind the door and Joelle could hear keys jingling. In moments, she had waddled out into the hall, a set of keys in her hand. She closed her door behind her.

"Come on," she said resentfully, and motioned Joelle to follow her.

They said nothing on the ride up in the elevator. When they stepped out onto the third floor, it was quiet. As still as the inside of a church.

"I don't hear anything," Oostie said, but Joelle thought she might actually be a little bit scared herself.

She fitted the key into the lock of Room 323 and turned. Joelle kept close behind her, peering over her shoulder.

"Nobody," Oostie said, after taking one quick glance inside. She flung open the door and stepped inside. "You see? I told you. Nobody."

Joelle followed her into the room and looked around. It was small, like all of their rooms, with nowhere to hide. The closet was open. No one in there. The bathroom door was open. No one was hiding in the shower. The beds were secured to the floor with wraparound wood. No place to hide under there.

Mrs. Oosterhouse let out another long dramatic sigh, but Joelle thought she was relieved. "I don't know what it is that turns seemingly rational college girls into raving hysterics."

"I heard it," Joelle said firmly. "I heard someone screaming in here."

"Maybe it was from outside."

"No." Joelle was not convinced. "It came from this room."

"You can see that's impossible! No one is here!"

Joelle looked around. The place seemed to be just as Bonnie Warner had left it. Her clothes still hung in the closet. Books were still piled on the desk. The bed was made. A stuffed teddy bear was propped against the pillows. The police had been thorough, but they had left everything as it was.

"Then someone was here earlier," Joelle said, refusing to back down. "And they left when I went down to get you."

"Come on. I shouldn't have let you in here. But I wanted to settle this thing once and for all."

Joelle reached out and took hold of Mrs. Oosterhouse's arm. "You've been here long enough. You know this isn't just one girl's delusion. You know what happened in this room twenty years ago! You know there's something bizarre going on!"

The older woman gave her a hard face. "I know no such thing."

"Bonnie Warner was killed by witches. That's the buzz around the school. There is something—unworldly—happening on this campus!"

Mrs. Oosterhouse smiled coldly. "Now I know you're crazy."

Something in the older woman's eyes terrified Joelle. She let go of Mrs. Oosterhouse's arm and stepped backward.

"You're part of it, aren't you?" she said softly. "That's your job . . . to guard this room."

Mrs. Oosterhouse continued to smile at her. "We have to leave now," she said calmly.

Joelle said nothing. She followed the older woman out of the room, anxious to get out of there. She said nothing more as Mrs. Oosterhouse relocked the door. She simply hurried back into her own room, and barricaded herself inside.

If what she suddenly suspected were true . . .

No. It's crazy. Maybe she really was hysterical.

But Oostie—her eyes—her smile—

She was just laughing at me, thinking I was a lunatic . . .

But when Joelle had claimed Bonnie had been killed by witches, that was when Oostie's attitude had changed.

Because maybe I hit on the truth.

Or close enough to it.

Joelle picked up her cell and pressed in Tish's number. "Where the fuck are you?" she asked frantically when she got Tish's voice mail. "Get back here as soon as possible. I've heard it. The screaming. Oostie took me into the room. I think she's in on it—all of them maybe—"

She heard a beep. Joelle looked down at her phone. CALL DROPPED.

She heard something else.

The door across the hallway opening again. There was a sound the doors made when they were unlocked and opened. It was very recognizable. And with the floor being so quiet, the sound had been unmistakable.

Joelle peered through the little hole in her door. She saw someone—she couldn't make out who—going back into Room 323.

Oostie had come back. It must be her. Joelle opened her own door and stood bravely in the hallway.

"I know you think I'm crazy," she called into the room across the way, "but I want answers. I'm going to talk to Dean Gregory."

The door to Room 323 had not closed all the way. It remained ajar, and Joelle could see light from inside. It was not the electric light she had just seen when she was inside the room moments before. It was—could it be? *Candlelight.*

She pulled the door open a bit more and looked inside. Indeed, someone had set a candle on the table at the far end of the room. With the overhead lights turned off and the sun having set outside, the candlelight flickered eerily, casting shadows all across the room.

"Is this what you meant, Joelle?" came a voice.

Joelle took a step into the room, trying to discern who was speaking.

"Is this what you meant by witchcraft?"

Suddenly, without warning, the door in her hands surged forward, threatening to pin her in the door frame. She leapt aside to avoid it—but that meant she was now in the room, and the door clanged shut with the familiar locking sound.

"Let me out of here!" Joelle screamed. She tried the door handle, but it wouldn't budge. She banged on the door. "Please, someone! Is someone out there?"

"No," came the voice from the darkness behind her. "Only in here."

Joelle spun around.

"Who's in here?" she asked, straining to see in the dark, her voice shaking uncontrollably. "Mrs. Oosterhouse—is it you?"

No answer now. Except for the candle, all was darkness. The darkness of nightmares.

She lunged for the window, but it was locked, too. She tried frantically to open it, to shout for help—but it was no use. She could smash the window—but with what? Her hands? But then what? She was too high to jump . . .

Something stirred in the darkness.

She was definitely *not* alone.

Joelle fumbled along the wall for a light switch, but couldn't find one. She began to cry out.

"Don't cry," came the voice again, a voice she did not recognize, a voice that seemed to be both man and woman at the same time. "You're here with us now, Joelle."

"Who are you?"

"You are here . . . in the most important room in the most

important dorm. We didn't expect you, but we're glad you came."

Something moved toward her from out of the shadows. In the glimmer of candlelight, Joelle saw something that went far, far beyond the scope of her imagination. All the nameless terrors she'd ever felt, all the creeping anxieties she'd ever experienced, all of the doubts and fears and nightmares of her life came rushing back at her now. Joelle screamed— and even as she did so, she knew if anyone heard her, they'd simply think it was the ghosts of haunted Room 323. Now, she realized, she'd be one of them.

23

While the Church still has not accepted the
Medjugorje sightings as "official," thousands of
the faithful continue to flock there. Business is
thriving in the once-remote and unknown little
town, renting rooms and serving food to the
pilgrims, as well as selling them religious
souvenirs and trinkets.

Ginny frowned at her computer screen. She'd written that
paragraph over three weeks earlier, and every time she tried
to think of a way to continue from there, nothing would come.

I've got to get this book done, she thought, rubbing her
eyes. She swore under her breath and reached for the thick
file with all of her notes on Medjugorje. She started flipping
through the pages, looking for anything that would trigger
an idea in her mind, some way to finish the chapter on Medjugorje.

The book was now two years overdue, and while neither
her publisher nor her agent was putting any pressure on her,
she knew that wouldn't last forever. Every time her phone
rang, she feared it was one or the other, calling to let her know

that their patience had finally run out and she was going to have to pay the advance money back. *Maybe I should be pre-emptive and give the money back before they ask,* she thought, discouraged, as she closed the file.

She'd learned early that writing wasn't something that could be forced or pushed out. It either came or it didn't. She closed the computer file and sat there for a moment, tapping her pencil on the top of her desk.

It's been a rough week, she thought to herself in justifica-tion. *I mean, it's not every week one of your students disap-pears without a trace and you have to be interviewed by the cops and the FBI. Poor Bonnie.*

There had been no news. Bonnie was still missing. And Ginny still felt some guilt about it. *If only I'd insisted she ride home with me . . .*

Stop it, she scolded herself. *Bonnie was a big girl. She was used to making her own decisions.*

She was just like me, Ginny thought, remembering herself as an ambitious college student, working her way through her studies, determined to make the most of them, to one day be a famous scholar—convinced that was the most impor-tant thing in the world.

She'd really believed that. Until she'd given birth—and watched in agony as her beloved son died in her arms. That's when she knew what was really important in life.

She knew on some level that her anguish and guilt over Bonnie was just another manifestation of her grief over Eric—and using it to explain her procrastination was just another excuse. She'd been procrastinating on this book ever since Eric died.

I'll try to work on it tomorrow, she finally decided, reach-ing for the syllabus for her Women and the Bible class. She had a lecture in a few hours, and she needed to refresh her memory.

There was a light rap at her door.

It was probably Dean Gregory. He'd sent an e-mail this morning saying they still needed to discuss the night she'd seen Bonnie, and she'd replied she was available anytime and by the way, there were a few other things she wanted to discuss. Like his offensive behavior to her in front of Joyce Davenport.

"Come in," she called, steadying herself for a confrontation.

But it wasn't Gregory. Ginny glanced up and scowled as she recognized the woman entering her office. Gayle Honeycutt—that treacherous local reporter who'd made her first days in Lebanon so miserable.

"What are *you* doing here?" Ginny asked.

Gayle smiled. "Obviously, I want to talk to you."

"I have nothing to say to you." Ginny waved her hand absently. "And I'm busy, so if you don't mind—"

"Look, Dr. Marshall, I don't blame you for being pissed at me." Gayle stood over her, implacable. "But you have to understand—you're a writer after all, and so you should get it. You write for your audience. I write for mine. The people who read the *Lebanon Observer* don't care about your theories or what your research has found. These people go to church every Sunday. They believe every word in the Bible came from God and is literal truth."

"So you wrote down to them," Ginny said. "That's brave of you."

Gayle sighed. "Okay, that headline was bad. It wasn't my idea, nor would I have agreed to it—but surely you know how a newspaper works, and how little control a reporter has over things like that." She took a seat beside Ginny's desk. "I'm also very sorry about what happened after the article came out." She tried a smile. "I've since read your books, and for what it's worth, I think you're right."

"Spare me your apologies and excuses." Ginny glared at her. "What did you come here for?"

"When I interviewed you, you mentioned you were working on a big book about the Virgin Mary. Is that right?"

"Yes." Ginny leaned back in her chair. "Sightings of the Virgin Mary, miracles, the cult of the Virgin. Why?"

Gayle smiled. "What would you say if I told you, right here in Lebanon, there is a thirteen-year-old girl who claims she saw the Virgin Mary?"

"I'd say most religious girls see her every night in their prayers."

Gayle's smile widened. "But what if I also told you that girl had stigmata? That she's in the hospital right now, and doctors can't explain her condition?"

"What's the girl's name?"

"Bernadette deSalis." Gayle leaned in toward her. "You're the local expert. This is a big story—but I have to be careful."

"Since when do you care about being careful in your reporting?"

"Nobody knows about it yet, but when they find out, this community will really get riled up." Gayle shivered. "The girl is the sister of my son's best friend. Monday morning, she was taken away to St. Agatha's Hospital up in Senandaga around eight in the morning. Obviously, I've known the family for a long time, but they aren't returning my calls. But I've confirmed, through sources, that the girl is under observation at the psych ward at Senandaga."

Ginny bit her lip. "You're certain about this? She's really manifested stigmata?"

"Hands and feet. The whole bit. The girl says the Virgin gave it to her to make people believe."

"Well," Ginny said, "if she's really got stigmata, then I'd be interested to speak with her."

"Exactly. If I can get you to confirm it, there's a story. If not—then my editors wouldn't run this."

Ginny smiled. "So in other words, you need me."

"Well, I thought you might be interested since you're working on a book." Gayle's eyes twinkled. "Maybe we can help each other."

"Why would they want to talk to me?" Ginny asked. "Thanks to you, I already have a reputation as an unbeliever in this town."

"Well, they're very confused. The family. The father especially. The mother is a devout Catholic and thinks it's a miracle. You should try to talk to the father. His name is Pierre deSalis." She spelled it for Ginny. "They're listed in the phone book."

"I might try to contact him," Ginny said. "But that doesn't mean I'd tell you anything he might share with me in confidence."

Gayle pouted. "But I gave you the tip."

"Scholars don't work like journalists," Ginny told her. "And we can all be grateful for that."

"But if I call you for a quote, you get publicity for your book." She smiled mischievously. "And maybe I can work into the story how respectful of religion you are, and make up for all that bad press before."

"You can call," Ginny said. "Maybe I'll have been to see the deSalis family, maybe not. And maybe I'll be able to tell you what I've learned, and maybe I'll just say, 'No comment.'"

"Come on, Dr. Marshall. I know you'll be a sport." Gayle stood. "I'm a working mom, after all, just trying to make a living to keep food on the table for my kids."

"I really *am* busy," Ginny told her. "I have a lecture to prepare for."

"Okay. Thanks for your time. I'll call you in a few days."

Ginny just nodded as Gayle let herself out, closing the door behind her.

A Virgin sighting right here in Lebanon, she thought, chewing on her pencil. *Complete with stigmata.*

Ginny smiled to herself.

Maybe I'll get the damned book done after all.

24

"So, it went well?" Malika was asking. "This seems to be turning serious."

Sue rubbed cold cream into her face and looked over her shoulder at Malika standing in the doorway to their bathroom. "Well," she said, "we'll see if he asks me out again."

"Why would he not?" Malika laughed, leaning on the door frame, her voice teasing. "Is it not every high school boy's dream to date a college girl?" She sighed. "Do I get to meet this boy someday? Or does he have two heads or something?"

Sue looked back into the mirror. Tonight had been her third date with Billy. They'd gone, as they always did, to Senandaga to see a movie. The movies playing at the twin cinema in Lebanon hadn't interested either of them for the third week in a row. They were second-run films, and somehow it seemed more exciting to get away to the "big" city. Tonight, as they'd done both other times, they'd eaten dinner at a small Italian place near the megaplex, and once again failed to convince the waiter they were old enough to order a bottle of wine.

It didn't matter. Sue really liked being with Billy. They'd held hands during the movie, and he'd bought her popcorn, and he'd jumped as much as she did during the scary parts. It was really very sweet. *So this is what dating is like,* Sue thought.

She realized pretty quickly that, for all Billy's jock arrogance, he was still a country hick—which only endeared him to her more. He opened the door of his mother's car for her. (Sue had tried to get him to agree to let her drive her own car, but he'd insisted he pick her up.) If he caught himself about to say "shit" or "fuck," he stopped and apologized to her. It was all, well, quite chivalrous.

Becca Stansfield would probably call Billy boring. He hadn't so much as made a pass at Sue yet. Billy wasn't anything like she thought a guy would be—what she'd been led to expect by her friends back in high school. Three dates, and he hadn't once tried to put a hand up her sweater or down her pants. Every time he'd drop her off in front of Bentley Hall, he'd kiss her—but with his hands on her shoulders.

Who'd have thought that she'd meet her first boyfriend in the little town of Lebanon?

Once, when she'd complained about her awkwardness with boys to her grandmother, Sue had merely gotten a smile and a pat on the head as response. "There's plenty of time for that later," her grandmother had said, "after you get your education. You have your whole life ahead of you."

They had been sitting in the living room, her grandmother next to her on the couch. Gran was embroidering a tablecloth for some charity or another, her needle flashing in the sunlight as it went in and out of the linen, pulling golden thread behind it. "The last thing you want is to fall in love too young," she told Sue, "and throw the rest of your life away."

"But didn't you get married at eighteen?" Sue asked.

The love story of her grandparents was something she'd heard so often she could practically repeat it word for word. They'd been from rural northeast Alabama, "waaaaaay back in the hills," and had met when they were in grade school. They'd started going steady when they were in the seventh grade, and were married right after graduating from high school. They'd moved down to Tuscaloosa, where Granpa had gone to the University of Alabama and Gran had worked to support them both while he studied and went to class.

"Look how wonderful that turned out!" Sue reminded her grandmother. "I mean, neither one of you even had electricity or indoor plumbing when you were growing up, and now look where you both are! A gorgeous apartment on Central Park, and servants, and Granpa is one of the top men in his field, and the two of you have always been so happy together."

The needle stopped moving. "We all make choices," Gran said.

Her voice—Sue would never forget it—was dull and lifeless. She saw that her grandmother was looking across the room at the shrine to her daughter. "Sometimes, the choices you make seem like the right ones at the time."

For the first time, Sue had wondered if maybe not everything between Gran and Granpa had always been so rosy.

Gran took Sue's hand. "Yes, we have come a long way . . . but you have to remember, those years in Tuscaloosa were very hard ones for both of us. We made some decisions . . ." The old woman's voice trailed off, and then she shook her head. "No, Sue, dear, trust me. There's plenty of time for that later."

She started working with the needle again. Sue studied her.

"Do you mean that maybe you wish you had made some other decisions along the way?" she asked her grandmother softly.

"Regret is a pointless exercise." Gran was sewing faster now. "Trust me, Sue. There will be time for you to think about boys later."

"Well?" Malika was asking. "Do I get to meet him?"

"Of course. Next time. Billy's very sweet. You'll like him."

Sue washed her face and turned off the water, grabbing a towel and walking back into the bedroom.

"I wouldn't mind meeting a man myself," Malika moaned, flopping down on her bed. "Damn girls' school!"

"Come on." Sue laughed, sitting opposite her and brushing her hair. "There are plenty of boys in Lebanon—and there's a rumor there are even some male grad students here, though I've never seen one of them. Where are they hiding?"

"No offense, Sue, but I do not want a *boy*," Malika sniffed, "I want a *man*—a man who knows what he's doing. Last summer, I met this man in Rome, Leonardo . . ." Malika smiled and closed her eyes. "I just hope my parents are still stationed in Rome this next summer." She winked. "Italian men know how to treat a woman—not like clumsy boys."

"Billy's just fine for me right now," Sue replied. She pulled her laptop across the bed toward her and clicked on her e-mail program. Nothing. Still no response from Joyce Davenport. Nearly three weeks and no reply. *She's a busy woman,* Sue told herself. *She'll answer when she gets a chance.*

Both girls were exhausted. School was finally starting to feel like school. They'd both had tests today, and both were a little unsure about how they'd done. The work was getting more difficult. Both had early classes the next day, too, so the lights went out and both tried to get to sleep. Within moments, Malika was breathing in the steady cadence of sleep. But not Sue.

Sue stared up at the ceiling. After she finished reading Joyce's book, she'd e-mailed her to thank her. *I'd really like to talk to you about my mother,* she'd typed at the bottom before signing her name. She'd stared at the computer screen for a minute or two before clicking SEND.

Had she really thought Joyce would respond right away? She probably gets hundred of e-mails a day. Maybe she hasn't even read it yet. Maybe an assistant got the e-mail and hasn't passed it on to her.

Maybe I should try calling her. She gave me her cell phone number. But if she did get my e-mail and simply hasn't had time to respond, I'll seem like a pest.

But she had made such a point of meeting me. Why have me come backstage to meet her if she didn't really want to get to know me?

When she'd mentioned to Malika that she was still waiting on an e-mail response from Joyce, all she'd gotten in response was a snort. "I told you, she is a mean-spirited bitch. I would think reading her book would have made you aware of that."

Yes, she had seen a meanness to Joyce in her book. A small-mindedness. But she'd also seen a strong, independent woman who wasn't afraid of speaking her mind. Who, like Gran, may have made some decisions she regretted—but for whom regret was a pointless waste of time.

Despite everything else, Sue liked that about Joyce Davenport.

The wind was howling outside. A major thunderstorm was rolling in from the north, and according to the weather report, was supposed to last all night. Sue heard the rain come, slamming against the windows, which rattled in their frames. Malika stirred, but didn't awaken. Malika almost always fell instantly asleep the second her head hit the pillow. Sue admired—even envied—her peace of mind.

In the past three weeks, much of Sue's fear about the room upstairs had eased—at least until recently. It had begun to seem like a silly obsession—a misplacement of anxiety and fear about being away from home for the first time. Girls laughed and gossiped about the "haunted" room. They weren't really frightened by it. As Bonnie's disappearance faded from the news, the girls on campus stopped talking about it—and her empty room no longer seemed so fascinating. It was just a room.

And not since that day she'd gone upstairs had Sue seen a face at the window. All of this served to make her feel she'd been silly for being so afraid.

But yesterday a twinge of the old fear came back. It was nothing, Sue tried to tell herself. She was sure it was just a coincidence. But yesterday Malika mentioned something she'd forgotten to tell her—that three weeks ago, Joelle Bartlett had come looking for her.

"I'm sorry," Malika said. "It totally slipped my mind. But what made me remember was someone mentioned to me today that she'd left school."

"Left school?" Sue asked. "Why?"

"I don't know. It's odd, because this was her senior year."

"Well, her roommate must know the reason."

Malika shook her head. "You haven't heard? Tish was expelled."

"What?"

"Yeah. No one had seen her around either for days, and finally, one of the teachers said she'd been kicked out for signing Bonnie Warner into the welcome ceremony."

Sue had been stunned, unable to respond.

So both girls who'd lived across from Room 323—both girls with whom Sue had shared her story about seeing the face—were now gone.

Dead girls.

No, stop it, Sue told herself again, turning over in bed. *They are not dead! They just left school.*

They are *not* like Lori and Melissa.

Sue closed her eyes and listened to the wind and the rain. She tried to think about something more pleasant.

Like Billy.

She liked him. She liked him a lot. When she was with him, she could forget everything else. He was good—a cocky little showoff, sure—but a good, decent boy. The kind Becca Stansfield had told her didn't exist anymore.

Sue was very grateful Billy hadn't tried anything with her. If he had, if he'd tried to push her into going further, she probably wouldn't have gone out with him again.

For the truth was, sex didn't really interest her. She had no yearning to discover what it was like. When her friends at Stowe had talked about wanting to have sex, Sue had always felt as if they were speaking a foreign language she didn't understand. She wondered occasionally if there was something wrong with her, if something inside her was missing somehow. Sex scenes in books and movies never did anything for her. Once, her friend Linda Deviney had found her father's stash of porn videos, pilfering one for them to watch—and it had left Sue repulsed. Watching the blowsy woman with the sagging breasts and the hairy man with the large penis grunt and sweat and make agonized faces had turned Sue's stomach. *This is what everyone is so obsessed with?*

She'd never had crushes on movie stars or pop singers, not really. She could look at somebody like Brad Pitt or Orlando Bloom and *appreciate* the way they looked, but it was never anything deeper or more emotional than that. Certainly, the boys she met had done nothing for her. Her crush on Tom Parker had been about his mind—about the intensity he had when he talked about astrophysics—it wasn't about his eyes or his muscles or his butt, the things other girls talked about. For a fleeting few moments a few years ago, Sue had even considered the possibility that she might be a lesbian—but then discarded that notion since girls' bodies left her even more disinterested than boys'.

But Billy—he was *different.*

Billy made her smile. He made her relax and chill out more than any other guy ever had—or girl, for that matter. When Billy put his arm around Sue's shoulders in the darkened movie theater, it felt comfortable and right. She felt warm inside, happy. When he kissed her, she liked it. She found herself looking at Billy's big strong hand as it hung from her shoulder rather than watching the movie. She was mesmerized by the uneven fingernails, the blue veins threading across the top, and the fine white hairs on the outside. When he held her hand as they walked out of the theater, making her laugh and smile as she looked deep into his frosty blue eyes, she wondered if this was what falling in love was like.

Sex she could live without.

But falling in love—that she found very nice indeed.

It was with Billy on her mind that Sue fell asleep.

And as the thunder and lightning crashed over Bentley Hall, Sue dreamed.

She and Billy were in his mother's Toyota Camry on their way back from Senandaga. They'd been to an action movie. Sue had hated it, and she was giving Billy a hard time about dragging her along to watch it with him.

"Bang bang, shoot 'em up, things go boom," she teased as they took the off-ramp to Lebanon. "Why can't boys ever get any further than that? Don't you guys care about plot?"

Billy grinned at her. "I care about plot. The movie had a plot."

"With holes in it big enough to drive this car through," she said, laughing more than she would have in real life. In real life, she probably wouldn't have teased Billy quite so much. But in her dream, Sue had known Billy a long time.

All her life, it seemed.

Maybe even longer.

His hand went from the side of the steering wheel to her knee. She looked down at his hand, and then back up at him and smiled. She felt a tingling where his hand was touching her bare knee, a vague sensation of warmth that started slowly creeping up her leg. "That's nice," she barely whispered, catching her breath and looking over at him.

This is what it's supposed to feel like, this is what a woman is supposed to feel when she wants a man. I'm not frigid, I just hadn't met the right guy yet.

"I love you, Sue," Billy said, moving his hand further up her leg.

She felt a strange sensation between her legs, in her lower abdomen, like hot liquid poured all over her.

"I love you, too, Billy," she said, and placed her left hand on his right knee. His leg was solid and strong, yet somehow soft to her touch, and he began to shift a little in the driver's seat.

"I want you, Sue," Billy said.

"And I want you, Billy," she whispered back.

But her eyes were on the dark road in front of the car, and she barely had time to scream—

—because there was a bicycle in front of them and on it,

a girl with long blond hair and a baseball cap, looking back over her shoulder at them, and her mouth was screaming, screaming just like the girl in the window. And then there was a terrible thud and for a brief moment, the girl's face hit the windshield and her eyes locked onto Sue's. After that, the windshield was all covered in blood.

Sue sat up in bed screaming.

"Sue!"

Malika's voice.

She was feeling around for the light, but the power must have gone out. The digital green clock on the side of Sue's bed was dark. Outside the storm still raged.

"Sue, are you all right?"

Her heart was thudding in her ears. She tried to find the words.

"A dream," she mumbled. "A bad dream."

"It's okay." Malika was at her side now, having gotten out of bed and come around to hers. "It's probably the storm that freaked you out."

Lightning suddenly lit up the room, and then a few seconds later came a huge crash of thunder. The building literally shook.

"A really bad dream," Sue mumbled.

"It's okay, Sue," Malika was saying. "Put it out of your mind and go back to sleep."

Sue lay back down. Her heart was still racing, but she seemed unable to fight off the sleep that was already overpowering her. She was vaguely aware of Malika going back to bed, and then she was asleep again.

The dream wasn't over.

She was outside. Just where, she wasn't sure. The night air was cold. There was no moon, and the clouds blocked out the stars.

"Sue," came a voice.

It was Billy.

And his eyes were glowing red.

"Billy?" she asked, her voice shaking.

He laughed— a low, guttural sound.

Sue's entire body went cold.

"Billy, what's—what's wrong with your eyes?" she stammered, taking a step away from him. *Run, run, you've got to get away from him . . .*

Because suddenly she knew.

This is what really happened to Bonnie Warner.

"There's nothing wrong with my eyes, Sue."

Billy's voice was lower, deeper than it usually was.

"Come on, Sue, let me take you home . . . come let me drive you home. Don't you want to go home, Sue?"

Her entire body was frozen in place. She willed herself to run, to get away, but somehow she couldn't move.

"Come on, Sue," Billy purred, and he took her hand— only his hand wasn't warm—

—*it was cold, and it didn't feel like skin, it felt like scales . . .*

Sue yanked her hand away.

"Get in my fucking car!" Billy raged.

Sue turned and ran. She could hear Billy's footsteps behind her. She ran hard, she ran faster than she'd ever run before. Something was wrong, something was terribly wrong. She didn't know what, but all she knew was she had to get away from him.

He's going to kill me, just the way he killed Bonnie Warner!

She saw the gates of the college in the distance. There were lights on in Bentley Hall, warm welcoming lights, safety.

Almost there, almost safe.

She heard laughter from behind her, and it wasn't Billy laughing.

She glanced back and what she saw—

It wasn't human. It was a thing of blackness, of cold, mad hatred and fury.

Sue screamed.

And then she was falling, falling hard—having tripped over two bodies on the ground. She came face-to-face with them.

Joelle Bartlett and Tish Lewis.

They were dead. But even worse—they looked deflated. Like plastic balloons that had been popped. As if all the life had just been sucked out of them.

Sucked out—by that—that *thing*—that was bearing down on her!

Somehow, Sue staggered to her feet and kept running. She ran through the gates of the college, the hot breath of her pursuer on her neck. In front of Bentley Hall, she looked up at the window of Room 323.

And yes, there was a face.

Only the face wasn't screaming.

It was her mother's face—kind and smiling—exactly as Sue had seen her in all those old photographs. Her mother was smiling, gesturing for Sue to enter.

"No," Sue said, backing away.

"Go ahead, Sue," came the voice of the thing behind her. "Don't you want to go home?"

She turned around. It was Billy. Billy in all his sweet boy-ishness. He smiled.

And revealed a mouthful of fangs.

As he leaned forward to kiss her, Sue didn't resist. She couldn't run. Not anymore. She was too tired. Besides, if she gave in to him, she'd get to go home, he promised. And there, her mother was waiting for her. Billy put his arms around her, and placed his cold lips against hers. He smelled of dead things, of rotting flesh, of death.

Sue surrendered.

And then she sat up in bed, shivering, just as lightning lit up the room.

Lightning—but no thunder now. The storm had passed.

But Sue's fear had returned.

25

In the morning, Sue awoke with a start, even if the power outage had ensured the alarm clock just sat there, blinking uselessly. She lay there unmoving, watching as Malika dragged herself out of bed and into the bathroom. Sue listened as the shower came on.

A bad dream, she thought to herself. *That's all it was, just a bad dream.*

The dream had been too monstrous.

You're just being silly, that's all, she told herself. *It was the storm. And all that thinking about Billy before bed, worrying about the whole sex thing—it's easy to explain. Anyone with a basic understanding of psychology would tell you that your subconscious mind—fearful of sex—turned Billy into a monster, a threat to you.*

But what about the Bonnie Warner stuff—where did that come from?

And Mother?

The shower shut off, and Malika opened the bathroom door to let out some of the steam. "Come on, lazybones," she called. "Time to rise and shine."

With great effort, Sue got out of bed and walked across

the room to the window. She looked out onto the campus. The sun hadn't fully risen yet, and there was a steady drizzle of rain. Dark and gloomy. Sue sat on the sill, wrapping her arms around her knees and leaning back against the wall, watching the water run down the glass.

All at once, pain shot through her head.

"Damn." She tried to stand, then stumbled and fell against the side of her bed. The pain was blinding, intense, like no pain she'd ever felt before. She was aware of nothing except the pain, like her brain was being ripped in two. She held on to the side of the bed, her face twisted, unable to think because of so much pain . . .

And then it was gone as suddenly as it had started.

She gasped, trying to catch her breath. She tried to call to Malika, who she could hear humming to herself in the bathroom as she brushed her teeth. But she found she couldn't make a sound. She attempted to stand—

—and then the pain returned, like a lightning bolt through her head. My God, it hurt so bad, as if her brain was being torn apart inside her head, as if something was going on in there that she couldn't stop or control. She could barely breathe.

And then it was gone again.

Except now her stomach was churning. She knew she was going to be sick.

Like a cannonball, she forced herself to her feet and ran into the bathroom, scaring Malika with her intensity. She fell to the floor before she could make it to the toilet, and she began crawling across the tile, fighting the violent heavings of her stomach just as the terrible headache returned.

The pain . . . oh God, the pain.

The tiles felt cool to her burning skin, and she hoisted herself up through the fog of pain—everything seemed to be tinted red—and hugged the toilet, opening her mouth and retching. The pain in her head didn't abate as her stomach emptied, even as she continued to heave and vomit after there was nothing left to come up.

"Jesus!" Malika was shrieking. "Sweet Jesus!"

Sue slid to the side of the toilet, lying facedown on the floor, the hard yet cool tile feeling good to her burning face.

And then, mercifully, the pain in her head was gone again.

"Sue," Malika called, stooping down and cradling her head in her arms. "Baby girl! What the hell is wrong?"

"I—I don't know . . ."

Malika made a face and turned her face away from the toilet, even as she managed to reach out and flush away the vomit. "Come on," she said. "Let's get you back to bed."

She helped Sue to her feet and across the room, easing her down on the bed.

"My head," Sue mumbled. "I had this wicked headache—and then—I knew I'd be sick . . ."

"Food poisoning," Malika said. "It looks like food poisoning to me. What did you eat last night?"

"Lasagna," Sue managed to say.

She and Billy had eaten at their favorite little Italian place near the movie. She could taste the sour bile of half-digested pasta, meat sauce, and cheese in the back of her throat.

"It must have been bad," Malika said. "We ought to report them. It could be salmonella."

"No," Sue said. She didn't know why she was so certain it wasn't food poisoning, but she was. "It wasn't the food."

"Have you ever had that kind of a headache before?"

"No, I definitely have not." She was feeling better—at least, she knew she wasn't going to be sick again. She managed to sit up, and Malika propped her pillows behind her back. "That was the real problem. The headache was so bad it made me throw up. It was the headache, not the food."

"Well, we need to get you to the infirmary," Malika told her.

Sue knew she was right, but all she wanted to do was stay right where she was. She was afraid if she moved, the pain in her head would come back. She didn't think she could take another bout of that pain.

But finally, she allowed Malika to help her into a pair of sweats and a T-shirt, and traipsed out into the rain with her across the campus to the infirmary. The nurse on duty took one look at Sue and must have seen how pale she was, because she immediately took her by the shoulders and got her to lie down.

"You can go on to your classes," the nurse told Malika. "I can take care of her from here."

"Is that okay, Sue?" Malika asked.

"Yeah," she said, nodding. "I'll be fine. There's a test in Dr. Marshall's class today that I can't miss. I'll skip biology and rest up for it."

"Okay." Malika gripped her shoulder once and headed out.

The nurse, meanwhile, was placing a cold damp cloth across Sue's forehead. "Want to tell me what brought this on?" she was asking.

The nurse was a small woman, small yet round in her white uniform, with short dark hair and large breasts that seemed to push the uniform top to its breaking point. Her name tag read POPPY COCHRANE.

"Well, I've had headaches before, but nothing like this," Sue explained. "After I threw up, I felt better. Just really weak."

"It could be an allergic reaction. You've never had a problem with the foods you ate before?"

"No, in fact, I've eaten the exact same meal at the same place the last two Saturdays before."

"Well, maybe the meat was bad this time out." Nurse Cochrane nodded her head. She opened the file in front of her, and a frown crossed her round face. "This is odd."

"What?" Sue frowned. "What are you looking at?"

"Your medical history."

"You have my whole medical history there?"

Nurse Cochrane eyed her. "Of course. We have it for all our girls. It's a requirement. Your grandparents had it sent up before you even arrived."

Sue made a face. "How would you know it was my grandparents? Wouldn't you have assumed it was my parents who sent it?"

The nurse smiled. "It says it right here. Grandparents are guardians."

"Oh. Okay." Sue sat up, removing the cloth from her head. She was feeling better. "So what's so odd?"

"You've never been sick." Nurse Cochrane looked over the top of the folder at her. "Nothing."

Sue shrugged. "I've had colds."

"No chicken pox, no measles, no mumps, no flus, no hospitalizations, no broken bones except for that little trouble with your nose." Nurse Cochrane closed the file. "You're a medical miracle, Miss Barlow."

Sue shifted in her seat. "So, I'm healthy. Is that a problem?"

"Well, no, of course not, that's not what I meant." The nurse gave her a beaming smile. "It just means you're a phenomenally lucky young lady. Children, as you may know, are incredibly susceptible to diseases—and most children run fevers, catch colds, get the chicken pox—I don't think I've ever seen a file like yours once in my entire career. And other than regular checkups and flu shots, you've never really had to see a doctor in your life. That's really amazing."

"Is that all?" Sue started to stand up.

"Well, I think I'd like to make an appointment for you with Dr. Bauer when he's in tomorrow—see what he thinks. He might want you to go up for a CAT scan in Senandaga, just to be on the safe side."

"CAT scan?" Sue suddenly felt defensive. "It was just food poisoning."

Earlier, with Malika, she'd been opposed to that idea, certain the headache had brought on the sickness, not the other way around. But now . . .

"There's nothing wrong with me," she told the nurse.

She didn't quite believe it. But some strange sensation inside her didn't want to know what might exactly have gone on in her head earlier this morning.

It had felt as if her brain was being torn in half.

"It was just a bad headache from eating bad meat, you said so yourself," said Sue. "And now it's gone and I puked out all the poison and I'm fine. Having to go to the hospital and have all kinds of tests would just upset my grandparents. No need to get everyone all upset. They'd worry—and would make me go to every specialist under the sun, and I'd rather not get everyone all worked up over a headache."

"It's your decision, but still—" The nurse removed an appointment book from the drawer of her desk and opened it. "Do you have class tomorrow at three?"

Sue shook her head. "No," she admitted.

"I'd like you to see Dr. Bauer then." She wrote Sue's name in the book. "Until then, stay away from that restaurant. And if you get another headache, get over to the emergency room. Lebanon General is a very good hospital."

"An appointment with the doctor is not necessary," Sue told her.

"I'd be remiss if I didn't make it." She narrowed her eyes at Sue. "What are you afraid of finding out, Miss Barlow?"

Sue quickly stood and thanked the nurse. More than anything, she just wanted out of there. She felt absolutely fine now. She hurried through the rain, her untied sneakers sloshing through the mud.

What are you afraid of finding out?

"Nothing," she said out loud to herself in the elevator. "I'm just afraid of failing Dr. Marshall's test."

Back in her room, she called Billy's cell. He was in school, of course, so she knew she'd get his voice mail. "Hey, it's Sue," she said. "Listen, were you sick last night? I had a wicked headache and then hurled all over the place. Maybe it was the food? Hope you're okay. Talk to you later."

She flopped down onto her bed. In a way, she hoped Billy had gotten sick, too. They'd had the same lasagna. If he got sick, it would confirm the idea that it was food poisoning. Sue felt awfully mean thinking it, but she hoped right now Billy was puking his guts out.

She needed to study if she was going to pass this test. Sue found her notebooks on the floor and picked them up so she could flip through her notes. She liked Dr. Marshall's class. Her lectures were interesting, and the subject matter Sue found fascinating. She'd never really given much thought to the things Dr. Marshall brought up about the history of the Church. She'd learned at Stowe about the Reformation and the religious wars that had torn Europe asunder in previous centuries, but it had never occurred to her to question the actual books of the Bible, and to wonder if they actually said today what they originally said two thousand years ago.

Some of the other girls in the class didn't like the things Dr. Marshall had to say, and there had been some heated discussion. Wilbourne had a lot of fundamentalist Christian girls, and most of them took what Dr. Marshall was saying very personally. "Jesus was the ultimate questioner of authority," Dr. Marshall would say. "He'd welcome a challenge to orthodox teaching. You might still end up believing exactly what you believe today, but until you actually examine your faith, you can never know for sure."

Sue didn't participate in these discussions in class. She just listened, but took it all in. She knew that her grandfather wouldn't approve of the class—or Dr. Marshall. "Anyone who attacks Christianity attacks the basic foundation of this country," he'd said once at the dinner table, "and is therefore anti-American."

But Dr. Marshall wasn't attacking Christianity. That she'd made clear once after class, when Sue sometimes stopped at her desk to talk about the day's discussion.

"Challenge—even dissent—should not be construed as an attack," she told Sue, who'd nodded.

"I think," Sue had told her teacher, "that those who cry that they are being attacked by such discussions are the ones least secure in their own faith.'

Dr. Marshall had smiled. "Very astute, Sue. I wish you'd share such thoughts in class. You'd add quite a bit to the discussion."

But Sue preferred not to speak in public. She'd probably stumble over her words or mangle her point. She preferred just to listen to Dr. Marshall—so eloquent, so articulate, so passionate.

It's odd, Sue thought, *that I can admire both Dr. Marshall and Joyce Davenport.* Both so different—but in their passion and conviction, the same.

Her cell rang, startling her out of her reverie.

She glanced at the Caller ID, hoping it would be Billy. But it wasn't. She flipped open the phone. "Hello, Gran."

"Sue? We just had a call from the school nurse. Are you all right?"

"Oh, man, I can't believe she called you," Sue groaned. "Yes, I'm fine. I had a minor case of food poisoning. I think it was bad meat lasagna."

"Was it served in the cafeteria?"

Sue couldn't tell her grandmother about Billy. "No. A friend and I—we went off campus to see a movie and ate at an Italian restaurant."

"Well, is she sick, too?"

"I don't know. I called—*her*. And left a message."

Gran sighed. "Well, I know what a healthy girl you are, Sue. I just wanted to make sure you were all right."

"Hey, Gran, is it true I was never sick? Like I never had the flu or anything like that when I was really young and now I can't remember?"

"Yes, it's true, Sue. As I said, you're a very healthy girl."

"Come on. I've had colds . . ."

"Mere sniffles. Your grandfather and I took very good care of you. We made sure you never got sick. And your healthy constitution meant that you could fight off things that more average girls could not. Don't you remember Brenda Upton's birthday party?"

Brenda Upton's birthday party.

Sue hadn't thought about that in years.

"Right," Sue said vaguely as recollection flooded her mind.

"Well, don't eat at that restaurant again," Gran was saying. "We want you to stay well. Don't eat off campus anymore. Who knows what those backwoods restaurants are like?"

Sue made a grunt in response, then thanked her grandmother for calling.

She wished she hadn't made her remember Brenda Upton's birthday party.

Sue had been nine years old when Brenda invited her. Brenda's father was one of Granpa's junior partners at the firm. She didn't like Brenda—a stuck-up little girl who was always throwing fits when she didn't get her way. Sue stayed as far away from Brenda as she possibly could. She certainly didn't want to go to her party.

But Granpa had insisted. "How would it look if the senior partner's granddaughter didn't go? Jim Upton would think I don't appreciate his work, that's how it would look, and we can't have that now, can we?"

So Gran had taken Sue shopping and bought her a beautiful party dress of white satin and red velvet, with new stockings to match. "Your grandfather is senior partner," Gran told her as she combed Sue's hair. "You have to make a very good impression on them all, to show them how important your grandfather is."

As soon as she arrived at the party, Sue knew she was overdressed. None of the other girls were wearing dresses; most of them were in jeans and T-shirts. Most of the girls at Brenda's party were other little girls Sue didn't like, so she spent most of the party sitting in a corner, just watching and hoping it would be over soon. She ate cake, drank punch, clapped politely as Brenda opened her presents, and wished fervently for the day to be over. Finally, it was, and when Gran asked her, Sue had lied and made it seem like she'd had a great time.

But unbeknownst to them all, one of the guests at Brenda's party had been coming down with the chicken pox. Sue couldn't remember which girl it was now, but there had been a frantic phone call, and Gran had come into Sue's bedroom with a terribly pale look on her face. She seemed horribly distraught, as if she had failed Sue in some deep and profound way.

"If we had known, we wouldn't have let you go," she said. She stroked Sue's hair, a rare gesture of affection, one of the few Sue remembered from her childhood. "Your grandfather thinks you're so strong that you'll be able to fight it off. But you might get sick, dear. And if so, we will nurse you through it. We'll see that you get better." She kept stroking Sue's hair. She seemed to be reassuring herself as much as Sue. "I told all of them that you'd be fine, that we'd get you through it, that no one needed to worry."

Remembering that now, Sue wondered whom Gran had meant—who the people were that her grandmother was so desperate to reassure. At the time, however, she had been too frightened to wonder—too scared that her face would soon be covered with the dreaded pox.

Only, she never got sick.

"I told you," her grandfather had crowed. "I told you she was strong enough."

Every other girl who'd been at the party got the chicken pox. Every one of them missed school the entire next week.

Except for Sue—the only one who didn't come down with it.

That doesn't prove anything is weird about me. Sue shivered, rolling over onto her back to look up at the ceiling. *It just means I'm immune somehow to that, and to all the other stuff kids get. It's not a big deal.*

But it's not *normal.*

She'd never missed a day of school. At the end of the year, she always got a prize for perfect attendance. The only other times she'd ever thrown up, in fact, were a couple of episodes of motion sickness on Granpa's boat out on Long Island Sound.

She felt like a freak.

"Hey!"

Sue looked up. Malika had come back. She came through the door with a large paper cup sealed tight with a lid.

"I brought you some chamomile tea," she said. "How you feeling, girl?"

"Much better, thanks," Sue told her, accepting the tea. She took a sip. It was too hot to drink, so she set it on her bedside table.

"I thought I'd pop back between classes to check on you," her roommate said. "What did the nurse say?"

"She agreed it was food poisoning." Sue decided not to tell her about the appointment with Dr. Bauer. "But I'm fine now."

"Will you be able to make it to Marshall's class for the test?"

"Oh, sure. I was just doing some last-minute cramming for it now."

"We should probably call that restaurant—"

Malika was interrupted by a rap at the door. "Miss Barlow?" said a voice from the other side. A male voice.

Sue and Malika exchanged a curious glance. Sue nodded to her roommate that she should open the door. Malika peered out through the peephole and then quickly pulled the door open.

It was Dean Gregory.

"May I see Miss Barlow?" he was asking Malika.

"Here I am," Sue said, standing.

The dean rushed into the room, followed by Mrs. Ooster-house. He was a tall man with a small, pinched face. He seemed to have been in a hurry to get to Bentley Hall, as he wore no jacket and his white shirt and blue tie were speckled with raindrops. Mud covered his Bass Weejuns and had splashed up on his wool pants. Oostie waddled close behind him, a little out of breath. Had no one answered the door, Sue assumed Oostie would have used her master key to let the dean inside.

"What's wrong?" Sue asked.

"Nothing, we hope," Gregory said, smiling at her. "I heard you weren't feeling well today, Miss Barlow."

Sue and Malika exchanged quizzical looks. "I had a headache," Sue said.

"Bad enough that you went to the infirmary."

Sue was astounded. "Do you check up on every girl who goes to see the nurse?"

Gregory's smile stretched across his small, weasely face. "Your grandfather called me," he explained. "I was just making sure you were all right."

"My grandfather? You know my grandfather?"

"Well, of course," Gregory told her. "He's one of Wilbourne's best supporters."

Sue gave a little laugh. "By supporter, you mean benefactor?"

Gregory nodded. "Mr. Barlow has always been extremely generous to Wilbourne."

"So that explains it," Sue said, turning to Malika. "Why they sent me here. They were so clever, pretending they wished I was attending a school closer to home. They wanted me to come here all along."

"And we're glad you did," Gregory said. He laughed. "Excuse me, but we haven't officially met." He extended his hand to Sue, who reluctantly shook it. "Let me welcome you to Wilbourne, Miss Barlow. I would have gotten around to meet you sooner—I was looking forward to it, in fact—but when I got the news that you might be ill, I knew it was long past time to come by and see you."

"Thanks," Sue said, terribly uncomfortable.

"Nurse Cochrane said you have an appointment with Dr. Bauer," the dean said. "Please let me know what he says. And if you need anything from us, please don't hesitate to call on me or Mrs. Oosterhouse."

Oostie gave Sue a cheeky grin.

"I'm sure I'm going to be fine," Sue said.

Gregory beamed. When he smiled, he looked less like a weasel and more like a bat—beady little eyes and a mouthful of teeth. There was a faint cheeselike odor hovering around him—perspiration meets wool and rain. Sue found him utterly repulsive.

"Well, you rest up today," Gregory told her. "Don't exert yourself."

"I have a test today I need to study for," Sue said. "Dr. Marshall's class."

Gregory shook his head. "I've already spoken to Dr. Marshall, and asked her to excuse you from the test. You can make it up later."

Sue felt herself getting angry. "That's not necessary! I'll take the test today!"

"Tut, tut, Miss Barlow. The most important thing is that you get better." He turned to Malika. "Please see to it that she does nothing but rest today."

"This is ridiculous and totally unnecessary," Sue objected.

"Please take my card, Miss Barlow," the dean was saying. "If, in the future, you should need anything, please don't hesitate to call. It's my private number."

He placed the card on Sue's desk, then turned to head out the door, Oostie following obediently behind. "Rest, Miss Barlow," he ordered her. "I assured your grandfather you'd get nothing but rest."

He shook his finger at her and smiled. Then he was gone.

"God *damn*," Malika said.

Sue sat down hard on her bed. "What the fuck was that?"

"I've never once had Dean Gregory come looking for me," Malika said. "I don't even think he knows my name."

"My grandmother was so smooth on the phone. She knew my grandfather was calling the dean."

"You had no idea that Granddaddy was bankrolling Wilbourne?"

Sue shook her head. "None."

Malika sat down beside her on the bed. "Hey, there are worse things than having the dean of students on your side."

"But I don't want to be treated any differently than anyone else. I want to take that test today!"

Malika sighed. "You didn't tell me about that doctor's appointment. Maybe it is better for you to just rest up today. Why stress yourself?"

"Dr. Marshall probably thinks I'm some snotty rich girl now, getting the dean to do me favors." Sue flopped back down on the bed. "I'm really fine. It was just a headache."

But she couldn't lie to herself. It had been more than that. Something had happened in her head this morning—something she didn't want to think about.

Nor did she want to think about her grandfather's involvement in Wilbourne. Why did it trouble her so?

When Billy called a half hour later to say that no, he hadn't gotten sick, Sue felt even worse. She gave in to Malika's insistence that she get back in bed and watch reruns of *The Golden Girls*. But her mind was far, far away from the antics of Dorothy, Blanche, and Rose.

She was thinking again about her dream . . . and about all the dead girls she had seen.

26

Every small town has its secrets.

People in Lebanon liked to joke that there were no secrets in their town—that everyone knew everyone else's business. Gossip could be mined pretty much anywhere in town. People talked at the Yellow Bird, at Earl's Tavern, at the A&P. They shook their heads over tragedies, clapped their hands when beaming moms revealed their studious offspring had made the honor roll. They'd never admit, however, to being secretly gleeful when someone flew a little too close to the sun and fell to earth—the people of Lebanon were good people, above all else.

Yet despite all the talk, there were still secrets in Lebanon, dark things people definitely didn't want their neighbors to know.

Everyone in town knew that brawny Bud Tomlin, who owned Bud's Shell, was catcher on his slow-pitch softball team and led the county league in home runs. But no one knew—least of all his wife Bettie—that Bud's real reason for staying up late some nights after Bettie and the kids were sound asleep was to cruise Web sites for pictures of naked girls under the age of thirteen, masturbating two or three times before erasing all traces of where he'd been. No one knew that sometimes, when he was finished, Bud wept with guilt—and that some nights he would put a gun to his head and consider pulling the trigger.

Everyone knew that Barbara Schoenfeld was a great cook and that her cakes and pies always brought the highest dollar amount at the Methodist Church's bake sales. Everyone knew she spent three or four hours a week in aerobics classes at Lebanon Fitness Center trying to keep her trim figure—and most thought her husband Nate was one lucky man. What no one knew was that every Sunday after church, while her husband was off haunting garage sales and flea markets for things to sell in their secondhand shop, Barbara would meet nineteen-year-old Tim Westlake in the back room at Schoenfeld Antiques. No one knew that Barbara would undress him and have sex with him on her husband's desk—sometimes on top of unpaid bills and invoices. No one knew she kept Tim's underwear every time as a trophy, locking the briefs away in a drawer in her kitchen. No one knew that sometimes when she was baking, Barbara would take out the most recent pair and hold them up to her face, inhaling the boy's scent deeply as she thought about what she'd do with him the next Sunday afternoon.

Everyone knew and liked Wally Bingham. Everyone knew he worked hard and missed his wife. Everyone knew Millie Carter—the devout, bereaved widow of former First Selectman Jesse Carter, who wore a locket around her neck with Jesse's photo inside, who played the organ at the Episcopalian Church and sang sweetly with the choir. But no one knew that on those rare nights when Wally took a night off, he'd give Millie a call, and off would come the locket and on would come some sexy fishnet stockings, and the two would meet down by Earl's Tavern. Making sure no one saw her, Millie would sneak down the alley and let herself into Wally's apartment with her own key.

Everybody knew Ken Von Stein had turned the fortunes of Lebanon High football around in the seven years he'd been head coach. Everybody knew and liked his wife Evie, and his adorable and smart three children who were in the grammar school. Everyone looked at the Von Steins as shining examples of everything that was right with Lebanon. Everybody was proud of the four conference championship banners that hung in the high school gym, won by Ken's teams in the last five years. But nobody knew that when making love to his wife, Ken was actually thinking about the boys on his football team walking around naked in the locker room after practice. Nobody knew that sometimes some of the football players were mystified to discover that their dirty jocks had disappeared from their lockers overnight. Nobody knew that every Tuesday night, after the other players had gone home, David Hemingway, the fullback, would slip into Ken's office and drop his jeans, letting the coach service him. Nobody knew how much Coach Von Stein hated himself every time he did this, yet somehow he couldn't stop himself, even though he knew he could lose his job and his family and go to jail if anyone ever found out.

Everybody knew that Cat Marsden was overprotective and smothering of her thirteen-year-old son Jimmy. That wasn't a secret to anyone—that had had been going on ever since Cat's husband had run off when Jimmy was just a baby. What nobody knew was that Hank Marsden hadn't really run off on his wife. He'd meant to, but Cat had shot him twice in the head before he could get out the door, and had buried his body in the basement of the Marsden house.

Everybody knew that Claire Holland had died a slow and painful death from a cancer that had rotted her from the inside out. Everyone had liked Claire—she'd been head cheer-leader and Homecoming Queen at the high school and had never had a bad thing to say about anyone. Everyone knew that her husband, Sheriff Miles Holland, was still mourning her death three years later, and it was beginning to look like he'd never get over it. They didn't know that when she had finally died he was relieved—and not just because her suffering was over. He was also relieved because his own suffering had ended as well. They didn't know how often he'd prayed for Claire to die, and how incredibly guilty he felt about it. No matter how much he tried to convince himself he prayed for her death just so she'd be released from her pain, he knew that he'd prayed so fervently because he wanted to be freed of the burden of taking care of her. People didn't know that every time Miles went to lay flowers on his wife's grave, he asked her to forgive him. They didn't know the guilt was slowly starting to take a toll on his own sanity. They didn't know how often Miles wished he were in the grave with her.

Everyone knew that Dean Theodore "Ted" Gregory ran Wilbourne College like a small personal fiefdom, an autocracy he'd been granted by an obliging board of trustees, nearly all of whom had been specifically selected by Gregory. There was a nominal president of the college, of course, Mrs. Marion Edwards Taft, but she was over eighty now, and her duties had gradually devolved to Ted Gregory. It seemed to most people in Lebanon that Gregory had always been at Wilbourne; his father had been on the board, and Ted had been made a professor of English right out of college. Everyone knew that Gregory had an intense dislike of being contradicted; he sometimes overruled fellow committee members when organizing fund-raisers for Lebanon's St. Mark's Lutheran Church. Few ever objected; Ted Gregory knew how to get things done. He and his wife Mona were pillars of St. Mark's, and the other church members understood how very committed

Ted was to spreading "the word of the Lord," as he called it. If that sometimes meant he had to run roughshod over people— usually secular-minded people who had no appreciation for the word of the Lord—then so be it.

Except for those who attended St. Mark's, not a lot of people in Lebanon knew Ted and Mona Gregory. They were, after all, "Wilbournians." But they knew their two twin sons, Bruce and Bryce, who'd been straight A students and star athletes at Lebanon High. Such good-looking boys they were, and so filled with promise for the future. People some-times asked Ted and Mona how the boys were making out at college, and they'd be told, "Marvelous, just marvelous." But what they didn't know was that Bruce had dropped out of Ohio State midway through his first semester and disap-peared; Bryce had left the University of Michigan a heroin addict, and was now a male prostitute on the streets of De-troit.

There was, in fact, a great deal that the people of Lebanon didn't know about the Gregorys. They didn't know that late at night, in the Dean's House on campus, Ted and Mona locked their doors tight and closed all the curtains, and then sat on the floor chanting strange words and singing queer rhymes. They didn't know that spilled between them on a marble altar was blood—and that more blood was stored in vials hidden in their dining room cabinet, behind the fine china and crystal. They didn't know about the secret room that the Gregorys had built in the basement of the dean's house. No one knew about that room—except for Bruce and Bryce, and it was that room that had sealed their tragic fates.

Everyone knew the history of the town of Lebanon—how in 1687, a group of people had left Boston and forged a new village out of the wilderness in upstate New York. Every schoolchild read that story of Lebanon's beginnings, how the town's founders had been a sect even more conservative than the rigid Puritans, and how they'd been forced to practice their religion in secret. Everyone knew there was a memorial to the patriarchs of the first four families of Lebanon in the Town Square, and that every June 20, Founder's Day, the town celebrated the bravery and commitment of these pious men. The original faith of Lebanon's founders had not lasted long beyond that first generation, but still these good men had endowed the town with a deep commitment to God, family, and neighbor, and for that, every year, they were hailed.

What people didn't know—what had been erased from history books—was that the "good founders" of Lebanon had left Boston just one step ahead of an angry mob that torched their houses, and that, had they been caught before they fled, they would have been hanged. Nobody knew that the religious expression the town fathers sought had nothing to do with worshipping God. They also didn't know that the original faith of Lebanon's founders had not, in fact, died out—but that it was still alive, thriving in fact, on the campus of Wilbourne College.

27

All Tish Lewis knew was that it was dark.

And cold.

How long had she been in this place? And where exactly *was* she?

She had long since stopped screaming. All it had done was leave her throat sore and throbbing. No one had come in response to her screams, not even that red-robed figure that brought her meals twice a day and hauled away the smelly pail that Tish used for a toilet. At first she wouldn't eat—fearful that she would be poisoned—but then sheer hunger had overtaken her and she'd wolfed down the bread and raw vegetables with a savagery she hadn't known she possessed.

When was that? A week ago? Two? Time meant nothing in the face of endless night. Tish begged the figure in the red robe to let her out of the room, but the figure never spoke. It just clamped the iron door shut as it left, and Tish could do nothing but shiver and cry in the dark.

Why? Why was she being held?

Ransom? That's what she thought at first. Someone had kidnapped her and was demanding money from her father.

But that was before she began to hear the chanting through the door. The terrible singing.

That was before she heard the scream.

It was a girl's scream. She knew that. And she thought she knew who the girl was, too.

Her roommate, Joelle.

That's when this had started. Between bouts of utter terror, when all Tish could do was cry and shake, she tried to force herself to remember the events that had led up to her being brought to this room. She had gotten a voice mail from Joelle. Her roommate's words were burned into her brain:

I've heard it. The screaming. Oostie took me into the room. I think she's in on it—all of them maybe—

And then the message had ended abruptly.

Tish sat in the dark, on the moist earthen floor, and held her knees, rocking a little as she once again tried to remember. *I went back to the dorm after getting Joelle's message. She wasn't in the room. I went out into the hallway and saw the door to Room 323 was open. I stood in the doorway and looked in.*

And I saw—

And I saw—

"What did I see?" Tish whispered to herself.

She knew it was horrible—something far beyond her comprehension—and it had terrified her. More than terrified her. It had overcome her. She had screamed, passed out, and woken up here in this place. Her mind would not allow her to remember exactly what she had seen. Or, more accurately, what she had seen had been so terrible, so beyond description, that her brain lacked capacity to fully comprehend it.

Tish began to cry again. She was starting to lose hope that she'd ever get out of this room alive. What worried her most now was *how* her death would come, not if. They had taken her for a reason—they'd taken Joelle, too, and Tish was certain it was Joelle's scream of death that she had heard. They'd taken both girls to kill them.

But who "they" were and why they wanted to kill them was unknown. And it was the unknown that Tish feared most.

28

Perry Holland was worried about his father.

As September turned into October, the leaves turned from green to vibrant shades of orange before they dropped from the trees. The days grew shorter and the wind colder, and Sheriff Miles Holland seemed to be aging right before Perry's eyes. It was as though he'd woken up one day to discover that his father had turned into an old man overnight. The circles under the sheriff's eyes had grown deeper and darker, his hairline seemed to move back an inch at a time every week, and more and more lines carved themselves into his face. Worse still was the emotional aging. Sheriff Holland didn't seem to pay attention when people talked to him. A look of complete indifference settled on his face. Sometimes, words had to be repeated to him more than once, and he'd forget what you told him in a moment.

Sheriff Holland had always take great pride in his job, and in the uniform he wore. But ever since Bonnie Warner disappeared, Perry thought, his father's uniforms had become increasingly wrinkled, and sometimes even looked dirty. Sometimes, he went days without shaving—and started skipping showers as well. Often, Miles would sit in his office for hours, just staring into space. People in the sheriff's department were starting to whisper. Sometimes, Perry would walk into a room where his coworkers were talking, and they would suddenly fall quiet, and he knew they were talking about his father.

He hasn't really been himself since Mom died, Perry thought as he turned his patrol car down the street where he'd grown up. *But it's gotten worse—far worse—in the last month and a half.*

His sense of unease heightened when he turned into the driveway. Several weeks' worth of newspapers were yellowing on the lawn, which hadn't been mowed in weeks. The flower beds his mother had taken such great pride in were overgrown with weeds.

Perry turned the ignition off in the car. It was nearly dark, with long shadows of pine trees cast across the house. But still, Dad hadn't turned on any lights. Perry sat and stared at the place where he'd grown up. He had lived here until he moved into his apartment on the other side of town. This is where he'd watched Saturday morning cartoons, where Mom had made her fabulous pot roast on Sundays, where Dad had grilled ribs in the backyard, where Perry and his friends had watched football games on the weekend.

Dad never let the yard go like this, ever, Perry thought. *Maybe it's becoming too much for him. I should make more of an effort.*

With a start, he realized he hadn't set foot in his parents' house since the gathering after his mother's funeral. He saw Dad at work, and they often shared dinners at the Yellow Bird. But he had not been back to the house since the funeral. Perry took a deep breath. *I still associate the house with Mom. That's why I can't face it. But how much harder has it been for Dad to keep living here?*

Perry was an only child; his birth had been hard on his

mother, and they'd given her a hysterectomy before she brought him home. "They said I couldn't risk another pregnancy," his mother had told him once sadly. "I wouldn't live through it." They'd been a close family. If his parents had ever argued, Perry never witnessed it. Both of his parents had done the best they could, which, thinking back now, seemed very good indeed to Perry.

I'm a terrible son, he thought, unable to budge from the car. *The last thing Mom said to me was, "Take care of your father."*

He forced himself to open the car door and headed up the walk. Kicking aside the damp leaves on the steps, he slipped his key into the lock, ringing the doorbell as he opened the door.

"Dad? It's Perry."

The living room was dark, the curtains drawn

"Are you here?"

"In the kitchen, son," his father answered.

With a sigh of relief, Perry switched on the overhead light in the living room and headed to the kitchen in the back. His mother had always kept the kitchen spotless and neat. As he took in its condition now, Perry sighed. Dishes were stacked in the sink. The kitchen table was piled with papers. Something had gone bad in the fridge, but Dad didn't seem to notice.

"Dad, what are you doing in here in the dark?"

His father was sitting at the kitchen table, straining his eyes as he read through a stack of papers in his hand.

Miles Holland looked up at him. "Oh, right. I guess I was so engrossed here I didn't notice the sun had set."

Perry switched on the lamp over the table. An amber light suddenly suffused the room. Perry looked down at the papers that were piled haphazardly. Old, battered file folders. A stack of newspaper clippings. Photocopies of photographs.

Perry sat down at the table. "Dad, I'm worried about you. Sitting here—"

His father waved a hand. "Son, I'm on to something."

"Dad, look, you're not eating, you're not taking care of yourself . . ."

"Perry, I tell you. I'm on to something."

His son made a face. "On to something about what?"

"The college," Miles muttered, shuffling some papers around. "Those missing girls . . ."

"Dad, only one girl is missing. Bonnie Warner."

"You're wrong. Two more girls." He pushed a report toward him stamped TOP SECRET.

Perry glanced down at it. "Joelle Bartlett . . . Patricia Lewis," he read. "Dad, why didn't you tell me?"

"As a favor to the college," he said, clearly unhappy with the decision. "It was a state police call, not mine. An agreement was made to keep the disappearance of two more girls secret for now, so as not to panic the campus and the town."

Perry was flabbergasted. "Dad, if people find out—hell, *when* people find out—they will be royally pissed. And with reason. If some maniac is running around abducting college girls, the public should know."

"Yes, I agree. The dean understood that eventually this would come out, but he asked that we sit on the news for a bit." He shook his head. "The muckety-mucks at State Police HQ agreed—but it's a temporary decision."

"How long have they been missing?"

Miles shrugged. "Not sure. The damn college administration is being cagy. They didn't even make the report. It was the girls' parents who got worried when calls they made to their daughters weren't returned. Finally, they called the college, which at first said the girls were very busy with exams. Then, finally they admitted to the parents that they hadn't been in class, but they've been vague for how long they'd been gone."

"Jesus," Perry said.

"And get this, Perry. The girls were roommates. And they lived right across the hall from the first girl who went missing—the one that left all the blood all over the street."

"So you suspect a connection."

Miles nodded. "The state is trying to take over the whole investigation. But I just can't let the thing go."

Perry sighed. He understood his father's determination. Bonnie Warner's disappearance still ate at *him,* too. He couldn't forget seeing her at the Bird that night, when she'd turned down his offer for a ride. He'd followed up every lead he could, questioned everybody who was out on the road that night, hoping to find some clue.

"I've been digging," his father told him. He began gathering the papers on the table into a pile. "Son, there's a cycle . . . every twenty years or so." Miles's voice was animated, and he actually sounded like himself for the first time in weeks. "Something happens to the girls up there at the college every twenty years or so."

"What are you talking about?"

Sheriff Miles laughed. "I know it sounds crazy. I've been thinking that myself for the last few weeks. But it's been there in the back of my head all this time . . . when Bonnie Warner disappeared, I said to myself, 'This has happened before . . .' "

"Dad, what do you mean?" Perry stared at his father. "A girl disappeared before from the college?"

"You don't remember?" His father returned his stare. "You were young, but it made the news. It was twenty years ago, almost to the month."

Perry closed his eyes for a moment. "Yeah," he said. "I vaguely remember a girl going missing there . . . it was right after you were elected sheriff."

"That's right. It was one of my first cases. Margaret Latham. An all-points bulletin went out searching for her."

Perry was nodding. He had been just eleven years old, but he remembered the gruesome details. "They found her eventually, right . . . badly mutilated."

"That's right. Limbs cut off, blood drained. Body was dumped in Lake Bessett. No one ever charged with the crime."

Perry shook his head. "But that hardly makes it a cycle, Dad. One girl's murder doesn't necessarily connect to the disappearances of three others twenty years later."

"I have a long memory, Perry. That's why I've made such a damn good sheriff. People forget things. But I remember. I make connections." He handed Perry a sheet of paper. "I recalled that another girl was reported missing soon after Margaret Latham disappeared. See the report?"

Perry glanced down at it. "Yes, but this girl eventually turned up okay. It says here her parents told police she had run away from the college and returned home."

"Yes . . . but *why* did she run away?"

"Come on, Dad, now you're really starting to sound nutty . . ."

"I have a long memory!" he shouted. He seemed genuinely angry. "I've been in the vault, combing through all our old cases. I've been at the library, going through microfilmed newspapers. This has been a recurring pattern at that school. I remember!"

He shoved a well-thumbed folder, cracking with age, across the table at Perry.

"If you read that, you'll see that almost twenty years before Margaret Latham's disappearance, there was another curious event at Wilbourne. People forget. But I remember."

Perry leafed through the contents of the file. A girl in a 1960s flip hairdo smiled up at him from one photo. In another, she stared glassy-eyed at him, her face swollen in death. Perry shuddered.

"I had to really rack my brain to remember," his father was saying, "but I did it. It was like there was something in there that kept me from remembering—that keeps everybody in this goddamn town from remembering. But still, I knew it was there. Deep down, the memory was there—and the files corroborated it."

"Okay, so girls have gone missing or murdered from Wilbourne before. Still, to call it a cycle—"

"You need more, son? When I suspected I might be on to something, I went back again in the files. Sometimes it was twenty years. Sometimes it was only nineteen. But sure enough . . ." He began tossing files at Perry, who practically had to catch them in his arms, they came so fast. "1962. 1943. 1923. 1904." Miles grunted. "That's when the sheriff's department was founded, so I don't have records to go on before then. And the local newspaper only goes back to 1897. But how much do you want to bet, if we went down to the town clerk's office, we'd find some death records of Wilbourne college girls—mysterious deaths—murders—circa 1884–1885?"

Perry leaned forward and placed his hand on his father's forearm lightly. "Dad, I think you might be tired. Maybe you should go lay down, get some rest."

"I don't need any goddamn rest! I need to figure out what the hell is going on up at the school!"

Perry stood. "Have you eaten anything tonight, Dad? Let's go get a chili burger and fries at the Bird—"

"Haven't you heard what I've been telling you? Come on, Perry. You've got to admit this is too weird to just chalk up to coincidence." He banged the table with his fist. "Explain why the townsfolk seem to forget. Explain why you didn't remember Margaret Latham going missing until I reminded you."

"Dad, I was eleven."

"Then explain to me why the selectmen didn't remember! Not even Veronica Thomas, whose father was the sheriff before me! She never called me to say, 'Gee, Miles, this sounds a lot like that case we had eighteen years ago.' Explain to me why no one in town seems to remember these things. Even more—why no one up at that goddamn school ever seems to wonder why every generation they lose two or three girls to violent deaths!"

Perry had to admit that was a very good question. Evidence of the girls' deaths sat right there on his father's kitchen table. But Wilbourne College had never acknowledged its recurring problem.

"Well," Perry said, thinking out loud as much as responding to his father, "if they did acknowledge it, enrollment would certainly decline."

Miles looked at him with a hard, intense stare. "I have a feeling enrollment is the least of their concerns."

"Dad," Perry said. "You think the school has something to do with the deaths, don't you?"

"Or at least covering them up."

The sheriff stood, rubbing his forehead.

"You okay, Dad?" Perry asked.

"Headaches," Miles grumbled. "Too much reading."

"Let's go to the Bird. You need to get out of this house."

The older man was still lost in thought, however. "The strangest part is why we don't remember. It doesn't make any sense. It's not like so much happens in this fucking town that you can't remember something bad happening. At the time, these were all big news stories. I don't understand it . . . it just doesn't make any sense."

"Dad, you need to eat."

"I'm not hungry." He put a hand to his head again. "Damn headache. Maybe I will go lie down and take some Motrin."

"Good idea," Perry said. "I'll clean up this mess. Then maybe I can make us both some eggs."

Miles shook his finger at him. "You gotta admit I'm on to something, Perry."

"We'll talk about it after you rest awhile."

His father grunted, then headed down the hall to his room.

Biting his lower lip, Perry started scrubbing the dishes in the sink. Food had dried like glue in pans. Milk rings stared at him from the bottoms of glasses. He decided just to fill the sink with hot water and let the dishes soak.

Hauling the trash out to the can, he scolded himself. *Why wasn't I paying more attention to Dad? Why wasn't I being a better son? Why couldn't I see he was on the verge of cracking up before?*

But he couldn't deny that what his father had discovered was very interesting. Very interesting indeed.

A good memory was one of the most important tools in solving crimes. Perry knew that. His father was right. So he needed to pay attention to the feeling he'd gotten when he looked at one of those files. He'd seen one of the names before.

But where? When?

Back at the table, he lifted a yellowed folder he knew had come from the station files. Yes, this was the one. The girl who'd disappeared but later turned up okay at her parents' home.

BARLOW, MARICLARE was written on the tab.

Barlow? That name is familiar. Why?

Perry sat down and scratched his head. *Where do I know that name from?* He opened the file and looked at the date it was opened.

Twenty years ago.

He heard his father saying, *"Every twenty years or so something happens to the girls up at the college."*

And then it came to him.

The girl in the white Lexus. Perry had pulled her over the night before school started. Her name was Barlow. Susan Barlow, with a Manhattan address. She'd flirted a little bit with him, and he'd found her attractive.

Might there be connection between her and this Mariclare Barlow, who was also listed with a Manhattan address?

Barlow was a fairly common name, and Manhattan was a big place. But Perry had enough curiosity to read the entire file. His eyes widened as he read.

Dear God, he thought. *Could Dad be right?*

Every twenty years or so . . .

The overhead light flickered. Perry shuddered as he continued to read.

29

Ginny climbed the stairs to her apartment, spitting mad.

I should have resigned on the spot, she thought to herself.

Fumbling with her key, she let herself inside, balancing her book bag slung over one shoulder and two paper bags of groceries in her arms.

I'll never forgive Gregory, she said as she stewed. *Never.*

They'd finally had their long-awaited face-to-face confrontation about Bonnie Warner, as well as a few other things.

"Do you want me to tell you I was planning on reporting her for being off campus? Is that what you want me to say, Ted?"

Ginny sat opposite the dean, who was ensconced in his tall leather chair behind his desk. His small pink hands were folded over his chest.

"I would hope that was truly what you were planning, Ginny," he said to her. "It would have been the only responsible thing to do."

"Fine. Then I'll tell you that's what I was planning to do. I never got a chance to do so, because I found out from Sheriff Holland that morning that she was dead. Or at least presumed to be, with all that blood. And frankly, that weighed more heavily on me than the fact that she'd broken one of the silly college rules."

Gregory had smiled at her, that toothy mammal smile. "We have rules for the students' protection and safety, Ginny. They're not silly."

"If I could do anything differently, it would be to have insisted that Bonnie ride home with me. If she had agreed . . ." Ginny's voice trailed off. She hated thinking about that poor girl and the fate she suffered.

"She was a headstrong child," Gregory said. "So I've been told. I never met her."

Of course not, Ginny thought. *She wasn't the grand-daughter of a rich benefactor like Sue Barlow . . .*

"Here's the dilemma as I see it, Ginny." Gregory leaned forward, his beady eyes locking onto hers. "I'm sure Bonnie's parents would be very distressed to know a teacher here saw her off campus the night she disappeared and did not report her right away."

"Right away? The administration was closed for the night."

"You could have called me directly."

Ginny laughed. "And what would you have done? Gone out looking for her?"

"Perhaps." Gregory leaned back in his chair. "The point is, if you had taken action rigft away—"

"That's an unfair charge!" Ginny's voice was loud, but she didn't care. "The best I could have done was report her the next day."

"I'm not sure if the Warners will see it that way." He gave her a tight smile. "They're threatening to sue Wilbourne, you know."

"Then you'd only be giving them ammunition if you told them I saw her."

Gregory nodded. "You'd probably be named a party in the case."

Ginny stood, approached the dean's desk, and gripped the sides with her hands. Her eyes bore into Gregory's. "What is this all about? Stop beating around the bush."

"Just a simple request that you drop the courses on the divine feminine next semester."

"What?"

"You heard me. The board of trustees isn't happy with such teaching at Wilbourne. Now that Fred Dodd has retired and I found Nancy Wallison to replace him, the board is quite unanimous in its desire for academic consistency."

Ginny stood, feeling a little dizzy. "What the hell does that mean?"

"Oh, come now, Ginny. You knew very well when you took this job that Wilbourne was a conservative school. We offered you a job to keep some diversity in our curriculum. But that was a priority of the old board of trustees. Now the board is less interested in promoting 'alternative' views."

"Look, Gregory, you are absolutely right. I took this position knowing that Wilbourne had a history of being conservative. I also knew that it had a history of academic freedom and a commitment to educational diversity. Being conservative, might I remind you, need not equal being small-minded or intolerant. It is only recently that the conservative movement in this country has been co-opted by Christian fundamentalists who have dictated how we must think and what we must believe."

Gregory was looking at her almost with pity. "Dear, dear Ginny. I think you ought to stick with religious theory and not get into politics."

"It's become hard to separate the two," she retorted.

"I'm not asking you to keep to any sort of line. Only that you submit to me a revised curriclum for next year."

Ginny was astonished. "Is this how it's going to be then? First, you personally intercede for a benefactor's granddaughter, who happens to be a student in my class, and demand she be given preferential treatment . . ."

"The poor girl was sick, Ginny."

"It was her place to work that out with me, not yours!"

He shrugged. "In any event, I do appreciate your flexibility on that matter."

Ginny had agreed to give Sue Barlow an extension, but it had been against her better judgment. She had always liked Sue—thought she was smart—and indeed, a few days later, when she took the make-up test, the girl had aced it. How apologetic Sue had been about Gregory's involvement. Ginny didn't blame her. Gregory was, quite simply, an impossible prick.

"I don't know," Ginny said, turning to leave Gregory's office. "I can't commit here and now to turn over my academic authority to the administation. Frankly, I'm too angry to even discuss it further with you.'

Gregory had smiled his infuriating weasel grin. "That's fine, Ginny. You think it over. Let's talk again by Friday, all right?"

He was threatening me, Ginny thought as she settled the groceries onto the counter. *He was holding over my head the fact that I saw Bonnie on the night of her disappearance.*

So let him tell her family I saw her! I couldn't have prevented what happened! They could read about it in the police report anyway.

Still, Ginny knew she should put a call in to her lawyer. Not only about Bonnie—but about the tactics Gregory was using to control her teaching. Her contract guaranteed her academic freedom.

She was tired and all she wanted to do was put the groceries away, open a bottle of wine, and find a little bit of mellow before sleep. The wind was cold, whipping against the side of the house and cutting right through to her bones. Winter, it seemed, was going to make early inroads on autumn.

She noticed the red light on her answering machine was blinking. She hit the play button as she put the groceries away.

Beeeeep. "Ginny, this is Angela. Just wanted to check in with you and see how the book's coming. I just got off the phone with Dan and he wants you to know they are really going to get behind this book—he really thinks this is going to be a big seller, that it's really going to push you over the top. They have plans to get you on almost all of the major television shows, and there's a possibility of a History Channel or A&E documentary. So look. He was just wondering when he'd be able see a few chapters. I can't keep putting him off. You know I really hate to be a nag about this kind of thing, but I can't keep assuring him that everything is going well when I haven't seen anything myself and you don't return my calls. So, please, please, please, Ginny, give me a call when you get this, no matter what time it is, okay? I'm a little worried. Is everything all right up there? Call me."

"Oh, Christ," Ginny said out loud, holding a jar of peanut butter in one hand and a bag of coffee beans in the other.

Angela Cohen had been her agent from the very beginning of her publishing career, back in the days when she was working on her Ph.D. at Harvard. Slogging her way through on her doctoral thesis, Ginny was advised to find a literary agent. "Publish or perish, my dear," her advisor, Dr. Guenther, a wise old professor with a heavy German accent, had told her. "If you already *have* a contract to publish your thesis, it's kind of hard for them to deny you not only your letters, but a teaching position here. And I'm sure there are any number of respected academic publishers who would love to have a shot at publishing you."

It had seemed a bit premature, but Ginny had learned early in her collegiate career to listen to faculty members giving advice. She'd bought a book on literary agents, typed up a synopsis of the book, and sent it out to twenty nonfiction agents. She honestly thought nothing would come of it. When Dr. Guenther asked her about it, she could just shrug and say, "I tried."

She was never sure how Angela Cohen came across her query letter, but she had, and she was not only interested in representing Ginny—she was excited and enthusiastic. "This book has *best seller* written all over it," Angela had enthused over the phone after reading a few sample chapters. "I just love how you take on the guys who started the early Christian Church—it's just great, and it's going to be controversial, it'll get all the fundamentalists' panties in a twist for sure."

"That's a good thing?" Ginny had asked, worried.

"Honey, controversy sells books like you would not believe." Angela had told her. "Ginny, you and I could do good things together, trust me on this, okay?"

And over lunch at a swank bistro in central Manhattan a few weeks later, Ginny took the plunge and signed a letter of agreement for Angela to represent her.

The last thing in the world she expected was for Angela to get her a six-figure contract with a major publisher in New York. But that's what she did. *The Sacred Feminine* earned her not only the Ph.D. she had coveted for so long, not only a teaching position at Harvard, but also one hell of a lot of money. Suddenly, Ginny was in demand for talk shows and speaking engagements all over the country. Scuttlebutt around the faculty was that tenure was a given, and sure enough, it came through . . . but Angela and the publisher were already pushing Ginny on a second book. "I never meant to be an author," she'd protested to Angela. "I want to be a teacher."

"Publish or perish, dear, you know it as well as I do." Angela was insistent, and as much as she hated to admit it, Ginny knew she was right.

For her next book, she decided to do a study of sightings of the Virgin Mary . . . but after getting started on the research and visiting a few of the places where shrines now stood—as well as a trip to Los Zapatos, Mexico—she stalled out on the book. She went on to write other books, but then Eric got sick, and her marriage crumbled, and Ginny, depressed and desolate, had finally fled to the wilderness of Lebanon, still unable to finish the book she had been working at on and off for twenty years.

Dan Rosen, her editor, was very understanding. "Ginny, after all you've been through, the last thing I want to do is push you to finish something that you aren't ready to finish." *The Sacred Feminine* was still selling well for them, and Ginny knew she remained an asset to the company. "Take your time," Dan told her. "Just keep me posted on your progress." He extended the deadline for her, and would extend it again two more times. Now the third extended deadline was coming up in March of next year, and Ginny had written little more than she had when she'd gotten the first extension.

She walked into the living room, pulling off her sweater and throwing it across the sofa as she turned her computer on. "Damn, damn, damn!"

Ever since Eric got sick, nothing has gone right.

But even as the thought crossed her mind, Ginny knew she was making excuses, yet again using Eric's death as a scapegoat. Failing to finish the book was her own fault. Eric had been dead for two years now. She'd blown off the deadline, asked for more time, and played on the sympathies of her agent and her editor. She couldn't play that card anymore. The truth was, she didn't have the slightest idea how to write the damned book. Sometimes she considered just paying the advance back and washing her hands of the whole mess. There was no shame in just being a college professor.

That is, if she kept her job now that Gregory was making things difficult for her.

But what else was there? All her hopes for the book were fizzling. *I couldn't even get Bernadette deSalis to talk to me,* Ginny thought, staring at her computer screen, her face reflected in the monitor.

In the month or so since Gayle Honeycutt had dropped that bomb on her—a local visitation, complete with stigmata—Ginny had gotten nowhere with the girl or her family. Whenever Ginny called, Mrs. deSalis hung up on her. Thanks to Gayle's fucking article, Mrs. deSalis considered Ginny "anti-Christian," and wanted nothing to do with her. She'd tried stopping by, but usually only found one of the deSalis boys at home, and they'd just grumble that they "didn't know nothing." Once, she'd lucked into Mr. deSalis, who Gayle had thought her best bet. The poor man's eyes were bloodshot, and he looked as if he hadn't slept in days.

"I've researched these kinds of cases, Mr. deSalis," Ginny had pleaded. "Maybe I can be of some help."

The man had just sighed. "I knew word would get out. I'm sorry, Dr. Marshall. I refuse to let my daughter become a freak in the eyes of the town."

"She's not that at all," Ginny said. "If I could just talk with her . . ."

"My wife won't allow it," Pierre deSalis told her. He

seemed so tired, as if all his life force was spent. "And what my wife says goes—at least concerning Bernadette."

Ginny felt that if she could just get in to meet Bernadette deSalis, she might find some new motivation, some new inspiration, to restart her book. But what avenue was left open to her? She couldn't exactly barge into their house—or wherever the girl was being kept—and demand Bernadette talk to her.

Bernadette, Ginny kept thinking. *Just like at Lourdes.*

She stood, turning away from her computer and pouring herself a glass of wine. A leave of absence, she thought to herself. That's what I need. There's no way I can continue here under Gregory's threats to control my classes. Maybe that's the handwriting on the wall. Get out of here now—go back to Hammond and finish my book.

A semester off would be just enough time for her lawyers to build a case against Gregory for breach of contract.

She took a sip of wine. Could she do it? Really walk away from teaching? What choice was Gregory leaving her?

She had just about decided to call Angela and talk it through with her when her doorbell rang. *Odd*, Ginny thought. *I never have visitors here.*

Probably a salesman, or a Jehovah's Witness, she told herself, setting her glass down on the counter and heading toward the door.

But when she opened it, the man she saw standing there was someone she recognized . . . from very long ago . . .

"Dr. Marshall?"

She looked at him, trying to place his face. He was Latino, with dark black hair shot through with streaks of gray, and he seemed a little stocky, though it could have just been the heavy gray overcoat he had buttoned up the front. He wore black slacks over black leather hiking boots, and his big almond-shaped eyes were warm and soft.

"Yes?" Ginny asked. "May I help you?"

"You do not remember me," he said, and smiled. "But then, I should not expect you to after so many years. And we only knew each other so very briefly."

His English was lightly accented, and he spoke it perfectly in cadence. There was something about the smile—and then it hit her. Ginny's jaw dropped.

"Father Ortiz? From Los Zapatos?"

"Ah, you do remember. I am glad. May I come in? I would like so much to speak with you."

"Yes, of course," Ginny said, stepping aside as he entered. *I certainly never thought I'd see him again.*

"Thank you for receiving me unexpectedly," he was saying. "I wanted to call but your number is not listed, and I did not want to wait to reach you tomorrow at the college."

Ginny couldn't imagine what caused his urgency. "Sit down, Father," she said. "May I get you anything?"

He removed his coat and draped it over a reclining chair. "No, thank you," he said as he sat down. "It is good to see you, Dr. Marshall. The years have been very good to you."

Ginny blushed, running a finger through her hair. "Oh, please, you're far too kind." She sat down opposite him on the sofa. "Now, for heaven's sake, tell me what you are doing here in Lebanon."

He stared off over her shoulder for a moment. "Dr. Marshall—"

"Please. Ginny."

"Ginny." Father Ortiz smiled again. "I will start by apologizing to you for not saying an appropriate good-bye to you in Los Zapatos. The archbishop was very insistent that the girls and I get to Mexico City immediately."

"No need to apologize, Father." Ginny laughed again. "I certainly understood—the nosy American researcher was hardly a priority, especially when the archbishop calls."

He shifted in his seat. "I have, you know, followed your

career with great interest—and a little pride, I must confess—since then. I have read your books, and they are very interesting." He made a short laugh. "Of course, the official Church position is that you are a heretic, but I know many of my fellow brethren in the Church have read and debated your works."

"Well, that's all I ever wanted. To bring about discussion."

He leaned forward, winking at her. "And you needn't worry, Ginny. I am not here to convert you or lecture you—unless of course you want to recant and come back into the embrace of Mother Church? No?" He laughed again as Ginny sat back in her chair, a tight smile on her face. "I thought not, but it never hurts to ask, as you say in this country."

Ginny's smile turned warm. "But none of this explains why you are here tonight, Father, or what was so important it couldn't wait until the morning."

He studied her for a few moments. "Why did you never publish the book you were working on in Los Zapatos?"

It was Ginny's turn to shift uncomfortably in her seat. "I'm still working on it." She glanced over at her computer, then back at Father Ortiz. "Funny you should ask about it. I've been sitting here tonight trying to figure out how to move forward on it."

"I've always anxiously awaited that particular book, Dr.—er, Ginny."

Ginny found his gaze and held it. "Why did you come here, Father?"

He cleared his throat. "I understand you have been trying to see Bernadette deSalis?"

Ginny narrowed her eyes. "And how did you know that?"

He laughed. "Ah, God knows everything—and perhaps He whispered it to me? No?" He made a bridge of his fingers. "I am acquainted with the deSalis family. I was brought in when the local bishop learned of her experience. And so I have interviewed her extensively."

"You've moved up pretty far in the church hierarchy from your humble days in Los Zapatos, Father. You're here to investigate the sighting."

He nodded. "I suppose some consider me now an expert. But it is you, Ginny, who are the real expert. You would be doing me a huge favor if you interviewed Bernadette, and compared her story to those of other girls you have studied."

"I don't understand," Ginny replied. "In Los Zapatos, you wouldn't let me anywhere near the girls who saw the Virgin. And now, you're offering to let me interview Bernadette." She leaned back in her chair. "Come on, Father, what gives?"

"Suffice it to say, Ginny, that Mother Church has her reasons." He gave a slight shrug of his shoulders. "Will you come?"

"Well, of course I'd like to interview her. Is it true she also has the stigmata?"

Father Ortiz nodded. "There is much to discuss when you come."

"Terrific. When?"

The priest rose from his chair. "I will call tomorrow and make the arrangements. I wanted our first meeting to be in person. I wanted to see for myself if you were still the good, honest woman I met in Los Zapatos." He smiled. "Thank you, Ginny."

Ginny walked him to the door. "Thank *you*, Father."

He turned to look at her, and his face was grave. "Save your thanks for after you have spoken to Bernadette, Ginny. You may not be so grateful after you hear what she has to say."

What he meant, she didn't understand—but it didn't matter. Somehow, the fates had intervened and given her a second chance on the book. She watched Father Ortiz walk down the stairs into the night, then picked up the phone to call Angela.

This could justify another extension, she thought, refilling her glass of wine.

30

Tish Lewis had become very good at hearing things in the dark.

She had learned to discern voices, even at a great distance, from somewhere far off in this place where she was being held. The voices drifted through cracks in the wall, seeped in through the floorboards above her head. Tish had determined she was in a basement, and from the voices she heard, she believed she was still on the Wilbourne campus.

That's Dean Gregory's voice, Tish had realized a few days earlier. *And that's his wife. And that's the nurse from the infirmary, Poppy Cochrane . . .*

They were chanting. Exactly *what* they were chanting, Tish couldn't make out. But it was some kind of ritual. The same kind of ritual during which she'd heard her roommate Joelle scream some time before.

They killed her, Tish thought.

Dean Gregory and the others killed Joelle.

Even worse.

They had drunk her blood.

They were drinking blood out there. Two phrases had

floated down to Tish's ears quite clearly: "Take this and drink" and "The blood is our life." It had taken Tish a long time to decipher what they were saying, but now it was clear. Each person said it in turn. Each time she heard it, Tish retched.

The horrible truth had dawned on her. They were passing around a cup and drinking the blood of girls they had killed.

But they're keeping me alive. Why?

Twice every day, the red-robed figure brought Tish bread, vegetables, and water. *They're keeping me alive,* Tish reasoned, *so they can kill me, too, when the time is ready.*

And drink my blood.

They probably expected her to go mad in her cell. And who wouldn't, trapped in this place, so small, so dark? The only light filtered through the small slats above her head, a dim, dusty, golden light that allowed Tish to make out the rough contours of her hands, of the metal pail she used as a toilet, and the walls that enclosed her. Crawling around the earthen floor, Tish had estimated her cell was almost square, about five feet by five feet. No bigger than a closet. They expected she'd go mad in such a small space. They expected her to lose her mind, so when her time came, she wouldn't be able to fight them, wouldn't be able to put up a last-ditch defense of her life.

Well, Tish though to herself, *they're wrong. They hadn't reckoned on dealing with a strong-willed Southern girl.*

She kept her wits by thinking. Constantly thinking. Listening for sounds, and identifying them. *That's a refrigerator coming on above me,* she realized. *That's the creak of a floorboard. That's the opening of a door.* She learned to listen so carefully that she could determine how many people were in the house, walking above her, each of their footsteps having a different sound.

And she listened for voices. Some she didn't know, but

she forced herself to listen and examine each one. She identified four.

Dean Gregory. Mrs. Gregory. Nurse Cochrane. And that new woman on the board of trustees, Nancy Wallison, who'd spoken to Tish's civics class just last month . . .

Joelle had been right. They were all in on it—whatever "it" was.

There was a familiar creak outside the locked iron door. Tish's ears perked. She knew what it was, and the rumble in her stomach confirmed it. She was like a caged animal whose body had come to expect food every day at the same time. It was mealtime for Tish. The red-robed figure was descending the stairs into the basement. Tish counted off the seconds in her mind, and right on schedule came the second sound, when the figure jangled its keys outside the door.

In seconds, the iron door was swinging open, and the figure, robed and hooded, its face always hidden, carried a tray in.

The figure never spoke, but Tish had learned to study it carefully. By now, because Tish had reverted to silence, they must have thought she was mad. But her mind was clicking away, storing away any data that might prove useful later.

Whoever's under that robe moves slowly, Tish thought. Stout. Maybe even fat. I could outrun it given the chance.

The figure placed the tray on the floor. Tish bent over it, eating the bread like a dog might, tearing it apart with her teeth, not using her hands. All the better to make them think she had regressed.

The figure bent—with some difficulty, Tish noticed—to retrieve the pail. Tish watched as the figure left the cell, clanging the door behind. Tish took a sip of water from the large mug that had been brought to her. She knew it took only a few seconds for the figure to return with the pail, having emptied it presumably in some nearby toilet. If Tish were ever to make a move, it would have to be when the figure came back through the door at that point. That would take it the most by surprise. But how?

For now, Tish decided to bide her time, but she couldn't wait much longer. Who knows when they planned to make her their next victim?

The figure came back inside. Instead of setting the pail back down as it normally did, it stood over Tish for a moment looking down at her.

Tish, playing crazy, looked up at the figure with animal eyes.

"Pitiful slut," the figure spoke, the first time Tish had heard its voice. "Useless creature."

Then the figure set the pail down on the floor and left the room, clanging the door shut behind.

And Tish, her ears so sharply attuned, knew immediately who was under that robe.

Oostie.

Their good matron, Mrs. Oosterhouse.

Immediately, Tish had to pee. That often happened after drinking. As she pulled down her ratty, dirty jeans to squat over the pail, she felt encouraged.

I could take Oostie, she thought. *I could totally take out Oostie.*

But then she felt something sharp sticking in her thigh. She winced, looking down. One end of the pail's metal handle was coming loose. In the very dim light, Tish studied it. It broke off in her hands. Its edge was sharp—very sharp. Just a slight touch to her fingertip had drawn blood.

With a little effort, she secured the handle back to the side of the pail. It might come undone again, but she thought it would hold long enough for Oostie to carry it out of the room to dump it one more time.

But it would also serve as a weapon—a very sharp weapon—providing Tish was fast enough and strong enough.

And she had every intention of making sure she was.

31

Billy Honeycutt looked at his watch. Sue was late for their date.

He was sitting on a bench in the center of town. It was getting close to five, and Sue had promised to be there by four thirty. Billy hated the fact that he couldn't just pick her up on campus. Those archaic rules of Wilbourne prohibited visitors except during very specified hours, and then only on weekends. Every minute Sue was late cut into the time they could spend together, given that the campus curfew was nine o'clock on a weekday night.

Billy sighed. He liked Sue. Liked her a lot, in fact. But he had thought dating a college girl would be a little more glamorous than it was. When he was dating Heidi, he was the Big Man at Lebanon High, strolling around town with his arm around her. Heidi was considered the foxiest girl in Lebanon, and Billy had nabbed her.

And now here he was, sitting on a bench all by himself in the middle of the afternoon.

Still, Sue was a breath of fresh air to him. Heidi would pout if Billy didn't kiss her right away. She was always try- ing to out-whore her friends by wearing short shirts to expose her belly button, pretending to be Britney. But Sue seemed oblivious to the whole game of sex. Billy liked sex—no question about that—but Sue was sophisticated. She came from Manhattan. For her, Billy reasoned, sex was just part of the mix. It came when it was supposed to. No need to flaunt it.

Billy liked that. Call him old-fashioned maybe. But he'd always felt pressure to measure up with Heidi. To be the cock of the walk. Sometimes she'd insist on making out— and to be honest, Billy really would have preferred to be watching the Yankees on television. Not that he didn't like sex—not that he didn't often initiate it himself—always making sure to reassure Heidi that he loved her—but sometimes he didn't want her around, would have preferred she and her big breasts stayed out of his sight for a while. Heidi, of course, could always tell when he wasn't really into it, and she'd flee from the room in tears, wailing that he didn't love her anymore. Billy would be forced to follow her and profess his undying love.

It was such a relief not to have to go through all that charade anymore.

Heidi hadn't taken the breakup well. "You've been lying all along, Billy Honeycutt!" she charged. "You've been stringing me along and lying about loving me and using me only for sex!"

Billy just sighed. None of that kind of drama with Sue, thank God.

He looked at his watch again. 5:01. Where was she?

He hoped she hadn't gotten another one of those headaches. When she'd described it to him, Billy had been really worried. "That's just not normal, Sue," he told her. She agreed, but the campus doctor, when she went in to see him, had given her a clean bill of health. So maybe the headache had just been a fluke.

Sue was smart. She was fun. She made Billy feel like a

grown-up. He didn't have to preen or pose. He didn't need to put on a show for her. She seemed to like him just for who he was. They talked about movies, and politics, and where they hoped to travel someday. Sue never made Billy feel stupid when he mixed up cities, states, and countries. (He thought Oregon was a city and San Diego was in Mexico, and he got all mixed up when it came to European countries.) Heidi would have laughed at him and called him a dolt. But Sue just explained the difference, and told him one day she'd really enjoy showing him Paris. Especially something she called the Shomp Deelasay. Billy smiled thinking about it, about walking hand-in-hand with Sue down the streets of Paris.

"Well, hello, Billy."

He jumped. Behind him, arms akimbo, was Heidi.

"Oh, hey," he said, danger signs flashing in his mind.

"Waiting for your new girl? Or is she standing you up?"

He frowned. "She is not standing me up."

"I came by half an hour ago and saw you sitting here. And you're *still* here now."

"So? A guy can't sit on a bench on a nice day?"

Heidi made a face. "Not a guy like you. Why aren't you at football practice?"

"It's a day off. Besides, it's none of your business."

Suddenly, Heidi broke out into tears. "Oh, Billy," she cried, throwing her arms around him. "This is such a mistake! We should be together!"

Her bouncy breasts, barely covered by a seersucker top, pressed up into Billy's face. Heidi clung to him, her long blond hair tickling his ear.

"Let go, Heidi," Billy told her.

He pushed her arms away from him, but she moved in closer, trying to kiss him on the lips. Her perfume filled up his nostrils.

"Jesus, Heidi," Billy said, managing to finally push her

away. And just as he did so, he saw Sue sitting in her car across the street, watching the whole scene.

"Fuck," he said, standing up.

Heidi saw Sue as well. "Is that her? Is that Miss Fucking Wilbourne?"

Billy watched as the two girls made eye contact. Sue seemed to be glaring at Heidi as she sat behind the wheel of her white Lexus. She seemed to be in no hurry to get out. She didn't seem the least bit upset, or eager to interrupt this little scene. She seemed intensely interested. Of course Sue was far too cool, far too sophisticated, far too Manhattan to react, to act like a spoiled, provincial little girl. She just kept glaring at Heidi until Heidi stamped her foot, shouted "Fuck you both!" and hurried off down the street.

Only then did Sue get out of the car.

32

Sue felt a strange emotion watching Billy with that girl.

Jealousy.

She'd never felt jealous over a boy before. Sure, she'd felt jealous of friends who got to vacation in some exotic place her grandparents refused to take her, and sometimes she'd be jealous of a girl's new shoes or really fabulous bag. But those were momentary feelings—they'd passed in a few minutes. This was raw. This was intense. Sue felt like scratching the girl's eyes out.

Stop acting like a stereotypical female, she scolded herself as she got out of the car. The girl was rushing away down the street. Billy clearly wasn't interested in her.

Or maybe he was.

Maybe he was, until he saw me.

Sue struggled to keep her emotions in check as she crossed the street.

Who the hell was that girl anyway?

"Hey, pretty lady," Billy called.

Sue smiled and let him kiss her on the cheek. "What was all that about?"

Billy scowled. "Ex-girlfriend."

Sue looked down the street to where Heidi was now just a small, pitiful figure in the distance. *She was trying to get Billy back,* Sue thought. *She was trying to take him away from me!*

And despite herself, she felt a surge of jealous anger. Once again, she couldn't take her eyes off the girl.

"Sue," Billy said, touching her shoulder. "Don't worry. She means nothing to me now."

Sue turned back to look him in the eye. "Just how many broken hearts have you left in your wake, Billy Honeycutt?"

"Not that many." He winked at her. "I know, hard to believe, given how good-looking I am."

He laughed, but she didn't return his levity. There was a voice whispering inside her head, *They slept together.*

She swallowed and closed her eyes. Images began flashing through her mind, horrible snapshots she didn't want to see.

A warm summer night, with the moonlight shining into the backseat of Billy's mother's Toyota. Billy and that girl— Heidi, that's her name—are making out. They are parked on a dirt road, and the scent of apples is in the air. On either side of the road, branches hang heavy with the unripened fruit. Both Billy and Heidi are shirtless. His head is down, nuzzling at one of the girl's large breasts. Her head is tilted back, her eyes are closed, and soft moans are coming from low in her throat. With his hands, Billy is working the clasp of her shorts. Just as the shorts come open, she reaches down and pushes his hands away from her.

"What's the matter?" Billy asks.

"I—I'm not ready for that yet."

"Aw, come on, Heidi." He grabs one of her hands and places it on the swollen crotch of his jean shorts. "You feel that?"

She pulls her hand away and sits up. "Billy—"

"I don't see what the big deal is."

"The big deal is you don't love me."

"Of course I love you, Heidi." He's lying to her, he doesn't love her, but his need is so powerful, his desire for release is so urgent, that he will say anything, do anything, to get inside of her and relieve his need.

She turns to him. She's a virgin. Not because of a deep commitment to saving herself, to keeping her purity, but because she's never felt in love enough to give herself so completely to any boy she's ever dated. But Billy—Billy is different.

"Do you really love me, Billy?" she asks.

He takes both of her hands in his and looks deep into her eyes. "Of course I love you, Heidi. I never say anything I don't mean." And then he kisses her.

And she stops resisting him.

"Sue? Are you okay?"

She shook her head and came back into herself. She gave Billy a weak smile. "Sorry." She glanced back over at Heidi, who she could barely make out now down the street. *Poor girl,* she thought. *I shouldn't have been thinking such bad thoughts about her.*

"You okay?" Billy asked.

"Just daydreaming, I guess."

He slipped his right hand over hers. "About me, I hope."

He's never tried to get me to sleep with him, Sue thought. *Why? Is there something wrong with me?*

They walked hand in hand for a while without speaking. They passed the drugstore and the A&P, and rounded the corner in front of the post office.

"I was afraid you weren't going to show up," Billy said finally.

"Oh. Right." Sue was struggling to get her thoughts under control, to yank them away from images of Billy and Heidi.

"I'm sorry I was so late." She brightened. "But I finally heard from Joyce Davenport."

Billy stopped walking. "Well, awesome. Did she tell you anything about your mother?"

Sue shook her head. "It was just a short e-mail, responding to mine from weeks ago. She said she was sorry it took her so long to get back to me, that she's been on tour, but said she would call and we'd set up a time to talk."

"Cool."

Sue sighed. "Yeah, I guess so. Anyway, I was late because I wanted to write her back right away, and I told her I'd been reading her book . . ." Sue laughed. "And you know what? She must have been online, because this time, she e-mailed me right back! And she was thrilled, of course, that I was reading *Smear*."

"Obviously, you didn't tell her what you thought of it," Billy said, laughing.

Sue had filled Billy in on what she perceived to be Joyce's prejudices. But she hadn't told him that she had been starting to revise her opinion, at least a little.

"You know," Sue admitted, "I can't figure her out. On the one hand, I think she's horrible. And the other . . ." Her words trailed off.

"What?" Billy asked.

"On the other," Sue said, "some of what she wrote makes a lot of sense to me. And I told her that, too, in my next e-mail to her. And she e-mailed right back again, saying she couldn't *wait* to talk to me!"

"Looks like she's found another follower," Billy said.

Sue smiled. Billy was sweet and he was cute, but he just wasn't very bright. He couldn't explain the difference between conservative and liberal to save his life. Completely apolitical. "Well," she said, "I'm not sure I'm a follower. But

I just feel maybe . . . maybe she speaks for some people, and maybe I should listen to what she has to say."

"Sounds reasonable to me."

"That's just it. I can see where Joyce and people like her can be unreasonable. But people on the left can be just as narrow-minded." Sue stopped walking again to make her point. "Take my roommate, for example."

"Malika? But I thought you liked her . . ."

"I do, but . . ." Sue's words trailed off again. "Well, you finally met her the other night. What did you think, Billy?"

"She seemed nice."

"No, come on, really."

Billy laughed uncomfortably. "Okay, maybe she was a little . . . I don't know . . . my Mom calls it 'crunchy.'"

Sue looked at him intently. "Crunchy?"

"Yeah, you know, like crunchy granola. The type who eats granola and thinks killing animals for food is murder." Billy smirked. "She was wearing those Birkenstock sandals, and she had a that pin on her jacket that read STOP GLOBAL WARMING NOW."

Sue was nodding. "Yeah. That's Malika."

Malika was so damn serious. Their conversations always seemed to veer into world politics. Malika had very little interest in any viewpoint other than her own. Her own way of thinking was the only correct one. Isn't that what she said about Joyce Davenport?

"Americans are so insular," Malika would explain whenever Sue disagreed with her. "You never look at the big picture, because no matter what may happen in the rest of the world, to Americans, it is only of interest if it directly affects your country."

Sue had grown impatient with such talk. Joyce Davenport had several paragraphs lambasting those foreign students who came to this country, took advantage of our great educational system, and then bashed America in turn. In fact, Malika's beliefs could be boiled down to one common denominator: *America is bad—America is very, very bad.* And if Sue challenged her, or asked her a question she couldn't answer, she became very superior. "That is just *wrong,*" she'd reply.

Malika was, as Sue's grandfather said, the epitome of the "limousine liberal." Her parents were wealthy, and when they came to this country, they acted like those uppity blacks—

Sue stopped in mid-thought.

Uppity blacks? How racist can I be?

She was stunned that such a thought could cross her mind. It was exactly the kind of thing that her grandfather would say—*and* the kind of thing Joyce Davenport would imply. Joyce was far too smart to put it in so many words, but it was there, between the lines of much of what she wrote.

Just because I might find some value in Joyce's work, Sue thought, *I don't want to become like her.*

Or—Sue shuddered—*like Granpa.*

She'd Googled Joyce's name the night before, and found dozens of Web sites about her. Some were worshipful—but a far greater number attacked her and what they called her "lies." One site was actually called "JoyceLies." There were cartoons with Joyce's face superimposed on an animated jackass or onto the body of a leather-clad SS guard. All of her extreme views came under attack. She opposed any rights for gay people. She thought most women had proven they didn't deserve the right to vote. And she said that if other races felt discriminated against here in the United States, they were always welcome to migrate back to their ancestral homelands.

That would certainly show them, Sue found herself thinking again. Really. Like some black person would be better off in Rwanda than here.

"It's just so difficult," Sue said.

They had been walking in silence again. Billy looked down at her. "What's difficult?"

"Figuring out how I feel," Sue said. "About Joyce, about her writings, about . . . myself . . ."

Part of me believes one thing, Sue thought, *and another part of me—a more emotional part—thinks maybe Joyce and Granpa are on to something. It's almost as if my brain is torn in half . . .*

And then she remembered her headache—when it had felt exactly and literally like that, her brain being ripped in half.

"You know what I think it is?" Billy asked. "I think because Joyce was your mother's friend, you want to really like her. That's what it is. You want to like her and find good things about her."

Sue nodded. Billy was right. Maybe he wasn't so dim-witted after all. She smiled up at him, cupped his cheek in her hand.

"I'm glad we met, Billy," she said.

He beamed. "Yeah," he said. "Me, too."

An image once again of him and Heidi flashed through Sue's mind. She pushed it away. But not before she felt the stab of jealousy again.

"You want to go over to the Yellow Bird for a Coke?" Billy asked, bringing her hand up to his lips and kissing it. "I told Mike we might stop by."

Mike. Billy's best friend, Mike deSalis. Sue's twinge of jealousy faded into one of sadness. She'd only met Mike twice, and briefly. "I don't think Mike likes me," Sue said. "I can just tell."

"Sure he does." Billy made a face. "You two just don't know each other very well yet. That's all."

He's lying, Sue thought to herself. *Mike doesn't like me and he's told Billy so.*

"Mike doesn't like me, Billy." Sue was adamant about it.

"He's just going through some family stuff. His sister is sick."

"Bernadette?"

Billy looked surprised. "Yeah. How'd you know her name?"

"He must have mentioned it . . ."

Billy shook his head. "No. He won't even say her name anymore."

"Well, then, I don't know how I could possibly know his sister's name," Sue said. "I mean, I barely know Mike."

"Well, come on, let's go. He'll be in a better mood if I buy him a chili burger and fries. Once you guys get to know each other, you'll be best of friends."

Billy was tugging at her hand to get a move on, but Sue stood her ground.

"Did he like Heidi?"

Billy sighed. "Sue, please . . ."

"He did, didn't he?" Sue asked.

"It doesn't matter."

Once again, jealousy rose up from Sue's belly like bile.

"Please, Sue, let's go," Billy pleaded. Finally, she relented, traipsing alongside him down the street toward the Yellow Bird.

It didn't occur to either of them that Billy had never told Sue his ex-girlfriend's name.

33

Heidi Swettenham burst through the doors of Martine's Boutique looking as white as a sheet.

"Heidi!" Martine gasped, standing over Rachel Muir, whose head was tipped back into the sink, peroxide cooking away on her gray roots.

"Can I sit down for a minute?" Heidi asked, gripping the back of a chair.

"Yeah, sure, honey. You sick?"

Heidi sat down hard. "I felt like . . . like I was getting these sharp pains . . ."

Martine walked around Rachel Muir's outstretched legs. "Here, honey, drink some water." She filled a small conical cup from the cooler and handed it to the girl. "You look pale."

The hairdresser saw that she'd been crying, too. The girl's eyes were red.

"You been having boy problems, I think," Martine said, taking back the empty cup and tossing it into the trash can. "Aren't you dating Billy Honeycutt?"

"I . . . was . . ."

"Well, you just sit there, honey, and if you don't feel better, I'll call your mama. She's due in for a cut and curl any-way."

Martine headed back over to Rachel Muir. The two women shook their heads at each other, in sympathy for a teenaged girl and her broken heart.

"When I was your age, Heidi," Martine was saying, "I had this boyfriend just like Billy. A regular Casanova, he was. The girls flocked around him like moths to a flame. But you get over them . . . "

She looked back in the girl's direction.

Heidi had slipped off her chair and was lying on floor. She wasn't moving.

Martine screamed.

34

"You want anything else, Mike?" Wally Bingham called from across the counter.

The Yellow Bird was empty, except for Mike deSalis. The supper shift was finished, and Marjorie was in the back, doing dishes. Everyone else had cleared out except for Mike, who'd been sitting in a booth for over two hours, just staring into his glass of Coke, which had been refilled at least ten times.

"No," Mike replied. "I'm just waiting on Billy."

Wally looked at his watch. "Well, if he was coming by for supper, I'm getting ready to close up the kitchen."

Mike sighed. "He's with his new girlfriend. They're always having serious conversations."

"You know how guys are with new girls," Wally said.

Mike just shrugged.

Wally looked over at him, and thought to himself, *The boy doesn't look all right.*

He walked around the counter and dropped down into the booth across from him. "Is everything okay, Mike?"

The boy looked at him. His eyes were glassy, his face pale.

"I'm fine, Mr. Bingham. I'll get out of here in a minute if Billy doesn't show up."

"Look, Mike, I noticed when you went to the bathroom a little while ago that you were weaving a little bit." He gave him a look of concern. "Level with me. You been drinking? High on something? I won't tell the cops. I just want to make sure you get home okay."

Mike looked at him, his eyes rolling a bit. "No, Mr. Bingham, I didn't. I don't know—I just don't feel that good today."

"Let me call Billy. What's his cell number?"

"Billy." Mike laughed, and his head lolled a bit. "Billy's too busy with that girl from Wilbourne to bother with me anymore. Just please, can I sit here for a minute longer? Maybe could I—could I have a glass of water?"

"Sure."

Wally hustled back behind the counter. *I can't let him walk out of here. Maybe I can get Marjorie to give him a lift home.* He glanced back over at Mike. The boy's head was down on the table now. Wally carried the ice water back over to Mike and set it down in front of him.

"There you go, son."

Mike picked his head up, and smiled at Wally. It was a pasty, weak smile, but his eyes—his eyes . . .

Jesus God, Wally thought.

The boy's eyes were bright red.

And in an instant, Wally could see flames. Everywhere he looked there were flames. He could smell the smoke, and hot cinders were falling from the fires that blazed across the ceiling. He could see even beyond his café—every building downtown was on fire. Even the trees and the grass in the square were aflame. There was a roar as the gas tank of a truck ignited and blew sky high. Wally could hear screaming voices begging and crying out for help. And then suddenly, there was the sound of a trumpet blaring, so loud that it hurt Wally's ears.

"Thanks, Mr. Bingham."

The flames were gone. Wally felt as if he might lose his balance as he stood there watching the boy drink the water.

What the fuck kind of hallucination was that?

"I have the worst dreams," Mike was whispering, looking up at him. He sounded drunk. "They are so terrible, Mr. Bingham, and I'm so tired all day, and I'm going to lose my scholarship . . . And my head—my head hurts so bad sometimes, it feels like it's going to split wide open and sometimes I wish it would—"

Wally steadied himself against the back of the booth. What the hell was going on here?

The bell over the door rang, and just as Wally started to turn to see who it was, Mike grabbed his arm, digging his nails into the skin.

"Hey!" Wally cried, trying to yank his arm away. He turned back in shock, only to see that Mike's eyes had widened in absolute terror, his mouth forming a perfect circle. His pupils were completely dilated, and his face was drained completely of color.

"Grill still open, Wally?" Billy Honeycutt was calling from the doorway. A blond girl stood at his side

But Wally couldn't take his eyes off Mike. The boy was gasping for air. With a final jerk of his shoulder, Wally managed to wrench his arm out of Mike's grasp. Bloody half-moons were cut into his skin from Mike's nails.

Mike was stuttering as if in utter terror, his finger pointing at the front door.

"Mike, it's Billy," Wally told him.

But Mike only started screaming. He stood up from the booth as if to run, but he seemed unable to move. He fell straight backward. For Wally it seemed almost in slow motion. He grabbed out for the boy, but his fingers just brushed against his shirt. There was a horrible thud as Mike's head hit the floor. Wally felt nauseated as Mike's head actually bounced up before falling again with another thud.

Both he and Billy were immediately at Mike's side. "Mike!" Billy was screaming. "Mike, are you okay?"

Mike opened his eyes and smiled up at them, "Everything is going to be all right now," he said in a startlingly clear voice. Then his eyes rolled back into his head.

Behind them, the blond girl was screaming.

Years of military training kicked in and Wally started performing CPR.

"Call an ambulance!" he shouted at Billy as he started pumping Mike's chest. "Don't die, Mike, don't die, please God, don't die . . ."

35

With shaking fingers, Sue flipped open her cell phone and pressed 911.

"You have to get an ambulance to the Yellow Bird diner!" she shouted at the operator. "Mike deSalis just collapsed, and they're trying CPR, but I don't think he's breathing. Please hurry!"

She hung up, watching Mr. Bingham pump Mike's chest. Billy was saying, "Come on, Mike, come on, Mike."

Marjorie, the waitress, had appeared behind the counter, her hands wet and soapy. "Should I call his parents?" she asked.

No one answered her.

Sue felt helpless, useless. She knew CPR—she'd learned it at Stowe in swimming class—but there was nothing for her to do. Mr. Bingham was working on Mike, but seemed to be having no luck. What had happened to Mike? He'd stood when he saw them come in, pointed at them, then fallen down. Sue saw the agony on Billy's face as he looked at his stricken friend. She wanted to go to him, put her arms around him, and hold him, but she was afraid of getting in the way.

"Come on, come on," Mr. Bingham said, his forehead

glistening with sweat as he started pumping on Mike's chest again.

Sue sagged down into the booth nearest the door and wiped her eyes with her hands. She didn't want to watch anymore, couldn't watch anymore. She took some deep breaths.

Why do I feel as if this is my fault?

It was crazy, but that's how she felt.

"Come on, Mike!" Billy was shouting. "Come on, buddy, I know you can do it!"

Sue heard Marjorie dialing a phone in the kitchen, then speaking in a low, hushed voice. Was she calling Mike's parents?

Outside, an ambulance siren. Sue jumped up and ran to the door, but the ambulance was heading in the other direction.

"No!" Sue cried, running outside waving her arms. "Over here."

She could see the ambulance at the end of the block now, stopping in front of Martine's Boutique.

Sue began to run. "Fools!" she screamed. "I said the Yellow Bird!"

Her legs took great strides as she ran. She knew every moment was critical. Crossing Baker Street, she barely looked in each direction, just took a chance and ran across the side street, keeping her eyes on the ambulance. Paramedics were rushing out of it by now, carrying equipment into the boutique.

"No!" Sue shouted. "Over here!"

She reached the door of the boutique. She looked inside.

Paramedics were bending over a girl on the floor, as the hairdresser in her white smock and a customer with wet hair huddled watching in a corner.

Sue saw the girl's face.

It was Heidi.

Billy's girlfriend.

Behind her, she heard the whine of another ambulance. She glanced up the street. This one stopped outside the Yellow Bird.

Sue pulled back, staggering out onto the sidewalk.

What is happening?

And why do I feel as if I am the cause of it all?

She was afraid. Suddenly, she was very afraid.

36

"She's in here," Father Ortiz said, gesturing for Ginny to follow him.

Ginny took a deep breath. Passing through the kitchen in the deSalis's small house, she inhaled the fragrance of lilacs. It was far too late in the season for lilacs, but when Ginny rounded the corner into the living room, she saw that dozens of vases were filled with the aromatic purple flowers.

"Strangest thing," Father Ortiz told her over his shoulder. "A day after Bernadette came home from the hospital, all the bushes in the yard began sprouting new flowers."

Ginny's eyes came to rest on the young girl seated on the couch. She seemed to be expecting Ginny. Her hands were folded in her lap clasping a rosary. She was dressed in a long white dress, and her dark hair was tied back in a long ponytail. On either side of her on the couch sat her parents.

"Bernadette," Father Ortiz said, "this is the lady I told you about. She is a good lady. Her name is Virginia Marshall." He smiled. "Her parents named her for Our Lady."

Bernadette smiled.

"Hello," Ginny said. She didn't extend her hand. She just looked down at the girl, who looked back at her with interested eyes.

"Hello," Bernadette replied, and gave her a bright smile.

This was not the little girl she had expected to find. Gayle Honeycutt had described a girl who was near comatose. Father Ortiz had told Ginny that for days Bernadette had been mostly unresponsive. But now she was alert and smiling.

"Bernadette," Father Ortiz was saying, "I was hoping you'd let Dr. Marshall ask you some questions."

Pierre deSalis seemed anxious. "You sure, Father?" he asked. "You sure this won't upset her? I don't want Bernie getting upset. She's coming along so much better now . . ."

"I won't upset her," Ginny said. "I just want to hear whatever she might want to tell me."

"And she has a great deal to say!" Mrs. deSalis told her, eyes wide, almost crazy. "She has a message from Our Holy Virgin Mother. A very important message!"

"Please, Dr. Marshall," Father Ortiz said. "Sit down." He gestured to the chair opposite Bernadette. Ginny took a seat.

"Is that so, Bernadette?" Ginny asked. "Do you have a message you want to share?"

"Yes, I do," she said clearly and evenly, her hands still folded in her lap. "Our Lady told me about you, Dr. Marshall."

"Did she?" Ginny asked.

Bernadette nodded. "She told me one would come along who could help. Who needed to hear the message." She smiled broadly. "And that one is you."

"Well," Ginny said, "I'm all ears."

"First, I need to ask," Bernadette said. "Are you a believer in Our Lord Jesus Christ?"

"That depends on how you define believer," Ginny replied. "I respect the teachings of Jesus. I think Jesus was a great teacher, with a great message for mankind."

Bernadette smiled. "But was he the Son of God?"

"Certainly as much as Buddha, or Mohammad, or as much as you and I are children of God," Ginny said. "If you are asking whether I believe in Jesus' divinity—well, I'd have to be honest and say that I have no way of knowing that."

Bernadette's smile only grew. "I am pleased that you are honest, Dr. Marshall. That is very important. Our Lady said that the one I could trust would be an honest person. And I can see that you are. You don't simply say what you think I might want to hear in order that I might talk to you."

"I won't lie to you, Bernadette, just as I'm sure you won't lie to me."

The girl closed her eyes, then opened them again. "I see that you teach about the sacred feminine."

"Yes. Have you read my book? Has Father Ortiz told you about my work?"

"Not a word," Father Ortiz told her.

"I have read nothing about you," Bernadette said. "I didn't even know your name until you just walked in. But I know what you teach, Dr. Marshall."

Ginny shifted in her chair. "Tell me more."

"When I saw the Blessed Mother, she did not look the way I had always imagined her," Bernadette said. "You know what I mean. Dressed in blue, surrounded by a halo, hands clasped in supplication, demure and saintly." The girl laughed—a laugh far older than her years. "Do you know how she appeared to me, Dr. Marshall?"

"Tell me, please."

Bernadette smiled. "She was riding a lion, and she carried a bow and quiver, and a sword."

Ginny's mouth opened, but words did not form right away. "Ishtar . . ." It was the only word she could utter.

"Was that her name?" Bernadette seemed to be asking a genuine question. "I did not know her name . . ."

"Ishtar," Ginny repeated. "The great Mother Goddess of the ancient Babylonians, invoked for battles."

"Yes, Our Lady was dressed for battle, for indeed a battle awaits," Bernadette told her. "A few nights later, she appeared again to me in my dreams. Only this time, she rode a tiger, and she had eight arms—and in each hand, she carried a weapon."

"Durga," Ginny said, stunned. "The Mother Goddess of the Hindus. The destroyer of demons . . ."

"Precisely," Bernadette said.

"Then you didn't have a vision of the Virgin Mary," Ginny told her. "You had visions of ancient goddesses . . ."

"But what is it that you teach about the sacred feminine, Dr. Marshall?" Bernadette asked, leaning toward her almost imperceptibly.

Suddenly, Ginny understood. "That ultimately they are all the same," she breathed. A chill ran through her body.

Bernadette smiled. "When I look at her over there," she said, nodding across the room, where a statue of the Virgin sat surrounded by lilacs, "I see her as clearly as I did when she appeared to me. Though we cannot see it, her sword is still strapped to her side. I am confident of that. She is not as submissive as she appears. Like any mother, she will fight for her Son—for *all* of her children."

Ginny was stunned. It seemed impossible that this girl should know so much. If Bernadette was telling the truth—if Father Ortiz was telling the truth—then this was the most radical Virgin sighting Ginny had ever encountered.

"But tell me," she said, leaning forward toward Bernadette, her hands imploring. "What was the message that she gave you? What is this battle you say is approaching?"

Ginny steeled herself for the answer. This was the part that Father Ortiz had seemed most anxious about. The answer to this question was what he most feared.

Just then the phone rang, shattering the silence. Everyone—except for Bernadette—jumped. Mr. and Mrs. deSalis looked at each other, startled and annoyed by the interruption, yet neither moved to answer it. The phone rang again. And then again. And again.

Finally, Mr. deSalis stood and rushed across the room into the kitchen. In a hushed voice, he answered the phone.

They could hear him in the living room. "Mike?" His voice was a whisper. "What's wrong with Mike?"

"And so," Bernadette said, overhearing, a terribly sad look crossing her face. "It begins."

From the kitchen Mr. deSalis shrieked, "No!"

His wife stood now and hurried into the other room as well. Father Ortiz followed.

Bernadette motioned to Ginny to draw near.

"I will tell you now," she whispered. "For you must hear Our Lady's message. The time is late. We must begin."

Ginny stood and moved over to sit on the couch beside Bernadette, in the spot vacated by Mrs. deSalis.

"Tell me," she said.

And so Bernadette did.

37

"He dropped right over there," Marjorie was telling Miles and Perry Holland. "I came out of the kitchen and Mike was on the floor, and Wally was doing CPR."

"Was it a heart attack?" Perry asked. "It would be strange in a kid so young, but not unheard of."

Marjorie shrugged. "Well, that's what they're still trying to find out."

Miles brought a forkful of hash browns to his lips. "Kid's been in the hospital now for four days," he said just before taking a bite. "You'd think they'd figure out what was wrong with him by now," he added, mouth full.

"Well," Marjorie said, leaning on her elbows on the counter, "what's really odd is that at the same moment, down the street at the boutique, one of Mike's classmates was having a similar attack. She just dropped, and she's been in the hospital now the same amount of time he has."

"Who's that?" Perry asked.

"Heidi Swettenham. The girl Billy Honeycutt dumped for that Wilbourne girl."

Perry paused, holding his cup of coffee in midair. "What Wilbourne girl?"

"Oh, I don't remember her name." Marj started wiping down the counter. "I'm getting old. What's the use of being the town gossip if you can't remember names? Susan . . . Sue . . . something."

A little bell went off in Perry's head. "Not Sue Barlow?"

"Yes," Marj said, nodding. "That's the one. Know her?"

Perry shook his head. "No. I just gave her a warning for speeding, that's all."

He and his father exchanged glances. Perry had filled Miles in about the daughter of Mariclare Barlow attending Wilbourne this year. But they'd both dismissed any thought of following up on the coincidence, since Mariclare Barlow had returned home safe and sound twenty years ago. Unlike the other girls, she didn't remain missing or turn up murdered and dismembered.

Even if what had happened to her on campus was surely horrendous enough.

But now . . . there was Sue Barlow's name again. Perry couldn't help thinking that there was something about her that he needed to find out. But what?

"Okay, Marj," Miles was saying, pushing back his plate. "It's time for us to start our shifts. Thank Wally for another superlative high-calorie breakfast."

Marjorie cleared away their plates. "I'm just glad to see you cleaned up for a change, Miles. That scruffy look went out with Don Johnson."

Miles clapped Perry on the back. "The boy here is keeping me in shape."

Perry smiled. He was pleased that his father seemed back to his old self. He was eating better, taking care of himself. Working together on this case seemed to have galvanized him. Without telling the state cops in charge of the investigation—big lard-asses who were doing nothing to find Bonnie Warner—

Perry and Miles had trudged down to the basement of the town hall and begun pouring over old death records.

It hadn't taken them long to find something. "Lookee here," Miles had said, his voice low. "Millicent Berwick. October 18, 1887. Cause of death, multiple stab wounds. Found on the Wilbourne campus."

"And here," Perry had said. "Just a week later. Phoebe Singleton. Wilbourne student. Cause of death." He'd gulped. "Severed head."

"Every twenty years or so," Miles had said, awed.

They had been right.

But what did it mean?

They headed out of the diner. Perry zipped up his nylon jacket. A sudden cold wind had whipped up, swirling leaves in the street.

"Early winter this year," Miles observed, shivering.

The trees were a riot of color, mostly oranges and yellows. There was nowhere more beautiful than upstate New York in autumn, Perry's mother used to say. The morning sun sparkled through openings in the leaves.

"I'm going back to the station to make a few calls," Perry told his father.

Miles nodded. "I'll take the first patrol around town. Make sure nobody's robbing the bank or slaughtering any more pretty co-eds."

Perry smiled. "I'm glad you're feeling better, Dad."

Miles shrugged. "It's been good spending these last few days with you, son. And I think your mother is happy about it, too."

"You never stop thinking about her, do you, Dad?"

Miles's smile faded. "No, I don't. But lately . . ." His smile flickered again. "Lately, it's been getting easier."

Perry gave him a thumbs-up. He watched as his father

slid behind the wheel of his patrol car and drove off. They exchanged a wave. Then Perry hopped into his own car and drove back to the station. He nodded at the secretary, checked to make sure he had no messages, then closed the door to his office and sat down on his desk.

He looked down at the file marked BARLOW, MARICLARE.

He opened it and read it again. It still had the power to sicken him.

He'd found a number for her parents in New York. They'd be Sue Barlow's grandparents. He'd thought about just calling Sue herself and asking her a few questions about her mother, but he suspected she didn't know what had happened to her mother on campus twenty years ago.

So he picked up the phone and called New York.

"Hello?"

"Mrs. Barlow? This is Deputy Sheriff Perry Holland from Lebanon, New York."

The line went quiet.

"Mrs. Barlow?"

"Has something happened to Sue?" the woman asked in a small voice.

"No. ma'am. Your granddaughter is fine, as far as I know." He could understand the woman's fear when she heard his voice. Had she gotten a similar call twenty years ago?

"Then why are you calling?"

"Mrs. Barlow, you may be aware that a girl has gone missing from Wilbourne. In fact, three girls are missing, although that hasn't been publicly acknowledged yet."

Perry knew that within a day or so the state police were planning on holding a news conference to disclose the names of Joelle Bartlett and Patricia Lewis. The families were exerting pressure, and word had leaked out on the Internet. He decided telling Mrs. Barlow about it now wouldn't matter—

in fact, it could only help to explain the reasons behind his call.

"So I'm looking back into the files of the department, and I'd like to ask you a few questions about your daughter Mariclare."

"But Mariclare came home." The woman's voice was icy.

"Yes, I know, but I thought she might be able to tell me a little about what happened while she was missing—"

The woman on the other end of the phone line made a clucking sound in her throat. "She simply ran away from the school. There was no kidnapping or anything like that! She ran away and came home to us."

"Still, I'd like to talk with her," Perry said. "I mean, about what happened to her on campus . . ." His voice trailed off, unable to articulate the words. "There was some thought here in the department at the time that it might be related to the other girls who went missing and then were killed. That the same perpetrator who—"

"You'll need to talk with my husband, and he's not home," Mrs. Barlow said tersely.

"Well, actually, it's your daughter Mariclare I'd like to speak with . . ."

"Mariclare is dead!"

Perry was silent for a moment. "I'm very sorry, Mrs. Barlow. I didn't know that. Could you tell me when she died?'

"Years ago. Many years ago."

"When your granddaughter was very young?"

"Right after she was born."

Perry was doing subtraction in his head. A horrible thought came over him.

"Mrs. Barlow," he said. "If you can't speak with me, maybe you'd give me a number where I can reach your husband?"

"He's a very busy man. He doesn't have time—"

"Mrs. Barlow," Perry interrupted. "Did you hear what I said?

Three girls have gone missing from the campus where your granddaughter is living. We suspect there may be some kind of pattern going on. Every twenty years—"

"That is absurd!"

Perry was losing his cool. "Are you not the least bit concerned about your granddaughter, given that twenty years ago your daughter was brutally raped on the very same campus?"

There was no hesitation in the old woman's reply. "Wilbourne takes good care of its girls," she said.

Perry couldn't believe his ears. "I'm sorry to have bothered you, Mrs. Barlow. I'll be calling your husband at another time."

She hung up on him.

She might call the state police and complain, Perry knew. But at the moment, he didn't care. He knew now his father was one hundred percent right.

They were indeed on to something.

Perry's eyes dropped back down to the file spread out on his desk. He read again the paragraph at the top of the report.

Screams were heard from Room 323 in Bentley Hall repeatedly, but the girls on the floor did nothing because of ghost stories about the room. It's campus lore that the room is haunted. At ten minutes past midnight, Mariclare Barlow emerged from the room, according to three eyewitnesses, girls who lived on the same floor of the dorm. She was naked, bleeding profusely from the vagina, and her face and arms were battered and scratched. She seemed in a state of shock. She told the three eyewitnesses that she had been raped, but did not say by who. No intruder was seen either entering or leaving the room. The eyewitnesses called for the dorm monitor, Mrs. Annette Oosterhouse, but by the time Mrs. Oosterhouse arrived, Mariclare Barlow had locked herself back in her room, telling the other girls she had to "go back to him." But when Mrs. Oosterhouse opened the door, there was no one in the room.

38

"Hey, Danny," Miles called from his police car window. It was Saturday, and the kids were riding their skateboards on the sidewalk in front of the post office. "Careful you don't run that thing out into the road."

The boy nodded. He was probably eight years old by now, Miles reckoned. The sheriff could remember when Danny was born, and when his older brothers and sisters were all born. He had a good memory. That's why he was a good sheriff.

"Whatcha gonna be for Halloween?" he asked Danny.

"Spider-Man," Danny shouted.

"Good for you," Miles said. "He was always my favorite."

Halloween. Miles couldn't believe it was almost here. How fast time went. He rolled up his window and continued his cruise down Main Street. He'd put an extra deputy on for Halloween night. There was occasionally some vandalism— soaping car windows, smashing pumpkins, that kind of thing. Nothing too bad. Lebanon was a quiet, well-behaved town.

Except every twenty years or so.

Why hadn't anyone made a big stink about this pattern before? One of the selectmen, one of the town officials?

There were ladies over at the Lebanon Historical Society who made it their life's business to know every scrap of history that happened in this town. They could rattle off statistics for every presidential election back to Lincoln—but no one had ever mentioned that every twenty years, a handful of college girls went missing or were found brutally murdered. Of course, every time it happened, there was a big fuss, with a town meeting being held the last time it happened, with feminists rallying against the rape of Mariclare Barlow and pressuring Wilbourne to beef up security. Miles remembered the rally—his wife had taken part, in fact—and the newspaper coverage was still there, for anyone to read, on microfilm. But within a few weeks, the town stopped talking about it, and then it all just seemed to slip from collective memory. Even Miles's memory—at least for a time.

"Not anymore," he whispered to himself as he drove, his eyes gazing out at the golden trees that lined his vision. "I'm not forgetting anymore."

He turned down Laurel Grove Road, a narrow, winding, mostly dirt road that cut from the center of town through the woods to the Wilbourne campus.

What was it? What went on at that college? Some kind of ritualized killings? Some secret group? Some kind of sect?

And why did everyone forget?

Who had the kind of power to cause that?

"State cops would call me nutso," Miles said out loud.

But he wasn't crazy.

He knew that much.

Even as he saw the figure on the side of the road, he remained convinced of that.

It was a girl, riding a bike—except she had no head.

"Dear God," Miles breathed, slowing the police car to a stop.

Then he heard the roar. He bolted from the cruiser, gun

drawn. The sound came from behind him. He turned to see what it was—

And a hand—more like a talon—gripped his throat. It lifted the sheriff off the ground.

Miles, in excrutiating pain, looked down to see his assailant.

What he saw was indescribable.

Not human.

Not animal.

Not—of this world.

It was darkness—darkness come to life—that was the only way Miles could perceive it.

Miles screamed.

"Scream all you want," the demon told him. "It is music to hear."

But there was another sound, too. That same roar. The creature that held him seemed concerned by it. Miles was able to see in the periphery of vision what it was—

A lion.

Dear God . . .

And a woman beside it, armed with a sword.

The thing holding Miles hissed, snapping the sheriff's neck before disappearing.

The last conscious thought Miles had before plunging to the earth was that he was dead—but that the lady with the lion had saved him.

And brought him home to be with his wife.

39

Among the materials that Sheriff Miles Holland had assembled as part of his investigation over the last few weeks were various accounts of the history of Wilbourne College, culled from newspapers, catalogs, and school yearbooks.

He had suspected that none of them told the full story.

He was right.

The Wilbourne School for Young Women was founded in the fall of 1879. The brainchild of Sarah Wilbourne, the college was established to educate young Lutheran women—in order for them to make contributions not only to American society, Mrs. Wilbourne explained to her church benefactors, but also to the world community. The college's motto, penned by Sarah Wilbourne herself, was *Service with integrity, courage, and intelligence.* It would all be wrapped in a devout Christian theology, which, Mrs. Wilbourne told her students, was what allowed them to serve at all.

Sarah had originally come to Lebanon by train from Manhattan in 1877, scouting locations for the school she was determined to found. She was favorably impressed by Lebanon's location, its access to the railroad, and the acres of apple orchards surrounding it. Even more impressive, she told town leaders, were Lebanon's deep Christian traditions. After she purchased a huge plot of land just outside of the city limits—Mrs. Wilbourne was a wealthy society widow from Manhattan—the architects and contractors began building. Local children often gathered to watch the majestic marble and brownstone buildings rising up from the verdant hills.

The school opened in 1879 with just thirty students, but with many more high hopes. Miss Wilbourne instilled impeccable standards. Students were required to maintain at least a B average, or they were asked to withdraw. The faculty consisted of a few Lutheran ministers and many more devout laymen whom Sarah herself had personally recruited. When Sarah died forty years later, she left her considerable fortune to further endow the school and to ensure its growth and continued excellence.

Since then, thousands of young women had walked past the bronze statue of Sarah that had been erected on the main lawn. Few of them ever even glanced at the image of the woman who started it all, who made it possible for them to be at Wilbourne College. When Wilbourne's board of trustees voted in 1921 to go sectarian, leaving the Lutheran theology in the past, Sarah's legacy seemed outdated to some. Still, her name was always invoked at graduation ceremonies with the reverence generally reserved for the holy saints in Catholic churches.

Yet Sarah Wilbourne had been anything but a saint—and the notion that she might be would have made her laugh scornfully.

Her origins were murky, lost in the mists of time. One would-be biographer, a woman named Kathryn Lang, had done her best to track down Sarah's past, and although her notes were donated to the Lebanon Historical Society and therefore preserved for Miles and Perry Holland to see, Lang herself had died in an automobile accident before she was ever able to write the book. Lang had been unable to discover where or when Sarah had actually been born, but found newspaper articles that documented her marriage, when Sarah was just nineteen, to the widower and wealthy financier Silas Wilbourne. She was described as an orphan and quite beautiful, with porcelain skin, wide blue eyes, and thick silky blond hair that she wore long. Silas Wilbourne, thirty years Sarah's senior, had discovered her working in a jewelry shop in Brooklyn when he came in to buy a diamond bracelet for his daughter. He was entranced by the girl's beauty, and returned to the shop the next day to purchase a pocket watch for himself. He returned a third time the following day, he said, for a very special jewel: Sarah herself. He invited her to join him for dinner.

Before long, New York society tongues wagged about the beautiful young nobody with whom Silas Wilbourne was smitten. He escorted her to plays, parties, and fancy society dinners. He bought her expensive clothing and jewelry. Some society ladies presumed Sarah had become Silas's mistress, but Kathryn Lang believed Sarah's devout Christian faith would have prevented her from sexual relations with Silas, and that she was holding out to become the next Mrs. Wilbourne.

Kathryn Lang was right about the facts, wrong about Sarah's reasons.

For, in fact, there was no evidence that Sarah was a Lutheran—or any kind of religious woman—until she began soliciting the church for money for her school. Wilbourne was a high Episcopalian himself, and they married in an Episcopal church. But Silas had little interest in religion, rarely attending services, and Sarah, as the dutiful wife, simply followed his lead. Indeed, in everything, Sarah seemed to subjugate herself to her husband's will. She seemed determined to prove that those who were skeptical about their marriage were wrong. She had managed to overcome the objections of her husband's children (both of whom were older than she was) and New York society, all of whom warned Silas against this mésalliance. It was only a matter of time, everyone reasoned, before Sarah tired of her older husband and the marriage descended into the depths of Shakespearean tragedy.

But they underestimated her—a mistake many made throughout Sarah's lifetime.

Sarah Wilbourne was no one's fool. She was very well aware that her entire future depended on how she conducted herself in her marriage. She didn't care about being snubbed by the Astors or other society women. If she and Silas weren't invited to dinners or parties by the so-called "best" people in New York, she'd put up with it. She didn't care if her stepchildren openly despised her and slandered her all over the city. Their treatment of her turned their father against them, which was perfectly fine with Sarah—but she also understood her own conduct must be above reproach. No minor flirtations with any man, nothing that could possibly be misconstrued or built into something more serious. Her husband was madly in love with her and denied her nothing. Sarah intended to keep it that way.

And so Silas showered his young wife with gifts, and eventually he liquidated his business—at a huge profit—in order to spend more time with her. They toured Europe, Egypt, and India—and everywhere they went, observers couldn't help but notice their devotion to each other. Men tried, from time to time, to seduce the pretty Sarah, but she cut them off with scarcely veiled contempt. As the years passed and she continued to be a devoted wife, the women who disapproved of her slowly started to come around. When Silas died, leaving her a very wealthy woman, Sarah grieved very publicly, and those around her took notice. His two children, horrified to discover they'd been cut off without a penny in his will, tried fighting her in court, desperate to wrest some of the family fortune away from her, but by now, society had rallied around Sarah. "Had my husband wanted them to have something," Sarah told a reporter, "he would have provided for them. But he wanted them to have nothing, and simply because he is now dead does not mean I will cease abiding by his wishes." A story circulated that Sarah, after the court ruled in her favor, approached her stepchildren, opened her purse, and handed each of them each a quarter. "That is the last cent of your father's you will ever see," she said before turning on her heel and walking away.

Now she was finally free to fulfill what she revealed had been her dream all along: the foundation of Wilbourne Collge. She sold the big house on the Upper West Side, and built a house for herself in Lebanon—the house that eventually became the dean's residence. Her only concern now was the school.

The town of Lebanon never knew quite what to make of the wealthy benefactress suddenly in their midst. The ladies of the town tried to befriend her, and while Sarah was always polite, she kept her distance. No one, for example, was ever invited into her house; she gave no luncheons or parties of her own, except for whatever functions the school might host. The only people who usually saw Mrs. Wilbourne were the students and faculty of the college. Curious townspeople who tried to glean information about her and what went on in her house made no headway with her servants, who were always brought up from Manhattan, never hired locally. In the place of actual information, gossip and rumor tried to fill the gaps. Mrs. Wilbourne, some whispered, had taken a lover: a groundsman from the school perhaps, or—horror of horrors!—one of the unmarried lady faculty members.

The fact that Sarah, still a youthful, pretty woman in her

early thirties, never remarried caused many eyebrows to rise. At a lunch raising money for the Ladies' Christian Charities, one guest asked her about it. With a slight smile, Mrs. Wilbourne replied, "The college is my husband, and the only husband I need." But around town, stories of guests from "the big city" were common—strange-looking men and women who arrived in Lebanon on the train or by coach, dressed all in black, their eyes always averted from the locals. Still, the gossip never reached a boiling point, for after all, Sarah Wilbourne's money had helped the town, and not only by founding the college. She built the town library, funded a new city hall building on the square, and always wrote substantial checks for whatever charity approached her.

But no one knew what really went on in her big house on campus. No one ever really knew Sarah Wilbourne, and that was how she preferred to keep things.

One clipping found among Kathryn Lang's notes was most curious, however. A visitor to the college in 1904 had congratulated her on the occasion of Wilbourne's twenty-fifth anniversary. Describing the event in *Collier's* magazine, the writer reported a strange smile on Mrs. Wilbourne's face after he commented on the generation of "good, Christian girls" the school had turned out. "It was almost," the writer observed, "as though she were laughing at the suggestion—as though there had been another motivation for building that college."

Kathryn Lang had underlined that observation and highlighted it in yellow, probably just a few days before she died.

Sheriff Miles Holland had also read it with a keen interest.

No one knew that Sarah Wilbourne had been impressed with Lebanon for reasons that had nothing to do with its pristine location and access to the railroad. No one had made

the connection between Sarah Wilbourne and those long-ago
city fathers who'd been driven out of Boston with threats of
burning at the stake.

When Sarah Wilbourne died, she left her mansion to the
college as a residence for the dean. She also left specific and
stringent instructions on the hiring requirements for any future dean—having handpicked the ones who served during
her lifetime. Her plans for the college stretched well into the
future. She died quite contented, knowing she had succeeded
far beyond what she—and the others—possibly could have
hoped.

40

The news of Sheriff Miles Holland's death unnerved Ginny.

She had liked Miles. Liked him a great deal. And, unlike the lazy state police, he had been aggressively looking into the disappearance of Bonnie Warner—not to mention those of Joelle Bartlett and Tish Lewis. Ginny had been horrified to learn that two more girls had gone missing from the campus, and that the administration had kept the news from the faculty and students. But Dean Gregory had announced the dire truth yesterday, confirming reports that had been circulating on the Internet. Increased security had been added all around the school, but already some parents had insisted that their daughters return home now.

Ginny sat at her desk in her office, reading again the report in the newspaper about the sheriff's death. His neck broken. Bruises on his body as if he'd been dropped from a great height. State cops speculated he had been climbing a tree, maybe to see something. But that made no sense. His body was discovered in the middle of the road, far away from any tree,

"What the hell is going on here?" Ginny whispered to herself.

That's when the words of Bernadette deSalis came back to her.

It's absurd, Ginny told herself again. *It's impossible. A delusional girl, made more so by a fanatic mother.*

Even the sightings of other female divinities seemed proof of that. Bernadette must have been read about the goddess traditions, despite her insistence that she had not. She had read about goddesses like Ishtar and the others—and worked them into her delusions. Father Ortiz believed she was telling the truth, of course, but it was the job of a priest to believe. It was the job of an historian to doubt. To play the skeptic.

Ginny was trying.

Trying very hard to dismiss everything the girl had told her.

But if what Bernadette said was true . . .

Ginny shivered.

She would definitely interview her again. This was certainly a case for the book. But at the moment, the deSalis family was distraught about the health of yet another child, a teenaged son who'd suffered an apparent heart attack and who was still languishing in the hospital up in Senandaga. Ginny would check in with Father Ortiz sometime tomorrow, and see when it might be good for her to come back and finish talking with Bernadette.

Her phone rang. It was Dean Gregory's secretary, asking her to hold the line for him. Ginny had been dreading this call.

"Ginny!" came the Dean's voice, trying to sound warm and friendly. "How are you?"

"As well as I can be," she replied coldly, "knowing you deliberately withheld information about two missing students."

"Now, Ginny, it was done to prevent panic. Look at what's

happening now, with all these girls packing up and leaving before the semester is over."

"Can you blame them?"

Gregory scoffed. "Look outside. Do you not see all the added security?"

There were indeed security guards, big burly men in green uniforms, stationed all over the campus. Many of them were armed. "How can students learn in this kind of pressure, this kind of anxiety?" Ginny asked the dean. "I hope you'll allow the girls who leave to take incompletes, and not fail their courses."

The dean sighed. "All of that is being discussed."

"I just think it's only fair—"

"Ginny, I didn't call to debate this issue. I called to find out what you had decided about our conversation the other day."

She gave him a small laugh. "You mean whether to scrap my curriculum and submit to the censorship of the board of trustees?"

"I see you are still being stubborn. Let's talk on Monday, shall we, in my office?" Gregory's voice was so damn smug. "First thing in the morning? Bright and early?"

He had threatened her last time; Ginny felt a dose of his own medicine might be a good thing. "With all the negative publicity being given to your administration over the news of the missing girls," she said evenly, "I think it would be very unfortunate timing for a well-known teacher to start a fuss about academic freedom." She let the words sink in. Gregory was silent; he had no comeback. Ginny didn't think he would.

"Yes," she told him, "I'll see you Monday morning. Bright and early."

He hung up on her.

Ginny laughed.

41

"Look at them down there!" Malika shrilled, staring out the window at the security guards posted at various intervals between Bentley Hall and the next dorm. "I feel like I'm in Nazi Germany."

Sue was growing impatient with her roommate's critiques of the security presence, but did her best to ignore her. Her mind was worrying about too many other things—plus she had a geology mid-term to study for.

"This is overkill," Malika continued, and Sue cringed at her poor choice of words. "I mean, everywhere you look there are guards packing weapons. What happens if one of these guys cracks—if he thinks some deliveryman is the kidnapper and starts shooting?"

Sue couldn't take any more. She slammed her book shut. "Oh, come on, Malika. Three girls are missing. What did you expect the administration to do?"

Malika glared at her. "For one, not to lie to us! Telling us Joelle and Tish had just left school!"

"They were trying to prevent a campus panic."

"So instead they install a fascist state in our midst!"

"Fascist state! Good God, Malika, that's such bogus rhetoric!"

"Bogus?" Malika's eyes were ready to pop out of her head. "You've read the new regulations. We can't leave the dorms after five in the afternoon except to go to class. No visitors, period. And we can only go into town on weekends."

"Seems perfectly reasonable to me, given we're faced with an enemy we can't predict and know nothing about."

"Jesus Christ, Sue. You sound like George Fucking Bush, curtailing liberties in the guise of the so-called 'war on terror.' "

"President Bush was just trying to protect us!" Sue shouted—surprising herself since she'd never been a fan of Bush, and had listened with deep suspicion whenever her grandfather had praised him.

Malika sneered. "What's gotten into you?"

Sue looked away from her. "Maybe these girls going missing has opened my eyes. I'm just tired of limousine liberals like you spouting off against the people in authority who are just doing what is best for us."

Malika seemed not to believe her ears. "Did you just call me a limousine liberal?"

Sue stood to face her. "Yes, I did. I'm tired of people like you coming to this country and taking advantage of all our freedoms and then bad-mouthing our government."

Malika was speechless. She turned away, then spotted something on Sue's desk. A book. She grabbed it, turned back to Sue, and held it in front of her face.

It was Joyce Davenport's *Smear*.

"This is where you've been getting all that bullshit," she charged. "You've been reading this and it's warped your mind."

"No," Sue said, snatching the book away from Malika. "I don't agree with everything she writes. But yeah, okay, maybe some of it makes sense."

Yet even as she spoke the words, Sue realized she didn't really believe what she was saying. In fact, she was as pissed as Malika about the administration withholding information from them, and then slapping down the rigid rules about leaving campus. It had greatly affected her relationship with Billy—at a time when she was already worried about whether they'd hit a snag. But for some reason, she wanted to provoke Malika, to play the devil's advocate, to get her riled up and pissed off . . .

"You are not the same girl who came here two months ago," Malika grumbled, turning away from her again.

Sue didn't answer. She was saved from having to try to think of a comeback by a knock at the door. "Come in," Malika shouted.

It was her pudgy friend Sandy. "Malika," Sandy said, rushing into the room, eating an ice-cream sandwich, "some of the girls want to organize a protest against the administration and they wondered if you—"

"Why does it always have to be me?" Malika shouted at her. "It's always Malika they come running to when they want to get something done! Can't anybody on this fucking campus ever do something for themselves?"

Sandy looked surprised. "Well, it's just that you're so good at it . . ."

"Jesus!" Malika shrieked. "Look at how you're dripping that goddamn ice cream all over my bed! And my sweater laying right here—" Malika snatched it up. "Chocolate all over it! Damn you, Sandy!"

The girl looked crestfallen. Sue knew she idolized Malika. "I'm sorry," she said in a little voice.

"You shouldn't be eating that anyway! I thought you were going on a diet! Do you want to stay fat all your life? Is that what you want, Sandy?"

Her friend just looked at her, then burst into tears and ran out of the room.

"Jesus," Malika grumbled to herself.

Sue said nothing, pretending to be reading her geology book.

Malika sat down on the edge of her bed. "That was rotten of me," she said, to herself more than Sue. "I shouldn't have taken out my anger on her."

Sue remained silent. She didn't like how she was feeling. She didn't like that she had to suppress a smile that was forming on her lips.

"I'm going to go apologize," Malika said.

"Why should you?" Sue found herself saying. "She came in here trying to get you involved in one more thing when you're already so busy. And these fat girls can be so inconsiderate, the way she slobbered all over your sweater. It's almost as if they're jealous of pretty girls like you and me, always trying to ruin things for us. Don't you think?"

Malika stared over at her. Sue smiled.

"I don't know you anymore," Malika finally said, and got up and left the room.

I don't know myself, Sue thought.

She stood and went to the mirror. *I still look the same,* she thought. *But I don't feel the same.*

The fight with Malika had left her invigorated, thrilled. She felt high. She knew her challenge to Malika had made her roommate quick to snap at Sandy. And now Sandy was likely to snap at someone else.

I caused it, Sue thought, grinning at herself in the mirror. *I set the conflict into motion . . .*

Suddenly, she felt sick. Without warning, she started to cry.

The feeling of exaltation was replaced with shame.

"I don't feel that way," she said, remembering her words about "fat girls." She'd never thought of herself as pretty. She cried harder remembering how she'd called Malika a "limousine liberal." What good was name-calling? It was just a cruel tactic—one used for shock and attention.

Yes, indeed, Sue thought, looking over at the book on her bed. *Just like Joyce Davenport.*

"Why am I acting like this?" Sue asked out loud.

I'm scared, so I'm acting strange, she told herself. *I'm scared about three girls who have gone missing. Three girls I connect myself to, in one way or another. I told Joelle and Tish I'd seen the face at the window. And Bonnie—I'd dreamed of her the night she was attacked.*

And then there was Heidi. Billy's ex. *I had been thinking terrible things about her, filled with jealous and rage toward her—and then she collapsed.*

Just like Lori Powers—who skied into a tree after an argument with me—and Melissa Hardwick—who died after I vowed to "do something to her."

I wished both girls dead.

I killed them.

"No," Sue said. "That's crazy."

And Mike deSalis . . . Sue hadn't wanted to go see him at the diner. She was wishing all the way over there that he'd be gone. She kept stalling Billy, teasing him, forcing him to window-shop—all in the hope that Mike would be gone by the time they got there.

And then Mike, too, collapsed . . .

"I'm thinking crazy," Sue said out loud again.

But she'd just been acting and talking crazy, too, saying those things to Malika.

It's like all I wanted to do was stir up trouble . . .

"I've got to concentrate," she said, opening her textbook again. But within minutes she glanced up from the page and was looking over at her laptop. She chewed on her lower lip. Her e-mail screen was open, but there was nothing new. Nothing from Billy. Nothing more from Joyce.

Ever since the day with Mike, Billy had been distant. Sue was worried that maybe she did something wrong that day. *Should I have stuck around at the emergency room? Should I have ridden with Billy up to the hospital in Senandaga?*

Or did Billy just decide to dump me for no good reason at all? He had certainly moved on from Heidi to me without an apparent second thought.

She found herself getting angry with Billy for not communicating with her, for not answering her e-mails. *He can't treat me that way,* she thought. *I won't stand for it!*

But she calmed herself. How quick she was to get angry lately.

"It's not like me," she said, slamming her textbook shut once again. She didn't think she'd get any studying done tonight.

Reaching across her bed for her cell phone, she hoped in vain that there would be a text message for her. Sometimes she didn't hear the beep. But there was nothing new. She hit the speed-dial button where Billy's number was stored, and it rang a few times before his voice mail picked up. She flipped the phone shut.

Stop this craziness, she told herself. *If he wanted to see me or talk to me he'd call. Let it go and forget about him.*

But in that same moment, her phone rang. She saw it was Billy's number.

"Hey," he said when she picked up. "I see you just called."

"I was just worried about you, that's all."

He grunted.

"How's Mike?" Sue asked.

"No change," Billy replied. "Listen. Would you go with me to see him at the hospital tomorrow? I know you said in your e-mail you can't leave campus, but tomorrow's Saturday . . ."

"We can leave on weekends if we get a pass," Sue said.

"So will you go with me?"

Sue hesitated. "Have you been up to see him since that night?"

"No. His parents weren't letting visitors in." Billy's voice sounded horrible. Empty. Dried up. "But now they think maybe it'll help him if he knew I was there. Not that he's conscious. But they say sometimes, even in comas . . ." His voice broke.

"I'll go with you," Sue told him.

"Thanks, Sue. I just can't make the drive . . . by myself."

He told her he'd call in the morning, then they said goodbye. No niceties, no lovey-dovey stuff.

Sue sat holding her phone after hanging up, just staring straight ahead.

Then, all at once, she leapt from her bed and hurried to her computer. She quickly typed out an e-mail.

I need to talk to you—soon. It can't wait.

Then she hit SEND—to Joyce Davenport.

42

Across campus, not far away, a weak, hungry Tish Lewis finally heard the familiar creak of the stairs.

It had been days since the figure had last come to bring her food. Maybe weeks. Time was blurring together for her. She was losing her grip on reality—perhaps what they wanted.

She had been primed to strike. To fight back. Had they known? Could they read her mind? Was that why they stopped coming?

Why had they stopped feeding her?

Tish's cell was now filthy with the smells of her own body. Water had begun dripping in from somewhere above. The place reeked, and Tish was cold.

But still alive, she told herself. *Still alive.*

The key was in the lock. Tish did her best to keep her wits, to stay strong.

The iron door swung open and the red-robed figure came inside.

Was it Mrs. Oosterhouse? If it was someone else—someone stronger—Tish wasn't sure she'd have much of a chance.

"Think we'd forgotten about you?" the figure asked.

It was rare for it to speak—but its words reassured Tish. It was Oostie.

"Here, slut," she said, placing in front of Tish a plastic tray holding a piece of crusty bread and a glass of water. "Don't die quite yet. We've come up with another plan for you."

Tish devoured the bread and gulped down the water. The red-robed figure lifted the pail, now overflowing with Tish's waste.

"Filthy slut," the figure said as it passed Tish, closing the door after exiting.

Sudden terror struck Tish. Might this be my last meal? If so, there'd be no need to return with the pail. And then no chance for me to fight back—

In the days she'd been left alone, Tish had kept her sanity by sharpening that broken handle. She'd unhook it from the pail and scrape it against the brick wall. It was now sharper than most knives. It would do the job—if she was given a chance.

To her great relief, the door creaked open again, and the figure returned with the pail. It set the pail down, then turned once more to Tish.

In the split second it took for the figure to bend down to retrieve the now-empty tray and glass, Tish leapt—grabbing the pail and swinging out with it, whacking it against the figure's head. Stunned, the figure staggered against the wall, giving Tish just enough time to unclasp the handle, and stab it deep into the figure's gut.

Mrs. Oosterhouse let out a bloodcurdling howl of pain.

With great effort, Tish gripped the handle and cut upward. It wouldn't be enough just to stab her. She had to cut—inflict as much damage as she could. She had planned it all out in those long hours in the dark.

"You . . . .slut!" Oostie shrieked, as the sharp metal handle sliced through her tissue, piercing her stomach.

Warm blood covered Tish's hand.

"Why was I kidnapped?" Tish demanded. "Why did you kill Joelle?"

"Help me," Oostie tried to scream, but her voice was too weak. She was sliding down the wall where Tish had attacked her.

"I swear to God I'll rip out your guts," Tish told her. "Tell me what's going on in this house! Tell me how to get out!"

"You can't escape," Oostie managed to say.

"You were planning to drink my blood, you freak! Just like you drank Joelle's!"

"Not yours," Oostie said. "Not after I confirmed the stories about you were true. You're no virgin! Your blood is no good to us!"

With a sudden, merciless yank, Tish pulled the handle out of Mrs. Oosterhouse's belly, causing a terrible popping sound. The chubby dorm chaperone fell hard to the floor on her big fat ass.

"But you were still going to kill me," Tish said. "You and Dean Gregory. And who else? Is the whole administration involved?"

"You can't escape," Oostie said. "Help!" She tried to scream again. "Somebody help—"

"I'll put an end to that," Tish said, and with one well-aimed swipe, she cut Oostie's throat, severing her jugular. Blood spurted forth like an opened fire hydrant. Oostie's mouth moved a few more times, but no sound came out. Then her head sunk down on her chest.

Holding tight to the bloody handle, Tish stepped out of her cell. She was in a basement. Old furniture was covered with drop cloths. Metal file cabinets rusted against a far wall. The small windows that were set high in the walls were papered over with cardboard.

Tish found the stairs.

She had no idea where they led, or who might be upstairs waiting for her. But she began to climb, the sharp pail handle that had saved her life held out in front of her.

43

All the way up to the hospital that next morning Billy barely said a word.

Sue had offered to drive, but like the typical boy he was, Billy had insisted on taking his mother's Toyota. Sue had tried making conversation, but Billy would just grunt. *Why am I even here?* she thought a number of times.

When they pulled into the parking garage of the Senandaga hospital, Billy turned off the ignition, placed his head down on the steering wheel—and started to cry.

Sue was stunned.

"Billy," she said, reaching over and touching his shoulder. "What's wrong?"

He looked at her with the tears just pouring from his eyes. "What's *wrong*?" he asked. "Everything is wrong. And it's all my fault."

"Your fault?"

He nodded. "My best friend is in there, probably dying. But not just him. Heidi is in there, too. And she's probably dying as well."

"Billy," Sue said, stroking his hair. "How can that be your fault?"

"Both of them were upset. Upset with me! You saw Heidi with me just minutes before she collapsed. She was all worked up and crying. I caused her heart attack!"

"They haven't diagnosed it as a heart attack," Sue reminded him. "They don't know what's wrong with Heidi. Or Mike. You had nothing to do with—"

"Mr. Bingham told me that Mike had been upset that I was late. He said Mike felt I hadn't been around much for him—even though I knew what he was going through, worrying about his sister . . ." Billy sobbed again.

"Billy," Sue reasoned, "you can't blame yourself."

"It's me!" Billy cried. "I caused this!"

"It's not you," Sue said.

It's me.

But blaming herself was equally crazy. Neither of them had the kind of power that could cause spontaneous illness in people. To imagine they did was pure insanity.

"Doctors are speculating there may have been something going around at your school," Sue said. "That's why both Mike and Heidi were struck."

"They don't know what's wrong with them! Why they're both in comas!"

Sue smiled kindly. "Do you really think you can cause people to fall into comas?"

When she said it that way, Sue even convinced herself that her own feelings of guilt were ridiculous. Billy just sighed, looked away, and wiped his eyes with his sleeve.

"Let's go in," he said,

Senandaga General Hospital wasn't much of a hospital by any stretch of the imagination. There was a wing with rooms for patients and an emergency room, but other than instant care—resuscitations, stitching up wounds, and setting broken bones—most patients had to be sent on to one of the bigger hospitals in the county.

Sue's eyes squinted as they entered, the fluorescent lights nearly blinding her. Billy told her he'd be okay, that she could wait for him in the lobby as he went in to see Mike. Sue gave him a quick kiss. She wondered if he'd go to see Heidi as well. They didn't discuss that part.

If he does, there's no problem, Sue told herself. *I won't be jealous.*

I can't be jealous.

Look at what happened last time.

After Billy had headed off down the hall, she put a dollar in the soda machine, hitting the button to dispense a can of Diet Coke. She found a seat opposite an old man who appeared to be sleeping. Sue popped the lid of her Diet Coke and took a sip, idly pulling a battered copy of *People* magazine onto her lap. Brad and Angelina were adopting another baby.

Ten minutes later, her eyes lifted from the magazine. It was strange—one of those intuitive moments when you just know someone is looking at you. Sue's eyes met those of another girl, several years younger than she was and sitting opposite her in the place where the old man had been sleeping. Sue hadn't been aware of the man leaving, nor the girl arriving.

"Hello," the girl said to Sue.

"Hello," Sue said back.

The girl had thick dark hair that reached all the way down her back. She wore a white blouse over a pair of jeans. Her hands were in her lap, holding rosary beads.

"Are you Sue?" the girl asked.

Startled, Sue nodded. "Yes. Yes, I am. And you are?"

"Bernadette deSalis, Mike's sister." Bernadette gave her a smile.

"Oh," Sue said. "Billy must have told you I was out here."

Bernadette didn't confirm it, just smiled again.

"How is your brother doing?" Sue asked.

"He's going to be fine."

Sue sighed with relief. "Well, that's great. What does the doctor say?"

"Oh, nothing. But I know Mike's going to be fine."

Sue studied the girl sitting opposite her. Goose bumps rose inexplicably on her own arms. There was something about Bernadette—something Sue found unsettling.

Get away from her. Now.

She shrugged off the instinct, but still—

This was the one who was sick. Who'd been in the hospital herself. No one knew what was wrong with her . . .

"It seems odd, doesn't it?" Bernadette asked.

"I'm sorry," Sue said. "What seems odd?"

"That not long ago it was I who languished in the hospital, and Mike came to see *me*." Bernadette smiled again. That smile was freaking Sue out. "And now it's the other way around."

She read my mind, Sue thought.

"But Mike's going to be fine. I just wanted you to know that."

"I'm . . . I'm glad."

Bernadette laughed, a sweet tinkling sound that set Sue's teeth on edge. "I know you were there when he collapsed, so I know you must be particularly worried about him. But I can assure you, Sue. Mike will be fine. And so will Heidi Swettenham."

Get away from her now.

Sue stood, knocking the magazine from her lap to the floor. "I'm—I'm going to get some air," she said.

"It was nice to meet you, Sue," Bernadette said, extending her hand.

Don't take her hand.

But that's rude. Billy would be furious if he learned I snubbed his best friend's sister . . .

She reached over. Her fingers touched Bernadette's.

And time seemed to stop.

Sue could hear her own breathing, but her vision blurred, just before everything went completely dark. She opened her mouth to scream, but no sound came out. Her throat was dry, and all of the strength seemed to drain out of her body. The only thing she could make out was Bernadette's face. The whole room had vanished in blackness, but the girl's face still filled Sue's vision.

Bernadette's eyes were closed, her mouth slightly open, and there was a humming sound coming from her throat, a humming that Sue could barely hear over the sound of her own lungs working, rasping as they drew in and expelled air. A light seemed to surround Bernadette's head. The girl's long dark hair began to rise into the air as the light intensified, blinding Sue in its intensity.

You won't win, Sue found herself thinking, screaming silently at the girl. *I'm stronger than you are—*

And then her hand disengaged from Bernadette's, and the room returned to normal.

Sue staggered, her knees buckling. She sat down hard on the floor. Vaguely she was aware of Bernadette getting up from her chair and approaching her.

She forced herself to look over at the girl. Bernadette had knelt beside her. Her eyes were closed, her lips moving. Sue tried to get to her feet, but her head spun and she sank again to the floor.

She's praying, Sue realized in amazement, looking at Bernadette. *She's praying over me!*

A nurse's aide had rushed over when she saw Sue fall. "Are you okay?" she asked.

Sue looked up at her. She was young, African-American. "Help me up, please," Sue said. The aide gripped her by the arm and helped her stand. "I guess I fainted."

Bernadette was standing now, too. "Poor Sue," she said. "You must be really worried about Mike and Heidi."

"You come on back with me," the aide was saying. "I want to check your blood pressure."

"No, really, I'm fine," Sue said, her eyes locked on Bernadette.

"I think you should let me check—"

"No!" Sue snapped. "I'm fine! Please leave me alone. I just fainted, that's all. I haven't eaten much this morning."

"I can't force you," the aide said. "But maybe you ought to get a sandwich from one of the vending machines."

"Please," Sue said, gentler now. "I'll be fine."

Sue sat down, the aide moving away, looking back over her shoulder at her, while shaking her head.

Bernadette sat beside Sue.

Sue stared at her. "What did you do to me?" she asked in a low, hard voice.

"I didn't do anything." Bernadette looked at her with innocent dark eyes. "Maybe your blood sugar is low—not only from lack of eating, but from worry."

Sue said nothing. She just stared straight ahead, wishing Billy would come back.

Bernadette leaned in to her. "It's not your fault, you know."

"What are you talking about?" Sue snapped. "Why do you think you know so much about me?"

Bernadette smiled kindly. "You—you really don't know, do you?" She peered at Sue, her eyes narrowed. "No, you don't." She shook her head. "It doesn't make any sense to me." She cocked her head as though she were listening to someone, and then nodded. "That makes it even more wrong. Yes, you're right, I do understand. I will pray for her."

She's insane, Sue thought, her eyes widening. *She's listening to voices no one else can hear.*

"You don't have to be afraid of me." Bernadette moved to touch Sue's arm, then seemed to think better of it, and stopped. She clasped her hands back in her lap with her rosary beads. "Maybe I can even help you, Sue."

"I don't need any help," Sue told her.

"No one wants to harm you, Sue. That's not a part of the plan."

"Plan?"

She's crazy, that's it, she is completely insane. The best thing to do is to get as far away from her as possible.

"God's plan." Bernadette shrugged. "We are all just pawns, you know. He moves us around in His infinite wisdom. That's why He sent the Holy Mother to speak to me—that's why He allowed you to be born, despite the great danger to you and all the rest of us. It's not for us to understand."

Sue was fed up with her. "What the *hell* are you talking about?"

"You can't help what you are, after all." Bernadette went on as though Sue hadn't interrupted her. "And now I understand somewhat better than I did before. You don't know—you really don't know."

"I'm going out to the car to wait for Billy," Sue said, standing.

"They never told you the truth, did they?"

Sue glared down at her. "Who?"

"Your grandparents." Bernadette's eyes widened in sympathy. "Oh, you poor thing. When the Holy Mother told me about you, I couldn't understand how you could do these things, how you could live with yourself. But now that I understand, it's so much worse." Her eyes filled with tears. "Because you don't know. They're just using you—just as they used your mother."

"You don't make any sense!" Sue shouted.

"And yet they are victims, too, I suppose. The true villain is the darkness that comes into their hearts, the darkness sent by . . ." The girl looked at Sue with strange, wide eyes. "I call him Lucifer Morning Star. Does the name mean anything to you, Sue?"

"You're crazy."

"Lucifer Morning Star. Who one night met your mother and . . ."

"You crazy bitch, stop saying these things!" Sue shouted, covering her ears with her hands. "What do you know about my mother? My mother is dead!"

"No, she isn't," Bernadette said sadly. "I'm so very sorry, Sue."

Sue turned and ran out of the room. She couldn't listen to any more of this. She ran down the hallway and out into the parking lot, but her stomach heaved before she could make it to the car. The Diet Coke came spewing forth from her mouth and her nose, burning the insides of her nostrils. She sank to her knees on the pavement and started to cry.

She doesn't know what she's talking about, Sue told herself over and over again. *She's a crazy girl! That's why they had her locked up!*

But how did she know about my grandparents?

What lies did they tell me?

They told me that my mother is dead.

Sue stood, bracing herself against the wall.

But my mother is alive.

44

Perry Holland loosened his tie and forked a french fry into his mouth.

Marj was standing behind the counter watching him eat with eyes filled with sympathy. She still had on her Sunday best—her dark navy blue dress with the short rope of pearls at her throat. She hadn't changed from the funeral. Neither had Wally, who'd simply doffed his sport coat to whip up Perry's chili burger and fries. They'd insisted Perry come back with them to the Yellow Bird and eat. He'd gone days without a good meal. Every day, in fact, since his father was murdered.

"That's it, Perry, you eat up now," Marjorie told him.

"It was a nice service, wasn't it?" Perry asked.

"Sure was. So many people turned out. This town loved your father."

Perry nodded.

The sheriff's death had sent shock waves through Lebanon. Miles Holland had been popular, and for days afterward, his death was the prime topic of conversation around town. Discussion of things like Thanksgiving plans, the high school football team's loss in the state playoffs, Heidi Swettenham's miraculous recovery—all of those conversational gambits were forgotten as the townsfolk talked breathlessly about the sheriff's tragic death. Those who knew him best were in shock. "What was he doing climbing trees on Laurel Grove Road?" they asked. "I'd heard he was losing his mind." This only seemed to confirm it.

Perry knew now that his father's mind had never been clearer. That was what made his death so difficult. Perry had been prepared for his mother's death, watching the cancer slowly diminish her for months, the chemotherapy brutalizinbg her as much as the disease itself. When she had finally stopped fighting and slipped away, it had been a merciful release. Perry had mourned and wept for her, but at that time he'd also had Jennifer to hold him at night until he went to sleep.

But his dad's death—this was out of the blue, completely unexpected. Perry had fallen into a kind of black hole in the days leading up to the funeral. He'd stopped answering the door, forcing well-meaning friends and neighbors to leave covered plates for him on the front step. Casseroles and pies, cobblers and lasagnas—more food than Perry could ever possibly eat in a year. He had no room left for all of it in his refrigerator. He'd started dumping it into his trash can, letting the dirty plates pile up in his sink.

Like father, like son, he thought ironically.

This morning Marjorie had come by, wearing her imitation pearls under her dirty gray coat. Perry had been sleeping on the couch in his underwear, and Marjorie stood over him with a stern expression. "Get showered and dressed," she said, removing her coat and tossing it on the couch. "I'm not going to let you be late for your own father's funeral. I'll make some coffee."

"I can't go," Perry protested.

"I said get in the goddamned shower." Marjorie walked

over and cupped his chin in her right hand. "You look like hell, Perry. Your father deserves better."

Perry didn't have the energy to argue with her, so he got up off the couch and walked into the bedroom. He turned the shower on, and looked at himself in the mirror. *You do look like hell. You need to shave and shower and get your act together.* He turned on the faucet and washed his face thoroughly, splashing it with hot water. He walked back into the bedroom and got out the black suit he'd bought at the JCPenney's in Senandaga for his mother's funeral. He laid it on the bed, and found a pressed white shirt, still in the bag from the dry cleaner. *I haven't worn that shirt since Mom's funeral.* He felt hysteria rising in him, but he closed his eyes and fought it back down. He walked back into the foggy bathroom and climbed into the shower.

When he'd stumbled back out into the kitchen, there had been a plate of scrambled eggs and bacon waiting for him on the dining table. And now here she was, cooking for him again. The funeral had passed in a blur. Nothing felt real anymore to Perry.

Marjorie seemed to be reading his thoughts. She reached across the counter and took his hand. Hers was rough and red, her fingernails chewed down below the quick.

"We never expect death, Perry," she told him softly. "Even when someone's been ill, like your mother, we always hope that somehow we can cheat it, that it won't happen if we pray hard enough or hope hard enough. But it's a part of life. We don't want to think about losing the people we love, because it's painful. But pain—" Marj hesitated, squeezing his hand harder. "Pain is also a part of life. It's why we go to church, why we read the Bible. We try to make sense out of a senseless world."

Perry felt his eyes burn.

"Go on now," Marjorie urged. "Eat your lunch."

He took a bite of his burger, then set it down. His fries were soaking in a pool of ketchup. Truth was, he just wasn't hungry.

"That was a nice bouquet that Jennifer sent," Marj said. "I think she still has a thing for you, Perry. I don't want you to be all alone and moping now. You should call her—"

"I'm sorry," Perry said, blinking. "Call who?"

Marjorie shook her head. "You weren't listening to a word I said."

"I'm sorry." Perry sighed. The funeral had been hard. Saying good-bye to Dad, watching them lower his casket into the ground, a military trumpet player sounding "Taps."

"It's okay, hon," Marj said. "It's going to be a while before you're back to feeling like yourself."

Perry doubted he'd ever feel like himself again. What was worse than his grief, though, was the roiling anger down in his gut. *Dad wasn't climbing any trees! He was dropped! He was picked up by something and dropped! He was murdered!*

A couple of the state cops who were investigating the Wilbourne girls' disappearances had come up to Perry and told him they appreciated all the work Miles had done on the cases. "Then why not follow up on his leads?" Perry barked. They promised they would, but Perry didn't believe them.

And would anyone find Miles's killer? Perry doubted it. It hadn't even officially been ruled a homicide. No fingerprints. No sign of a fight. Just some crazy theory that Dad had climbed a tree and fallen—

Why the fuck would he be out climbing trees on Laurel Grove Road?

Perry knew why his father had been on that road. He was driving out to the college. Because that's where the answer was—the answer to who kidnapped those girls. And that's where Perry knew he would find the same answer to the question of who killed Sheriff Miles Holland.

Perry stood. "Thanks for the food, Marj, but I have to go."

"You hardly ate anything! Where do you have to rush off to?"

"I've got a case to solve."

The blood was suddenly pulsing through his veins again. A rush of adrenaline seemed to propel him off the stool.

I need to find out who killed my father!

Marjorie wrung her hands. "Sweetie, the state cops are working on it—"

"The hell they are!" Perry calmed down, managing a smile for her. "Thanks for all your concern, Marj. But I've got someone I just have to see."

He was out of the diner before she could make another objection.

Perry sped out of town, driving past the spot on Laurel Grove where Dad's body had been found in the middle of the road. If he fell out of a tree, he'd have had to leap to land that far out in the road.

No. It had been no fall. Someone—or something—lifted Dad off the ground, snapped his neck, and dropped him. That's what the coroner said. Just because the state police could come up with no plausible way that could have happened didn't mean it wasn't true.

At the Wilbourne gate, Perry flashed the guard his badge, and was waved through.

He'd planned on calling Dean Gregory and making an appointment to talk to him. But why give him time to prepare? Better to catch him without warning.

Of course, since it was Saturday, he might not be in his office. If that were the case, Perry would try him at his house. Or find out where he was—and wherever the fuck he was, he'd confront him there.

Turned out, however, that Gregory was easy to find. He was working on a Saturday. Lots of shit had been going down on the campus of late. Perry suspected he was in his office working on a little damage control.

"I'm sorry, Dean Gregory isn't seeing anyone today," the secretary told Perry. "I can give you an appointment Monday, Deputy . . ."

"This can't wait," Perry said, pushing past her into Gregory's office.

The dean was at his desk, poring over a pile of folders. He looked up as Perry entered, clearly annoyed.

What a weasel face, Perry thought, discarding any notions about innocent until proven guilty. *This guy is implicated in all of it. I'm certain.*

"Deputy," Gregory said, folding the papers he'd been looking at and placing them in his top drawer. "How sorry I was to hear about your father."

The secretary rushed in behind Perry. "Sir, I tried to tell him you were busy . . ."

Gregory waved her away. "It's okay. I always have time for the law."

The secretary shut the door behind her.

"Sit down, Deputy," Gregory said, making a grand gesture with his hand.

"I prefer to remain standing," Perry told him. "What I have to ask you won't take long."

"All right." Gregory smiled up at him, his rat's teeth showing from between his thin lips. "Ask away."

"How do you explain the pattern of deaths and disappearances on this campus every twenty years?"

The smile didn't leave the dean's face. "Well, actually, it hasn't quite been every twenty years. Sometimes it's been nineteen, sometimes twenty-one . . ."

"How do you explain it?" Perry asked, raising his voice impatiently.

"I can't. Can you? After all, you're the law."

Perry frowned. "I just find it a very odd coincidence—"

"Well, so do I. That such a small, seemingly tranquil town should harbor a killer . . ."

"Don't blame the town!"

Gregory sat back in his chair. "Well, surely you're not blaming the college. After all, we've been the victims here, and the local and state police have never apprehended a culprit." He narrowed his beady little eyes at Perry. "I should think I should be barging into *your* office and accusing *you*."

Perry kept his cool. "Is that what you think I'm doing? Accusing you?"

"Well, I should hardly know for what." Gregory sighed. "These killings date back over a hundred years, since almost the very beginning of the college." He made a great show of sadness. "When I think of those poor girls, so many over the years . . ."

"And it's not mentioned in any of your literature."

Gregory gave him a wry smile. "Would *you* publicize such a thing, Deputy? I'm just waiting until some enterprising reporter finds all this out and writes a sweeping history of the tragedies here. Enrollment will plummet."

"Yet no enterprising reporter ever *has* written such a story," Perry said. "Don't you find that odd?"

"Yes," Gregory said, nodding. "Yes, I do."

"Why do you suppose that is?"

"I'm not sure. But I suppose it's inevitable."

"My father was one of the few who even remembered that such things had happened here before," Perry told the dean. "When he jogged people's memories, they'd recall the murders—but only if he reminded them. People just don't seem to remember them on their own."

"Strange, isn't it?" Gregory gave him a sympathetic look. "I suppose it's human nature to try to block out such tragedy from our minds."

"Well, I think the community would benefit from knowing the full details. If there is a connection in these cases—
even dating back over a century—I think we need to bring it
out into the open."

Gregory eyed him coldly. "Are you saying you're going to
the press?"

"I think that might be wise. If anyone knows anything,
they can come forward."

Gregory held his gaze. "I wish you wouldn't, Deputy.
Think of what it would do to this school."

"Yes," Perry said. "I am thinking about that."

"Your father had given some of his data to state police
investigators," Gregory told him. "They asked me about it. I
told them the little I told you. And they agreed it was best
not to dredge all this up. I would hate for you to reprimanded
for going over their heads in this investigation."

"Don't worry about me, Dean," Perry said. He gave him a
terse smile. "Thanks for your time."

He could feel Gregory's eyes on him as he turned around
and walked out the door.

Outside, the sun was doing its best to warm up a chilly
day. Most of the leaves were now off the trees. The campus
was blanketed in orange and gold.

Perry was heading back to his car when he heard someone
call his name. He turned. An attractive woman, mid-forties.
"Deputy Holland?"

"Yes," he said. He didn't recognize her.

The woman approached him and extended her hand.
"Dr. Virginia Marshall. I just wanted to give you my condolences. I recognized you from the funeral."

He shook her hand. "You were there?"

"Yes. I was very fond of your father. A good man. He was
very good to me when I first came here to Lebanon."

Perry smiled. "Yes, I remember you now. You wrote that book—"

Dr, Marshall sighed. "Yes. *That book*. The one that stirred up all that controversy."

"I remember." An idea came into Perry's mind. "What was the name of the reporter who wrote that piece?"

"You mean sensationalized it?"

"Yeah," Perry agreed. "What was her name?"

"Gayle Honeycutt."

"Right." Perry made a mental note.

Dr. Marshall looked intently at him. "Deputy, I know how hard your father was working to find the truth behind the disappearance of those missing girls. And now his death . . ." The professor shivered. "Something very strange is going on, and I hope you will keep alive his passion to find out what it is."

"You have my word on that, Dr. Marshall."

"I'm glad to hear it." She smiled. "My condolences again."

"Thank you."

Perry watched her walk away. Then he slid in behind the steering wheel of his car and drove off campus. Once through the front gates, he picked up his cell and dialed 411.

"Lebanon, New York," he said to the operator. "The number for Gayle Honeycutt."

45

Not surprisingly, Sue couldn't sleep that night.

Malika was still angry with her, and was spending the night in Sandy's room. Sue didn't blame her for being angry.

What's happening to me? she kept thinking, tossing and turning in her bed. *Why did I say those things to Malika?*

And what did that girl mean, that my mother is alive?

Billy had found her slumped by the car. Tenderly, he'd helped her inside. He'd explained that Bernadette was indeed a little touched in the head. She'd imagined the Virgin Mary had spoken to her. He'd encouraged Sue not to put any stock in what she had to say.

That still didn't explain why Sue had blacked out when the girl had touched her hand.

So much was unexplainable.

The face at the window.

The terrible headache.

The near certainty Sue felt that she was responsible for so much that had happened here.

And the most terrifying of all—the split personality that seemed to overtake her at times . . .

What is happening? she thought again, staring at the ceiling.

She had tried calling her grandparents earlier that night. She'd gotten their answering machine, and hadn't left a message.

What would I ask them anyway? Have you been lying to me all these years? Is my mother alive?

At least she could be grateful that she and Billy seemed back on track. He'd been so sweet, so caring, when he'd found her crying by the side of the car. He'd stroked her hair, told her that she meant the world to him . . .

Even though he'd been up to see Heidi, and had stroked her hair, too.

He hadn't told her that. Sue just *knew*. She could see it all very clearly, just the way it had happened. Mike had seemed to respond to Billy's presence, possibly even offering a small smile. At least Billy had thought so anyway. Encouraged, he'd gone down the hall to see Heidi. Her parents were only too glad to let him in. "Anything that might awaken her," Heidi's father had said. Billy had stood over the girl, stroked her hair, told her he wanted her to get well. He never told any of this to Sue. But she knew it all as a fact.

Lying there, thinking about it, seeing Billy touch Heidi's hair, she did her best to control her jealousy. Her jealousy scared her.

So much scared her now.

Especially Joyce Davenport's one-line e-mail back to her.

Dearest Sue, we will speak very soon. And then everything will make sense to you.

What did she mean?

What did Joyce Davenport know about her? About everything that was happening here?

She wasn't aware that she was falling asleep, that sheer exhaustion was overtaking her nerves and her fear. She thought she was wide awake, in fact, and walking down the hallway on the third floor, heading to Room 323, where voices were calling to her through the door.

Sue, come join us . . . We're having a party . . .

The hallway was cold, far colder than it ever was, and Sue could see her own breath in front of her. Across from Room 323, she saw that the door to Joelle and Tish's room was open, and they were inside, smiling, smoking some pot. They waved at her. "Go on," Joelle told her. "The door's open. We've been inside Room 323 and we had a *blast.*"

But Sue didn't want to go inside. She wanted to run. She started to cry.

They're just using you . . .

Bernadette's voice.

Sue stifled a sob as she reached the door. Despite wanting to run, she reached out for the knob, which was hot to the touch.

Bearing the pain, she turned the knob, and pushed the door open.

And looked into her mother's face.

She screamed and sat up in bed.

Tish Lewis sat there, staring at her.

"No!" Sue screamed again.

"Be quiet!" Tish demanded. "If they hear you, we're both dead."

Sue concentrated on the filthy, blood-caked girl sitting in front of her.

"Everyone's been looking for you," Sue said, remarkably calm.

Tish seemed frantic. "You're the only one I can trust. The only one I know for sure isn't in on this."

"In on what, Tish?" Sue asked, recoiling just a bit from the rank odor that permeated the girl's ragged clothes.

"They're a cult," Tish said. "Some kind of blood-drinking cult. Like vampires."

Sue gave her a small smile—a smile that felt strange even as she felt her lips making it. "Now, that sounds quite outrageous, Tish."

"I know. But it's true! You must believe me, Sue. You came to our room because you had seen the face at the window of that room. You were frightened, so you can't be part of them. Who knows who else is involved? Maybe everyone! Joelle called me—she went into that room, she said they were all part of it—"

Sue managed to stand. Tish followed her.

"Joelle went into Room 323?" Sue asked. "What did she see?"

"She saw enough that they killed her! They drank her blood!"

"Really now?" Sue asked.

"You've got to believe me. They were going to kill me, too. They kept me locked in a room in the basement of the dean's house. I managed to break out—I killed Oostie—Mrs. Oosterhouse—she was part of it, too!"

"Oostie? Harmless little Oostie?"

"They weren't going to drink my blood, though," Tish said, her eyes moving around the room crazily. "The fact that I wasn't a virgin saved me! I knew getting laid was a good thing!" She laughed wildly. "But I got out! And we'll get them! We'll get them all!"

"How did you ever get in here?" Sue asked, backing up toward her desk.

"I snuck out of the dean's house and hid in the bushes all day. Then I saw Malika. She was sitting on a bench and her purse was open. When she got up to talk to someone I snuck over and took her key."

Sue smiled, another strange sensation as it crossed her face. "Is that why Malika didn't come to the room tonight? And here I thought she was angry with me."

"I hid in the dorm basement and waited until it was really dark before slipping up here." She approached Sue with eyes filled with insanity. "You don't know who's working with them! I couldn't afford to take any chances."

"Of course not," Sue said.

She turned, picking up the phone on her desk.

"Who are you calling?" Tish asked in terror.

"Don't worry, Tish. I know exactly who can help us."

"You do? Who?"

Sue was silent. She waited for someone to pick up on the other line. When she heard "Hello," she said, "Hello, this is Sue Barlow. Could you come right away?" Then she hung up the phone.

"Who did you call?" Tish asked, backing away from her now. "Who can help us?"

"You'll see, Tish." She gave her a thoughtful glance. "Why don't you use the bathroom to wash up? You look terrible."

"No," Tish said, mumbling to herself. "I shouldn't have come here. I should have tried to get over the campus wall. But all those guards everywhere . . ."

"Now, now, don't start sounding like Malika," Sue said. "They're there for our own protection."

"Don't you see?" Tish cried. "They can't protect us! They're all involved. Dean Gregory! His wife! Oostie! The nurse from the infirmary!"

Sue blanched a little when Tish said that. *Nurse Coch-rane . . .*

Tish was ranting as if she'd completely lost her mind. "When I was in that cell, I heard so many voices I knew! Professor

Adamson—you know, the guy who spits when he talks in biology class! And the woman with the jet-black hair who works at the library! And that new lady from the board of trustees! And the guy who teaches American film! So many, Sue! So many!"

"So many," Sue repeated.

She glanced out the window. She saw movement below. She smiled.

"We've got to get out of here!" Tish shrieked. "You don't know what they'll do to us."

"Tish, calm down. I've called someone who will help."

"Who?" Tish was screaming at her now, grabbing her by the shoulders. "Who can help us?"

Behind them, the door opened.

Tish spun around.

"Noooooo!" she screamed.

Dean Gregory, in a green satin smoking jacket, entered, followed by three of his leather-clad guards.

"Thank you for calling, Miss Barlow."

Tish turned on Sue, eyes wide. "You're one of them! They got to you! I shouldn't have trusted you!"

"Well, Miss Lewis," Dean Gregory said, looking at her kindly as the guards surrounded her. "We've all been so worried about you."

"Let me go!" Tish screamed, as the guards took her by the arms.

Sue smiled over at Gregory. "Everyone will be very relieved to know she's alive."

"Indeed," the dean replied.

Sue looked down at the card on her desk, the one with Gregory's private number that he'd given her in case she ever needed him.

"No!" Tish screamed again, as the guards began moving her out of the room.

Dean Gregory smiled again at Sue and gave her a little bow. "Thank you, Miss Barlow. We're so very grateful to you."

"Of course," Sue said, returning his smile.

One of the guards had clamped a gloved hand over Tish's mouth as he took her out into the hall. A little rough, Sue thought, but there was no use in waking up the whole dorm.

After they left, Sue got back into bed. She looked at her clock. 3:15 A.M.

She had no trouble falling back to sleep. All her previous anxieties were gone. Everyone would sleep better now that at least one of those poor girls had been found.

46

On Monday morning, Ginny steeled herself for what she was certain would be the final confrontation between Dean Gregory and herself.

"Sit down, Ginny," the dean said, gesturing to one of the plush leather chairs in front of his desk. "Would you like some coffee? Some tea?"

She took a seat and looked at him. He seemed glowing, as if he were the happiest man in the world. He seemed—sated. That was the word that came to Ginny. As if he'd just indulged himself in a full-course breakfast and sat back now in his chair, full and satisfied. She had no idea what gave Gregory such a glow this morning, but whatever it was, she didn't like it.

"Let's cut to the chase, shall we?" she said. "I'm not about to hand over my curriculum to the board of trustees for their stamp of approval. So let's figure another way to proceed."

"And what might that be?"

"Under these conditions, I can't continue teaching at Wilbourne."

He seemed surprised. His small eyes opened wide. "What are you saying, Ginny?"

"That I'd like to take a year's sabbatical, starting at the end of this term. I want to finish my book, and figure out where to go from there."

He gave her a mock smile of regret. "And might you decide to leave us at the end of that time?"

"A new board will be in place by then," she reminded him. "I'll make that decision after I get a chance to hear from them."

She knew, in some ways, it was a retreat. She could cause a big stink, as she'd threatened to do. But it wouldn't serve her needs. For right now, what she wanted to do was *write*. Meeting Bernadette deSalis had given her the jump start she needed. And last night, Father Ortiz had called her out of the blue, asking that she visit the deSalis home right away. Bernadette wanted to speak. She'd had an experience visiting her brother at the hospital, and she wanted to share it with Ginny.

What an interview that had been. For the first time in many years, Ginny felt galvanized to write. She felt inspired. Thanks to the visions Bernadette claimed to have experienced, the book had come back to life.

Ginny just needed the time and space to write it. And as much as she loved her students, the pressures from Gregory and the stress of the missing girls—exacerbated by the administration's mishandling of it—were distractions she didn't need.

"Well," she said. "What do you say?"

"You know that sabbaticals are applied for well in advance. This is quite sudden."

She gave him a tight smile. "What do you say, Dean?"

He raised as his hands as if to say, "You win."

Ginny stood. "I'll have the paperwork on your desk by this afternoon. I expect that I will still be allowed to work with any students who have signed up for long-term projects with me."

"I'll have to consult with the board about that—"

Ginny shot him a look. "That's not negotiable. Some of these girls had expectations I'd be on campus next semester. I want them to feel they can still contact me by phone or e-mail."

Gregory again made the hand gesture of supplication. "Very well, Dr. Marshall. Whatever you say."

She nodded, and strode out of his office.

And *that,* she hoped, would be the last time she ever had to look upon that weasel's face.

Heading back to her own office, Ginny knew she wouldn't return to Wilbourne. Gregory was going to keep stacking the board with his people. She wouldn't want to remain in a place that clamped down on freedom of thought and expression. They'd mutually agree to terminate her contract one year from now.

But at least she'd get a year to finish her book without worrying about a paycheck or health benefits.

Hazel looked up at her as she came through the door to her office. "That reporter has been trying to get ahold of you," the secretary said. "I told her I didn't know when to expect you back."

"Gayle Honeycutt?"

"That's the one." She handed Ginny a note with Gayle's number. "Should I tell her you're still out if she calls back?"

"No," Ginny said, remembering Perry Holland asking about her the other day. "Put her through."

Inside her office, Ginny was happy for the first time in weeks. She began packing up her files into boxes. She'd never liked Wilbourne, not really, nor the town of Lebanon. The students had mostly been great, and she'd met some good folks like Miles Holland. But mostly, she had always felt like an outsider here. It was time to go home.

To Hammond. To the house that had been her parents'— in a quiet little town where Southern hospitality, not New

England rigidity, was a way of life. She could write her book there, and move on with her life.

It didn't take long for Hazel to buzz in with word that Gayle Honeycutt was calling again. Ginny took the call.

"You're hard to reach," the reporter said.

"What can I do for you, Gayle?"

"For one thing, you can tell me what's going on with Bernadette deSalis. Can you vouch for her? Was this an authentic sighting of the Virgin Mary?"

"No comment."

"Oh, come on, Dr. Marshall!"

Ginny sighed. "The family has asked that I not speak to reporters."

"You owe me more than that! I put you onto the story!"

Ginny felt herself getting angry. "I don't owe you anything, Gayle. In fact, a third party brought me in to meet Bernadette."

"Well, I'm writing the story anyway. It's all over town. If you don't like how it turns out, then it will be your own fault."

"Just make sure you spell 'No comment' correctly," Ginny told her.

Gayle laughed. "But what do you make of all these other sightings? Isn't it odd that they're taking place at the same time?"

Ginny was stuffing files into boxes, but now paused, the phone cradled between her shoulder and her ear. "What other sightings?"

"You don't watch the news, do you, Dr. Marshall? It's been all over the wires. It's like an epidemic of Virgin sightings. Ohio, Arizona, Oregon, Tennessee—and in Canada, too. And Mexico—the place you told me you studied—Los Zapatos."

"There's been another sighting in Los Zapatos?"

"Yeah, and in a whole hell of a lot of other places, too."

Gayle laughed. "Maybe you'd care to make a comment now, Dr. Marshall?"

"No," Ginny mumbled, clicking the mouse on her computer to get to the Yahoo! News screen. Sure enough, Gayle was right. A headline read, RASH OF MARY SIGHTINGS CALLED MIRACULOUS OR MASS DELUSION. Clicking on it, Ginny read the lead: "All over North America, reports of sightings of the Virgin Mary have left the faithful rapturous and skeptics charging fraud . . ."

"Dr. Marshall?" Gayle was asking. "Are you there?"

"Yes, I'm here . . ."

"Well, there's another story I'm working on, and maybe you would want to comment on that."

Ginny was deeply engrossed reading the article online. All of the cases involved young girls who claimed, like Bernadette, to have been told a fearful secret by the Virgin . . .

"What story is that?" she asked distractedly.

"These missing girls from Wilbourne. Perry Holland called me yesterday and told me there's a pattern going back decades. Every twenty years, give or take, a handful of girls from the school either disappear or wind up dead."

Ginny's attention snapped back to the telephone conversation. "What?"

"I remember a couple of them. I was just married, and I remember this Wilbourne girl, Margaret Latham, who was found dead and dismembered, all her blood drained out. Strange how I'd forgotten about it until the deputy reminded me. He has more information to give me."

"So you're saying, it happens on a regular basis?"

Gayle sighed. "That's what Perry Holland says. He has reports of cases going back over a hundred years, he says. I haven't seen all of his evidence yet, so I can't say for sure whether he's right. But I do remember Margaret Latham—

and that other girl, too, the one who got raped in her dorm around the same time. It was all over the news back then. How could I have forgotten? Mariclare Barlow was her name."

Barlow . . .

"So," Gayle asked, in a self-congratulatory voice, "have I convinced you to comment on any of this? I'm going to be calling Dean Gregory, of course . . ."

"He's the one you should speak with," Ginny told her. "I can't possibly comment on something that happened before I arrived here."

"Well, you read up about those strange occurrences with the Virgin, Dr. Marshall." Ginny laughed. "That's the first story I'm working on. Not too often that I get *two* sensational scoops at the same time! And if you decide you want to talk to me, you know my number."

"Yeah," Ginny said, her eyes returning to her computer screen. "Thanks for calling."

"Anytime!"

Ginny hung up the phone.

None of the girls had yet revealed what the Virgin told them, except to their local priest or bishop . . .

"But Bernadette told me," Ginny whispered.

Dear God. What is happening?

47

It was difficult to calm her mind and plan what she would say to her students. But finally, Ginny forced herself to put aside everything Gayle Honeycutt had told her and concentrate on her upcoming class.

"I want you all to be the first to know," Ginny announced when the students were all seated in front of her. "I am going on sabbatical next semester. I won't be on campus. I'll be leaving right after final exams."

There were groans and shouts of "Oh, no!"

"But Dr. Marshall," one girl in the back called out. "You promised you'd be my advisor . . ."

"Yes, I know, and I will continue to be available to advise any one of you who needs it." She smiled. "Take down my e-mail address now, and feel free to use it over the course of the next year."

She gave them her address, answering a few questions about why she was going on sabbatical ("I'm a writer, too, remember, and if I don't finish this book now, I never will"). Then she began the day's lecture—rather anticlimactic. Afterward, several girls gathered around to wish her well and to secure her promise, yet again, that she'd be only an e-mail or telephone call away. She assured them that would be the case.

Then she noticed Sue Barlow.

The girl was standing there staring at her, clutching her books to her chest.

"Hello, Sue," Ginny said.

Sue smiled but didn't reply.

"I know you expressed interest in taking my course next year," Ginny said. "I'm sorry that won't be possible. But if you'd like me to recommend some books—"

"No need, Dr. Marshall." Sue's voice seemed odd. The girl appeared glassy-eyed and almost robotic. "I've benefited greatly from your class, but I think now my interests will be diverging elsewhere."

"Oh," Ginny said. "I see."

Sue's smile widened. "You'll be leaving Lebanon? Returning to Louisiana?"

"Yes. That's where I'll be writing the book."

Sue nodded. "Well, best of luck to you, Dr. Marshall."

Ginny watched her leave. That was odd. Very odd. Sue had been one of her most enthusiastic students, rare for a freshman. Her essays were always interesting and well thought out, and in the last few weeks she had even begun speaking out in class, asking questions that were intelligent and sometimes even provocative. Ginny liked Sue; no matter that she might be a pet of Gregory's due to her grandfather's endowment money. She was still a bright, friendly girl.

Or, at least, she was.

Ginny didn't have time to ponder it. She wanted to get home to listen to the tape recording of her interview with Bernadette deSalis. She hadn't had a chance to listen to it all the way through, and she knew from experience that little details were often missed in the actual conversation, and could be picked up by listening to the recording. She gathered her papers and headed off campus.

Driving back to her apartment, she thought again about what Gayle Honeycutt had told her. These multiple Virgin sightings—what could they mean? Were they a symptom of mass hysteria? Had Bernadette read about one of them, and thus imagined her own encounter?

Or was something else going on?

Ginny wasn't religious—but neither was she a disbeliever. Too much of what she had studied all these years could never be explained "logically" or "scientifically." As an historian, her job was to record and interpret—not to pass judgment or rule out scenarios simply because they didn't fit into her personal beliefs. Bernadette's visions of Mary had gone beyond the standard Christian tradition. She'd seen the Divine Mother in her various incarnations. And now there were other sightings, all around the world—

Ginny glanced over at her briefcase. Inside were printouts of news reports from as far away as China. Gayle Honeycutt had underestimated the story. It wasn't just North America. It was the entire globe. And in reports uncannily like Bernadette's story, sometimes the Blessed Mother appeared as a deity other than her traditional Christian self. In China, a girl claimed a visit from Quan Yin. In India, Durga had made another appearance, complete with her eight arms.

And in each case, the Divine Mother had relayed an incredible secret. Just as she did to Bernadette.

But that secret . . . Ginny thought, shuddering. How could she possibly believe *that*?

If I believe that the Divine Mother is making appearances around the world, why should I doubt what she has to say?

And could it have anything to do with these girls' disappearances? Gayle had said Perry Holland had found evidence girls had disappeared from Wilbourne before. Was there any connection?

Suddenly, Ginny slammed on her breaks. Ahead, in the gathering twilight, a group of children were crossing the road. They were dressed as witches and ghosts and tiny little red devils, carrying pitchforks.

Halloween. That's right. It's Halloween.

One little devil boy looked over at her through the windshield. He grinned. Ginny shivered.

Back home, she tried to relax. A little pasta, a little red wine, and some good music. That's what she needed before she settled down to listen to the tape.

She always listened to Stevie Nicks when she wanted to unwind. "Just like the white winged dove," Ginny sang, pouring a jar of spaghetti sauce over the noodles she'd boiled. She refilled her glass of wine and carried her plate into the living room.

The tape recorder sat on her desk. She'd called both her agent and her editor to tell them about this latest development, and both were ecstatic. Ginny wondered if they'd caught the reports of the multiple Virgin sightings. The universe seemed to be writing her book for her. Ginny surely would have another best seller on her hands.

Unless, of course, the Virgin's warning went unheeded.

Could it really happen? Ginny thought as she ate her dinner and washed it down with the wine.

As "Edge of Seventeen" morphed into "Stand Back," Ginny deposited her plate in the sink and refilled her glass. She took a deep breath, then headed back into the living room to switch off the CD.

"Sorry, Stevie," she said. "Now it's time for Bernadette."

She sat down at her desk and hit PLAY on the tape recorder.

GINNY: Thank you again for agreeing to be interviewed,
Bernadette, and agreeing to be recorded. For the record,
my name is Dr. Virginia Marshall, and I am writing a
book about sightings of the Virgin Mary, and am
currently a professor of theology at Wilbourne College.
For the record, can you state your name and your age and
tell me a little about your family?

BERNADETTE: All right. My name is Bernadette Marie
Claire deSalis, and I am thirteen years old. I will be four-
teen in February. I am the youngest child of Pierre and
Madeleine deSalis. I have three older brothers.

GINNY: Thank you. Now, you've told me that you saw the
Virgin Mary back in September, is that correct?

BERNADETTE: Yes, I did.

GINNY: Will you describe what happened?

BERNADETTE: It was the night before school started. Every
night, before I go to bed, I pray to the Blessed Mother to
give me the strength to believe in the Lord and to follow
His teachings. I also pray for my family, and for the
world in general—for the sick, for the poor, and for the
starving.

GINNY: And you do this every night?

BERNADETTE: Yes.

GINNY: So what made this evening different than any other
evening?

BERNADETTE: (*laughter*) Besides the Virgin Mary appearing
to me?

GINNY: Yes. Is there anything you can think of that made
the night different from any other night?

BERNADETTE: No. It was a Sunday like any other Sunday.
My mother and I went to Mass, then we did some shopping in Senandaga for school clothes—did I mention
school was starting the next day?—and then we came

back home. Mom made dinner. It was like any other night really.

GINNY: And your prayer was the same as it always was?

BERNADETTE: Yes. I don't know why the Blessed Mother chose to appear to me that night, Dr. Marshall, although I know God in His wisdom chose that night for a reason. He has a plan, and I am part of it.

The doorbell suddenly rang, startling Ginny. She hit the PAUSE button, hurried to the door, and discovered a couple of trick-or-treaters. The girl, no more than five, was dressed as a ballerina. The boy, about eight, was yet another devil, complete with horns and pitchfork. Ginny could have sworn it was the same child she'd seen on the road. He grinned at her the same way.

"Trick or treeeeeeeet!" they screeched.

She hadn't gone shopping for candy. "Hang on," she said, and rushed into the kitchen. She banged through her cabinets looking for something, but all she had were cans of tuna fish and boxes of ziti. She went back to the kids and gave them each a five-dollar bill.

"Cool," the boy said.

After that, Ginny turned off all her lights. By the glow of the moon, she refilled her wineglass. She had a slight buzz going—it was her third glass after all—but she needed to unwind. She sat in the dark and thought about what was happening.

Could it be true?

Father Ortiz believed it could be. "It's been prophesied," he told her.

Ginny had scoffed. "The Bible has been mistranslated so often that I can't put stock in any prophecy."

Father Ortiz looked at her. There was fear in his eyes.

"You've written about the lost books of Revelation, have you not, Ginny?"

She nodded. "The ones that the Vatican supposedly keeps hidden, out of fear of panicking the faithful?"

Father Ortiz nodded. "What if I told you I'd seen them? That I'd read them?"

"I'd ask you if you thought they were forgeries, or later additions by some fanatical sect."

He smiled. "I am not an expert."

"So give me your opinion."

He demurred. "I've said too much. I simply want to impress upon you that this situation is . . . serious."

"Then why hasn't the Vatican swept Bernadette off to Rome?" Ginny asked him. "Why not put her in hiding somewhere, as always seems to happen to those who see visions? Why get me involved?"

That question, of course, had come before Ginny had learned of the sightings taking place all over the world. But clearly, the Vatican had known about them right from the beginning—and was unnerved by them. That's why they were calling in experts like herself. Ginny was probably just one of many being consulted all around the globe. The fact that the Church was as unnerved as she was . . .

Ginny sighed, switching the tape recorder back on. It was *not* reassuring.

GINNY: So tell me about God's plan.

BERNADETTE: I can only tell you what the Holy Mother told me.

GINNY: All right.

BERNADETTE: It is the beginning of a great battle. A terrible, malignant evil has been manifesting in the world for some time now. And now one has come who will bring great destruction to all men and women. It is the One who has been prophesied.

GINNY: Are you speaking of the Antichrist? As foretold in the Book of Revelation?

BERNADETTE: I am.

GINNY: And who is this Antichrist? Do you know?

BERNADETTE: I do.

GINNY: So tell me his name.

BERNADETTE: That I am forbidden from telling. At least for now.

GINNY: So are you able to tell me anything about him?

BERNADETTE: Perhaps one thing.

(Pause.)

BERNADETTE: The Antichrist is not a him, but a *her*.

48

When Tish Lewis finally awoke, she was hanging upside down on a cross.

She couldn't scream. Her mouth was gagged. She was naked.

A fire blazed in front of her. Figures in red robes moved about in the dark room, illuminated now and then by the fire's glow. They were chanting.

Tish struggled, but she was tied securely with strong rope. She knew her end was at hand.

She prayed it would come quick.

"Master!"

The voice in front of her was familiar. Dean Gregory.

"Master, for you!"

Gregory let his robe fall open. Even though she was upside down, Tish could see clearly that the dean was naked, with a blood engorged erection.

She began to cry.

"On this, your sacred night!"

Gregory approached her. The group was chanting, urging him on. Nurse Cochrane, Professor Adamson, even the dean's wife.

But not Oostie, Tish thought with some satisfaction. *I killed Oostie. One less monster in your coven.*

That was Tish's last conscious thought. Mercifully, her brain shut down as Gregory raped her. Her eyes never opened—not even after Gregory pulled away, the darkness in the room seeming to vibrate, to pulse with life.

The darkness became the demon itself, and it swallowed what was left of Tish's body.

49

Outside, the sky looked like snow. *Impossible,* Sue thought. *It's still too early in the season.* November had just begun. Yet the gray, heavy sky looked ominous enough.

She looked over at Malika, studious as ever, her nose in a book. They'd never really talked about their argument, just fallen back into a careful routine with each other. They didn't talk much. Mostly just "hellos" and "good-byes" and the occasional grunt in between.

"I'm heading into town," Sue told her.

"They'll stop you at the gate."

"I have the guard fooled. I pull a cap down over my forehead and he thinks I'm a driver for one of the bigshots."

Her roommate lifted an eye to look at her over her textbook. "You're breaking the rules," she said softly.

"Promise you won't squeal?"

Malika returned to her reading. "I'm not the type. I challenge authority."

There was just the slightest emphasis on "I" and it pissed Sue off. "And are you implying I do not?"

"I'm merely referencing your support for these armed fascist goons on campus."

"Oh, please," Sue said. "Have you ever talked to one of those guys? They're quite sweet. As if they'd ever do anything to harm one of—"

A strange image flashed through her mind. A guard—clamping a gloved hand down over a girl's mouth.

Had she dreamed it? She didn't remember.

"I'm sorry, I don't trust them. Grow up a black woman in this country and you'll learn that you can't just blindly trust a group of white guys with guns."

That statement just pissed Sue off all the more. "Look, would you really rather the administration did nothing?"

Malika threw down her book. "That's exactly what they did! Nothing! For weeks! Not a word to any of us about Joelle and Tish going missing! Just lies!"

Sue gave her a bemused face. "Tish Lewis isn't missing."

"What do you mean?"

Sue began to answer, then realized she didn't know. Why had she said Tish wasn't missing? As far as she knew, Tish still hadn't been found . . .

Or had she?

"I guess it's just a feeling I have," she said, puzzling to herself. "I guess I think she'll turn up."

"Well, I'm not nearly so optimistic."

Anger flared again. "That's what's wrong with you, Malika! You're always so pessimistic, always so ready to see the bad side of things!"

"Tell me a good side to any of this!"

Sue glared at her. "You know, maybe your problem is that you just haven't gotten laid lately."

Where did that come from? Even as Sue said the words, she was aghast at what she was saying. Certainly *she* hadn't gotten laid—she had never gotten laid. But she was deliberately giving the impression to Malika that she and Billy were having sex. And the weirdest part—she was enjoying doing it!

Malika stood up to face her. "That is uncalled for, Sue Barlow!"

Sue laughed, even as part of her hated herself for doing so. "You know, Malika, I'm beginning to wonder if maybe you just don't like men. Maybe in fact you're a lesbian. Ever consider it?"

Her roommate's eyes were nearly popping out of her head. "I am not a lesbian!" she shouted.

"Not that there'd be anything wrong with that, right, Miss Limousine Liberal? Excuse me, Ms. Limousine Liberal."

"Fuck you, Sue!"

Sue laughed. "I'm beginning to think you want to."

She gathered up her pocketbook and cell phone.

"If anyone reports me for going off campus," she said, one last parting shot, "I'll know it was you."

She closed the door behind her.

Once again Sue made it past the guard.

Driving into town, she was mystified as to why she had deliberately provoked Malika in that way. But she had to admit, she enjoyed it.

"That bitch thinks she knows everything," Sue said to herself. "I'll show her a thing or two."

Oh, her roommate got her so mad . . .

She found a spot to park on Main Street. She was supposed to meet Billy at the Yellow Bird. She looked at her watch and saw that she was early. She'd go in anyway, and grab a booth.

She took one close to the door. "I'll just have a strawberry shake," she said when Marjorie offered her a menu.

She sat there and stared out the window. The square was deserted. She watched the bare trees bend and swing in the strong wind. The sky was still dark. *It's going to snow,* Sue thought.

And sure enough—a few wispy flakes began turning in the air.

"Well, will you look at that?" Marjorie said as she placed her shake in front of her. "The first snow of the season. Gets earlier every year."

"It won't amount to much," Sue said.

"Let's hope not," the waitress said before moving away.

Sue took a sip. She was surprised at how angry she still was at Malika. Part of her said the fight had been all her fault, that she'd goaded her roommate into it by calling her a lesbian. But what if she had? Malika had only gotten what she had coming to her.

"She'll learn," Sue whispered.

"Do you mind if I join you?"

A voice startled her out of her reverie.

She looked up and instead of seeing Billy, she saw an older man. Sixties probably. Small, some kind of Hispanic. She resisted her Manhattan upbringing—that instinct drilled into her from childhood to not talk to strangers, to dismiss him with a wave of her hand and a curt "no." Why this older man wanted to sit in the same booth with her was rather peculiar and even a bit creepy—but Sue was intrigued. She gave him a slight shrug. "Be my guest," she said.

"I'm Father Ortiz," he said as he slid into the booth across from her. He smiled at her as he opened his coat and shrugged it off his shoulders, revealing his priestly collar.

"You're a priest?" Sue asked.

"I am."

"Catholic?"

He nodded. "Right again."

Sue gave him a strange look.

"I just wanted a moment of your time, Miss Barlow."

"How do you know my name? My boyfriend will be here in a minute—"

"This won't take long," said Father Ortiz. "I understand

you had a rather interesting encounter with a friend of mine recently at the hospital."

"I don't know what you're talking about."

"You seem sad," he replied as though she had said nothing. "Is everything all right?"

He seemed genuinely interested. Sue thought that his eyes looked kind.

"I don't know you," she told him.

"But I know you, Miss Barlow. I know that you must be very confused right now. Even frightened."

"Why would I be frightened?"

"It's not hopeless, you know. It doesn't have to go the way they are expecting. You still have your own self-will. You still have a soul—"

"Okay, now I'm thinking you're crazy. Who are 'they'? I'm thinking I should call the waitress and have her kick you out of—"

"I suspect you are not usually so belligerent. Does it frighten you? Concern you?"

Sue stared at him. "Your friend at the hospital. You mean that freak, don't you? Bernadette deSalis? How dare she speak of my mother!"

"It must have been hard for you to grow up without your mother."

How does he know so much about me?

Sue narrowed her eyes at him, ready to tell him to *get the fuck out of her face!*

But suddenly—she softened.

"I wish I had known her," she said, slumping.

"There's been a lot of tragedy lately," Father Ortiz said. "You're a caring girl, I can see that. I know you don't want any more to occur."

Sue picked up the wrapper of her straw and began shredding it. The priest was making her uncomfortable, despite the kindness in his eyes and the gentleness of his voice. There was something about him—*he's dangerous to you*—that unsettled her.

Still, he seemed to have answers . . .

"It's almost like," she said, struggling to get the words out, "the college is under some kind of curse."

"As though there are dark forces at work there?"

Father Ortiz's smile was still kind, but his eyes narrowed a fraction, and the twinkle in them seemed to go out as he spoke. "Tell me, Sue. Do you believe in evil?" He tilted his head to one side slightly. "Evil as a force that exists in the world?"

Sue shifted in her seat, and looked down at her melting milk shake. The straw wrapper lay in shreds next to her glass. "I suppose that without evil, good cannot exist," she replied. The words came from nowhere. "They need each other. They define each other."

He laughed gently. "Many theologians have debated and written about this very question—indeed, far greater minds than mine."

Sue was growing increasingly uncomfortable. "Why did you sit down here with me? Did you come here specifically looking for me?"

"I admit I did. I was at the hospital in Senandaga just now. Mike deSalis is being sent home as we speak. He has made a full and complete recovery." Father Ortiz smiled. "Your boyfriend was there, cheering him on, and I heard him say he had to hurry back here to meet you."

"And so you came to tell me this?"

The priest nodded. "I wanted to see your reaction."

"I'm happy, of course. Mike is Billy's best friend."

"Heidi Swettenham is also going home."

Sue stared at him.

"Both are better," the priest told her, "because they were cured through the intercession of Our Lady, the Blessed Virgin Mary."

Billy was at the hospital to see Heidi. That's why he's late. That's why he's not here.

"Only Bernadette kept the faith," Father Ortiz said. "All along, she knew her brother would be all right. As would Heidi." He leaned in close to Sue. "So there are other forces at work, too, Miss Barlow. I just wanted you to know that."

"Bernadette," Sue said, her voice low.

"Yes, Bernadette. The girl you called a freak." He reached over and placed a hand over Sue's. "She's quite concerned about you."

She pulled her hand away. "She doesn't know me! She told me lies about my mother . . . ."

Lies that Sue had blocked out of her mind, refused to think about . . .

"Father Ortiz," said a new voice.

It was Billy. Sue was never more delighted to see anyone.

"Hello, Billy," the priest said, standing up. "I was just keeping your girlfriend company until you got here. I've already given her the good news about Mike."

Father Ortiz turned to face Sue.

"Pleased to have met you, Miss Barlow," he told her.

Then he headed out.

Billy slid into the booth in his place. "What was that all about? You seem bugged by him."

Sue couldn't reply right away.

Do you believe in evil, Sue?

"Billy," she said all at once. "I have to get back to campus."

"Why? You think they know you left—?"

"No," Sue said. "I just have to get back! It's Malika!"

She stood, rushing out of the booth, forgetting to pay. Billy threw down a five on the table and followed her out onto the street.

"What's wrong with Malika?" he shouted.

"She's sick!" Sue screamed, running toward her car. "I've got to get to her!"

"Then I'm coming with you!"

She didn't object. They both hopped into Sue's car and sped back to Wilbourne. Guests weren't permitted during the day like this, but Billy would just have to pose as one of the grad students. By now the guard was used to seeing the Lexus going in and out, so he didn't even try to stop them as they came through the gate. Billy kept asking her how she knew Malika was sick, but Sue couldn't answer him. She was crying too hard.

She skidded to a stop in the student parking lot. "If she's dead," Sue cried, "it's all my fault!"

Billy hurried to keep up with her as she ran across the pavement. "What the fuck is going on, Sue?"

But she didn't take time to answer him. Up the steps in Bentley they ran, several girls doing wide-eyed double takes when they saw Billy. Sue didn't even wait for the elevator, just took the stairs three at a time.

And once inside her room, she saw she was right.

Malika was on the floor, gasping for breath.

"Malika!" Sue shouted, Billy hot on her heels.

She bent down over her roommate. Malika's eyes had rolled toward the back of her head.

"I'll call 911," Billy said.

"Malika," Sue called. "Can you hear me?"

She cradled the other girl's head in her lap.

"I want you to live! Do you hear me? I want you to get better! You will be *fine*! Do you hear me? You were my first friend when I came to Wilbourne. You are still my friend! I want you to live, Malika!"

"Paramedics are on their way," Billy reported, flipping his cell phone closed.

"I want you to live, Malika!"

And the girl's eyes suddenly popped back to life, and she drew in one long breath, letting it out with sudden relief.

"Malika?"

"Sue?"

"Thank God."

She helped her onto the bed.

"I was just reading," Malika said. "And then I couldn't breathe."

"You're all right now," Sue told her.

Billy was dumbfounded. When the paramedics arrived, they checked Malika's vital signs and pronounced her fine. In perfect health.

"It's like you willed her to snap out of it," Billy said as Sue escorted him back to the car. They had to get him off campus quickly before someone spotted him. "But how did you know she was in trouble?"

"Intuition," she said. Her voice was flat.

Billy got into the passenger side of Sue's car.

She would have died, Sue thought.

And I would have killed her.

Her cell phone dinged in her purse.

She pulled it out. A text message. She clicked on the icon.

Do you believe in evil, Sue?

She stared at the glowing letters. She didn't recognize the number it came from.

"Yes," she said out loud, before slipping in behind the wheel.

50

Perry Holland knew all along that Bonnie Warner would be found eventually. He could even have predicted that she'd be found in the lake, her body drained of blood.

"Hope the other two don't end up in here, too," said the state cop in charge of the investigation, watching as the coroner's department examined Bonnie's decomposed, mutilated, water-logged body on the muddy shore. A couple of kids had found her, washed up, tangled among the cat-o'-nine-tails. The slate-gray November sky seemed to reflect the melancholia every-one felt.

"Twenty years ago," Perry reminded the cop. "another missing girl was found in this same lake in the same condition."

"I'm well aware of that, Deputy. Trust me. We're on top of this. This has become an official murder investigation now, not just a disappearance."

Perry sighed, and headed back to his car.

Sure, you'll be on top of it for a few more days, maybe a couple of weeks. Then you'll forget about it. I don't care if it is a murder investigation. You'll forget about it just like your predecessors did twenty years ago. Just like the whole fucking town did. The whole goddamned state.

Everybody, that is, except my Dad.

This time, Perry was going to make sure *nobody* forgot about Bonnie Warner and Joelle Bartlett and Tish Lewis.

And Miles Holland.

He started the car. He had put off phoning Gayle Honeycutt for a couple of weeks, leery about the consequences he could face from the department if it found out he was talking to the press without authorization. He wasn't sure he could trust her to keep his identity a secret. But when word came in this morning that Bonnie's body had been found, he knew he could wait no longer. He'd phoned Gayle to meet him at his father's house this evening.

Of course she'd jumped at the invitation, and promised him complete anonymity. Perry had promised to give her all the information she'd need to write a major article—one that would draw national attention. He was well aware that he was going against regulations, but it was the only way to keep the story alive, to prevent it from falling back into obscurity the way it did every generation. He was taking a risk—especially now that they were officially dealing with a murder—but he felt he had no other choice.

All of the files on every disappearance, every murder, that had ever occurred at Wilbourne were waiting for Gayle back at Perry's father's house. Perry had spirited the files out of the station's archives, one by one, over the last couple of weeks. Again, this was against regulations, but Perry knew he'd need to have complete privacy to go over them with Gayle. He trusted very few people these days. The state cops were in and out of the sheriff's station all the time lately. It wouldn't do for him to be seen talking to a reporter.

I'll avenge your death, Dad, he thought as drove back into town. *And I'll solve the mystery you were killed for investigating.*

In just a little more than a week, Perry would be celebrating Thanksgiving for the first time alone. No Mom. No Dad. No Jennifer. And the thought made him very blue indeed.

It was just as he was feeling his bluest when he spotted a dark green BMW at the corner of Main and Elm streets barely slowing down for the stop sign. The car breezed right through as if its driver owned the town.

Perry knew whose Beemer that was. He turned on his siren and went after her.

"What's wrong?" Mona Gregory asked after pulling over, rolling down her window, and staring up at Perry. "What did I do wrong?"

"You know that big red octagonal sign back there, Mrs. Gregory?" Perry asked her. "It says STOP. That means you put your foot on the brake and stop your car."

"Oh," she whined. "Didn't I stop? I though I stopped . . ."

Around town, Mona Gregory was known as "Mousy Mona." She was a small woman with graying dark hair that she wore cropped short. She never had much to say for herself, always standing demurely behind her husband in a conservative dress and pearl earrings.

"No, Mrs. Gregory," Perry told her. "You didn't stop."

"Are you writing me a ticket?"

"Yes, ma'am."

"Please, just a warning? My husband will be very upset . . ."

Perry said nothing, scribbling out her ticket, tearing it off his pad, and handing it to her through the window.

"Oh, dear," Mona said, accepting it.

"What's the big rush, Mrs. Gregory? Did you hear about Bonnie Warner being found?"

"Who?"

Perry frowned. "Bonnie Warner. One of the girls who were missing."

"Oh," Mona said, still staring at her ticket. "No, I hadn't heard. Oh, well, I suppose it will at least give her family some peace. They can bury her and move on."

Perry was silent as he looked down at Mousy Mona. Finally, he said, "I didn't tell you she was found dead, Mrs. Gregory."

Mona's eyes darted up to him. "Oh, well, I—" She flushed. "I suppose I had been expecting the worse, and so I—" She was trembling now. "Was she found alive, Deputy? How wonderful if so . . ."

"No," Perry told her plainly. "She was found dead."

Mona had no response. She just returned to staring at her ticket.

"Drive more carefully now, Mrs. Gregory," Perry told her.

He headed back to his car. That was odd. Very odd indeed.

He watched as Mona put her BMW back into gear and drove off. He stood there for a moment, watching her go. Then he got back into his patrol car and drove off.

He went off duty at five, made himself a frozen dinner, and sat in front of his television. There was a teaser for the local news. Footage of the police at the lake, the plastic-faced anchorwoman shrilling, "Missing Wilbourne student found dead and dismembered. More news at ten."

"Yeah," Perry growled, "and then that'll be the end of it."

It was getting close to seven, the time he'd scheduled to meet Gayle at his father's house. Driving there, Perry thought again of all the papers and folders Dad had found, all neatly stacked, labeled, and cross-referenced.

The documentation of more than a hundred years of victims, sitting neatly on Dad's kitchen table.

Victims of whom? Of what?

He'd just turned onto his father's street when a cold chill

ran through him. He could see the house, his father's car still in the driveway. Gayle was not yet there. Perry parked in the street, not knowing why he felt so terrified all of a sudden. He gripped the steering wheel until his knuckles turned white.

They're watching you, Perry. They're not going to let you expose them.

Dad's voice.

That was when the house blew up.

51

The explosion was heard all over Lebanon.

Bernadette deSalis was in her room, writing at her desk. The entire house shook with the deafening blast from a few streets away. The young girl turned her eyes to the crucifix over her bed. *It's begun,* she thought. *Please, Lord, have mercy on your humble servants and show us the way.*

A few blocks away, Darby Pequod was forging a title to a stolen car, and sat up in his chair as if he'd just been shot in the back. His mother Marjorie, a couple of houses down from him in the Banks, was watching a rerun of *Law and Order,* and had just fallen asleep with a cigarette in her mouth. She would credit the explosion with saving her life.

At the Yellow Bird, Wally Bingham had just locked the front doors and was getting ready to clean up when the entire building rocked with the noise. *What the hell was that?* he wondered, unlocking the door and going out into the street to take a look. The downtown was quiet, but over the trees toward the west, a mushroom cloud of black smoke was rising.

Gayle Honeycutt thought it was a terrorist attack. She saw the house go—like a golden rocket shooting into the violet night sky. She had just turned onto the street, and pulled her car over immediately to the side of the road. It was now raining golden balls of fire everywhere in the neighborhood. "Jesus!" she shrieked. She kept repeating it over and over. "Jesus! Jesus! Jesus!" Then she rushed forward, notebook in hand, to record everything she saw and heard.

At Bentley Hall on the Wilbourne campus, the sound was far away, but still loud enough for girls to run to their windows. Malika, propped up in bed studying with pillows behind her back, looked up from her book and over at Sue.

"What was that?" she asked.

"I don't know," Sue replied, heading to the window and glancing out. "Something's on fire . . . I can see the flames through the trees, and the sky over town is really black."

"It was an explosion," Malika said.

Sue watched the black smoke billowing into the night sky. She couldn't take her eyes off it. It was both terrifying and utterly beautiful. She was fascinated by it.

"Why don't you call Billy?" Malika suggested. "His mother will know what it was. What if it was a gas station? That can cause a really bad fire . . ."

"I don't want you worrying about anything," Sue told her, snapping closed the blinds over the window. "I want you to rest."

"Sue, I'm fine." She smiled. "It's been weeks since I had that attack and you're still treating me like an invalid."

"Well, they've been testing you for all sorts of things . . ."

"And you know very well every doctor has given me a clean bill of health." Malika leaned her head back into the pillows. "I'm just glad we're friends again. But for the life of me, I still don't know how you knew I was having that seizure that day . . ."

"Intuition, I guess," Sue said.

Though she knew it was something more than that.

Much more.

I can see things.

I guess I've always been able to see things.

I can see things . . . and I can make things happen.

That's why she was not going to call Billy.

She doubted she'd ever call him again, in fact. Over the last couple of weeks, Billy had been spending time with Heidi again. He was going to see her now that she was home, bringing her flowers, keeping her cheered up. Sue knew he felt guilty about Heidi's illness, believing somehow that he'd caused it. Heidi's parents credited him with helping her pull through it, by showing up to visit her at the hospital. Now they were hopeful he'd continue keeping her on the mend, and so he did, sitting there at the side of Heidi's bed, making her laugh, telling her jokes, even kissing her good-bye on the forehead.

Billy hadn't told Sue any of this. She just knew.

And she was jealous. And angry.

That's why Heidi still isn't strong enough to walk, whereas Mike deSalis is up and back to school.

And that's why Sue had to contain her anger. That's why she had to stop thinking about Billy. She knew what might happen. Next thing they all knew, it would be Billy on the floor, gasping for breath.

So let them have each other, Sue thought bitterly. *I hope they're deliriously happy.*

And that they both choke to death the next time they kiss! No!

Sue closed her eyes, pretending to study.

I can't think that way. I can't allow myself to have thoughts like that!

Her computer suddenly dinged. She looked at it. Her mailbox indicator was bouncing. She opened her e-mail.

At last. It was a reply from Joyce Davenport.

Sue:

Yes indeed, it's time we talked. I understand your urgency. I'm sure you are going through many confusing, even frightening, experiences. But trust me. You must go through them. It is the only way.

I am going to be in New York in a couple of weeks. I'm assuming you will be in the city for the holidays as well. Why don't you come hear me read from my book at the Politico Bookstore in Times Square on the day after Thanksgiving and then we can have lunch afterward?

We will talk about everything and anything then.

Sincerely,

Joyce

Sue read the e-mail again, and then a third time.

What did Joyce mean?

I'm sure you are going through many confusing, even frightening, experiences. But trust me. You must go through them. It is the only way.

Did she mean just the usual experiences every college girl faces her first year in school, her first time away from home?

Or did she mean more than that?

How much did Joyce know about the forces at work here—the forces Sue were now convinced had some kind of control over her?

Was she being paranoid?

All she had to do was look over at Malika, propped up in her bed, still shaken from her ordeal, to convince her that she was not.

She clicked on RESPOND, and typed quickly: *Joyce, I'll be there. Thanks, Sue.*

She clicked SEND.

She got up just as her cell phone beeped.

Another text message.

Her hands shaking, she picked up the phone.

It has begun.

With a cry, she threw the phone away from her.

From outside, sirens could be heard, and the sky continued to turn black.

52

Gayle Honeycutt's fingers moved furiously over the keyboard of her computer. She was determined to get the story of the explosion onto the wires before anyone else.

I was there! She was thrilled by her good fortune. *I was right there to give an eyewitness account.*

"Front page," she was murmuring to herself as she typed up her story. "And surely splashed across newspapers throughout the region . . ."

Her cell rang. She saw from the Caller ID it was Perry Holland. Poor guy had gone berserk watching his father's house blow up. He kept ranting that "they" did it, that "they" didn't want him talking to her.

"Who are *they*?" Gayle had asked.

Perry had been unable to respond. He was just wide-eyed and shocked, mumbling to himself. But an hour later, he was suitably composed—if Gayle could call it that—to call her on her cell, ranting again about "them." From what Gayle could make out, he seemed to think some unnamed group of unknown people were plotting behind his back, and they were connected to everything from Bonnie Warner's murder to his father's death. "Like a cult," Perry raved. "I think they're like a cult."

That was all Gayle needed to hear to tune him out. Whenever people started rambling on about "cults," she knew they were crazy. Later, she'd talked to the fire chief, who suspected it was a gas leak. Perry Holland had dismissed that idea with his paranoid theories. Gayle had simply rolled her eyes. Now the crazy deputy was calling her again. She'd let the call go to voice mail. Sure, there might be an interesting story in this history of murders that Perry claimed had happened at Wilbourne, but she had more pressing matters first.

Her cell rang again. Caller unknown. It could be Perry calling back, blocking his number. But she'd also left messages for the fire chief to confirm a few facts. She answered.

"Gayle Honeycutt?"

"Yes," she replied.

It was a woman's voice, one that seemed very familiar, though Gayle couldn't place it.

"If you think this story about the exploding house is big news," the caller said, "I suggest you meet me for something really big."

Gayle laughed. "Who's this?"

"Meet me tomorrow and you'll see."

"I need more to go on than that."

The caller chuckled. "You're tired of supporting those two kids all on your own, aren't you, Gayle? You work so hard . . . slaving away at some second-rate newspaper in the backwoods. You should be writing for *The New York Times,* Gayle." A pause. "And you could be."

"Who *is* this?" Gayle asked again, suddenly thinking she knew the voice.

But why would *Joyce Davenport* be calling *her*?

"Everything you've dreamed about could be yours," the caller said. "Just listen, Gayle, and I'll tell you how . . ."

53

During the third week of November, a cold front moved down from Canada, obliterating any lingering traces of autumn. The trees were now completely bare, and the skies were perpetually gray. Even if the official declaration of winter was still a few weeks away, it had for all intents and purposes already arrived. The residents of Lebanon reached for their thermostats, their fingers shaking from the cold. Coats, hats, gloves, and scarves were dug out from the backs of closets. Alarms were set a little earlier in order to warm up cars and scrape frost off the windshields. Children suffered from runny noses, and cold remedies began flying off the shelves at the drugstore.

And now, the week of Thanksgiving, a huge snowstorm was predicted—the earliest such storm anyone in the region could remember. Six or seven inches were possible—enough to paralyze the town, making the roads impassable. The power company sent workers out ahead of time to make sure the lines were strong enough to withstand the winds the storm might bring.

As the temperature dropped, Perry Holland sat in his rocking chair, staring out the window into the hard gray sky. The doctor had given him a pill to help him sleep without the dreams, where he saw his father's house explode again and again.

In the days following the explosion, he'd waited impatiently for the fire department's report on the fire. He had wandered like an aimless ghost through the devastated neighborhood, where dozens of windows on other houses had blown out, and where debris had rained down on yards, cars, and rooftops. Perry had found shards of his mother's china and charred photographs of happier times nearly a block away.

The fire department had gotten there in a matter of minutes, and the fire—and the smaller ones started by falling, burning debris—had been contained very quickly. Gayle Honeycutt seemed not to appreciate the magnitude of the loss—all of the files about all of the Wilbourne murders and disappearances had been in that house—and instead was busy running around, jotting down notes and observations, seemingly thrilled to be an eyewitness to a local disaster.

"No lives lost," the fire chief was able to proclaim hours later. But that was small consolation to Perry. The fire inspector determined that a gas leak and faulty electrical wiring were responsible. Given the state of disrepair Dad's house was in, it was possible. But Perry believed it as much as he believed his father had been out climbing trees on the day he died.

As long as Perry lived, he would never forget watching the house he'd grown up in blow sky-high, flaming debris raining down all around him. The explosion had rocked the car, the windshield spiderwebbing with cracks from the concussion. His ears rang from the loudness of the blast, his eyes popped wide in disbelief. He'd turned the car off, leaving it in the middle of the street, and run toward the flaming wreck of the house.

They've done it, Perry thought. *They've kept anyone from finding out the truth.*

But just who they were, Perry still didn't know.

When he tried to tell Gayle what he suspected—that there was something, some kind of cult, at work in Lebanon—she was disinterested. No one believed him.

He was alone now, completely alone in the world. No family, no wife, no children.

The future looked incredibly bleak.

But the pills the doctor gave him helped a lot. They numbed him to the pain, the depression, the horror of it all. He was given two weeks off from the department with pay—even though already there were whispers that he had removed official documents from the archives. Perry just sat in his apartment, slipping into the fog of chemicals. He slept a lot, with the ringer on the phone turned off. Even a visit from Marjorie Peqoud had failed to rouse him. Her face had barely penetrated through the Valium fog.

All he could hear was his father's voice.

Perry, every twenty years or so something bad happens up at the college to one of the girls. Sometimes they disappear, sometimes it's a rape, sometimes they die, but it's a cycle. I swear to God, there's something going on up there. I know it doesn't make any sense—a serial rapist-murderer who only strikes every generation? A bizarre copycat? But goddamn it, son, there's something not right up at the college, and I'm going to get to the bottom of it.

All the files his father had pulled, going back as far back as the department's records went . . .

All of them went up with the house.

But Perry had *read* the damned files. He could recite them almost by memory. Yet he felt unable to speak, as if all the air had been sucked out of his lungs.

It was easier just to take his Valium and rock in his chair.

Perry, you were going to avenge my death. You were going to find out the truth!

The fire department . . . the state cops . . . everyone just wanted to move on, explain everything away. Already, Bonnie Warner's murder had moved off the front pages. History was repeating itself.

They're in on it. People well placed in the fire department, with the state police . . . they're part of it.

Dad's voice again.

"But that's just crazy," Perry said out loud, just as a soft rapping was heard at his front door.

He ignored it. Probably just Marj again with a casserole. She'd leave it on the step with a note. He couldn't bear to see her.

How far did it go? Perry wondered. How deep? How many people were involved?

The Gregorys certainly. And there must be more up at the school. Those beady-eyed private security guards Gregory had brought in from Manhattan—they must be part of it, too.

"Now you're going paranoid," he said to himself.

The rapping continued on his front door.

"And crazy, too," he said. "Sitting here talking to yourself."

The knocking had grown more insistent.

"All right!" Perry shouted. "Hold on a minute!"

He forced himself up and out of his rocking chair. He crossed the room and pulled open the door, expecting to see Marjorie standing there with a casserole dish. Tuna probably. Boy, was he sick of tuna casserole.

But it was a teenage girl with long dark hair.

"Deputy Holland?" she asked.

He nodded, trying to place her face. He knew her, but . . .

"I just wanted to say I'm sorry about your father," the girl told him, leaning up to give him a hug.

Perry put his arms around her.

"Your father was murdered," she whispered in his ear. "You

are right to suspect what you do. I just had to come over and tell you that."

He let her go and stared down at her. "Bernadette deSalis," he said. "That's who you are."

"That's right." She smiled kindly up at him.

"The girl who saw the Virgin Mary . . ."

She nodded. "It's begun," she told him. "But you'll be safe. Our Lady promises you will be."

"What do you mean?"

"That's all I can say," Bernadette told him, turning and hurrying back down the walk to where her bicycle waited on the curb. "But you're right in your suspicions, Deputy Holland. All of them!"

"Wait!" Perry called after her. "What do you mean?"

But she was already on her bike and pedaling down the street.

He stood there watching her as she disappeared around the block.

And then it began to rain.

54

Billy Honeycutt lay in bed staring at the ceiling.

Why has she stopped calling me?

Sue hadn't responded to any of his messages—phone or e-mail—in more than two weeks. Since Bonnie Warner's body was found, a campus-wide clampdown had prevented anyone from outside the college from setting foot on college grounds without being properly authorized. Billy had been completely cut off.

And he'd really been starting to like her, too.

His mother was rapping on his door. "Just because you're on Thanksgiving break doesn't mean you can sleep the whole day away," she called. "Come on, I've got chores for you to. Up and at 'em!"

He groaned.

"I'm making pancakes," she called. "If you want any, you better get your ass in gear."

"Life sucks," Billy said aloud to no one in particular, getting up and stretching. He switched his stereo on with the remote, and headed into the bathroom.

I've just got to accept that it's over, he told himself as he started the shower. *It was fun while it lasted. I should just be glad that Heidi's taking me back.*

Mike thought Billy was well rid of Sue. "There was something odd about her," Mike told him the other day. "Something that seemed—off somehow."

"You're fucked," Billy argued. "She was a sweet, nice girl."

"Every time I looked at her, all I saw was hate."

Billy just repeated that his best friend was "fucked."

Yet—it had been Sue—or the sight of her, entering the Yellow Bird—that had given Mike such a convulsion that he had landed in the hospital.

Since being released, Mike had been different. The doctors might not have found anything wrong with him, pronouncing him completely healthy, but Billy had known Mike his entire life—and Mike wasn't the same. Before everything that happened, Mike had had a quick sense of humor. He was always laughing. He could always find something funny to say. It was why he was so popular at Lebanon High.

But now, Mike always had this remote look on his face, like he wasn't paying attention. His mind seemed to be somewhere else—and he hardly ever smiled anymore, let alone laughed or made jokes. Billy felt he didn't even know Mike anymore. Mike never wanted to hang out, go do things, and on weekend nights he chose now to stay home rather than join Billy and their friends. He stopped going to parties, and seemed not to care who was dating whom, or how the football team was doing, or what his schedule of classes would be like next semester.

"What's happened to you?" Billy had finally asked him last night. "What's different about you?"

Mike had just given him a blank stare. "Ask your girlfriend."

Billy couldn't understand why Mike blamed Sue for what

happened. Okay, so he didn't say that in so many words—but he called her "hateful" and "deceitful," and Billy would never forget the look on Mike's face that day in the diner when he saw Sue enter. Billy had dated girls before that Mike didn't like—Heidi Swettenham for example. Mike thought she was a moron. But it had never been an issue between them before. Why Mike had taken such a violent dislike to Sue never made any sense to Billy. "She's bad news, man," Mike had told him last night—and at that, Billy had let the matter drop.

He let the water cascade over his hair and body. *But I liked her. I liked her a lot. What did I see in her that Mike didn't see?*

And yet, scrubbing his hair with shampoo, he thought of something else: Heidi had just seen Sue, too, right before her collapse.

What am I thinking? That Sue goes around giving people the evil eye and then they fall to pieces?

But still, he couldn't stop thinking about her. He couldn't stop dreaming about her at night, strange fantastic dreams that faded from his memory within moments of waking up, leaving him feeling slightly disturbed . . . and with an aching erection.

And there was no one he could talk to about it.

Certainly not Mike. The old Mike would have made jokes and teased him about it all and made him feel a lot better—but the old Mike was gone, maybe never to return. And as for his mother—no, she was so damned happy that he wasn't seeing "that college girl" anymore that Billy hated to even have her name came up when his mother was around. But it was weird how his mother—who'd never liked anyone he'd dated, and had always discouraged him from dating at all—was now pushing him to date other girls.

"Stop moping, she was wrong for you," Mom said one

night at the dinner table, slicing a meat loaf and not looking up. "She was too old for you, for one thing, and she's from a different world anyway—spoiled pampered princess like those Hilton girls. That would have ended badly anyway. You're lucky you got out of it when you did. Why don't you ask out that sweet Brenda Harris? I saw her at the A&P the other day—such a pretty girl, and nice, too."

"Brenda Harris is a dweeb," Billy had replied, irritated. "And why do you care who I date anyway?"

"I just hate seeing you waste your time on girls who are wrong for you."

"I wasn't going to marry Sue." he'd snapped. "And it's my life, isn't it?"

She looked up from what she was doing and gave him the smug look he hated. "As long as you're under my roof, mister, no, it's not."

He stepped out of the shower and towel-dried himself. Brushing his teeth, he stared at himself in the mirror.

"I've never been dumped before," he said to his reflection. "I guess that's what it is."

He'd had a steady string of girlfriends since the eighth grade, moving from one effortlessly to the next. Yes, he broke a few hearts along the way, but he'd never felt about any of them the way he felt about Sue. He'd moved on from his other girls without a second thought—but this, this was *different*

In the kitchen, he ate his pancakes without talking, his mother on one side and his younger sister Meghan on the other. "Now, Billy, I want you to take down all the lawn furniture today. We're going to get walloped with a snowstorm tonight, and I want the grill and the tables and chairs all safely put in the basement. *Comprende?* "

"Yes," he sighed.

"I'm heading to the office because I have a deadline I just have to meet." She smiled over at him, then at Meghan. "It's all going to change now for us. I won't have to work so hard. We can buy a nice house, a new car . . . "

"You getting a raise?" Meghan asked.

"Better than that." Gayle only smiled enigmatically. "I'm getting a new job."

"When?"

"Soon. It's been promised to me. By some very important people."

Billy just sighed. Mom was always coming up with crazy schemes that were supposedly going to make them rich. They never did.

"Okay, enough jibber-jabbering," Gayle announced, standing up. "Clean off these breakfast dishes. And Billy, get to work right away out back. It could be snowing by noon."

He sighed again and mopped up the last of his syrup with a piece of sausage.

In a few minutes, his mother's car was backing out of the garage and Billy trudged out onto the back porch. He hoped to be finished with his little task quickly and then he'd call Mike—or maybe another one of his friends. Mike probably wasn't interested in hanging out.

"He might be," came a voice.

Billy spun around. There, in the driveway, on her bike, was Bernadette deSalis.

"What?" Billy asked. "Who might be what?"

"Mike," Bernadette replied. "Mike might be interested in hanging out."

Billy approached her, dumbstruck. "You just read my mind . . ."

She smiled. "Don't worry about Mike. He's just adjusting. He saw a lot of things in his coma he can't really talk about yet. There just aren't words. But he'll come around."

Billy stared down at her. "How the fuck did you do that?"

"Do what?"

"Read my mind!"

The girl smiled. "Oh, I guess I was just lucky."

"No," Billy said. "It's the Virgin Mary stuff, isn't it? Ever since then, you and Mike . . ."

"One can't be in the presence of the divine and remain unchanged," Bernadette said.

"So you believe it really happened."

"Of course it did." Bernadette lifted her eyes to the gray sky. "I know it's been difficult for Mike. I keep praying that he will find his way."

Billy said nothing, just looked down at her. Finally, he tapped the side of her head gently. "Are you okay in there, Bernie?"

"Right as rain." She smiled at him for a moment, but then her face darkened. She was looking over his shoulder, and he turned slightly to see what she was looking at. There was nothing behind him.

"What is it?" Billy asked.

"She's here," the girl said quietly.

"Who's here?" Billy had to admit to himself that Bernadette was really creeping him out.

"The one you think about constantly."

Billy felt his face flush.

"Beware her, Billy," Bernadette warned.

It began to rain, a cold icy downpour all at once. A prelude to the storm that was to come.

"I have to get back home," Bernadette said, pushing off on her bike. "Billy, when I said to beware her, I meant it very sincerely. But still—you've got to find a way to see her."

"Who?" Billy said, the rain pouring down over his face.

"You know very well who I mean. You've got to find a way. You and she—it's not a part of their plan, you know."

The girl was pedaling away down the street as the rain fell even harder.

"Why do I have to beware her?" Billy called after her.

"Just whatever you do," Bernadette called back, "don't tell your mother!"

And then the rain was so hard and so fierce, Billy could scarcely see. He hurried back inside. Within an hour, the temperature had dropped, and the rain had turned to snow.

55

"I'm going home!" Ginny sang to herself as she unlocked the door to her apartment, juggling several books in her arms while snow accumulated on her shoulders. "I'm getting out of this godforsaken town and *going home*!"

Not even the unsettling encounter she'd had with Deputy Perry Holland could shake her good mood. She was done with this place. Good-bye Wilbourne!

She'd miss the girls, of course, Ginny thought as she settled her books on the dining room table. But not the administration. Not that nefarious, smarmy Ted Gregory.

"I'm going home and I'm going to write my book!" Ginny said out loud, glancing around the apartment, planning what to pack first,

When she'd left campus today, it had been practically deserted, as it always was the Wednesday before the holiday. There was no one to officially bid Ginny good-bye. Some girls had left early, taking the entire week off, but even the most dedicated students who'd stayed for last minute cramming before the holiday were gone by five, the time Ginny drove out through the gates. Probably for the last time, she told herself.

Ginny had canceled her last week of classes, scheduled to resume after the Thanksgiving break, and given her students a final project that would serve as their final exam. The projects would be mailed to her in Louisiana, and she'd read them there, submitting her final grades to the registrar by mail. Wilbourne had an early finals schedule anyway—most girls would be home by the second week of December—but Ginny had decided she couldn't wait even that long. She wanted out. She wanted to start writing about Bernadette deSalis and the dozens of Virgin sightings that were happening all over the world.

She'd already started shipping things to the house in Hammond, and had spent most of the day today cleaning out her office. The backseat of her car was filled with boxes, and she planned to spend Thanksgiving drinking wine and packing boxes. Friday morning, bright and early, she was setting out for Louisiana.

Home. She hadn't thought of Louisiana as home in years. Her accent was long gone, stomped out of her by her postgraduate work at Harvard. In Harvard Square, it hadn't taken her long to learn that to her colleagues and students, "Southern accent" equaled stupid. As far as Ginny had been concerned, Louisiana was the past. She'd fully intended never to look back.

But once she made up her mind to go back to the house where she'd grown up—back to small-town Hammond, Louisiana—she found herself looking forward to it. The house was a perfect place for her to get the book done—and the more she worked on the book, the more confident she became that it was going to be the biggest thing she'd ever done. And that meant no more Wilbourne College, which was more than fine with Ginny. She was tired of the brutal winters—this latest cold snap and the early snow seemed to settle into her bones and joints. No matter how high she turned up the thermostat, she couldn't get warm.

Of course, it might have been the words of that crazy Perry Holland that still gave her the chills.

"Professor Marshall! Professor Marshall!"

He'd looked like a madman waving down her car. He was unshaven, disheveled. His shirt was untucked and his greasy hair hung down into his eyes. Cautiously, Ginny had slowed her car and rolled down her window.

"They're out there!" he'd said, eyes wild. The snow swirled around him. He wore no coat, and was shivering.

"Who's out there, Deputy?"

"The killers," he told her. "They're a cult. They meet here, on the campus. I'm sure of it. They kill girls. They kill every twenty years. They killed my father!"

"Deputy, I'm sorry, I can't help you . . ."

He gripped her window with dirty hands. "They made sure all evidence was destroyed. They blew up the house! They're out there watching!"

Ginny recoiled, her hand on the knob to roll up the window again. "Deputy, why don't you talk to Gayle Honeycutt? She can write the story for you . . ."

"No! She's in on it! They must have gotten to her. She won't write anything now, she says! They must have promised her something . . ."

"Deputy, I'm sorry, I've got to be somewhere . . ."

Ginny had managed to roll the window halfway up when Perry's fingers grabbed it.

"That's what they do!" he shouted, his nose and mouth just inches from her. "They promise a person what they want! To be rich! To be powerful! That's how they got people in the state police, the fire department . . . that's how they keep the news from spreading."

"What news, Deputy?" Ginny asked indulgently.

"The news of the cult they're running right here at this school! The cult that kills girls like Bonnie Warner every twenty years!"

"Really, Deputy, I have to go . . ."

"Gregory's one of them!" Perry was shouting as Ginny's window rolled all the way up. "He's running the cult! It's like a devil thing—or witches. That's why the girls went missing! That's what happened to Bonnie Warner!"

Poor man, Ginny thought, looking in rearview mirror as Perry stumbled in the snow and flailed his arms. *The deaths of his parents, the explosion at the house have driven him mad.*

Not that Ginny wouldn't like to believe the worst about Gregory and Wilbourne. In many ways, it was a cult. Gregory had stacked the board of trustees with ideologues like himself, crowding out freethinkers like Ginny. If there *had* been previous murders on campus, Ginny found it quite believable that Wilbourne's repressive, tightly controlled administration would do everything in its power to cover them up and prevent the memory of them from filtering down to new classes of students. It was a story that was worth exposing—but Perry Holland no longer seemed such a reliable source.

"Poor man," she said as took a bottle of wine from the shelf. But even her sympathy for Perry Holland could not dim her sense of celebration. She'd drink a toast to her time at Wilbourne—and to bidding the school good-bye.

I won't be returning at the end of my sabbatical, she thought. *Not with this dean, with this board. My contract will simply expire.*

She was struggling with the corkscrew when there was a knock on her door.

"Damn." She put the bottle down on the kitchen counter and walked over to the door. She peered through the glass. At the bottom of the steps was Father Ortiz, white snow dusting his black hat and coat.

Ginny pulled open the door. "Father Ortiz, hello! Just in time to join me for a glass of wine!"

"I got your message that you were leaving town," he said, entering, wiping his shoes on the mat.

"I'm glad you came by. I was planning to call you before I left. Here, let me take your coat."

She hung his coat on the rack and gestured to the priest to sit in the living room. "Will you join me in a glass of wine?"

"Thank you," Father Ortiz said.

Ginny smiled. She'd grown quite fond of him. Of course, the fact that he'd gotten her the interview that was going to make her book the definitive one on the subject didn't exactly hurt. But there were other reasons to like him. He was kind, smart, funny. He'd taken to stopping by Ginny's apartment from time to time for a glass of wine and some theoretical theological discussion. For a Catholic priest, Ginny found Father Ortiz to be fairly open-minded and intellectually curious, which she enjoyed.

Ginny finished opening the bottle, filled two glasses, and carried them into the living room. "Cheers," she said.

"Cheers," Father Ortiz echoed. They both sipped.

"How is Bernadette?"

The priest smiled. "Back to being a normal girl. Riding her bike, watching television, studying for school. Of course, she and her Mother say several Rosaries a day, and Bernadette sits in quiet mediation for about two hours a day. She has become wise beyond her years."

Ginny nodded, taking a seat opposite him. "She's been fascinating to interview. I hope to come back, perhaps in the spring, and interview her again."

The priest gave her a wry smile. "If we are all still here."

"Where do you plan on going?"

His eyebrows raised. "I was referring to Bernadette's prediction that we are in the presence of the Antichrist."

Ginny smiled. "Oh, yes, of course. So you meant 'we' in the broadest possible sense. If the *human race* is still here, you meant."

He smiled. "I admit to a bit of melodrama." He looked over at Ginny intently. "I am sorry that you are leaving now, at this particular time."

"Father, you know how much I've wanted to get away from Wilbourne. This sabbatical will change my life."

"Yes, of course. Where will you be going?"

"I'm heading down to my place in Louisiana to finish working on the book."

He closed his eyes, then opened them again. "I brought you to meet Bernadette in the hope that you could help me understand. I appreciate all the context you have provided, Ginny, all the details of other sightings over the years. But I must ask you for absolute honesty. After speaking with Bernadette all these times, what do you believe?"

"Well, it's not about what I believe, it's what the girls who have the visions believe," Ginny said. She'd told him this before.

He leaned forward in his chair. "I want to know what *you* believe, Ginny."

"Bernadette's a very sweet girl." Ginny took a sip of her wine. "I was struck by her sincerity. And by her seeming understanding that all religions are connected . . . that this was a sort of pan-spiritual experience, not simply rooted in Catholic dogma."

"That still doesn't tell me what you believe." Father Ortiz sighed.

"I'm sorry," Ginny said. "I guess I've trained myself not to believe *or* disbelieve."

The priest was nodding. "You're a skeptic. You would have to be to write about your subject objectively. Otherwise, it would have no value."

"I try to keep an open mind, Father. I don't judge either way."

"Yes, that is why your work is so respected." He nodded. "I have to tell you, I am really looking forward to your book, as are a number of my superiors. Does it surprise you to know you have fans in the Vatican?"

"Just who exactly are your superiors, Father?" Ginny set her glass down on the coffee table and leaned forward. She smiled at him. "I've researched you—or tried to—and found nothing. Do you work for some secret society in the Church that no one knows about?"

"Don't tell me you buy into those Catholic conspiracy theories?" He laughed. "Hardly, Ginny. I'm just a priest, a simple priest who works for the Congregation of the Doctrine of the Faith. Hardly more than an administrator."

"You're dissembling, Father." Ginny peered at him with a new respect. The Congregation of the Doctrine of the Faith was one of the most important offices within the Vatican. It was they who determined miracles, pronounced sainthood, and interpreted Church doctrine. "You wouldn't have come here to Lebanon if you were merely some clerk."

He gave her a smile.

Ginny smiled back. "I'm curious, Father—why are you still in Lebanon? In the past, in every instance of a sighting of the Holy Mother, the seers were quickly whisked off to Rome . . . which is what happened in Los Zapatos, where we first met all those years ago. And yet here you are. Bernadette is still here in Lebanon, too. Let's be frank with each other, shall we? Off the record?" She picked up her glass. "Do *you* believe Bernadette's visions?"

He toasted her with his own glass. "To frankness, Ginny." He took a sip, then held her eyes seriously. "None of this, of course, is for your book."

"Agreed. Off the record then."

His eyes moved past her as he seemed lost in thought. "Bernadette's visions . . ." He paused, returning his gaze to Ginny. "Yes, I believe them to be true. And since we are off the record, I will add this. What the Holy Mother told her was consistent with other secrets true seers have been told. There was no *earthly* way that Bernadette could have known these secrets, Ginny. Therefore, it stands to reason Bernadette's vision was a true one." He smiled. "Pure logic and deduction, Ginny."

"Then why has she not been taken to Rome?"

"Well, let's return to one of the primary theses of your work. The idea that the books of the Bible have been rewritten, over and over again, throughout history, for political purposes. You have written that what we today know as the Bible is not, in fact, purely Holy Scripture that came directly from God, but rather is a mix of words of men with agendas, is that not correct?"

She nodded. "Yes."

"Suppose I were to tell you that you are correct, Ginny."

"My only surprise would be your confirmation."

"Deep within the vaults of the Vatican there are original texts of the Bible, in the handwriting of the actual authors. They tell us many things not found in standard Bibles today. Throughout the millennia, the Vatican has kept these things secret—and not only for political purposes, as you believe, Ginny, but because it has been the opinion of the Papacy that the world—that mankind—is not ready for the truth they reveal."

"It's not for the Pope to decide what the world is or is not ready for . . . and a decision made thousands of years ago might not still be valid today."

"Spoken like a true American." Father Ortiz laughed. "Suppose I were to tell you that probably the most incendiary of those texts contains prophecies—prophecies that are not vague and symbolic, but word-for-word constructs of what is to occur at the time of the Antichrist."

"I—" Ginny couldn't find words. "Word-for-word constructs . . . ?"

"Suppose I were to tell you that a copy of that text somehow managed to leak out of the Vatican over a hundred years ago, and that there is a group—a society if you will, perhaps you might call it a cult—which is determined to force the prophecy to come true sooner than what is predicted . . . sooner than what God's will intended?"

A chill went down Ginny's spine, and her mind began to spin. "But—but that's just crazy."

"I thought you were trained not to believe *or* disbelieve," Ortiz said.

She just nodded.

"Suppose," the priest went on, "many centuries ago, when the Church was still being founded, and the Bible still being put together, it was determined that the true text of the Book of Revelation could *not* be revealed to the populace at large for fear of panic."

"I'd say that fear of panic was perhaps only one of the Church's fears."

He gave her a look. "And you'd be right. The Book of Revelation—in its complete, unabridged version—connects all religions. It places Christianity in context with Hinduism and Buddhism and paganism and every form of god-worship since the dawn of humankind. And we learn from its pages that the Antichrist, as we call the demon, comes not simply to overthrow Christianity, but all men who are good."

"Such knowledge would undercut every religion's claim to superiority," Ginny observed.

"But unite them as well," Father Ortiz said. "For the threat predicted by Revelation is very specific."

"Word for word, you said."

The priest nodded. "Over the years, there has been intensive debate within the Vatican as to whether or not the true text should ever be revealed. It has always been determined that the text needed to be kept secret. And so we have guarded that secret, and watched . . . . we have always watched . . ."

"But you say a copy of the text leaked out of the Vatican? A hundred years ago? How was that possible, Father?"

"Ah, Ginny, I said *suppose.*"

She shook her head. "I promised this would be off the record. Tell me what you know."

"All I know for certain is what Bernadette has told me."

"She believes the Antichrist is here on earth now. And that the Antichrist is not a man but a woman."

"Yes," Father Ortiz agreed.

"Do you know who she is?"

The priest nodded.

"Who?"

"If Bernadette has not given you her name, I am not allowed to say."

Ginny groaned. "Then what's the point in this conversation? Father, these other appearances around the world—are they reporting the same thing? That the Antichrist has arrived?"

"Yes, they all have the same message."

"Then why aren't you off investigating all of them?"

He smiled. "You asked why I was still here in Lebanon."

"Yes. Exactly."

"Don't you see?" Ortiz asked her.

It dawned on her. Ginny shuddered. "Are you saying . . . the Antichrist is here in Lebanon?"

The priest nodded. "All of the sightings have reported the same. They have pointed here."

Ginny laughed. "I knew this town was strange, but I never thought . . ."

"You shared with me the result of your research into another rash of Virgin sightings, Ginny. From about twenty years ago."

She nodded.

"I have seen the Vatican reports on those sightings. Most of those also pointed to this place, predicting that in twenty years time, we would see the rise of the Antichrist."

"Why here?" Ginny asked.

"Well, we've long suspected that the Antichrist would come from somewhere in America. Revelation—that is, the unex-purgated version—tells us that many will rise attempting to claim the mantle of the Antichrist. Throughout history, many have indeed tried—Hitler comes to mind. But they have failed."

"Are you saying Hitler was an Antichrist? The son of the devil?"

"Perhaps."

"I think mankind is capable of enough evil that we do not need demonic explanations."

Father Ortiz nodded. "But man needs an instigator for his basest instincts to come forward. Someone to fan the flames of hatred, bigotry, anger, fear. Now suppose . . ."

Ginny shook her head. "We're back to suppositions again."

"Suppose, just suppose, that there is a cult that has risen in this country in the years since the text of Revelation leaked out of the Vatican," Father Ortiz said. "A cult devoted to the Book of Revelation and the end times. What if, Ginny, there is a group in this country which, in its misguided faith, believes it is doing God's will by trying to bring about the Rapture—the end times, with all the destruction and death foretold in the Book of Revelation?" His face grew sad.

"And suppose, just suppose, they, in their misguided fervor, have allied themselves with the forces of evil to breed an Antichrist?"

"The stuff of horror movies, Father." Ginny finished her wine, got up, and refilled her glass. "Has Bernadette told you all this?"

"She hasn't needed to. I've read Revelation." He shuddered. "But she has confirmed that forces are at work to bring about the Rapture, as the fundamentalist churches call it. Good, faithful, religious people are being conned into doing the devil's bidding!"

"That's happened for aeons."

"Yes. Look about you, Ginny. These so-called Christian televangelists, raising so much money, blaspheming the Word of God. You've seen the likes of, say, the Reverend Bobby Vandiver? You've had your own experiences with the Reverend, have you not?"

"Bobby Vandiver." Ginny took a deep breath. He'd attacked her and her work, calling her a blasphemer. But Ortiz was right: Vandiver and his ilk were the true blasphemers, amassing great wealth and power by preaching eternal damnation and filling their pockets with the donations of the faithful—simple people who were desperate to make sense of a senseless world, to find faith and spirituality and redemption. Ginny hated how such hucksters influenced their followers on how to vote, how they manipulated them in their own quests for political power. Vandiver was infamous for stating over and over again that the United States was a *Christian* nation, not a secular one, that there should be no separation of church and state. Even with such extreme rhetoric, Washington politicos still kowtowed to him, knowing his influence over large segments of voters. Vandiver claimed to speak with God; he pronounced hurricanes as God's punishment for sin; he called the terrorist attacks on 9/11 "God's vengeance on America" for turning its back on God and Holy Scripture.

Not so different from the Muslim fanatics who'd piloted those airplanes into the Twin Towers.

"Religious fanaticism can be corralled by any faith," Father Ortiz said. "And used for distinctly unreligious ends."

"So you're saying that there is a cult in this country, powered by some in the far-right religious movement, that has actually summoned the Antichrist?"

Ortiz nodded. "For the rank and file, it means their long-awaited Rapture. For the leaders, it means untold riches, power, fame, glory."

Ginny could not respond.

The priest set down his wineglass and offered her a small smile. "But of course, it is only a supposition."

"How have they brought the Antichrist to life? How was it accomplished?"

Father Ortiz stood. He walked over to the coat rack. "I do not know the details. I'm not sure I want to. They would have had to make some sort of bargain with the demon. Ritual sacrifice perhaps. Probably over many years. And then a girl to bear the unholy seed."

He slipped his coat back on, turning to face Ginny.

"You see, the demon—the force of evil—thrives on discontent. On hatred, on warfare, on discord, on chaos. The leaders of the cult know this, and so they stir up the faithful, exhorting them to go after abortionists, or homosexuals, or blacks, or immigrants, or feminists . . . The hatred, the conflict, is lifeblood for the demon. The leaders know this. So they stir it up. And in return, the demon makes them richer, more powerful."

"What will happen to them when the Antichrist wipes out the world?"

He was buttoning his coat. "That's not what Revelation actually predicts. The world won't end. Only the good will die."

"So the leaders of the cult—they will go on. And their sheep? The faithful who thought they were doing God's work?"

"They'll get their end times," Ortiz said. "Only it won't be so rapturous."

"You've told me quite a fascinating story, Father," Ginny said, speaking over the priest's shoulder as he opened the door to leave.

"Thank you for all your expertise, Ginny," he said, looking back at her. "It has been very helpful. Now I must use it to try to prevent what is to occur."

"You've got to find the Antichrist," Ginny said.

"Oh, I've met her. Now I just need to find a way to deal with her."

Ginny gave him a weak smile. "Right now," she said, "I'm glad I'm not a believer."

He smiled back at her. "But you are not a disbeliever either." He headed back down the stairs. "Godspeed in your travels, Ginny. We will keep in touch!"

"Yes," she called after him.

Godspeed to you, too, she wanted to say, but didn't.

Then Ortiz was gone, a black figure moving out through the white snow.

Ginny returned to the living room and sat down.

No, she finally said to herself. *It's just a crazy theory, there's nothing to back it up, no evidence. Ortiz is as much a religious fanatic as the people he criticizes if he, in fact, really believes all this.*

Could he have been toying with her?

Someone who works for the Congregation of the Doctrine of the Faith would not reveal the great secrets of the Vatican to me.

The Antichrist . . . .here in Lebanon!
How absurd!
Still, Ginny shuddered.
She couldn't wait to get the hell out of town.
"Pun not intended," she said as she began packing her bags.

56

The subway was packed full of holiday shoppers, and Sue found herself hanging on to an overhead railing as the train sped downtown toward Times Square. She'd always liked looking at the other people on the subway—she never tired of it. She was always fascinated by the multitude of faces and races she saw on the subway. Part of her enjoyment, she knew, was a backhanded slap at her grandfather, who always hated the subway and wouldn't take it for any reason. "All those dirty, nasty people down there, and it's not safe. It's like going down into the bowels of hell," he'd said more than once.

He hadn't changed. After being away from home for three months, Sue had almost forgotten how much of a presence her grandfather could be. But yesterday, at the Thanksgiving table—he had seemed so large, so commanding, all white hair and flaring nostrils.

"Blessed be God and these Thy gifts," he had intoned, saying grace over the roast turkey and sweet potatoes. A Jamaican maid carried in platters of vegetables from the kitchen as Sue and her grandmother bowed their heads. Granpa's voice seemed to echo off the walls.

How strange it felt to be back home. The apartment she'd grown up in felt alien to Sue. *Is this how everyone feels the first time they come back?* Her grandmother had been especially doting, asking after her health—but Granpa had finally told his wife to leave Sue alone. "She is a grown woman now," he'd said strangely. "Our custodianship is almost over."

The subway jostled, and the lights blinked on and off for a moment. Sue wondered what her grandfather had meant. After that, her grandmother had seemed to keep her distance for the rest of the day. That night, Granpa summoned Sue to his study, and he gave her a box.

"What's this?" she asked.

"You are going out into the world now," he said. "You will face many dangers."

Sue opened the box. It was a gun. She gasped.

"I don't want a gun!" she cried. "I hate guns!"

"I taught you how to use one," he told her. It was true: He had. He'd insisted some years ago that Sue know how to shoot in case the need ever arose.

"There is a safety," Granpa said. "You should have it. Especially now."

Sue assumed he referred to the murder of Bonnie Warner. "Don't worry, Granpa, there are security men all over campus . . ."

"I know," he said. "Keep the gun in a safe place. It is there if you should need it."

Sue put the box in her closet, hating the idea of a gun in her possession. After that, she went to bed, and this morning, when she awoke, neither of her grandparents were at home. She felt she barely knew them anymore.

Certainly, she didn't tell them what she was planning to do this day. She didn't tell them about her appointment with Joyce Davenport.

I'm about to find out about my mother. Even more—I'm about to find out about myself.

Sue was certain Joyce Davenport had answers for her. Answers that would explain what was happening. For Sue had come to understand that she was on the brink of discovering something about herself—and the things that she could do.

Was that what Granpa had meant? That she was now a woman—who could make things happen?

Things she didn't always like.

But still—things that made her feel very powerful.

Sue couldn't deny the ripple of excitement she'd felt as she'd driven out of Lebanon early Wednesday afternoon in the midst of the snowstorm. She didn't fear slippery roads. She didn't fear anything, in fact. *The roads will clear for me,* she told herself.

And they did. It might be snowing fiercely, but as Sue's Lexus made its way through the winding roads of upstate New York, ice melted and slush receded. She didn't so much as spin a tire all the way back to the city.

Luck—or something else?

She got off the subway at Times Square, and headed over to the bookstore Joyce had told her about. A mob of people stood waiting to hear Joyce speak. *Sheep,* Sue couldn't help but think. *They look like sheep.* Blank-eyed, they clutched copies of Joyce's books to their chests. Sue found a spot in the back, and watched with fascination as all the seats were filled. Then Joyce was up there in front, basking in the applause. Her rant was far more specific than the one she'd given at Wilbourne. Joyce blasted "godless liberals" who wanted to destroy "the American way of life." She called a well-known Congressman a "faggot" to the hoots and applause of the crowd. Those blank eyes were waking up, filled now with fire. Joyce went after illegal immigrants. "Tar and feather them!" one young man in the same row as Sue shouted. The people around her hooted. Sue could feel the hot energy pulsing from the crowd. It was both terrifying—but also, strangely, exhilarating.

Sue stood off to the side watching Joyce sign copies of her book after she had finished speaking. Sue marveled at the way these people responded to Joyce. They seemed to draw power from her. And she from them.

She certainly drew their dollars. The cash register never stopped ringing.

"Sweetie!" Joyce finally said as she caught a glimpse of Sue. "You're here!"

She flew over, flung her arms around Sue, and whispered in her ear. "Meet me across the street at the Hubcap Grill. I'll get rid of these sheep so we can speak privately."

Sheep, Sue thought, smiling. *She called them sheep, too.*

The Hubcap Grill was crowded when she walked through the front door, as most places around Times Square generally were. It was a specialty place that sold nostalgia along with overpriced food. It was patterned after a classic fifties-style diner. Shiny chrome stood out everywhere, with booths covered in red vinyl. A jukebox played only music from Elvis Presley, the Big Bopper, and Buddy Holly. Everywhere you looked, flat-screen televisions were mounted, each of them showing episodes of a different black-and-white sitcom from the fifties. Sue recognized *Leave it to Beaver, The Honeymooners,* and *I Love Lucy.* The others weren't as familiar.

She slipped into a booth way in back and ordered a Coke. After about ten minutes, she spotted Joyce moving through the crowd toward her. She was wearing a simple black pantsuit—*where's the sexy black miniskirt?* Sue wondered—with a short rope of pearls hanging onto her black blouse. The long black hair, styled dramatically over her shoulder at the book reading, was now pulled back into a ponytail. She'd washed off most of the makeup she'd been wearing, too. Apparently, the persona she adapted for public consumption was off duty now.

Her one concession seemed to be her mink coat, which she ditched as quickly as she arrived at the booth. "Too many of those freaky animal rights people around, you know?" Joyce laughed. "I've got to hide it under the table. If I hang it here on the rack, somebody's bound to throw ketchup on it, pretending it's blood." She sat down opposite Sue. "Minks are nasty little animals anyway."

"Great turnout across the street," Sue said.

"Oh, that's nothing, sweetie. I pulled in five hundred last night on Fifth Avenue."

"On Thanksgiving Night?"

Joyce beamed. "I've got 'em flocking behind me."

Sue smiled awkwardly. "Anyway, I appreciate you meeting me."

"Well, I'm only sorry it took so long. But everything happens for a reason." She narrowed her eyes and gave Sue an intimate look. "I've been wanting to see you for a very long time, you know."

A waitress handed them two menus. "Can I just get a glass of white wine?" Joyce asked as she opened her menu.

"I'm sorry, ma'am, we don't serve wine," the waitress replied.

Joyce made a face. "Then just bring me a fucking Diet Coke." She waved her hand as if dismissing the waitress.

Joyce sighed. "So, what do you think of Wilbourne? Have they been good to you?"

Sue nodded. "It's okay. I mean, I enjoy my classes, and some of my professors are great."

"Like who?"

"Well, like Dr. Marshall."

"Virginia Marshall?" Joyce let out a hoot. "Brilliant! Fucking brilliant! I'm so glad you had Marshall this semester!"

"I didn't think you'd approve of what she teaches."

Joyce grinned. "She gets people riled up. That's what it's all about, sweetie. Getting people riled up."

"Or getting people to think."

"Hell, no!" Joyce laughed again. "If they think too long, they start getting too many ideas!"

If they think too long, maybe they'll stop buying your books, Sue thought.

"Do you think you're getting a good education at Wilbourne?"

"I guess." Sue shrugged. "I mean, it's not easy—I really have to study and work hard to get good grades . . . and my teachers really push me, you know?"

"Wilbourne is a great school," Joyce replied. She smiled and raised her eyebrows. "And did you get a chance to read my book?"

Sue looked down at her Coke. "Um, yes."

"I gather you didn't much care for it?" Joyce barked out a laugh. "That's okay, Sue, you aren't my target audience. Did some of the things I wrote in it shock you?"

"No. Well, yeah." Sue looked Joyce directly in the eye. "There wasn't anything in it that I hadn't heard before. You and my grandfather agree on almost everything. It was pretty much the way you said things that I didn't care for."

"Because I'm a bitch?" Joyce laughed again. "Yeah, I can be pretty mean, right? That's the point, you know. I say things that people think but don't have the balls to come right out and say. Get people riled up. That's my motto." The waitress set down her Coke and Joyce took a sip. "But if you think I'm bad, you should see the things the liberals say about me sometime."

"I have," Sue said. "You seem to provoke quite a bit of controversy."

"And that's the point, sweetie! Get things stirred up! You know what my favorite Web site is? *Joyce Davenport is a Lying Cunt dot com.* Isn't that great? People get all passionate—and they start accusing me of everything—and then they get mad at each other and actually start arguing with each other! It's fantastic!"

The waitress was hovering to take their orders. Without looking at her, Joyce said, "I'll have the Cobb salad, no dressing. Sue?"

"I'll have the Reuben sandwich with fries." Sue smiled at the waitress and handed over her menu.

"A Reuben?" Joyce raised her eyebrows. "That's pretty fattening, Sue."

Sue smirked. "I'm not one of those girls who worries about my weight."

"Good for you." Joyce sighed. "But me—I have to watch my weight." She patted her stomach. "Don't think I'm not aware that if I gained about fifty pounds, I wouldn't get on television any more."

Sue was becoming impatient. "Please, Joyce," she said, "I want to know about my mother."

"Direct and to the point. I like that." Joyce laughed. "But I wouldn't have expected anything less from Mariclare's little girl."

"You knew her well?"

"Well, as I told you before, your mother and I were roommates at Wilbourne. I really liked your mother. I miss her."

I can't believe my mother would be friends with someone like you.

"I wanted to see you, to talk to you about her, many times over the years, but your grandfather wouldn't allow it," Joyce went on. "I understood. It hurt your grandfather too much to talk about Mariclare."

"But you decided to risk his displeasure when you sought me out at Wilbourne."

"Darling," Joyce said, reaching over and patting Sue's hand. "He gave me permission to do so."

"He did?"

"Of course. I wouldn't do anything behind your grandfather's back."

"He never told me," Sue said, Just like he hadn't told her he'd been in contact with Dean Gregory, that he'd intended for Sue to go to Wilbourne all along . . .

"Sweetie, I understood that everything would come out in time." She sat back in the booth, looking over at Sue. "That's why I phoned your grandparents to tell them we were meeting today."

"You did?"

Joyce nodded. "They agreed not to say anything to you."

Sue was dumbfounded. "What is going on? Why does it feel that there's all this stuff going on behind my back?"

"Sweetie, it's time that you learned everything. Of course, a bit at a time. Too much at once would be too much for anyone. Even me!"

"What are you talking about?"

"Your grandfather is allowing me a wonderful privilege in giving you this news, Sue. I'm forever grateful to him."

Sue was ready to jump out of her seat. "What news?"

Joyce was quiet for a moment. Finally, she said, "I went to see your mother last week. Told her I was meeting you."

"You mean . . . you went to the cemetery? My grandparents have never brought me, said it was too hard for them . . ."

"No, baby," Joyce said. "Your mother's not in any cemetery."

"Then where . . . ?"

The waitress was there with their food. She settled their plates in front of them. Neither Joyce nor Sue looked down. They just kept staring at each other.

"Sweetie," Joyce said. "Your mother is alive."

"No," Sue said, feeling as if someone had just kicked her in the stomach. "My mother and my father were both killed in a car accident when I was a baby." There was a dull buzzing in her head.

"No, baby."

"Yes!" Sue struggled to keep her voice steady. The words of Bernadette deSalis echoed in her mind: *Your mother is alive*. "My mother is dead!" Sue shouted.

"No."

Sue squeezed the older woman's hand. "Tell me the truth!"

Joyce leaned back against the booth. "That's what I'm trying to do, sweetie. Your mother is in a mental hospital in western Pennsylvania. It's called Fair Oaks, in a town called Star of Bethlehem."

"My mother—in—a—mental hospital."

Joyce nodded. "It was a terrible thing, what happened to her. You have no idea how many times I've blamed myself for what happened—if only I'd done this, if only I'd done that . . ."

"What—happened to her?"

Joyce took a deep breath. "We were roommates at Wilbourne—Room 323 in Bentley Hall."

So she had been right. Her mother had lived in the haunted room.

"One night, I was at the library studying. It was very late. If only I'd gone back to the room earlier . . ."

"Why?"

"Because maybe I could have stopped what happened."

Sue swallowed hard. "My mother was the girl who was raped in there, wasn't she?"

Joyce nodded. "When I got back, she was gone. She had

wandered off. We looked everywhere for her, the other girls and I and Mrs. Oosterhouse . . ."

"And she was never found?"

"Oh, yes. She was found. She was missing for several days, and then one day she just turned up back here in New York." Joyce's voice shook as she remembered. "Except she was no longer able to speak. She seemed catatonic. Even when she regained some of her voice, she didn't make any sense. The experience had driven her right out of her mind . . ."

"Did you see her after that?"

Joyce hesitated. "Not until after . . ."

"After what?"

"After you were born."

Suddenly, Sue understood.

Her rapist got her pregnant.

My father was a rapist.

"She's been in the mental hospital ever since. Your grandparents had every good reason to keep the truth from you. Please believe me. When you go back home after this, don't judge them. Listen to them. They'll tell you everything else you need to know."

"They'd let you—a complete stranger—tell me this about my mother? About myself?"

Joyce smiled. "It was a great honor. I told your mother I was going to tell you. I'm not sure how much she understood, but I told her. I told her you were growing up to be every bit the woman we all hoped you'd be."

"You still see her?"

Joyce nodded. For just a second, she looked uncomfortable. "Yes, I see her. Every couple of weeks I visit. I'm the only one who does."

Everything I've ever known about my mother was a lie.

"Sue," Joyce said, the energy returned to her voice, "you have a bright and wonderful future ahead of you."

*There was no car accident, none of that was true . . .
what else have they lied to me about?*

"Eat your lunch, sweetie."

Sue wasn't hungry. She pushed her plate away from her and started to cry.

"Don't cry, Sue," Joyce said as she began nibbling at her salad. "This simply opens the door for everything else."

"What are you talking about?"

"Go back and talk to your grandparents, sweetie. They'll tell you everything." She gazed over at Sue's Reuben. "Sure you don't want it? I might take a bite . . ."

"How is my mother?" Sue choked the words out. Her entire body was numb, her head was still buzzing, her stomach twisting in knots. "Can I see her?"

"Oh, definitely. All in good time." Joyce smiled. "Really, baby, your grandparents will tell you everything else that you need to know . . ."

Sue grabbed her coat and stood up. "I—I've got to go."

"At least wrap up your lunch to take with you," Joyce said.

"You can have it!" She ran out of the diner, not caring whether Joyce had intended to pick up the tab or not.

She didn't see Joyce take a bite of the Reuben, or pull her cell phone out of her purse. An eyebrow went up as she said into the phone, "It's done."

57

Ginny poured herself a cup of coffee, and resisted the strong urge to add Bailey's to it. Drinking first thing in the morning wasn't going to help anything, tempting though it was. Instead, she just added cream and sweetener, drank half of the cup, and refilled it. She looked out the window. It was going to be another gray, drizzly December morning in Hammond, the perfect background for her mood.

You're being ridiculous. Just think it through and you'll know what to do—what the right thing to do is.

It was seven in the morning, and she hadn't slept well. She hadn't expected to, despite all the wine she'd tossed down the night before. After she'd put Sue to bed, she'd stayed up trying to take her mind off the story she'd just been told, going over her notes and writing out in longhand an outline of what she was going to write the following day.

But no matter how hard she tried, she couldn't get Sue's story out of her head. Her mind just kept drifting back to it.

If it hadn't been for what Father Ortiz told me the day before I left Lebanon, I'd have never believed her for a minute. Hell, I wouldn't have listened to her for more than a minute. I would have just called her grandparents and been done

*with it. Her story is just too damned fantastic. How could it
be possible?*

That was the worst part, Ginny thought as she sat down at
the table. She was starting to believe it *could* be possible.

The rational side of her mind wanted to dismiss Sue's
story as the product of an obviously unstable mind. It was the
part of her mind that tried to dismiss all these Virgins sightings—Bernadette deSalis included—as just part of a mass
hysteria. Sue's ramblings were like something out of the Middle Ages, before science had disproved almost everything
religion held to be sacred truths. This was what Ginny's rational mind told her.

But her instinctive mind—the part of her that was raised
in the Church, that still remembered her catechism and still
kept a strand of never-used rosary beads in her purse, the part
that had prayed and lit candles for the life of her son—that
part believed. It all came together—Bernadette deSalis's visions, her prophecies, her declaration about the Antichrist.
Father Ortiz's stunning revelations. And even Deputy Perry
Holland's crazed rant about a cult committing ritualized murders at regular intervals at Wilbourne College . . .

*Father Ortiz was not talking in hypotheticals. Was he
preparing me for the day when Sue would show up here?*

Last night, she'd drunk a great deal of wine, hoping to
anaesthetize her mind enough to stop thinking about it all.
But when she'd finally called it a night and gone to bed, she'd
tossed and turned all night, unable to turn off her mind. The
thoughts just kept coming, nagging at her as she stared at the
ceiling. And when she had been finally able to drift off into
something approximating sleep, she'd had nightmares. Horrible nightmares of death and destruction, explosions and
fire . . . Ginny woke each time shaking and sweating in her
bed, almost *afraid* to go back to sleep.

This can't be happening. This can't be . . . none of this

can be true, there has to be some logical explanation for all of this that has nothing to do with God and the devil.

And what role does Joyce Davenport play in all of this? Why Joyce?

Sue had told her about her meetings with Joyce Davenport. In some ways, that was the oddest part. But at least on that score, Ginny had little reason to disbelieve. Joyce Davenport in league with the devil? Now *that* she could believe.

Is Sue's story true, or is she mentally unbalanced? Could she somehow be in cahoots with Bernadette to cash in on some kind of mass hysteria?

No. At the very least, Ginny felt certain, Sue believed every word of her story.

Two days before Sue's arrival, Dean Gregory had called Ginny. When she'd seen the Lebanon area code on her caller ID, she'd thought, *What the hell is he calling me for?* She'd debated not answering, just letting the voice mail pick up, but finally, curiosity got the better of her. Hearing Gregory's voice was unsettling enough, but the purpose of his call—to let her know that Sue Barlow was missing, had she heard from her?—was even more disturbing.

"Not another girl," Ginny had said. "What is going on?"

"We're all very worried, Ginny. Have you heard from her?"

"Of course not," Ginny said. At that point, she hadn't gotten any of Sue's e-mails. "Why would she contact me?"

"She was in one of your classes. She had a final to hand in to you."

This was true. But Ginny sensed the dean suspected more.

"She is a very special student, with very special needs," Gregory told her. At the time, Ginny had thought he meant Sue was the granddaughter of an important school benefactor. Now she wondered.

Could it be true? Was the girl sleeping upstairs really—

Ginny heard a bang. She jumped, her heart suddenly pounding in her ears. It was a shutter outside the window, blown loose by the wind. She relaxed in her chair, surprised at how jittery she was.

Dean Gregory . . . might he be in fact far more nefarious than she'd ever dreamed?

If Ginny had thought she'd put Wilbourne behind her, here it all was, right back with her. So much for her great plan to renew her mind and body and career. Since returning to Hammond two weeks ago, Ginny had structured her life into a healthy daily routine. Every morning, she ate fresh fruit and granola for breakfast before a vigorous workout at the gym. Three days a week, she rode the stationary bicycle; two mornings a week, she sweated through a yoga class. After showering, she worked for several hours, reviewing her notes and writing. The book was coming along even faster than she could have hoped. One night, while having her usual glass of wine, she'd looked at her notes and was amazed at how fast she was writing. *It's almost like God wants me to write this book.*

That thought had come from nowhere. Ginny laughed out loud. *God and His Mother both.* At the rate she was going, she would not only finish by her deadline, she'd beat it by several months. *And the work is good, probably the best I've ever done*—and that only motivated her even further.

And then Sue Barlow had shown up at her front door.

If I didn't know her from class, if she were someone I'd never met before, I would think she was completely deranged.

But is Bernadette deSalis deranged? Is Father Ortiz?

Ginny sat down at her kitchen table and poured herself more coffee.

She hadn't called Sue's grandparents. Sue had begged her not to—and so far, she'd acceded to her wishes. *If her story is true—Good Lord, her grandparents are the last people in the world I should let know anything.* But as a parent—as someone who'd been a parent—Ginny also empathized with the grandparents. They must be worried sick—if Sue's story wasn't true.

She rubbed her eyes and sighed. *The truth is, Ginny, if you'd not had that talk with Father Ortiz right before Thanksgiving, you'd think Sue was completely insane. You would have called her grandparents, you would have called the police, you would have called anyone and everyone who could get her the kind of help she needs.*

And maybe it was just too easy to believe that there was something evil going on at Wilbourne College. That was a personal reaction that Ginny needed to separate from Sue's story.

She stood, suddenly motivated, and walked into her office. *Treat Sue's story,* she told herself, *like it's a Virgin sighting for your book. Consider it rationally and objectively without emotion.*

From the top drawer of her desk she removed a spiral notebook and a pen. Sitting down, she opened the notebook and stared down at the blank page. Across the top she wrote, "IF SHE IS TELLING THE TRUTH." Ginny sat for a moment, worrying the end of the pen in her mouth. Then she continued writing.

58

Upstairs, Sue tossed in the bed, a prisoner of terrifying dreams.

Billy was beckoning to her from one side of a bridge. Joyce Davenport stood on the other. The bridge was falling and Sue had only time enough to make a quick sprint to safety before it plunged into the chasm below. But which side was closest? Toward whom should she jump?

She sat up in bed. Where was she?

Dr. Marshall's house, she thought. *I made it.*

Images from the past few weeks kept rattling through her mind as she tried to get back to sleep.

Wandering around Times Square after her meeting with Joyce . . . pulling out her cell phone to call Billy . . . but snapping the phone shut every time.

She dreaded going back to her grandparents' apartment. Joyce said they had more to tell her—but Sue couldn't bear to hear any more. Truth was, she was also terrified of what they might say. They had lied to her. She hated them.

At that moment, she didn't care to see either of them ever again.

All these years, they've lied to me about my mother. Why? Why would they do such a thing? To spare me the knowledge

*that my father was a rapist? That I'm a bastard, with a
mother locked up in a loony bin somewhere? Were they ever
going to tell me that she is alive? And why would they let me
find out the truth from Joyce Davenport, of all people—that
just makes it worse, so much worse. How could they have
done this to me?*

Sue desperately wanted to believe that Joyce, not her
grandparents, was lying, but there was no conceivable reason for Joyce to make up such a story. She'd told Sue to go
back to her grandparents, who'd confirm the story.

But Sue was in no mood for confirmations.

She finally got back on the subway around four and headed
back to the apartment. The train was packed full of people
carrying boxes and bags, their cheeks flushed red from the
cold, talking joyously to their friends. People wished each
other "Merry Christmas." But Sue couldn't look at anyone,
couldn't bring herself to even glance at their faces. She stared
out the dark window at the walls of the subway tunnel. She
almost missed her stop, jumping through the doors just before they closed.

Back home, she let herself in quietly. She could hear the
television in her grandfather's den—a football game—and
she hurried to her room without saying anything. She shut
the door soundlessly behind her, and locked it.

*One way to find out if Joyce is a big fat liar—and I don't
have to go to Joyce-Davenport-is-a-lying-cunt-dot-com for
this.*

The Lebanon newspaper had a Web site, but its archive
only went back as far as the launch of the site—a few years.
Gritting her teeth, Sue went to the Web site for the *Senandaga
Reporter,* and clicked on ARCHIVE SEARCH. Unaware that she
was holding her breath, she entered "Mariclare Barlow" into
the archive search engine, and clicked SEARCH.

No matches found. Make sure you have the spelling correct.

She swore under her breath. *Idiot, they don't print the names of rape victims in the newspaper.*

She typed in "rape victim Wilbourne College" and clicked again.

Several links came up, and she clicked on the first one.

LEBANON, N.Y.—A student at Wilbourne College was missing this morning after being raped on the campus late Friday evening, a spokesperson for the college announced today.

The student was allegedly raped in her dorm room at Bentley Hall by an unknown assailant, according to several other students who witnessed the young woman emerging from her room bloody and in shock.

"The college is cooperating with the local sheriff's department as well as with the state police to not only catch the perpetrator of this heinous crime, but to ensure the safety of the other students at the college," the spokesperson's statement went on to say.

Reports that the student had left Lebanon to return to her home in New York City were unconfirmed. Police list her as "missing."

The mood in this small college town is tense.

"This kind of thing just doesn't happen here," said Marjorie Pequod, a local resident. "Lebanon is a small town full of God-

fearing, law-abiding citizens. We just don't
have crime here—and everyone is on edge
now, especially the women. It's hard for
anyone here to even consider that this
was done by a local—the general consen-
sus around town is that it was some kind
of drifter, passing through town, who
wound up on the campus."

"If the rapist is a local, we'll catch him,"
Deputy Sheriff Miles Holland stated. "We
are working in concert with the state police to catch him. I am confident that we
will catch him and bring him to justice."

The police are not releasing the name
of the victim.

Sue stared at the computer screen, reading the story over
and over. The date was exactly right. Nine months later, Sue
was born.

Finally, she swallowed and went back to the list of search
results. She clicked on the other links, but nothing much was
new there, just a report that the missing student had indeed
returned to her parents' home in New York and that the assailant had not been found. There were promises that he would
be found, but then nothing.

The people of Lebanon appeared to forget the story.

Sue decided to print the accounts of her mother's rape.
She closed the browser window as her printer started spitting out pages.

*I have seen my mother's face in the window of her old
dorm room, which people think is haunted. I have seen her
face, screaming in the window, like she is trying to warn me
about something. But warn me about what? And why? How
is it possible that I see her face up there if she is still alive?*

The printer stopped. Sue grabbed the pages and shoved them into her backpack.

She was getting out of there.

She packed quickly. She knew her grandparents would soon be knocking at her door. They'd want to find out how her meeting with Joyce had gone. They'd want to tell her more things about her life—a life Sue no longer felt was her own. Her fear outweighed her curiosity.

I don't want to know anymore! I just want to get out of here!

At the last minute, she decided to take the gun her grandfather had given her, wrapping it carefully in cloth and placing it in her backpack.

She listened at her bedroom door. She could hear the television in the den, and her grandmother saying something to her grandfather. She slipped out into the hallway, and made her way to her grandfather's home office. Once inside, she carefully closed the door behind her and hurried to the wall behind her grandfather's massive oak desk. She swung the hinged painting of her grandmother aside, and stretched her arm up to turn the combination lock. As she spun the dial, she heard her grandmother's voice in her head. *Don't tell your grandfather that I gave you this. There are important papers in here, and what if there's a fire or something when you're here and we aren't?*

Sue heard the click, and turned the handle. The door came open.

She reached back for the strongbox.

If ever there's a fire or something, Sue, and we aren't here, you've got to come in here, open the safe, and take this metal box with you when you get out. It has all of our records in here—birth certificates and so forth, our wills— and they must be rescued. But don't ever come in here unless

*there's a fire, and you must never let your grandfather know
you know the combination. It'll be our little secret . . .*

Sue opened the strongbox.

Inside were three manila envelopes. One had her name on
it. Sue shook the contents out onto the desk top.

A birth certificate. Hers.

Sue picked it up and stared at it.

Mother's Name: Mariclare Madeleine Barlow.

Father's Name: Luke Morgenstern.

They knew the rapist's name?

Luke Morgenstern . . .

As realization dawned on her, Sue stifled a scream.

"No," she whispered as she stared at the document she
was holding with trembling hands.

The words of Bernadette deSalis came back to her.

Lucifer Morning Star.

59

Ginny wrote it all down in her notebook, everything Sue had told her, about meeting with Joyce Davenport, going back to her grandparents' apartment, finding the article about the rape online, and discovering the strange name on the birth certificate.

"I've always known somehow that I was *different,*" Sue had said last night, her voice low.

Ginny had just stared at her, not knowing what to say.

"I knew I couldn't stay in the apartment the rest of the weekend," Sue continued, oblivious to the expression of shock on Ginny's face. "I had to get out. I didn't want to know more. My instinct was just to run away."

"And so you did," Ginny said.

Sue nodded. "I wanted to go back to Lebanon. I wanted to see Billy. He was the only one I felt I could trust."

"And what were you thinking . . . about your parents?"

Sue gave her an odd smile. "I did an Internet search and came up with any number of Luke Morgensterns. Was I thinking that Satan might be my father? Because some crazy girl who'd seen the Virgin Mary said he was? You bet your life that's what I was thinking. That my mother was raped by the devil."

Ginny was speechless, but Sue just laughed.

"And then I decided it was all too crazy, too much like a bad horror movie, for me to even consider. If I said anything to anyone, I was going to wind up in a padded room right next to my mother. So, I decided that I *was* acting crazy. There's no such thing as Satan, right?"

Sue fell silent.

"I just wanted to get back to Billy."

"You drove back to Wilbourne that night?"

Sue nodded. "I snuck out of the house. Of course, then the calls started on my cell phone. I never picked it up. Gran and Granpa were frantic. But I made it back to school."

"Did you see Billy?"

Sue's face darkened. "Oh, yes. I saw Billy."

60

She called him when she was about an hour outside Lebanon.

"Billy?"

"Sue!"

"Billy, I need to see you . . ."

"I thought I'd never hear from you again! I'd given up!"

"You're the only one I can talk to, Billy. Please. Will you meet me?"

He'd promised. Enthusiastically. He'd seemed so happy to hear from her.

Even though he still saw Heidi, nearly every day . . .

Driving back to Lebanon, Sue felt the urge just to give in to her feelings. *Why not? If I want Billy, take him. If it means Heidi croaks, who the hell cares? I don't know her. Get rid of the bitch so she won't come around hounding my man anymore . . .*

Dear God, Sue thought. *Now I sound like Joyce Davenport.*

"You have a bright and wonderful future ahead of you," Joyce had told her.

Sue sensed she might indeed—if she wanted it.

Why am I so afraid? I have powers. I can do things. I shouldn't be afraid.

Other people should be afraid of me.

She drove directly to town, not even bothering to stop at the college first. Billy promised to meet her at the Yellow Bird.

"Sue," he'd told her on the phone, "you don't know how glad I am that you called. I've been thinking about you all the time. I really started to like you a lot, Sue, and then you stopped returning my calls . . ."

"We can be together now, Billy," she told him. "Meet me at the Bird. I need you. I need to be with you."

She sat in the booth she always took—the one nearest the front door. Marjorie recognized her, and brought her a vanilla shake without Sue even needing to ask for it. She took a sip and looked out the window, waiting for Billy. The snow was nearly all melted now. A bit of a warming spell had settled over the town after that early snowfall. Water dripped from the roof above. The sidewalks were wet.

For a moment, Sue imagined she was just a girl—just a girl like she'd been when she first came to this place. Innocent. No worries. Just a girl meeting her boyfriend for a shake, and maybe a walk holding hands through town.

Now—what was she?

"Hello, Sue."

She looked up. It wasn't Billy.

It was Bernadette deSalis.

"How did you know I was here?" Sue asked bluntly.

The girl smiled. "Just like I think you knew that I'd be here, too."

"No," Sue said. "I didn't know you'd be here. I'm waiting for someone else."

"He'll be along."

Sue eyed her cannily. "How do you know who I'm waiting for?"

"Just like you know certain things, Sue. Please, may I sit down?"

"Go ahead," Sue said. "There are a few things I'd like to ask you."

"I imagined you'd want to eventually," Bernadette said, as she slid into the booth opposite Sue.

"What can I get you, Bernie?" Marjorie asked, approaching the table.

Bernadette smiled up at her. "I'll have the same thing she's having, thanks."

After Marjorie moved away, Sue glared at the girl across from her. Bernadette's dark hair was pulled tightly away from her face in a ponytail. Her eyes seemed to bulge. "How did you know my mother was alive?" Sue asked.

"I told you, Sue. I know things the same way you know things."

"Well, apparently it's a little different. You've seen the Virgin Mary, but my father happens to be Lucifer Morning Star."

Bernadette laughed. "I guess that means we were destined to meet." Marjorie placed her shake in front of her. "And share vanilla milk shakes!"

"So you believe I'm the devil's daughter."

Bernadette nodded. "The Antichrist," she said matter-of-factly, taking a sip of her shake.

"This is *crazy*!" Sue's voice was loud. Several people in the diner turned to look at her.

"Have you ever read the Book of Revelation?" Bernadette kept smiling. "Believe me, Sue, I'm not here to convert you or anything. I'm asking you for a reason."

"Yes, I've read Revelation. For Dr. Marshall's class, in fact."

"But not the full version? I suppose not. We can get you a copy . . ."

Sue laughed. "Who's we?"

"Father Ortiz and I. You've met him."

Sue nodded. "Yes. He was sitting right where you are."

Bernadette leaned across the table. "Sue," she whispered. "We want to help you. It's not too late—it's never too late—and you can thwart the plans of those who plan to use you."

"Who wants to use me?" Sue stared at her. "Why should I trust you any more than I trust someone else?"

"Do you trust Joyce Davenport?"

"As much as I trust you. Which is zero."

"The seeds of evil are in you, Sue," Bernadette said, shaking her head. "But it's through no fault of your own. You can reject your destiny. Even Christ had the ability to refuse his calling. He could have succumbed to temptation and not fulfilled his ordained role. The Antichrist will also have free will . . ."

"I'm a freshman in college! I'm not the Antichrist!"

A man in the next booth turned and looked at her, made a face, then turned back around.

"This town has a long and ugly history, Sue," Bernadette told her. "So does the college. And you're in danger. I want to help you, because it's not too late to change things. You know the truth about your mother now, don't you?"

"Yes." Sue managed to croak the word out.

"Go see her."

"My mother . . ."

"Get in your car and go." Bernadette's voice was urgent. "Don't go back to the campus. It's starting, Sue. You have to get out of town."

The bell over the door jingled.

Sue looked up.

Billy.

Her heart raced.

She wanted to jump and run to him. She wanted to fold herself into his arms and forget all this madness.

Billy! It was so good to see him again.

A wide smile crossed his handsome face as he spotted her. He beamed.

"I'll leave the two of you alone," Bernadette said, standing, taking her shake with her.

"Hey, Bernie," Billy said as he approached. "What you doing here?"

"Just saying hello to Sue," she told him as she moved off.

Billy sat down. "Did she upset you?"

"No," Sue said.

Billy smiled again. "Goddamn, Sue. It is so good to see you. I've missed you. I really have."

She stared at him. "Have you?"

"Of course," he said. "Have you missed me?"

"Yes," she admitted, averting her eyes.

"So now we can be together again. That's what you said, right?"

She had said that. And she'd meant it. She'd wanted it. Needed it.

But it wasn't right. She cared about Billy. She might even love him. But what kind of relationship could she have with him now?

"I really started to like you, too, Billy," Sue said, looking again at him, at his soft, kind eyes. "I want you to know that."

His smile flickered, but didn't fade. "Don't say that in the past tense."

Sue looked away again.

"You said you needed me, Sue. It seemed like something was wrong. Are you okay?"

Her eyes misted with tears. "I've found something out about myself, Billy."

She moved her eyes back to his.

Their gaze locked.

"What, Sue?" he asked. "What did you find out?"

"Look into my eyes, Billy," she said. "What do you see?"

She could see so much by looking into Billy's eyes. She could see how much he loved her. She could see how much he had missed her.

And now, she saw how much he feared her.

"What do you see in my eyes, Billy?"

In the booth across from her, Billy stiffened. His face went white.

"What is it, Billy?" Sue asked.

Her voice was calm. She knew the answer to her question.

"Sue," Billy said in a low voice.

"Tell me what you see, Billy."

Suddenly, he gasped. He gripped the side of the table, unable to tear his eyes away from what he saw in her face.

"Do you still love me, Billy?" Sue asked.

She no longer recognized the sound of her voice.

Billy let out a sound. He whipped his face away from her eyes, then jumped from the booth. Stumbling across the floor of the diner, he looked back at her.

"You . . ." His voice trailed off. "You're not Sue."

Sue just stared at him.

Billy let out a whimper. Sue saw the utter terror in his eyes. So she was right.

Billy ran out the door. Marjorie looked after him, shaking her head, apparently concluding it was a lovers' squabble.

But Sue knew differently.

She lowered her head, and began to cry.

Bernadette was back, standing beside her.

"Leave town," she whispered. "Get out while you can. Go to see your mother. There is still time."

Sue just sat there crying, the enormity of the horror settling around her.

"Your mother," Bernadette repeated. "Go see your mother."

61

"So I got back into my car," Sue said, draining her wineglass and holding it out for Ginny to refill, "but I didn't leave town. Not right away."

"What did you do?"

"I went to the campus. Just what Bernadette warned me against doing."

"Why?"

"Because now I had some sense of my power. I wasn't afraid. I just wanted answers."

"Who did you want to see on campus?" Ginny asked.

"Who else? Dean Gregory."

62

Sue rang the doorbell at the dean's house.

This is where they killed Tish Lewis.

Sue knew it the moment her finger had touched the bell.

They killed Tish—but I condemned her to die.

The horror and the guilt and the shame sank deep into Sue's soul.

"Hello, Sue."

It was Mrs. Gregory, dressed in a red robe.

"Is the dean in?"

It was a weekend. Sue expected that Gregory would be at home, rather than at the office.

But he was out, his wife explained. "Would you like to wait for him?" Mrs. Gregory asked.

"Yes, thank you."

Mrs. Gregory stepped aside so that Sue could enter. "Did you have a nice holiday in New York?"

"Yes," Sue lied. She was certain that her grandparents had called Gregory to report she'd left abruptly. *He's out looking for me,* Sue realized. *I've got them all in a tizzy.*

"You're back on campus earlier than expected," Mrs. Gregory said. Sue realized the woman was nervous.

"Yes," Sue said, maintaining the charade. "I came back early to study for my finals."

"What a good student you are, Sue. Here, why don't you wait in the parlor? I'll call Ted on his cell phone . . ."

And rustle up his goons to overpower me . . .

"Mrs. Gregory, wait," Sue said. "I just have a quick question for you. Did you know my mother?"

"Your mother?" Mousy Mona's face blanched. Her shaky hand went to a button on her blouse, which she twiddled anxiously. "Oh, no, I'm afraid we weren't yet on campus then . . ."

"But you were involved, weren't you? You must have been."

Mrs. Gregory smiled nervously. "Involved in what, dear?"

"The cult of Revelation. The movement to bring about the end times. You must have been. Otherwise, your husband wouldn't have been named dean."

Mrs. Gregory fell silent.

"Was it worth it, Mona?" Sue asked, drawing close to the woman, almost menacingly. "What it did to your sons?"

In a flash, looking into Mrs. Gregory's eyes, Sue had seen the tragedy of the two Gregory boys. One was now dead—an overdose in just the last couple of days—though she didn't think Mona knew about that part yet.

"My sons," Mrs. Gregory said. Then she began to cry.

"What will you get when it's all done?" Sue asked, so close to Mona that she could see the whites of her eyes. "What have they promised you? Certainly, your husband isn't content with just staying dean of some backwoods women's college."

"I . . . I don't know what you're talking about . . ."

Sue could see she'd get nowhere with Mrs. Gregory, who just stood there bawling her eyes out. She knew now it had been a mistake to come here. She could get trapped. Gregory would keep her—

"Tell your husband I'm not going to play the game the

way he intended," Sue said, moving away from Mona toward the door. "I have a few ideas of my own."

"You can't leave," Mona managed to say.

"Watch me."

"No!" Mrs. Gregory's arm darted out, her hand gripping Sue around her wrist. "If I let you go, they'll punish me."

"Let go of me!"

Sue felt something rising inside of her—something that seemed to fill her brain and her body like water filling a glass. A force pushed into the very back of her mind. Powerful. It felt thrilling.

It felt *good*.

The power rose within her, and Sue's vision was tinted with red. Her entire body was tingling, the hairs on her arms standing up, and it felt good, so good, like nothing she'd ever felt before in her life. *This is who I am,* she thought. *This is who I am meant to be.* A smile played across her lips as Mrs. Gregory's tears suddenly turned to blood.

Sue wrenched her arm free.

And then the dean's wife was sailing through the air, smashing against the opposite wall with a horrible thud. For a moment, she stared at Sue, her face covered in blood. "You cannot escape who you are . . ." she said, before her eyes rolled back into her head and she slumped down, lifeless, to the floor.

63

"She was dead."

Sue put her wineglass down with shaky hands.

"I walked over to her, checked her pulse, but there wasn't one. She was dead, and I had killed her. *I killed her,* Dr. Marshall, and what was more, it felt good while I was doing it."

"Sue, when I spoke with Dean Gregory, he didn't mention his wife's death," Ginny told her. "I think he would have . . . maybe you imagined all of this . . ."

"Don't you see? He didn't care about her. She was just an obstacle." Sue laughed bitterly. "He has far greater things to worry about than Mousy Mona's death."

"Well, if it's true, then *you* have a great deal to worry about. A charge of murder."

"It was in self-defense." Sue laughed again, a sound that unnerved Ginny with its cavalier attitude. "Besides, the body was destroyed. There's no evidence. I'm certain of that. I've seen it in my mind."

Ginny shuddered.

"You're right to tremble, Dr. Marshall. I've become a monster. In that moment, I knew what I was. And I knew what

I had to do. I got off that campus as fast as I could. I stopped at an Internet café in Senandaga and got directions to Star of Bethlehem, the town where Joyce Davenport told me my mother lived. Curious name, no? Ironic. But I knew I had to follow that star. Bernadette told me to go see my mother . . ."

64

Star of Bethlehem, Pennsylvania, was just across the state line. According to the directions Sue had gotten off the Internet, it was about a six-hour drive from Senandaga. She spent that night in a motel a few hours from the border, paying cash for the room. Drifting in and out of a dreamless sleep, Sue steeled herself for what else she might discover about herself the next day. When the sun finally came up, she quickly showered and dressed and got back on the road.

The Fair Oaks Rest Home was on the far side of the little town. The building was large and made of red brick. The woman at the desk, overweight, in her late fifties, glanced up at Sue without smiling.

"Help you?" she asked.

"I would like to see—" Sue swallowed and took a deep breath before continuing. "I would like to see Mariclare Barlow."

The woman's eyebrows darted up. "Mariclare Barlow?"

"Is that a problem?"

Maybe she's here under an assumed name . . .

"No problem." The woman shrugged. "It's just that she

doesn't get too many visitors." She pushed a clipboard and a pen across her desk. "You need to sign in. I'll call up to see if she's finished with her breakfast."

She glanced down at the clipboard after Sue signed it.

"A relative?" she asked after noting the name.

"I'm her daughter," Sue said.

All her life, Sue had dreamed about her mother. She had playacted a moment like this, meeting the woman who had given her birth. She'd gazed at her photograph in the shrines set up to her, examined every little contour of her face, hoping to spot a resemblance. She'd imagined what her mother might be like, how she might have sounded, how she might have reacted to the daughter she never knew.

And now, all of that was about to be revealed.

Sitting in the spartan waiting room, uncomfortable on a hard plastic chair, Sue only felt numb. No excitement. No fear. No anticipation.

She felt nothing.

"Miss Barlow?"

An Asian nurse in a spotless white uniform had appeared in the doorway.

"If you'll follow me?"

Sue stood, following the nurse down a narrow, dimly lit hallway into a small room. At the door, the nurse paused.

"She didn't seem surprised when I told her you were here."

Sue didn't reply.

"I didn't know Mariclare had a daughter."

Sue lifted an eyebrow. "What should I expect?"

"She's usually very quiet. A very sweet lady, in fact. She's not a danger. Poor dear, she's simply delusional."

Sue gave her a weak smile, then walked into the room. A woman was seated at a table with her back to Sue. Long red hair streaked with gray fell down her back. She wore a cheap-looking, floral-patterned cotton housedress. As Sue rounded the table and got a look at her, she thought the woman—her mother—looked tired. Dark circles drooped under large, luminous green eyes.

"Hello, Susan," her mother said as Sue sat down.

Sue stared at her. There was a strong resemblance to the photographs she'd grown up with—bone structure doesn't go away with the passing of time. Mariclare's face was devoid of makeup, but her hair was carefully brushed and held out of her face with two plastic pink barrettes. Despite the streaks of red cobwebbed through the whites, her eyes were still very beautiful.

"She said you weren't surprised when you heard I was here," Sue said.

"I knew you'd come someday," Mariclare said. She smiled. "Joyce was here a few days ago. She said she was going to tell you the truth."

"Well," Sue said. "She did."

"Was it terribly hard for you?" her mother asked.

Sue gave her a tight smile. "That's putting it mildly."

"What a pretty girl you are," Mariclare said.

But I don't look like you, Sue thought.

I look like my father.

She didn't know what to say to this pitiful woman sitting in front of her. All her life she'd missed her mother, thought about her, wished she was still alive—and now that she was sitting across a table from her, she couldn't think of anything to say. She felt tears forming in her eyes, and bit her lower lip.

"They kept you away from me all these years." Mariclare said. She started drumming her fingertips on the table. "I guess they didn't want you to know your mother was a lunatic . . .

though they're just as crazy as I am. Your grandparents, I mean. They told you I was dead, didn't they?"

"Yes."

"And they sent you to Wilbourne."

Sue nodded.

"Mother called me yesterday. She told me if you came here, I should refuse to see you."

"I'm not surprised," Sue said.

Mariclare smiled. "But they can't tell me what to do anymore."

"Did they know what would happen to you at Wilbourne?"

"Do you mean, did they know I'd be the one? The one who'd be raped?"

Sue nodded.

"I think *he* did. My father. At least, I think he was *hoping* I'd be the one." She gave her a bitter smile. "It was a great honor, you know."

Sue couldn't speak.

"I didn't know anything. I was just like you, dear Susan. Just a naïve sheep being led to the slaughter."

"But now you know . . . you understand what happened to you."

Mariclare nodded. "When you've been fucked by a demon, you get a few things in return." She laughed, a brittle sound from deep inside her throat. "You can see things. Understand things. So much suddenly made sense. Those other girls who went missing or were killed at Wilbourne? Part of the bargain. Virgin blood, to keep the dark forces sustained. Keep them interested. Because to bring about the Rapture—"

"You mean, the end times? The prophecy of Revelation?"

Mariclare nodded. "That's right. To bring about the end times, they needed an Antichrist. And Revelation says it will be a girl, eighteen years of age, and her name will be Susan."

"It doesn't say that," Sue said. "I've read Revelation . . ."

"But not the *lost* books of Revelation." Mariclare grinned, almost smugly. "The ones the Vatican tried to hide for centuries. But some renegade priest smuggled them out. Formed his own little cult, headed up by a good little Satanist named Sarah Wilbourne." Her smile faded. "I got to see the lost books of Revelation. I actually got to read them. I told you there were a few perks to being fucked by Satan."

Sue recoiled. This woman was crazy. And yet . . . she made sense.

She made horrible sense.

Mariclare looked over her shoulder, gesturing toward the door with a nod of her head. "Here, they all think I'm quite insane, you know. Delusional. It's much easier to believe that I'm crazy than to think that I am telling the truth. No one wants to hear the truth, you know. Not when the truth is too frightening to contemplate. Not when the truth can't be fit into a box of logic and rationally explained away. No, it's easier to think poor Mariclare lost her mind when she was raped nineteen years ago. She became delusional because she can't handle the reality of what happened to her."

Sue was suddenly overcome with sympathy and compassion for her mother, and began to cry.

Mariclare seemed not to notice. "Not that it matters what they think. They can't do anything more to me than what they've already done."

"Mother—" The word didn't feel right coming out of her mouth, but Sue said it anyway. "There's got to be a way we can beat them. There is this girl. She told me there was still hope. She's seen the Virgin Mary—"

"A good Christian girl, I suppose. But the Christians haven't got the lock on God. This goes far deeper than just God and Satan, Susan. This is much more elemental. This is about the power of good and the power of evil. It transcends all religions."

"So what can we do?"

Mariclare shook her head. "They've been planning this for a long time. It goes back over a hundred years. And now, finally, is the time."

"Because of me," Sue said quietly.

Her mother nodded. "Every religion has its own diabolical messenger, the one who is destined to ignite the final battle between good and evil. The Christians call it the Antichrist."

"No," Sue said. "They call it Susan."

Her mother gave her a compassionate smile. "The girl you spoke of," she said, reaching across the table and taking Sue's hand. "The one who saw the Virgin."

"Bernadette."

"She's right. It's not too late. You don't have to fulfill the prophecies, you know. I told Joyce that you wouldn't succumb, but she said you would."

At Joyce's name, Sue's ears perked up. "Was she really your friend?"

"Yes, she was." Mariclare's face grew dark. "When we were girls, she was a happy child. Filled with sunlight. But then her father went bankrupt and all her dreams seemed dashed. She was failing in school. It was only the influence of my father that got her into Wilbourne." She closed her eyes. "But Joyce betrayed me. She left the room that night, knowing what was to occur. She'd already made her dark bargain with the people running the school. Success, fame—that's what she wanted. She never told me anything, never warned me. And because of that, she's gotten everything she's always dreamed of."

"Why do you see her then? Why do you let her come here?"

Mariclare smiled. "Because some part of her is torn with guilt. She knows what she did. She sees me, hoping to sway me over to her side—but I just sit here and laugh at her. I take some comfort in how she squirms."

All at once, she leaned across the table, her green eyes filled with passion.

"But you have free will, Susan! Just as I did! I could have joined their cult. I could have sung out the praises of the dark lord who defiled me. If I had, I would have been raised to the highest honors as the mother of his daughter. But I said no. I said *no*—and I still say *no*!"

"That's why they put you in here," Sue said.

"That's right. They hid me away because they couldn't kill me." She smiled. "You see, I've realized my own power— my own power for good." She opened her blouse, revealing wrinkled, freckled skin. Around her neck hung a crucifix. As well as a Star of David. A Wiccan pentacle. An Egyptian scarab. A medal of the Hindu goddess Durga. And other symbols Sue didn't recognize.

Sue looked from the symbols back into her mother's eyes. "But I'm not you," she said. "I'm not—human."

"Yes, you are, Susan. You are *my* daughter as much as his."

Sue sat back in her chair, struck by the realization.

"There is someone who can help you, isn't there? A teacher. Someone who knows, someone who will know what to do . . ."

Sue refocused her eyes on Mariclare. "Dr. Marshall . . ."

Her mother nodded. "Yes. I told you. I can see things. I can see her now. She's writing. I can see that she is good. Strong. Wise."

"She's left campus," Sue said. "She's gone to Louisiana."

"You have an address for her. I know you do. You must go to her, Susan. They will try to find you . . . to force you to do their bidding."

Sue stood up. "I—"

"Go, Sue. There's still a chance you can save yourself." She gave a small chuckle. "And maybe the rest of us, too."

They faced each other for a few moments in silence.

Then Sue leaned down and took her mother into her arms.

65

Ginny was writing in her notebook about Sue's meeting with her mother when she heard the girl coming down the stairs. She placed the notebook into the top drawer of her desk, and got up to meet Sue in the hallway. Sue was dressed and showered, her face scrubbed, her hair combed. She looked so much better than she had last night.

"Did you sleep well?" Ginny asked.

"Mostly. But this morning I started dreaming."

Ginny touched Sue's cheek. "Would you like some breakfast? A cup of coffee?"

"Coffee would be good," Sue said, and they headed into the kitchen.

They sat at the table drinking the hot liquid in silence for a few moments.

"Well?" Sue asked. "Do you think I'm insane?"

"I wish it were that simple." Ginny wrapped her hands around her coffee mug. "Obviously, your story is pretty fantastic."

"That's an understatement."

"I believe something is happening, Sue. Right before I left Lebanon, I met with Father Ortiz—"

"The one who spoke to me at the diner."

Ginny nodded. "Yes. I didn't tell you last night that I knew him. And I know Bernadette deSalis. I've interviewed her."

"My mother was right," Sue said. "You do understand."

Ginny smiled. "Understand? Hardly. But I know there's some basis to your story. I've been trying to call Father Ortiz all morning. But all I get is his voice mail."

"Do you think he can help me?"

"I don't know, Sue. But remember what else your mother told you. You have free will. No one can force you to do anything."

Sue rubbed her forehead. "That doesn't change what I am."

"What you've been *told* you are. I believe something is going on, something strange, but there's no proof that you're—" Ginny couldn't say the word.

"The Antichrist?" Sue looked at her. "But Bernadette told you about me, didn't she? I can see it in your mind, Dr. Marshall. She told you that the Antichrist was a woman."

Ginny sighed. "Yes. Yes, she did."

"And she told you more, too, didn't she? And Father Ortiz told you—"

"He told me the same thing your mother told you—that the true Book of Revelation has been kept a secret by the Vatican. He told me that there was a conspiracy to bring about the end times . . ."

Sue started softly crying. "It's true, Dr. Marshall. How can you believe otherwise? What's the point in pretending I'm not what they say I am?"

Ginny opened her mouth to speak, but was cut off by a knock at the door. They both jumped. Ginny motioned for Sue to be quiet and stood to look outside. It was a tall old man with bright white hair in a tweed sport coat. With some reluctance, Ginny pulled open the door and peered outside, hoping Sue was out of sight in the kitchen.

"Yes?" she asked. "May I help you?"

"I've come for my granddaughter."

Ginny watched as the old man's lips tightened and twitched. His nostrils flared.

"You must be Mr. Barlow," she said.

"I know she's here, Dr. Marshall. That's her car out front."

"Yes, she's here. But she doesn't wish to see you."

"She's my granddaughter! I'm her legal guardian!"

Ginny stood her ground. "You seem to have forgotten she's eighteen years of age. A legal adult who can make her own decisions."

The old man's eyes were nearly apoplectic. His face was turning red.

"Let him in, Dr. Marshall," came Sue's voice behind her. "I'll see him."

Reluctantly, Ginny stepped aside. She took note of the big black car in her driveway, and the burly jumpsuited driver who was leaning against it, his massive arms crossed over his chest.

Sue's grandfather now stood facing the girl in Ginny's living room.

"Come home with me, Sue," he said.

"Why? So you can tell me more lies?"

Ginny stood in the foyer watching the scene play out. Who was this man? Was he really in league with—the devil?

"We spared you the truth for your own good," he said.

"That's bullshit, and you know it." Sue looked at the old man with sheer contempt. "I know everything. I know what you want of me."

"Has this woman been telling you lies?" Mr. Barlow asked.

"I've been to see my mother, your darling Mariclare," Sue said. "But then you probably know that, don't you?"

"I just know that your grandmother is very worried, and wants you home."

"You can't force me," Sue said.

Her grandfather leveled his eyes at her. "I think I can."

In an instant, the front door opened and the burly driver was on Ginny, his hairy arm around her neck, choking off her breath.

"Kill her," Mr. Barlow said calmly, his eyes still on his granddaughter.

"No!" Sue screamed. "Leave her alone!"

"Then come with me," her grandfather said.

Sue was silent, not moving.

Ginny's heart was racing in her ears. The driver shoved her into the living room, away from the door. He pushed her to the floor and stood over her, a semiautomatic pointed at her head.

"If I go with you," Sue said, "you'll just kill her anyway."

"She knows too much," Mr. Barlow said.

Sue walked across the room, seeming to contemplate what to do.

"I suppose you're right, Granpa," she said. And in the blink of an eye she withdrew the gun he'd given to her from her blouse and fired off one quick shot—right through the driver's head.

Ginny screamed. The burly man staggered, as if doing a macabre little dance. Blood and brain matter was still raining down onto the carpet. Then he toppled over. He would have hit Ginny if she didn't leap out of the way.

Mr. Barlow was stunned.

"I'm a pretty good shot," Sue said coolly. "You taught me well, Granpa."

"Apparently not well enough."

This was a new voice. They all turned to look. Striding in through the front door, apparently having been waiting in the car, was Joyce Davenport, complete with black miniskirt and boots.

"Maybe if you'd been more vigilant, she wouldn't have grown up to be such a rebel," Joyce said, casting an angry glance at Mr. Barlow. Then she smiled at Sue. "But you do have spunk, Sue. That's good. You'll need it." She laughed. "They always used to say I had spunk. Now they just call me a bitch."

Joyce noticed Ginny on the other side of the room.

"Ah, Dr. Marshall. We meet again. How nice to see you. How's your book coming?"

Ginny decided not to parry words with her. Somebody had already been shot in this room, and she didn't want to be the second.

"I'm not going with you," Sue told Joyce.

Joyce spun on her. "Sue, stop this nonsense! It's your destiny! Do you have any idea how much power awaits you?"

"I don't care!"

"Hell, Sue, I'd *love* it if I were in your shoes!" She laughed. "I've certainly been called the Antichrist enough times by mealy-mouthed liberals! But I've just had to content myself with being the Anti-John the Baptist." She hooted again, seeming very pleased with her joke.

Sue pointed the gun at her.

"Oh, please, you're not going to shoot me," Joyce said, waving a hand at her.

"Why shouldn't I?"

Joyce shrugged. "Because I know so many things you want to know. Admit it, Sue. This whole destiny thing . . . it kind of appeals to you. It kind of intrigues you.'

Ginny watched from a safe distance. She couldn't get to a phone to call the police, and if she tried to run, she was certain she'd be shot. Mr. Barlow was probably armed, and who knows what Sue would do . . .

"I want no part of it," Sue said.

Joyce laughed. "So you'll end up like your mother. Is that

what you want? Do you think we'd just let you waltz off to do your own thing?" She took a step closer to Sue. "Do you think your *father* would just let you go?"

Sue made no answer. But the gun in her hand was now trembling.

"You'd end up crazy in some lunatic asylum like your mother. Is that what you want, Sue?"

"You put her there," Sue said. "You could have stopped what happened to her."

Joyce winced, but just slightly. Mariclare was right: she did feel some guilt. But not enough to stop her.

"It's your choice, Sue." She held out her hands as if they were balancing scales. "Crazy lunatic asylum . . . or untold power and glory. You decide."

"So many will hail you," Sue's grandfather told her.

"All those people who buy your books, who come to your readings," Sue said to Joyce. "All those people who get riled up by your rants and raves . . . they're all part of this . . . part of this cult?"

"We *wish*!" Joyce hooted. "Wouldn't that be amazing! But no, Sue. They're just sheep. I get them riled up. The televangelists get them riled up. They protest at gay weddings and blockade abortion clinics and hound illegal immigrants . . . They think they're doing God's work, but they're actually working for the Other Guy!"

Sue was struggling to keep a firm grip on the gun.

"Strife, conflict, bigotry, name-calling—this is what we thrive on! It's what *he* thrives on—your father. He loves discord. He is the Lord of Chaos and Conflict. It's so much fun to get the sheep riled up. Get them shouting on talk radio. Fill their hearts with anger and accusation. It's fun to stir up trouble between people. Admit it, Sue, you, too, enjoyed it. I know you have."

Sue remembered the thrill she'd experienced causing trouble between Malika and Sandy. As if it was a natural thing for her . . .

"You're not like other girls, Sue, and you never have been," Joyce told her. "You know that. You've never been sick. You can do things with your mind. You can't ever live the life of a normal girl." She took a step even closer to Sue. "And you can't love, can you? You have never been able to love a boy, or feel desire for him. What would life be like if you can't love?"

Sue was noticeably shaking now.

"And the one boy who might have loved you is now terrified of you, isn't he?" Joyce asked.

"How do you know about Billy?"

Joyce smiled. "He told his mother, who told me."

Sue began to cry. She dropped the gun, and Joyce picked it up.

"So isn't the choice apparent, Sue? What else is there for you? Your destiny is to be—"

What Ginny saw next took her breath away. She wasn't even able to scream.

Sue transformed. In an instant her whole body changed. She seemed almost to explode—and in her place stood a fearful creature, a swirling, crackling demon whose form was indistinct—as if darkness was suddenly given life.

Joyce jumped back, terrified.

Mr. Barlow cowered behind his hands.

I NEED NO GUN TO PROTECT MYSELF FROM THE LIKES OF YOU, came the voice of the creature. It sounded like nothing Ginny had ever heard before. A hollow sound, neither female nor male. It seemed to vibrate off the walls.

I WILL GO WITH YOU, BUT REMEMBER WHO I AM.

I WILL NOT BE TOLD WHAT TO DO.

I WILL GIVE THE INSTRUCTIONS, AND YOU MISERABLE SCUM WILL FOLLOW THEM.

IS THAT CLEAR?

"Yes," Joyce said, her voice trembling.

And then Sue was back. Looking none worse for the wear.

"Sue!" Ginny called. "You mustn't give in!"

Joyce rolled her eyes. "Can't we just kill her and get it over with?"

Sue turned her face to look over at Ginny. Their eyes held for a second. Ginny thought she looked different. Hard. Cruel. As if she'd given in to the dark part of herself.

"No," Sue said. "I don't want to kill her."

She reached out her hand, and in that one simple gesture, Ginny crumpled to the floor.

"But when she wakes up, she'll have forgotten that any of us ever came here."

Joyce looked down at Ginny's fallen body. "Are you sure you don't want me to kill her?" Joyce asked. "Think of the trouble it would stir up . . . all those accusations flying . . ."

"No!" Sue shouted. "She is to be left alive. And make sure that the driver's body is removed and properly disposed of. Clean up all the blood. I don't want any trace left."

Joyce made a face. "But who's going to clean it up?"

"You are. Get scrubbing."

She turned to her grandfather.

"And when she's done, you will drive me back to Wilbourne." She looked out the window into the bright light of day. "I have final exams to take."

66

Billy sighed and exhaled. Even in the darkness, he could see his frosty breath in front of his face. He shivered, cursing himself for the tenth time in as many minutes. *I should have said no,* he thought as he shoved his hands deeper into his coat pockets. *It's fucking freezing out here.*

"Why should I do what you're asking?" He'd thrown the question at Bernadette like a fastball, hoping she'd miss, hoping she'd be unable to answer, and the whole thing could be dropped.

But Bernie was ready. She hit the ball out of the park. "You should do it," she told him, "because you love her."

Standing there shivering in the cemetery just outside the walls of Wilbourne College, Billy remembered Bernadette's words. *Because you love her.*

"Do I?" he asked out loud, his voice sounding odd in the cold night air.

How could I love what I saw in her eyes?

"She's . . . not human," Billy had managed to say to Bernadette. What he'd seen in her eyes—red eyes, eyes filled with fire—was death. He couldn't explain it more than that. He saw death, and destruction, and damnation. He knew that sounded weird, but that's what he saw when he looked in Sue's eyes. *Damnation.*

His mother had seen the look of terror on his face when he'd run home from the diner after seeing Sue. She'd made him tell her what he saw. "She had the face of . . ." Billy struggled with the words. "The face of a devil!"

His mother had seemed fascinated, pumping him for all the details, but she also warned Billy to stay away from Sue. Then she was on the phone to someone, whispering furiously—spreading gossip about Sue, Billy presumed. She'd never liked her.

But when he told Bernadette the same story he told his mother, she had a far different reaction.

Bernie had come by, bundled in a down coat, red scarf, and pink mittens, and asked Billy why he'd run out of the Yellow Bird after seeing Sue.

He told her that Sue Barlow was not human.

"Oh, Billy, of course she is," Bernadette said. "She's as human as you or I. But she's in trouble. I know that. Bad trouble."

And so here he was, freezing his ass off in a cemetery, looking over the Wilbourne wall at the back windows of the dean's house.

Because I love her.

He didn't know if that was true. They'd known each for such a short time. They'd never had sex, never even made out all that much. But he *had* liked being with her more than any other girl he'd ever known. She had captured his heart in a way he'd never experienced before.

But now he was afraid of her.

Billy couldn't deny it. He now believed Sue had caused Mike and Heidi to collapse and get sick. Maybe it wasn't deliberate. But she had some kind of power. Some kind of diabolical power. He'd seen it that day in her eyes.

But if she could be helped . . . then he wanted to try.

Bernadette had insisted she could be helped. *Saved*, she'd said. "Sue can be saved, and you can save her, Billy."

What the fuck am I doing listening to a little kid like Bernie? Billy thought once again about just chucking the whole plan, beating a path out of the cemetery, and heading home, where it was warm and safe.

But Bernie had some kind of power, too. Billy couldn't deny how she'd changed. Something very strange was happening in this town, and Bernie and Sue were just part of it.

He pulled his woolen cap down further over his ears. His nose was cold. He looked over the wall at the top two floors of the dean's house, an imposing gray granite building. Townsfolk said the ghost of Sarah Wilbourne still walked the house. Billy remembered being a kid and being dared to go up and look in one of the windows on Halloween night. It had taken all of his nerve—and the taunting of his friends— to go up there and look in the window, but he'd seen no sign of Sarah Wilbourne—or, for that matter, of Dean Gregory and his mousy wife either. Still, having proved his coolness to his friends, he climbed back over the wall and strutted through the cemetery like the cock of the walk.

But now, standing here among the graves as the wind whipped through the trees, Billy felt surrounded by ghosts. The house itself was in good repair, but its crenellated roof and dark windows certainly made it feel like a place of evil.

And Sue was inside.

Bernadette had told him that Sue was returning to Wilbourne after trying to escape. "Escape from what?" he'd asked her, but Bernie was vague. She simply said that Sue was being brought back to Wilbourne and that terrible things would happen if Billy didn't stop them. He mustn't tell his mother or the police or anyone else. "If you do," Bernie said, "Sue will die. At least Sue as we know her will die."

"You keep saying not to tell my mother," Billy said. "You make it seem as if she's part of the conspiracy, whatever it is."

"Trust no one, Billy."

"Even you?"

Bernie had just smiled. "But you *do* trust me."

He just shook his head. "I don't know why. You're just my best friend's kid sister. But yeah, I do trust you, Bernie."

He knelt down behind a tree, trying to take shelter from the wind. There was a light covering of snow on the ground, and more was predicted for tonight. *I hope this is all over with before it starts to snow,* Billy thought as he pulled out his cell phone and checked the time again. Two minutes since he'd last looked. He shoved the phone back into his coat pocket and looked back up at the house again. All the downstairs lights were on, and from what he could make out, there were several people moving around behind the windows. A campus Christmas party maybe. Somewhere among them, Bernie had assured him, was Sue.

He needed a better look. In a sudden move, he began climbing the bare branches of the tree, confident his black coat and the moonless night would obscure him from the windows of the house. The limbs of the tree gave him a closer view of the dean's house than he could have obtained on the ground, and would also allow him to drop down on the other side of the wall if need be. Now he was able to make out faces in the lighted windows. Most of them Billy didn't recognize. But he picked out Dean Gregory—and wasn't that the state cop who'd been asking lots of questions around town about Bonnie Warner? He was drinking a glass of wine, laughing with the dean. And over there—*Goddamn!*—wasn't that Joyce Davenport, the political commentator he'd seen on TV?

The sound of tires on gravel distracted his attention. Billy peered through the branches to see a car pulling into the long circular driveway around the dean's house.

It was his mother's Toyota.

He watched, too stunned to move, as his mother got out of the car and sauntered up the front door. She was let inside.

His heart dropped into the pit of his stomach.

In moments, he could see her through the window, being handed a glass of wine by Joyce Davenport.

She's part of this—whatever this is.

He swallowed hard as another car pulled into the driveway. He reached for his cell phone and dialed. "Bernie," he whispered. "They're arriving."

67

Deputy Perry Holland peered out from between his blinds. These days, he did this eight or nine times a night—jumping at every sound, certain someone was out there, trying to break in. The wind was blowing hard and the night sky was covered in gray clouds. *That blizzard is going to break at any minute,* he thought. The weather forecast was predicting another snowstorm. *Two already—and it's not even Christmas.*

Christmas. He dreaded the holiday. If he felt alone and paranoid now, he could only imagine how he'd feel on Christmas Eve.

Jennifer had been calling him. She'd heard he was having "a hard time of it," as she put it, since his father's death. Perry imagined Marjorie had spoken with her. Jennifer asked in her last message if she might come see him. Was it just pity—or did she really want another chance with him? Perry didn't intend to find out. He was in no frame of mind to see the woman he'd once loved. *She'd run screaming from me anyway,* Perry thought.

He glanced in a mirror. *I look a wreck.* His hair was matted down, greasy and unwashed. His eyes were shadowed with dark circles.

Since he wasn't going into the sheriff's office these days, he didn't need to be cleaned up. All he had to do was stay in this apartment with the doors locked and the blinds drawn. There were *things* out there—and he was terrified of them.

Bernadette deSalis told me I was right in my suspicions. And she's seen the Virgin Mary. She knows. She knows the truth.

Another sound. Perry jumped. His gun was strapped to his waist, but he knew guns wouldn't protect him against the forces that had killed his father. Still, his hand went automatically to the gun's handle.

The rapping continued.

Someone at the door.

Every nerve in Perry's body tingled. *They've come for me. They're here!*

He peered through the blinds on the door.

It was a priest. He wore a heavy black coat, but his white collar was visible.

"Might I have a moment of your time, Deputy?" the priest was asking—shouting, really, over the wind.

"Who are you?" Perry called through the door.

"My name is Father Fernando Ortiz. I come seeking your help."

Why should I trust him? Perry didn't budge.

"Bernadette deSalis sent me," the priest said.

Perry opened the door a crack. Bitter cold air came rushing into the house.

"What has Bernadette told you?"

"That you understand. That you know what's happening here. The evil that threatens us all."

Perry opened the door, nodding for Father Ortiz to enter.

"We need your help," the priest said as Perry shut the door and turned to face him. "Tonight. We cannot delay any longer."

"What's happening tonight?"

"A girl will be killed."

Perry studied the man's deeply creased face. "Why not go to the police with your story?"

"You are the police," Ortiz told him.

Perry laughed. "Not exactly. I've been put on leave. They think I've gone a little nutso. And they're investigating me for removing official documents from the archives."

"Who knows this? Is it general knowledge?"

He shook his head. "Out of respect to my father's memory, all that's been officially said is that I'm taking some time off." He made a sound in his throat. "To grieve."

"Then they won't know at the college that you're not officially authorized. Dean Gregory, for example—he'll think you're there in your official capacity."

Perry's mind was clearing. "That's where you think this girl is going to be killed? At Wilbourne? Again?"

"It continues, Deputy," Father Ortiz said, nodding. "All of the research your father did is confirmed by what is taking place tonight on the Wilbourne campus."

"And you think I'm enough to prevent it? Won't we need backup? A few state police . . ."

"I don't trust the state police, and I don't think you do either." Father Ortiz looked impatient. "That's why I came here. We felt you were the only one we could trust."

Perry sighed, walking around the room like a caged animal. He'd been hiding out too long—and that's exactly what they wanted. They didn't need to kill him the way they'd killed his father. They simply turned him into mush. They chopped off his balls and sent him into hiding.

No more.

He turned and faced Ortiz. "I need to know more. What's going on up at the school? What's behind these deaths? What kind of cult?"

Father Ortiz's eyebrows came together at the bridge of his nose. "These atrocities have been going on since the school was founded. They are *why* the school was founded." He held up a hand to stop Perry from interrupting. "Oh, certainly, it is a fine institution. That's the brilliance of the plan, you see. For over a hundred years, it has been hidden in plain sight. Most girls go to school there, get a degree and a fine education, and go out into the world to make a difference. Only a very few are part of the dark side of the school. But now, the cult makes up a majority of the new board of trustees."

"Satanists?" Perry guessed.

"They worship Satan, but it is even more than that. They have tapped into the elemental evil that exists in this world. Satan is merely the name Christians use to describe this fundamental force. Evil predates Christianity by many aeons, and all societies have recognized the power evil can have when men give it free rein. These people are attempting to harness evil for their own greed and lust for power. But evil is not easy to control. It takes over—it grows larger—it consumes and destroys. They feed it—sacrificing virgins in a nod perhaps to ancient societies of devil worshippers. But now they've reached a turning point—they have engineered the birth of a creature who is literally the human embodiment of the elemental evil, and with her they believe they will be able to take over the world."

Perry stood staring at the silver-haired priest. "Father," he said, "I think you might be as crazy as people say *I* am."

Father Ortiz smiled. "And the story will only get stranger, Deputy. We mustn't delay any longer. Their plans are very close to completion—the moment they've been planning for almost one hundred and fifty years."

"You need to give me more specifics than that."

"I know it is a fantastic story to hear from a stranger. These days, it is difficult to convince people that good and evil are not merely abstract concepts—that they exist as powerful forces, independent of men. Call them God and Satan—call them what you like. But good and evil exist as forces outside of ourselves. We have become so educated that faith is no longer possible. Anything that cannot be explained in a rational and logical manner simply cannot be. But it is true. It was foretold, explained to St. John in a revelation from the Lord."

"I've read Revelation, Father, and I don't remember anything about—"

"You haven't read the *real* Book of Revelation." A gentle smile played at the corner of the priest's lips. "You read the rewritten version, the one the Vatican allowed to be seen. The true book, in its original Greek, is in a vault at the Vatican. When this college was founded, we knew what had been foretold was beginning. These people, who got a copy of the lost Revelation, decided to cash in, as they say, on the prophecies by making them happen on their time schedule, with their input and their control." He shuddered. "And so they play a very dangerous game."

Perry was rubbing his temples. "It's all so fantastic . . ."

"Let me posit this, Deputy," said Father Ortiz. "Isn't it entirely possible to believe in this conspiracy without believing that their goals are actual fact? Isn't it possible that a group of people can *believe* they are bringing about the birth of the Antichrist even if it isn't true? And isn't it entirely possible that they would also *kill* to preserve the secrecy of their goals?"

"Yes." Perry said.

"So even if your mind refuses to let you accept what is happening, you can see that we mustn't waste any more time . . . a girl's life is in danger."

Perry held his gaze for several seconds. "What is it you want me to do?"

"Use your badge to get us into the dean's house."

"Us?"

Father Ortiz nodded. "You, me . . . and Bernadette."

"I can't take a child into a place where a murder might occur! Or you either, for that matter."

"Yes, you can, Deputy! You know as well as I do that what is happening here is beyond the bounds of natural understanding! You know as well as I do that Bernadette is no mere child, not anymore—and that without her, we have no power against the forces they are summoning, even as we speak, on the campus of Wilbourne College!"

Perry let out a long sigh. "All right. I'll go to the dean's house and ask to look around. But you two will wait in the car." He glanced in the mirror again. "I need to wash up quickly. They'll know something is wrong if they see me looking like this."

"Okay," Ortiz said. "But hurry."

Perry stepped into the bathroom, closing the door behind him. Just as he did, Father Ortiz's cell phone chirped. He dug it out of his coat pocket, looked down at the Caller ID, and didn't recognize the number.

"Hello," he said.

He listened, and a broad smile stretched across his face.

"Thank God," he said. "I was wondering if we'd hear from you . . ."

68

"I'm sorry I didn't get back to you earlier," Ginny was telling Father Ortiz. "But I haven't been myself."

That was putting it mildly. Two days ago, she'd awoken in her living room, dazed and uncomprehending. She seemed to have missed a day—or at least a night. *The last thing I remember,* she'd thought to herself, *is sitting at my desk writing—and then someone was at the door . . .*

But nothing after that. *I guess I must have dozed off here,* Ginny told herself. *How unlike me.*

She looked around the house. Everything was tidy—tidier than she usually left it. The coffeemaker was washed and cleaned, rather than sitting with a black sooty mess from the day before, the way she usually found it in the morning. And it was late—almost noon—why did she sleep so *long*?

She walked around the house. The guest room was neat, the bed made. So was her own bed. "Now I know I did not make my bed," she said out loud. "I never make my bed."

The living room, once she walked back in, had the vague scent of cleaning fluids. On closer inspection, she saw that her rug had been scrubbed. It was cleaner in one section than it was elsewhere.

"Something happened here," she said to herself. "Only I can't remember what it was!"

For two days—two whole days—she walked through her life as if in a dream. She knew something was wrong—but to probe her mind too much was painful. It physically hurt. And she was scared, too—of what, she wasn't sure. But she was scared.

The worst part was that she couldn't write. All that momentum was out the window. She sat and stared into space. She didn't return calls. Not even when Father Ortiz left a message saying it was "vital" that he speak with her.

Finally, she forced herself to sit back at her desk and try to write. A call from her agent had spurred her into action. Her editor wanted to take a chapter with him to read over the Christmas holidays. Ginny stared down at her computer, but still couldn't bring herself to write anything.

Then she pulled open her top drawer.

A notebook.

"I don't remember this," she said, pulling it out and opening to the first page.

My handwriting. When did I write this?

The date at the top . . . two days previous.

The day she'd lost partially . . . those missing hours.

And then she started to read.

She read the whole account Sue had given her, as if she was hearing about it for the first time. Parts of it she couldn't believe—but when she reached the last page, she remembered everything. All of it.

The gunshot. The blood. Joyce Davenport.

And that horrible creature of darkness that Sue had become.

For twenty minutes, all Ginny did was cry and shake.

Then she was on the phone making flight arrangements to Senandaga.

"I barely made it in," she told Father Ortiz now, driving her rental car through the first flakes of furious snow. "They were worried the blizzard would close the airport, but it held off just long enough."

"It is God's will then," Father Ortiz said. "Ginny, I am so glad to hear from you. We were worried."

"I know everything," she told him. "I know about Sue Barlow. She came to see me."

"Bernadette felt certain she had," Ortiz said. "Please hurry, Ginny. Tonight . . . tonight Sue is being consecrated to her father. She will be asked to officially accept her destiny."

"Where should I meet you?"

"How far away are you?" Ortiz asked.

"Half an hour."

Ortiz gave her the address of Perry Holland's apartment. "We will wait half an hour for you, but no longer. Bernadette has just heard from her lookout. People are arriving at the dean's house."

Ginny told him she'd drive as fast as she could, given the snow. She snapped her cell phone shut. Perry Holland. He wasn't crazy after all.

Hang on, Sue, she thought. *You're not completely lost to us yet. You could have killed me. That's what a true evil nature would have done. Killed me, and enjoyed it. But you spared me—and you had to know my memory would come back.*

In fact, Ginny suspected, Sue was likely counting on it.

69

Sue sat in a room upstairs, listening to people arriving below. Laughter, loud voices, classical music playing in the background. Dean Gregory was offering everyone who came through the door a cocktail or a glass of wine. If Sue didn't know better, she might really think there was a Christmas party going on downstairs.

"This was the eldest son's room," she said all at once to Joyce Davenport, who was fixing her makeup in a mirror. "The one who died not long ago. An overdose. He'd been living in a homeless shelter on Long Island."

"Marvelous, isn't it?" Joyce turned to face her, a broad smile on her face. "Like a Shakespearean tragedy. Those boys were offered so much—and fell so low."

"After what they saw in this house," Sue said, no emotion in her voice, "they were shattered for life."

Joyce approached her. "They were weak. Just like their mother was weak. You did right in eliminating her, Sue."

Sue let her eyes move past Joyce and find their reflection in the mirror across the room. She felt numb. Her mind didn't seem to work the way it once did. Her emotions felt turned off. She was like an observer, not a participant, in her own life.

"They're all gathering downstairs," Joyce said, "waiting for you. This will be quite the ceremony. The beginning of great things for you, sweetie."

"My grandparents?"

Joyce nodded. "Seated in places of honor."

"Yes," Sue said. "I can see them."

And she could. Her grandmother was done up with her best jewelry and a dress of black satin. Her hair was piled on her head. Beside her, Granpa smoked his cigar, his ascot tie proudly puffing out of his jacket. Sue could see them clearly. They were being greeted by the guests as if they were a king and queen.

That's what Granpa had wanted. That's why he had allowed his daughter to be raped by the devil.

In Sue's mind, she saw several of her grandfather's colleagues from the law firm, their wives on their arms. They stuck close to Granpa, hoping to bask in his glow.

"All of my grandfather's success," Sue said, "that was part of the bargain, wasn't it?"

"Of course, sweetie. Everything he's ever wanted, he's achieved." Joyce drew close to her. "And that will be even more true for you, Sue."

She laughed. "But what is it that I want?"

The door opened. In walked Dean Gregory, resplendent in a black suit and bright red satin tie.

"Are you ready, Sue?" he asked. "Everyone is here."

She looked at him. *I killed his wife,* she thought, *but he remains at my command. He remains my dutiful servant.*

"Why?" she asked. "What's in all this for you, Ted Gregory?"

His pinched, weasely face looked momentarily surprised as he exchanged glances with Joyce.

"Sue's just wondering what comes next, I think," Joyce explained.

"We will all know great glory through you, Sue," Gregory told her.

"But how? What is the plan?"

Joyce laughed. "Well, it can go any way we choose. But I was thinking . . ." She smiled, her eyes dancing. "You'll graduate top of your class here at Wilbourne, Sue. Then you'll go on to law school, and be spotted by a promising politician as excellent advisor material. You'll dazzle Washington with your charm and command of the facts, and be appointed secretary of state when that same politician becomes president. And then . . . well, Sue, how does the idea of being the first female president of the United States appeal to you?"

"President . . . of the United States," Sue said.

"What better position for the Antichrist to hold? The leader of the most powerful nation on Earth?"

"What we will be able to do," Gregory said, literally rubbing his hands together.

"And I suppose I'll appoint you to the Supreme Court," Sue said, looking at her dean.

He just grinned.

Sue sighed. President of the United States. It was her destiny. That young girl who'd once dreamed of working for social justice—she seemed like a figment of her imagination now. A vague, fast-fading memory.

It was a thrilling idea. Sue felt a rush of ambition surge through her body. President of the United States . . .

It's good I can feel ambition. I'll certainly never feel anything else.

She understood now why she'd never known love for a boy before. *Because the daughter of Satan cannot comprehend love. It is not an emotion that I can experience.*

And without love—well, then, ambition—greed—power—these things would have to take its place.

"All right," Sue said. "I'm ready to go downstairs."

She stood. Joyce was holding a red robe for her. Sue slipped her arms into the sleeves. She caught another look at herself in the mirror.

Her eyes were no longer blue. They had become as red as her robe.

70

Ginny sat in the backseat of Perry Holland's car with Bernadette. Up front, Father Ortiz sat beside Perry. No one talked as they drove across town toward the Wilbourne campus. Bernadette was saying a Rosary.

Finally, Ginny spoke. "What are we expecting to find?'

"I'm not sure," Father Ortiz said. "But it will be some sort of ceremony."

"And you think we can just waltz inside and take part?"

"Hardly, Ginny. But you're still a faculty member and the dean will see you. And Perry has a badge."

"I'm going in," Perry said. "The three of you will remain in the car."

"Perry," Ortiz said. "Bernadette's parents have given their consent for her to join us. I have told them that her presence is necessary, and they trust me. Nothing can happen to the girl while she is under the direct protection of Our Holy Mother."

"Still," Perry told him. "You wait in the car until I give the word that it's safe to go inside. Understood?"

"Understood, Deputy," came Bernadette's voice.

Ginny looked over at her. Such a small girl. And yet

Ginny shared Father Ortiz's conviction that nothing could happen to her.

It was the rest of them that she worried about.

She remembered all too clearly the monstrous thing that Sue had become in her living room. She'd seen firsthand the power—and the evil—that they were dealing with.

Perry pulled up to the college gate and showed his badge to the guard.

"I need to see the dean," Perry explained.

"I'll call him," the guard said.

"Is that you, Tom?" Ginny called from the backseat. Tom O'Riley had been a guard at the gate ever since Ginny first started teaching at the college. She liked him; he liked her. "It's me, Ginny Marshall. How are you, Tom?"

The guard peered in through the window and spotted her. "Oh, hey, Ginny. I'm great. What're you doing in a police car?"

She smiled. "I just got back in from Louisiana and Deputy Holland was kind enough to pick me up in this snowstorm. I'm bringing my friends here to Dean Gregory's party. The party *is* tonight, isn't it?"

"Oh, sure," Tom said. "There's been dozens of people coming in all night. I had to check their names against a list . . ."

Ginny thought fast. "I'll bet Ted didn't have time to put my name on the list. I didn't think I'd be able to get in with all the snow. I just called him a little while ago to say I could make it after all."

Tom nodded. "Oh, that's fine, Ginny. Besides, you can come on campus anytime you want. You're faculty here."

"Thanks, Tom."

He pressed the switch and the iron gates swung inward. He waved them through.

"Good work, Doctor," Bernadette told her.

Ginny smiled.

Cars were parked all around the dean's house. Many had out-of-state plates. Connecticut, Massachusetts, Pennsylvania, even a couple from Canada. The house was ablaze with light, from the top floor to the basement. The snow continued to fall, blanketing the campus in a soft whiteness that sparkled in the moonlight.

"Now stay here until I check things out," Perry told them again, parking the car and turning off the ignition.

Ginny agreed to wait. There wasn't much she could do anyway. What was she supposed to do—march up there and call them all Satanists and grab Sue by the collar?

She wasn't quite sure what Perry could do either.

They watched him walk up the steps to the front door. None of them said a word.

The only sound in the car was Bernadette's steady murmur as she whispered the prayers of the Rosary.

71

Mom's in there, Billy kept repeating to himself over and over.

This crazy cult—this secret ceremony that's somehow going to hurt Sue—and Mom is a part of it.

As he sat in the tree, Billy's blood boiled.

His mother was a hypocrite. A lying hypocrite.

Was this what her new job was? Was this how she had gotten her "great opportunity" to make them all rich?

It sickened Billy to think of it.

"Well," he said to himself, "maybe it's time one more person joined their little party."

He dropped from the tree branch over the fence, the soft snow cushioning his fall. He stood up, brushed himself off, and began searching for a way into the house.

72

"Deputy Holland," Dean Gregory said as he opened the door. "What's going on?"

Perry kept his face blank. "I'd just like to ask what's going on here tonight."

The dean smiled, but did not open the door all the way. "Simply a Christmas party for a few friends. Why are you asking?"

"I'm looking for Sue Barlow. Is she here?"

The dean's face betrayed only a momentarily flicker of unease. "Sue Barlow? Oh, you mean one of our freshmen students?"

Perry felt certain, after talking with Ginny and Father Ortiz, that Sue's grandparents would be here tonight. So he took the chance. "Yes," he said. "I noticed a car registered to her grandfather outside, and she's not in her dorm. So is she here?"

"She might be," Gregory said. "There are at least a hundred people in the parlor. Why do you need to see Sue?"

"That's my business with her, sir."

The dean opened the door a bit further. "Well, yes, her

grandparents are here. Mr. Barlow is a major supporter of the school. Perhaps she's with them."

"May I come in and look for her?"

Gregory pulled open the door wide. "By all means, Deputy. Please come in. Have a glass of wine with us. Merry Christmas!"

73

"Hello, Gran. Hello, Granpa."

It was the first time Sue had faced them since discovering the truth. She noticed her grandmother's eyes flicker away for a moment, but her grandfather beamed, placing his hands on each of her shoulders.

"Tonight," he told her, "is a great night."

"Yes," Sue said, her voice cold. "The culmination of a dream, isn't it, Granpa?"

"It certainly is."

She felt no emotion for them except contempt. She smiled. She would enjoy humiliating them, dashing their dreams. They would benefit not in the least from her rise. She would see to that. She would order her grandfather's law firm shut down. Their plush apartment would be taken from them. They would be literally turned out into the street, and Sue would give the order to all of her followers to shun them.

Her smile stretched across her face. She would enjoy that. She would enjoy destroying the people who had destroyed her mother.

"By the way," she said as she moved away to greet the

others who had gathered in her honor, "I met Mariclare. She sends her regards."

Her grandfather's face remained stoic. Her grandmother turned away again, her hands trembled.

Sue just smiled.

"Sue," Joyce Davenport said in her ear, coming up behind her. "It's time."

74

Billy was able to pop open a basement window, and jumped down into the murky, damp darkness.

Across the vast expanse of the basement he spotted a dim orange light. Carefully, he approached, feeling his way. One time he stumbled over something metal, causing a large clanging sound. His heart pounding in his ears, he stood still, fearful he'd alerted the house. But the music and the laughter upstairs drowned out any sound he made. Carefully, he resumed his walk across the basement floor.

He reached the light. It was coming from under a door. He tried the knob, but the door was locked.

He bent down and peered through the keyhole.

What he saw inside the room made him gasp out loud and froze him into place.

Above him, he heard footsteps.

They were coming downstairs.

75

"Where is he?" Ginny asked, looking at her watch. "He's been in there over twenty minutes."

"Let us not worry needlessly," Father Ortiz said from the front seat. "Remember, Perry has a gun."

"Guns are hardly a defense against what we're facing," Ginny reminded him. "You know that, Father. And I saw it with my own eyes."

"They haven't summoned the demon yet," Bernadette said, looking up from her rosary beads. "But Perry is indeed in trouble. We're going to have to save him."

Ginny turned to look at her. "Are you sure?"

The girl nodded. "And it's going to have to be you, Dr. Marshall. That's what Our Lady is telling me."

Ginny felt a shudder of fear. "What is it that I have to do?"

"You have to go inside," Bernadette told her. "You have to get to Sue."

76

They proceeded down the stairs in a procession, each of them having donned their red robes, each of them carrying a candle.

In the great ceremony room in the basement, an orange glow permeated everything, changing the colors of their faces to the hues of hell.

Folding chairs were arranged in rows, and in front, as if on stage, a huge black canvas covered a structure whose shape was difficult to determine. Sue was led up to the front, where she contemplated the canvas for a moment before turning back to look out over the crowd taking its seats.

Deputies and state policemen that she recognized. Her grandfather's colleagues. School trustees, faculty members, even a couple of students she'd seen in the cafeteria. And . . . Billy's mother.

"Billy," Sue whispered to herself, and immediately pushed the thought away.

"Have a seat, Sue," Joyce told her, slipping her cowl down from around her face. They sat next to each other on the dais in front. "May I make a request? Would you see about chang-

ing the fashions of these gatherings? These robes are so me-
dieval. Why not something new and hip? There are lots of
New York designers who would just *die* to come up with a
new look for us."

"Joyce," Dean Gregory said quietly, holding up a finger.
"We're about to begin."

She shrugged and pulled her hood back around her head.

Sue felt nothing. No fear. No anxiety. No excitement for
what was to happen.

The irony of her indifference was not lost on her, however.

*All my life I've wanted to meet my father. And now here I
am, about to come face to face with him.*

And I feel . . . nothing.

"My friends," Dean Gregory intoned, standing before the
group, "tonight is the result of all of our plans, all of our
hard work. Tonight is the beginning of a new, more glorious
phase in our religion. Tonight we begin to reap the benefits
of all those who came before us. Many have worked their entire lives for this day to come to fruition, and as our founder,
the great Sarah Wilbourne, planned, it has now come to pass.
The day we have all longed for, the day when the world becomes ours!"

Sue looked over at Joyce, who winked at her from inside
her cowl as Dean Gregory continued.

"Tonight we sacrifice once more to our great master, to
bring him forth amongst us."

Sacrifice? Sue turned her face back to the canvas behind
the dean. Gregory nodded, and two of his security men yanked
on a couple of cords. The canvas fell, exposing a huge cross
made out of black wood.

And bound to the cross was Malika.

A flicker of emotion sparked in Sue's chest. She studied

the unconscious form of her roommate. She was naked, and her head was dropped down on her chest.

Then the emotion left Sue, and she turned back to look at the crowd.

The chanting began. Sue didn't quite know what they were saying. She supposed she would learn eventually. But she understood they were summoning her father—who would rape and kill Malika.

Sue smiled. *Maybe it will be exciting. Certainly, growing up, I never thought I'd witness a demon devour a human being. And Malika—serves her right, that goody-goody limousine liberal . . .*

Sue began to laugh.

"You see?" Joyce whispered. "I told you all this could be a lot of fun!"

The chanting intensified. Everyone was so caught up in their ritual, most with eyes closed, that no one but Sue noticed two security men walking down the center aisle, forcing along a hooded man in between them. When they reached the cross where Malika was strapped, they forced the man down on his knees, pulling off his hood.

It was the deputy. Perry Holland.

He pulled me over for speeding on my first day here, Sue thought.

Except that wasn't me.

That was a pitiful, scared little girl named Sue.

I am someone much greater than she.

Perry Holland's hands were handcuffed behind his back. He seemed to have been drugged. He swayed on his knees.

Dean Gregory stepped forward and pulled a switch at the side of the dais. The great black cross began to move. Wood and gears creaking, it turned, taking Malika with it, until it came to rest completely inverted. An upside-down cross. Malika's head now nearly touched the floor.

The chanting stopped. The air in the room was very close.

"For you, master! We bring you two tonight! They are yours!"

Perry Holland continued to sway on his knees.

And Malika was beginning to wake up.

77

Father Ortiz picked up Bernadette's cell phone, which was buzzing furiously.

"Yes?"

"They've got—they've got a girl tied to a cross!" Billy's voice, although a low whisper, was terrified. "And now they've got Deputy Holland."

Bernadette was lost in prayer in the backseat. Father Ortiz worried they wouldn't be able to stop what was happening.

I mustn't lose my faith, he told himself.

To Billy, he said: "Be careful, son. Don't let yourself be seen."

"I've got to stop this," Billy said.

"Dr. Marshall has gone inside. Bernadette says she is the key. She will be able to get to Sue."

"Give me the phone."

The priest looked over the backseat. Bernadette had stopped praying. Her hand was held out. Father Ortiz passed the phone over to her.

"Dr. Marshall is indeed the key," Bernadette told Billy, "but you have a part to play, too. You'll know when it's time to act."

She switched off the phone.

"Now, Father," she said, "it's time we do our part as well."

"What's that?" he asked.

She opened her car door and motioned for him to do the same with his. He followed her as she trudged through the snow to a spot right in front of the house. She dropped to her knees, nearly hip deep in snow, and began to pray.

Father Ortiz did the same.

78

One by one, the candles were snuffed out, and the room fell into darkness.

Only the two torches on either side of the dais remained illuminated. The cross on which Malika was strapped turned again, clicking back into its upright position. Malika was now fully awake, and she began to scream.

The pressure in the room grew fierce. It reminded Sue of those calm, close moments just before a thunderstorm.

And then she heard the rumble that seemed to come up from beneath the floor.

"He's coming," Joyce whispered, and grabbed Sue's hand. *My father* . . .

79

The front door, to Ginny's great surprise, had been open.

Or maybe, simply by placing my hand on it, I unlocked it, Ginny told herself.

She understood now she was not alone. All of her years studying Virgin sightings had left her coldly rational, steadfastly cerebral.

Now the part of her that wanted to believe came rushing back full force.

Holy Mother—you of the sacred feminine—walk with me.

Ginny hurried through the dean's foyer. From below, the chanting had suddenly ceased, replaced by a low, steady, rumbling sound.

She located the door to the basement. It was dark down there, and a terrible coldness blew from the stairway, almost like air-conditioning at full blast.

But she knew that coldness was not man-made.

Ginny took a deep breath and headed toward the door.

As she did, she passed a large gilt-framed mirror. She caught her reflection, and behind her—a woman in blue, carrying a sword.

She spun around. There was no one there.

But she knew she was not alone.

She started down the stairs.

80

Billy felt the house begin to shake. It felt as if something was moving under the concrete beneath his feet.

An earthquake.

Billy shuddered. He had never been so terrified in his life.

Hell was erupting.

And his mother was inside.

81

"Lord Jesus," Father Ortiz prayed in the snow. "I beseech you! Save this house and the people within from the demon's clutches!"

He wished he had Bernadette's faith. The little girl knelt serenely in the snow, mumbling her prayers. Ortiz was trembling, terrified.

So many times I didn't believe, he told himself. *So many sightings of the Virgin I simply called hysterical. So many times I told the Vatican that the lost Book of Revelation was a hoax. So many times I didn't believe . . .*

He could feel the earthquake now through the blanket of snow. The moon was gone. Snow fell more heavily as the power across the campus went out and everything was plunged into darkness.

Darkness that took life around them.

Darkness that began to close around Father Ortiz's throat.

"No!" he screamed.

"Pray, Father!" Bernadette shouted. "Pray!"

But it was too late. The darkness had him by the throat. The darkness seemed to grow limbs, and it lifted him high in the air, higher and higher—

And then, like it had Miles Holland, it dropped him head-first into the snow.

The last words that went through Father Ortiz's mind were: *I believe in God, the Father Almighty, creator of heaven and earth . . .*

Bernadette did not move as the snow around her turned red from the priest's blood. She continued to pray.

From the house came a great roar.

The roar of a lion.

82

Sue saw him first. The red eyes in the dark. The figure—both enormous and small at the same time—moving down the center aisle toward her.

We have the same eyes, Sue thought dispassionately.

He was called the Prince of Darkness, and now Sue could understand why. Darkness rolled down the center aisle—a deep, pulsating darkness. It was darkness that lived, that encased a beating black heart. Sue felt its damp coldness as it grew nearer.

Behind her, Malika screamed again, but Sue was barely aware of the sound. All of her attention—her entire being—was focused on the roiling darkness that loomed ever closer.

On either side, people fell from their chairs. Some dropped to their knees. Metal chairs clanged. Cries and gasps disturbed the silence as the breathing darkness passed down the center aisle.

The demon seemed to smile amidst the chaos. Not a smile in the physical sense—but Sue could sense its pleasure. It continued its approach to Sue on the dais.

Daughter, it said in words only Sue could hear.

Father, she replied.

The darkness reached out to her.

She put out a hand to meet it.

"Sue!"

The voice came like a spear thrown unexpectedly at them. Everyone spun around to look. Sue withdrew her hand, and the demon whirled around in a great rush of darkness, its red eyes growing large.

Then it was gone.

At the bottom of the stairs, looking into the room, stood Dr. Marshall.

"Sue!" she called. "It's not too late! You can stop this! You know you can!"

"Get her!" Dean Gregory shrieked to his guards, who made a beeline toward Ginny.

Sue's vision went red.

There was a terrible high-pitched thrumming in her ears.

My father . . .

He's gone!

Anger began to well up inside her. She stood, eyes blazing.

"Sue!" Ginny shrieked again, just as the guards set upon her. "You are your mother's daughter as much as you are his!"

My mother . . .

Sue spun around. Her eyes met Malika's on the cross.

With a wave of her hand, Sue caused the straps that held Malika in place to fall away. The girl slumped to the ground, free. Sue spun on Dean Gregory, who was running toward her. Her arm flew out, and without even touching him, she sent him staggering backward, propelled into the wall.

People were standing now, many trying to flee. Some were screaming. With another wave of her hand, Sue caused the door to the stairway to slam shut, locked, preventing anyone from escaping.

They will all die. All of them. Sue felt the power rising up in her. *All die. In honor of me!*

"Sue!" Joyce was saying. "Control yourself! This is all new for you, very heady . . . maybe we rushed things too fast . . . sit, Sue, sit . . . we'll take care of Virginia Marshall."

Sue turned to look at her. "No, Joyce," she said, delighting in her treachery. *"I'll* take care of *you*!"

And with a grand sweep of her hand, she sent Joyce flying across the room, arms outspread, coming to rest on the cross that Malika had just vacated. The straps reassembled themselves, securing Joyce in place. She screamed as the cross clicked into gear and inverted itself once again, leaving her upside down, her long black hair hanging in front of her face.

On the dais, Sue laughed maniacally.

She began pointing at people in the crowd, feeling the power surge down her arm and through her fingers. How wonderful it was to watch them crumble under her power, fall lifeless to the floor. She killed a state cop. Then her boring biology teacher. She laughed uproariously. The whole room was screaming, in a panic.

Her eyes came to rest on her grandfather.

"You made me like this," she said to him. "You made me a creature that would be born without the capability to love or be loved."

"Susan," he argued, terror on his white face. "You will be great—"

"I *am* great," she said, and with a flick of her hand, she blew the head off his neck. Her grandmother screamed as the old man's blood covered her.

"Sue!"

Amid the pandemonium, she heard a new voice. She spun in its direction.

"Sue!"

Billy.

It was Billy—standing in front of a door he'd just broken down.

Billy.

"Sue," he said. "You're wrong. I loved you. I did! I loved you!"

Their eyes held.

83

Dean Gregory was getting to his feet. As Ginny struggled with the guards who held her, she watched the dean waver across the room, heading for Sue.

He wants to subdue her, Ginny thought. *Harness her. He knows her power is great, and that she'll use it against all of them.*

"Holy Mother!" Ginny shouted. "Save your daughter! Sue is as much your daughter as his!"

In that instant, the two great torches on either side of the dais fell, bursting into a huge fire that separated Gregory from Sue and Billy.

In moments, the whole room was on fire.

84

"Billy!" his mother shrieked, grabbing his arm. "We've got to get out of here!"

But he kept his eyes locked with Sue.

He felt a calmness he'd never known in his life before.

"I did love you, Sue," he repeated. "And I think . . . I think you started to love me."

85

Yes, Sue thought. *Yes, I did.*

And she started to cry.

The door sealing off the room from the stairs flung open. People began scrambling to get away from the flames. Even the guards who held Ginny let her go, hoping to save themselves from the inferno. People were trampling over each other as they attempted to get up the stairs, just as the fire caught hold of the walls.

"Go," Sue said to Billy. "Take your mother and save yourself."

Their eyes continued to hold for a moment. Gayle Honeycutt was crying hysterically, tugging at Billy's sleeve.

"Sue," Billy said.

"Go," she told him again.

Billy turned, pushing his mother in front of him, and headed for the door.

Sue watched them go, the intense heat of the flames now reaching her face. She turned, and helped a sobbing Malika to her feet, removing her own robe and placing it around Malika's naked body. Her roommate was still obviously drugged and unable to walk. "You will be strong now, Malika," Sue told her. "Your legs will carry you. You will go up the stairs and save yourself."

Malika looked at her. "Sue, you must come, too . . ."

"No," Sue said, shaking her head. "My place is here."

She reached down and also brought Perry Holland to his feet. "You, too, Deputy. You, too, will find your legs strong enough."

Perry glanced at her a moment, shaking off whatever last inertia still hung over him. His handcuffs suddenly opened, freeing his hands from behind his back. Then, he gripped onto Malika's arm, and together they made their way out of the burning room.

Flames were jumping across the ceiling now.

Sue looked down at Joyce Davenport, upside down on the cross.

"Yes," she said. "You were right, Joyce. All of this can be *so* much fun."

Joyce screamed.

86

Upstairs, as smoke billowed up from the cellar and the sound of sirens could be heard in the distance, Ginny made her way among the screaming throng of people toward the front door.

"Not so fast, Dr. Marshall," came a voice. A hand reached out and grabbed her by the arm.

She spun around and came face-to-face with Dean Gregory. His head was bleeding and he was covered with soot.

He gave her a thin smile. "So pleased I could offer you so much material for another best seller," he seethed. "Too bad it will never see print."

He poked a gun into her ribs.

"I should have fired you long ago," he whispered in her ear.

Ginny tensed for the shot.

But instead—

A sword suddenly plunged through Gregory from behind. Ginny saw its blade emerge from his chest, and then the blood streamed down the front of his shirt.

His eyes registered surprise, then horror, then nothing.

He crumpled to the floor. Ginny looked around. The sword was gone.

And the Woman who had wielded it was nowhere in sight.

But Ginny knew she would never be far away.

As the flames began popping up through the carpet, Ginny hurried outside into the snowy night.

87

The fire engines arrived too late. The dean's house was en-
gulfed by flames in just minutes. Most of those who had es-
caped from the basement tried to flee, but Perry had angled
his car across the driveway, preventing them from driving
away. The snow continued to pile up, thwarting any attempt
to drive over the grass. Immediately, many people were pro-
claiming in loud voices that they'd had no idea the ceremony
was going to include murder. Perry listened with a stoic face,
taking down names. He didn't worry that he'd be undermined
by higher-ups who were secretly cult members. Two of the
state cops he'd recognized inside had perished in the flames.

Standing in the snow, Ginny watched the house burn, her
arm around Bernadette. The fire lit up the dark sky. The falling
snow turned to steam as it came close to the flames, produc-
ing a weird, otherworldly mist that hung over the entire scene.

Girls emerged from their dorms to stand in awe before
the blaze.

"Did the dean and his wife get out?" some of them asked.

"What caused the fire?"

"Why is Dr. Marshall here? I thought she'd left campus."

Ginny just pulled Bernadette tighter to her. She couldn't

bear to look at Father Ortiz's twisted form, facedown in the snow.

"So many tragedies," she whispered, tears falling down her cheeks.

It was Sue she cried hardest for. Sue—whose destiny overtook her, through no fault of her own. It was better this way. Better that she perish rather than face what she was.

There would be many questions. Perry was hopeful that the remaining members of the state police could be trusted. The fire wouldn't destroy all the evidence. Gregory's twisted activities in the basement of the dean's house would be exposed.

"I can't see her anymore," Bernadette said, her voice barely discernible over the high-powered whoosh of the hoses fighting the blaze.

"Who?" Ginny asked. "Who can't you see anymore?"

"The Holy Mother." Bernadette looked up at Ginny. "Ever since I first had a vision of her, I could always see her. I could always hear her. But not anymore."

Ginny pulled the girl toward even closer. "She's still there. She's always there. Maybe she feels now we can get by a little better on our own."

They stood there watching until the house was nothing more than a smoldering ruin.

88

"To think," Marjorie Pequod said as she wiped down the counter at the Yellow Bird, "all of this was going on right under our noses here in Lebanon."

"I never liked that Ted Gregory," Wally said from the kitchen, shaking his head and dropping some frozen french fries down into the deep fryer. "Or his wife either."

Marjorie shuddered. "Perry told me they found the remains of those two missing girls, Joelle Bartlett and Tish Lewis, in the ruins of the dean's house."

"The Gregorys were sick," Wally opined. "Sick and twisted."

Marjorie was nodding emphatically. "Well, it'll all come out in the story Gayle Honeycutt is writing." She folded her arms across her chest and raised an eyebrow to look at Wally. "She claims she was there that night at the dean's house as an undercover reporter. She claims she never really joined the cult—she just told people she did in order to get inside and get a scoop."

Wally laughed. "It's absurd really. In this day and age. People worshipping the devil as if he was real."

Marjorie's eyes moved up to the TV set on the wall, where

the Reverend Bobby Vandiver was preaching one of his infamous fire-and-brimstone sermons as below him, a 1-800 number scrolled across the screen for people to call in and donate their money.

Marjorie snapped off the television. "Maybe the devil is more real than you think," she muttered under her breath.

"To think so many good people got sucked in. Cops, teachers . . ." Wally shuddered.

"Well, at least one good thing came out of it," Marjorie said. "Perry being named acting sheriff. Wasn't it wonderful how everyone was crowing over him, praising him for how he rooted out the cult in our midst? He'll be elected officially this spring, you just watch! And to think people called that boy crazy!"

"For me," Wally was saying, "the creepiest part of all was how that TV commentator Joyce Davenport was found burned to death—hanging upside down on a cross! How twisted is *that*?"

Indeed, Joyce's death had ensured that Lebanon was all over the national news. Crews from all the networks had poured into the little town, filming the blackened husk of the dean's house. They reported that Joyce Davenport had been a graduate of the college, but her connection to the cult was unclear.

"I can't imagine Wilbourne surviving all this," Wally said, flipping a hamburger. "I mean—to think there's been a cult of devil worshippers operating at the place for decades!"

"Well, that Dr. Virginia Marshall seems like one smart lady," Marjorie said. "I heard the interview she gave on TV yesterday. The board of trustees—the ones who haven't been arrested, that is—asked her to serve as interim dean of students."

"Has she agreed?" Wally asked.

Marjorie nodded. "She said she would, so long as she didn't have to teach any classes. She has a book to finish, she said."

Wally grunted. "I'll bet she does. Everyone connected with this thing will write a book."

He placed hamburgers on each of three plates, then loaded them up with fries as well. "Order up," he told Marjorie.

"I just hope the town's back to normal by next week," Marjorie said, expertly taking hold of all three plates at once. "After all, it's Christmas."

She brought the burgers and fries to the three kids in the booth. Billy Honeycutt and Mike and Bernadette deSalis.

"Thanks, Marjorie," Billy said.

"You bet," she said. "Hey, Mike. You're all better, eh?"

Mike smiled. "Yes, ma'am. Fine as can be."

Billy clapped him on the back. "It's good to have my buddy again."

"And you, too, Bernie?" Marjorie asked. "Feeling fine yourself?"

The girl nodded. "No more visions," she said. But there was a tinge of sadness in her voice as well.

After Marjorie left, Billy took a bite of his burger and fixed his eyes on Bernadette.

"So," he asked, "what do you think happened to Sue?"

Sue. The name had not passed his lips since the night of the fire. He'd been wanting to ask Bernie about her, but hadn't dared. Mr. and Mrs. DeSalis had refused to let Billy's mother speak to the girl for the article she was writing, and Billy refused to be put in the position of knowing something his mother would try to pry out of him. Not that Mom could intimidate him quite as easily as she once had. He believed her when she said she hadn't known the cult planned on murder, but he had his doubts over her claim that she'd only gotten involved in order to land a scoop. He knew his mother too well, and she knew he knew her. There was a new balance between Billy and Gayle, and he was glad of that.

But now, after nearly a week, his thoughts had returned to the girl he had loved so briefly. The girl he'd never really had the chance to love—but whose feelings for him, and his for her, might have prevented something even more terrible from happening that night in the dean's basement.

Neither Bernie nor Mike said anything in response to Billy's question. They simply looked down at their plates.

"I know she must have burned to death," Billy said. "Even if they're still unable to identify her body."

"Then why are you asking, dude?" Mike said.

"I mean—well, do you really think she was what they said she was?"

Bernadette lifted her dark eyes to face him. "What does it matter now, Billy?"

"I just want to know—if she died—what happened to her."

Bernadette looked out the window, and seemed momentarily interested in something she saw there. Then she smiled, and returned her eyes to Billy.

"Remember what Dr. Marshall said," she told him. "Sue was as much her mother's daughter as her father's."

Billy just nodded, and began eating his lunch.

"Excuse me a minute, guys," Bernadette said. "I just saw a friend of mine from school. I'll be right back."

She slid out of the booth, struggling into her down parka. Outside, she crossed the street, and hurried after the figure in the blue jacket she'd spotted from the window.

"Wait!" Bernadette called.

The figure, wearing a wool hat and scarf, paused.

"Where are you going?" Bernadette asked.

She looked up at the other girl's face.

"I'm not quite sure," Sue answered.

Bernadette was certain Billy and her brother couldn't see who she was talking to. She smiled at Sue.

"I was positive that you survived," Bernadette said. "But I'm no longer absolutely certain about things. I've kind of lost my second sight."

Sue smiled. "You get to go back to being a normal girl. Lucky you."

"You can be a normal girl, too."

Sue scowled. "After all that's happened? After all I've learned?"

"You're just as much—"

"I know, I know." Sue looked back at the diner. "Just as much my mother's daughter." She sighed. "I just wanted to see Billy one more time, even from a distance. That's why I walked past the diner on my way to the bus station."

"Are you leaving town? Oh, no, Sue! There's so much you could tell us. The police, Dr. Marshall . . ."

Sue shook her head. "It's better that I go far, far away. There are those who are still out there. Very powerful people who want to bring about the end times. They'll be looking for me."

Bernadette grabbed her hand. No electric shock this time. Just the warmth of two hands coming together in the cold air. "You have free will, Sue—the right to choose," she told her. "I might not be in direct communication with the divine anymore, but this much I still know. You have the choice to do good, to do evil, or to do nothing at all."

"Yes," Sue said, her eyes betraying nothing as she looked at Bernadette. "I am aware of that."

"So—what then?" Bernadette's eyes pleaded with her. "What will it be, Sue? What will you choose?"

She didn't answer. She looked away, her face folding in anguish. She seemed not to know the answer.

Bernadette let her hand go, and Sue resumed walking.

"Where will you go?" Bernadette called after her.

"We will see," she said, without looking around, "where the road leads."

Bernadette stood there watching her until she was just a tiny dark figure against the bright white of the snow.

More Nail-Biting Suspense From Your Favorite Thriller Authors